A STUDY in REVENGE

ALSO BY KIERAN SHIELDS

The Truth of All Things

A STUDY in REVENGE

[A Novel]

KIERAN SHIELDS

 CROWN PUBLISHERS • NEW YORK

Copyright © 2013 by Kieran Shields

All rights reserved.
Published in the United States by Crown Publishers, an imprint of the Crown Publishing Group, a division of Random House, Inc., New York.
www.crownpublishing.com

CROWN and the Crown colophon are registered trademarks of Random House, Inc.

Library of Congress Cataloging-in-Publication Data is available upon request.

ISBN 978-0-307-98576-7
eISBN 978-0-307-985774

Printed in the United States of America

Book design by Lauren Dong
Jacket design by Tal Goretsky
Jacket photography © Topical Press Agency / Getty Images

10 9 8 7 6 5 4 3 2 1

First Edition

For my family

A STUDY in REVENGE

PART I

July 2, 1893

It is ever easy for us when motive and crime are in open connection: greed, theft; revenge, arson; jealousy, murder; etc. In these cases the whole business of examination is an example in arithmetic, possibly difficult, but fundamental. When, however, from the deed to its last traceable grounds, even to the attitude of the criminal, a connected series may be discovered and yet no explanation is forthcoming, then the business of interpretation has reached its end; we begin to feel about in the dark.

—HANS GROSS, *Criminal Psychology*

THERE WAS SOMETHING STRANGE ABOUT THE STONE, BUT Frank Cosgrove liked the feel of it. He'd first held it less than an hour ago. Since then it had remained hidden safely inside a cloth sack stuffed into a deep pocket of his coat. In the time it took him to make his winding, moonlit journey across Portland, Maine's maze of angled streets, he'd already formed the habit of running his fingertips over it. A handful of etched symbols marred a surface polished as smooth as glass. Even though the carvings proved otherwise, some corner of his brain was tempted to believe the impossible notion that the stone had never been worked by human hands. The stone had a calming effect; it took his mind off the dull ache that was working its way up his leg.

Still, Cosgrove would never think of paying good money for it, not even a tenth of the amount he was getting paid to steal it. That was the beauty of this type of thing, a one-off piece. Cash was cash, never more than a flat deal. But something like this stone, there was always someone with enough taste to pay a lot for it. They called it *taste*, but Frank knew that was just another word for a guy with one of two problems: Either he suspects he's got too much money on his hands or he's got a woman who wants him to prove it.

He turned right onto Walnut Street and stared at his pocketwatch in the moonlight. Five minutes to three; he was right on time. The uphill walk was starting to take its toll, and part of him regretted his selection of a meeting place, but the end was in sight. Another block ahead, just past the intersection with North Street, he saw the steep earthen embankment of the Munjoy Hill Reservoir. The massive four-acre structure marked a sort of outpost at the edge of the working-class neighborhood. The land to the north and east was about the last open, undeveloped space on the Neck, the peninsula that made up almost the entire city.

Besides being a quiet area where he was unlikely to be noticed this late, the reservoir had the added virtue of being a perfect dumping ground. If any police showed, he could heave the stone over the bank. The reservoir was forty feet deep inside and held twenty million gallons of water. He'd be out of Maine long before anyone ever managed to bring the stone back up.

Cosgrove made his way around the well-cemented hardpan that constituted the lower portion of the embankment. Farther along Walnut Street, a couple of houses stood in darkness. In the other direction, the grassy slope fell away to reveal the darkly shimmering surface of Portland's Back Cove. The wooden span of Tukey's Bridge crossed at the point where the nearly enclosed tidal cove narrowed and emptied out into Casco Bay.

As he neared the northeast corner of the reservoir, Cosgrove slowed his pace when a figure stepped into view. Even in the dark, he could tell that this wasn't his man.

"What's this?" Cosgrove's entire body tensed, preparing to bolt at any sign of trouble. "You're not—"

"Just a minor alteration, Mr. Cosgrove. You needn't worry; your money's all here." He shook a small leather traveling bag. The contents gave off a dull shuffling sound as they bumped against the bag's rigid frame. "You have it?"

"I wouldn't bother coming empty-handed, would I?" Cosgrove asked.

"No. That would be a mistake."

Cosgrove drew the cloth sack out of his coat pocket. He held it up for the man to see. The gibbous moon was enough for the outline of the object to be visible: a smoothed, oblong shape of about eight inches in length.

"That's good," the man said. "Very good, Mr. Cosgrove."

"The deal I had was for five hundred." The sudden appearance of a stranger was an unannounced shift in the plan, and Cosgrove couldn't hide his irritation. He'd been in jail plenty of times over the years. He viewed predictability in his business transactions as the one thing that would keep him outside a cell. Minor alterations to plans were not welcome, especially any attempt to change his payout.

"I'm well aware. Here." The man took a step and tossed the bag forward. It landed between them with a thud. "As soon as you're satisfied, we can conclude this bit of business."

Cosgrove crouched down on the thin, browning grass. He needed to peer close to better see the latches on the leather money bag. He set the cloth sack down, near at hand. If need be, the sack could be spun overhead; the weight of the stone at the bottom would make a crippling weapon. The rigid leather bag opened at the top, but he couldn't get the second of its two latches to turn.

As Cosgrove tried to force the bag open, he kept throwing glances at the man. "It's stuck."

"Turn both latches together but in opposite directions," the stranger said.

With the solution in hand, and the promised money so soon to follow, Cosgrove felt himself smiling. He focused on twisting each of the latches, one clockwise, the other counter. The bag top popped open. He reached in and pulled out the top stack of money, secured with a thin strip of paper around the center. Cosgrove had asked for ones and fives, since that would never raise eyebrows when he spent it. Something felt wrong to his expert touch; the weight of the bills was off. He held the stack close to his face with one hand and let the tops of the bills flick past his other thumb so he could check the whole wad. Only the few on the top and bottom of the stack were dollar bills. The center was nothing more than blank paper. Surprise ignited to anger in the mere second before he could speak.

"What the——"

Cosgrove was still close to the ground and saw only the flash out of the corner of his eye. He heard the bang at the same time as the blow hit him in the chest. It was as if someone had hauled off and swung a hammer, driving the head straight into his ribs. The force of it rocked him, and he tumbled backward, hands flailing as he tried to steady himself.

His vision went blank for a second; then he was looking up at the sky. He wanted to push himself off the ground, but his hands had instinctively gone to his chest. He stared at his left palm. It was wet, covered in slick, black oil. No, it only looked black in the dark. It was red. With the fingertips of his other hand, he brushed at his palm, but the dark stain wouldn't wipe off. What was wrong with his hands? He re-membered that he'd been holding something just a moment before. He looked to his left and saw the bills. The stack was ripped apart, and the papers were loose, skittering along the ground. Was this real? It had to be. He caught a glimpse of movement. The man was crouching nearby.

"What are you doing?" Cosgrove's voice was nothing more than a whisper. He stopped caring even as the words left his mouth. The man no longer mattered. Cosgrove rolled and flung his right side over. He landed facedown, tasted dirt and grass, and felt a searing pain spread through his chest. He could do nothing but watch as the fake bills started to flutter away in the night's gentle sea breeze.

[Chapter 2]

THE CORPSE SEEMED TO DEFY GRAVITY. THE BODY SLUMPED severely to the right, ready to slip off the side of the rickety wooden chair and collapse in a pile on the bare floor. The only thing holding the man up was the unlikely fact that the suit coat he was wearing had come down over the thin back of the chair. The buttons were undone, and the pull of the dead man's weight stretched the coat awkwardly, but the seams had not yet given out.

Deputy Marshal Archie Lean of the Portland police had been circling the body and staring at it for several minutes, making some sense of the horribly scarred and disfigured face. Cracked blisters dotted the blackened skin, the charred bits flaking away from the underlying musculature and bone. It wasn't so much that he expected to see anything new, but there was nothing else to draw his attention away. Apart from the chair and its disturbing occupant, the dingy second-floor room was merely an attic that had been finished off to its short peak with old barn boards. The space held nothing more interesting than empty booze bottles, old newspapers, and a few other scraps of litter. He circled his forefinger and thumb across his sandy, well-trimmed mustache. It didn't satisfy the restlessness in his hands. Lean wanted to light a cigarette but didn't want to disturb the air, which already held a strong smell, like that of a struck match or spent gunpowder.

According to the neighbors, the old house hadn't been occupied in six years. After the last owner's death in 1887, the place had passed to an out-of-state relation who had paid it no heed. The house had suffered badly enough from neglect even when it had a resident. The past few years had sped it on toward its inevitable condemnation. The property had been left to occasional use by vagrants and transients, and more constant abuse by neighborhood kids.

Lean heard the clatter of the horse-drawn carriage's wheels rattling over paving stones. He went to the room's single small window facing the front. There was no curtain, but Lean had to yank his handkerchief from his pocket, spit on the glass, and give it a firm rub in order to see through the stubborn layer of grime. Even from a distance, he recognized the man at the reins as Rasmus Hansen. The quiet but reliable man had formerly worked as the driver for Dr. Virgil Steig, before the latter's untimely death last summer. The old city surgeon had been a trusted ally and a good friend. His murder in the course of duty, a death that could have been prevented, remained a painful memory for Lean. Still, he allowed himself a hint of a smile at the thought of the carriage's current occupant.

He strode across the room, careful to avoid stepping on the sooty footprints that marked the dull, scuffed floorboards. Leaving the door open, he made his way down the creaking stairs. He kept his feet to the outer edges of each board, again to avoid damaging the prints, but also out of concern that the worn and cracked treads might not support his sturdy frame. The front parlor was mean and empty except for bits of trash along the baseboards and a clinging odor of dampness tinged with urine. Every stick of furniture that had ever been in the house was long since sold, stolen, or smashed to kindling and burned in the room's small fireplace.

Lean eased open the front door of the run-down little building and stepped outside, onto the crooked stoop. He stared once more at the blackened shape of a hand, fingers splayed, that was scorched into the door. A few people stood in a doorway along the narrow, unpaved stretch that led from the house down to Vine Street. More faces craned in from the sidewalk where this alleyway ended. A uniformed patrol officer, Harrington, made sure none of the overly interested neighborhood gawkers got any ideas about wandering close. Lean was glad for the timing of it, ten a.m. on Friday. The demands of the weekday had already thinned the early-morning crowd of schoolchildren and men walking to work.

After fumbling in his pocket for a match, Lean lit a long-overdue cigarette. He was glad that Harrington was the officer at hand. The man was a veteran whose combination of solid nerves and blunted imagination kept him from getting keyed up at crime scenes. At the moment, Harrington was staring in the direction of the newly arrived carriage.

A man in a lightweight frock coat had exited and now stood examining the house and its environs. Lean recognized the sharp features of Perceval Grey peering out from beneath the brim of a black brushed-felt hat. He recalled a similar arrival by Grey a year ago, in the dead of night, at the scene of a young woman's gruesome murder. That night he'd met the man for the first time in an atmosphere of desperation, skepticism, and irritation at Grey's condescending arrogance. Now he simply smiled, glad to see his onetime partner again.

"Y'know," Harrington began, without taking his eyes off Grey, "the more I think on it, the more I'm sure I've seen that guy up there." He jerked a thumb over his shoulder, toward the upper floor of the house. "Course, can't say for sure with his face the way it is."

"It's Frankie the Foot," Lean said with all the enthusiasm of a desperate card player forced to reveal his own middling hand.

"What?" The announcement was startling enough to yank Harrington's attention away from the new arrival for a moment. "That's impossible. Frankie's—"

"Yes." The look of utter disbelief that greeted Lean was exactly what he'd expected. "He certainly is."

"Then how the hell could he be here? And looking like that?"

"The question of the day, right there." Lean blew out a cloud of smoke and watched it disintegrate above him.

An uncomfortable silence settled over the deputy and the patrolman, as if Lean had just committed an embarrassing gaffe with a pronouncement that caught Harrington so far off guard. A guttural sound escaped from Harrington's throat as Grey approached and that man's slightly dark complexion, inherited from his Abenaki Indian father, became apparent.

"Not this one." Harrington's raspy voice was suddenly thick with disapproval. He sounded like a man readying himself for a confrontation. "Such a high-talking windbag."

Lean knew that Grey's work was earning him a reputation around the city, one not fully appreciated by the other members of the police department.

"It's all right. He's here at my request"—Lean fished about for the right way to justify calling on a private detective during a police investigation—"as a sort of expert on . . . unusual matters."

The look in Harrington's eyes still bordered on hostility, so Lean suggested the man take a stroll past the onlookers down the alley, to see if anyone had had a change of heart and now wanted to offer up something useful.

"Deputy Lean." Grey touched the brim of his hat, then cast a dubious glance at the ramshackle building. "Forgive me for showing up empty-handed. Your note didn't mention that this was to be your housewarming."

Lean chuckled. "Good of you to come, Grey."

"I was surprised to hear from you so soon."

Lean tilted his head. "We haven't spoken in nearly a year."

"Yes, but during that last bit of business, you voiced your hope that we wouldn't need to renew our professional acquaintance."

"Yes, well, I missed that radiant bonhomie of yours."

"Bonhomie?" Grey chuckled. "Good to see that the Vocabulary for Policemen correspondence course is paying dividends."

He looked again at the building. The paint was peeling from the sides. Dry rot was visible in the sills below the few narrow windows. Many of the panes were cracked, and all of them held several years' worth of dust and grime.

"Judging by the air of morbid curiosity among our crowd of onlookers, and the absence of any signs that a financially motivated crime would even be possible at these premises, I assume that the offense was one of bodily violence."

"Violence to the body would be a very apt description," Lean said.

"And yet there's something else at hand that concerns you?"

"Several bizarre pieces of evidence. The type of thing that, after our previous work together, I thought might be of interest to you."

Lean led the way over to the building. The front door was just a step up from the alley. The single granite block had been level at one time. Though the idea seemed foreign now, in the heat of July, the step had clearly fallen victim to decades of severe frosts that had caused the ground underneath to heave and buckle. Now it sloped noticeably to the right. It fit the building, which also sagged and slouched with age.

"This isn't just a stain," Grey said as he peered at the hand-shaped mark on the door.

"No—it's actually burned into the wood." Lean slid past, into the front room. The unkempt space was poorly lit, and the walls had gone a flat gray from lack of wiping. Years of scuffing by soles tracking in dirt had left the wooden floor dull and soiled. Still, a new series of blackened footprints stood out, leading from the front door across to the staircase on the far side of the room.

Grey knelt and examined one of the footprints closely. He ran a finger through the mark, then sniffed the sooty material. Lean felt a bit uncomfortable watching the man dirty the knees of his expensive-looking trousers. Grey came from money on his mother's side and, apart from his earliest years, had been raised to be a gentleman. He dressed accordingly, always in impeccably tailored suits. As if to balance the ledger, Lean straightened his waistcoat and tightened the tie he'd been loosening over the course of the warm morning.

With the close inspection of the ashen marks finished, Grey returned to the front door. He then crossed the room, comparing his own track to that of the blackened footprints.

"I'd say a man of average height, in no particular hurry, wearing mismatched shoes and intent on leaving a trail."

Lean nodded in agreement. "The body's upstairs."

Grey held up a finger, wishing to pause a moment as he checked the other two rooms on the ground floor. The back room was small and held nothing other than a door to a dark, narrow closet. The kitchen, which never boasted running water, had been greatly abused, with the drawers and cupboard doors all having been removed, presumably for use as firewood. The brief examination complete, Grey started for the staircase, but Lean stepped in front of him.

"Something I want to show you before we enter the attic."

The door at the top of the staircase was open, but Lean stopped short so he could close it. A small, four-paned window admitted enough light to reveal an image on the front of the faded, whitewashed door. Grey paused and studied the crudely drawn figure. A rough-shaped face, traced in ashes, stared back at them. It lacked a nose or mouth, the only features being two slitlike eyes that appeared to be drawn in blood. Above these was a small pentagram. The face narrowed at the chin, giving the look of a short, pointed beard. The head was topped with two curving horns, completing the malevolent, inhuman impression. Above the face, scrawled in greasy ash, was a two-word message:

" 'Hell Awaits,' " Grey read, then motioned Lean to proceed. "Onward now. Impolite to keep your acquaintances waiting."

They entered the room, and despite the grisly sight ahead of them, Grey focused on the scent that permeated the space. He continually sniffed the air as he approached the body.

"Like sulfur. Cheap eggs or expensive matchsticks—which have you been indulging in?"

Lean nodded at the body. "His fault."

Grey bent forward, close to the seated corpse, and sniffed again. "So it is."

He briefly examined the man's shoes, then stepped back. "That explains the difference in the footprints. He has a deformity—clubfoot, probably."

Grey began to slowly circumnavigate the room, patiently looking into every corner and occasionally stopping to consider the dead body from various vantage points. After a few minutes, he arrived back in front of the body, staring at a face scorched beyond recognition.

"All in all, this is quite the case of fire and brimstone, eh? Well, we can officially eliminate what it seems we were meant to assume as obvious. The man was, of course, not actually on fire when he entered the house. The footprints do not reflect his deformity. Also, they're too evenly and closely spaced. No one suffering the unbearable pain of being burned alive would have been able to walk up the stairs and find his way to a chair with so measured a step as this trail would have us believe."

Grey stepped closer and lifted the dead man's arms one at a time, checking the palms. The back of each hand was charred, but the palms looked undamaged.

"Furthermore, neither palm is burned, which refutes the right handprint on the outside door as being made by the victim. If such a ludicrous possibility even needed to be disproved."

After a close study of the face, which was swollen and horribly blistered, Grey tugged at the man's collar, enough to glance down his neck. "No burns on the torso."

"Arms or legs neither," Lean said.

Grey pointed to the dead man's mouth and then the right side of the head. "He's missing teeth and part of his ear, but they could well be old injuries. Difficult to tell with the extensive damage from the facial burns. Has the photographer been here? And the city surgeon?"

"Photographer's come and gone," Lean said. "Dr. Sullivan preferred to wait at Maine General and view the body there."

Grey's dark eyes flashed a bit of surprise. Lean thought he saw a hint of annoyance as well, even though Grey had no formal ground on which to object to the surgeon's choice. The deputy just shrugged.

"In any event," Grey said, "the scorch marks are placed selectively. His hair is only partly singed, the clothes are largely fine, though it looks like he may have taken a roll in the dirt. The soles of his shoes are slick with soot, but the laces are knotted loosely. They were tied by someone else, in a hurry and at an awkward angle. There's something seriously out of place with this body."

"I'm glad to see that your powers of observation have remained sharp," Lean said.

Grey raised an eyebrow at the comment, and the faintest hint of a smile appeared. "As has your keen wit. I'm not speaking of his being burned and dying, but rather the order of those two events."

He stared at Lean for a few seconds. "Each one of my observations has been obvious. No inference I've drawn from the scene has been surprising. You didn't need me to come here and tell you that all of this is a false design, some kind of hoax. So what is it that you're not telling me, Lean?"

The deputy feigned insult. "What's that supposed to mean?"

"It means that, based on our past dealings, I've come to expect that you have an opinion on this. Furthermore, you usually find it difficult not to share your opinions. Which leads me to believe that you must have an ulterior motive for standing there so quietly."

"Well, I know how you like to form an unbiased opinion of a crime scene, without the rest of us ruining the canvas with our foolish

observations and—what do you call them?—preconceived notions."
Lean allowed himself a smile. Though he knew it was a touch immature
and unprofessional, there was an undeniable bit of delight in knowing
some elusive fact that Perceval Grey was only able to guess at.

"Still waiting."

"His name is Frankie 'the Foot' Cosgrove. Knew him from those
missing teeth—and he lost that ear in a fight years ago."

"I recognize the name," Grey said. "Burglar, good with locks and
safes."

"Usually small stuff, though. Nothing worth getting killed over. But
he was shot early Sunday morning, the second. Single bullet to the chest.
Small service, then they buried him over in Evergreen on Wednesday."
Lean wandered across to stand behind the dead man. He rested a hand
on the back of the chair. "I was there in case any of his few friends started
mouthing off about him getting shot. Came away empty-handed—or
so I thought. Heard they had an open casket at the viewing the day
before."

Grey took in the expression on Lean's face. "I see. So at least you
know for a fact that the late Mr. Cosgrove here went into the ground
without a burn mark on him."

"You're right, Grey. I didn't need help in seeing through this ghoulish display." Lean left the body and slowly approached Grey, gathering his thoughts. "Maybe it's my lurid imagination getting the better of
me. Maybe it's the smell of the burned body, bringing back memories.
It's hard to get past that. But I can't help feeling that once again there's
something . . . *more* lurking beneath the surface. And what I do need is a
clue as to what it all means. Why would someone go to such lengths to
desecrate a dead body so horribly?"

[Chapter 3]

ONLY A FEW SCATTERED VISITORS MEANDERED ALONG THE manicured pathways that crisscrossed the two hundred–plus acres of Evergreen Cemetery. Grey and Lean stood close to the burial ground's eastern edge, where a few broad-canopied elms and maples provided a bit of shelter from any prying, morbid eyes. A uniformed officer was also present, watching the two gravediggers haul up the empty remains of Frank Cosgrove's casket.

The men set it down atop the small mound of freshly turned earth that was supposed to be covering the man's body for a peaceful eternity. Lean stepped close to get a better look at the plain pine box. The top third of the casket was shattered, and pieces of thin wood littered the area. Scattered about in the dirt and debris were the mangled remains of a wreath of flowers. Lean glanced at the diggers, who had already backed away from the grave. Even the patrolman had a skittish look about him.

"What do you think?" Lean asked.

Grey glanced up, then redirected his attention to the ground. He had one knee in the earth as he gathered up shards of the pine box, trying to fit them together like pieces of some ghoulish mosaic. After a minute, Grey settled on one section of pine board in particular, which he brought to the casket and held in various spots, trying to gauge its original location.

"Here's our answer." Grey held the pine board aloft to view it in the sunlight.

"Proof that Cosgrove was as dead coming out of the grave as he was when he went in?" Lean's loudly voiced question had its desired effect, drawing the patrolman and cemetery workers closer to hear what he knew would be a perfectly rational explanation of the events.

"Of course. Look here: The edges have been deeply scored to weaken the cover, and right here a small, perfectly round cut. Someone drilled a hole in the casket lid." Grey then handed the piece of wood to Lean. "Look at the interior of the bore hole."

Lean raised the board to let sunlight stream through the hole. He saw several thin strands. He plucked one away and held it in front of his nose.

"Rope fibers."

"Exactly," Grey said. "The perpetrator covertly placed a rope inside the coffin with one end threaded through this hole. The wreath of flowers decorating the top hid the rope end and also disguised his further tampering. The grave robbers only had to dig a narrow hole into the loose soil of Cosgrove's fresh grave, recover the end of the rope, and pull. The lid, weakened by cuts, would give way with ease, providing access to Cosgrove's corpse."

"Then they could recover the body without digging up the entire coffin, and the shattered lid gave the appearance that Cosgrove somehow crawled out of his grave. Very clever."

"Makes sense." A thick reluctance clung to the nearby patrolman's words.

"Still . . ." added a digger, who also volunteered a tilt of his head, which comprised the full measure of his insight into the matter.

"Still." Grey repeated the word like an accusation and gave Lean an incredulous look. "And there you have it. The scheme of our unknown corpsenapper achieves its purpose. An impossible event is disproved, but the belief that it happened still cannot be dislodged from the superstitious mind. People are scared. But who, exactly, is he trying to frighten? And why?"

Lean glanced at the gathered faces. He wanted them to hear Grey's explanation and so be able to spread the word that the dead body coming out of the grave was definitely a hoax. He did not, however, want them all over town doling out whatever potentially bizarre theory Grey might be about to conjure.

"Let's walk a bit," Lean said to Grey.

"Deputy, what about the hole?" the patrolman called after him. "And the box?"

"Leave the hole; we're going to rebury Cosgrove as soon as Dr. Sullivan's done with the body. The coffin . . ." He looked sideways at Grey, who shook his head.

"It's told us all that it can."

"Get rid of it," Lean ordered the diggers.

The ground sloped away in front of them, and they passed a series of grass-covered mounds rising out of the hillside. The front of each mound held the door of a granite-faced vault that looked out over the back end of the cemetery.

Lean broke the silence. "This whole business is a tremendous amount of work for someone to go through, and for what? A grudge against Cosgrove?"

"Seems unlikely. If someone was angry enough at him to dig up his body, burn it, and drag it all the way across the city, why would they have killed him so cleanly in the first place? The single shot to the heart was a rather workmanlike murder. It doesn't seem motivated by any personal animosity."

"Could be two totally separate culprits," Lean offered. "Someone didn't get his chance to settle a score with Cosgrove before he was killed. Took it out on him afterward."

"Possible." Grey had his head bent forward, studying the ground as they walked. "But consider where he was found. Taken from here into the city to be arranged in that abandoned house."

"There's nothing interesting about that property."

"Exactly. It stands to reason that the house was chosen because it would get attention. It provided shelter so that the criminal could make his arrangements, but the place is frequented by tramps and neighborhood kids, ensuring that the gruesome sight would soon be found. And few people spread rumors as quickly and wildly as do drunks or children. Add in the elaborate nature of the hoax: faking burned handprints and such. I suspect that these actions were not aimed at Cosgrove. This was intended for an audience that can appreciate the message—one that's still with us."

"A threat, perhaps. At Cosgrove's killer—someone seeking vengeance," Lean suggested.

"Or a message *from* the killer, scaring off Cosgrove's associates or threatening someone else who might have been a part of whatever got the man shot to begin with. All speculation. More facts are needed."

Ahead the ground evened out, and the men continued on toward a group of four ponds that marked Evergreen's far boundary. Benches and

arbors adorned a perimeter trail around the three closest ponds. Tiny islands dotted the waters, and short wooden bridges spanned some of the
narrow sections. A couple of families with small children loitered about,
tossing crumbs to the swarms of geese, ducks, and wayward seagulls
that patrolled the water.

"The devilish images and words, dead bodies being moved. It's hard
not to think about the last time," Lean said.

"Jotham Marsh and his followers. The idea had occurred to me."

The occult murderer they'd pursued last summer had been a onetime
member of Dr. Marsh's mystical society, the Order of the Silver Lance.
Marsh claimed to have previously severed ties with the killer over the
latter's desire to pursue the study of black magic. Lean had found the
man to be creepy and somewhat suspicious. Grey had a stronger reaction, thinking that Marsh had some blood on his hands by the time that
tragic investigation ended.

"There's not a shred of evidence that Marsh has any involvement
here," Lean said.

"True," Grey said. "But I wouldn't want to delay inquiries in that direction too long. I can't help but consider how things might have ended
differently last year if we'd fully understood the breadth of Marsh's society. The worst of dangers can arise from unexpected corners. We should
never again let Jotham Marsh and his cronies be a surprise."

The detectives entered onto one of the pond's walkways, passing
through a massive tree crotch overturned so that the two diverging
trunks formed a pedestrian archway.

"The only thing that's sure is that the guilty party needed access to
this coffin. You'll have to talk to the undertaker," Grey said.

"What, not curious enough to come along?"

"On the contrary, I'm quite intrigued. But I have a prior commit-
ment, one that's already been postponed twice."

"How pressing can it be if it keeps getting pushed off?" Lean asked.

"The man's lack of consciousness has prevented the previous two
meetings. I'm told he's unlikely to last the week."

"Well, I know when I'm beat," Lean said. "I'll let you know what the
undertaker has to say."

Chapter 4

THE BUTLER MET GREY IN THE GRAND ENTRYWAY OF HORace Webster's house and promptly handed over a small envelope. "This was left for you by Mr. Dyer, the attorney."

Before Grey could inspect the letter, the butler started walking. Grey slipped the envelope into his pocket and followed, down a wide hallway lined with dark wood paneling, toward a sweeping staircase. Grey noted the fraying edges of the worn rugs and the marble-topped table that held two expensive vases, the flowers wasting away like forlorn prisoners in beautiful porcelain cells. Although the house was well appointed, the décor was outdated. He recalled hearing that Mrs. Webster had passed away many years before; the house missed her touch.

The solid oak door to a side room opened ahead of the butler, who paused at the sight.

"Consider what I'm saying," said a plaintive voice from inside.

"I'll consider the source first, and, as usual, that settles the matter." The second man's response rattled through the hall like a cannon shot.

"You don't understand what's involved here," the first speaker insisted.

"There's a blasted fool involved, and more like you lurking behind, no doubt." A tall, solidly built man with gray hair and a handlebar mustache stormed into the hallway. He nearly barreled into the butler, who neatly stepped aside. The mustachioed man glared at the butler before noticing Grey.

"Who the hell are you?"

The butler cleared his throat. "Mr. Euripides Webster, this is Mr. Perceval Grey."

As Euripides took closer notice of Grey, his weathered face recoiled a bit. The man continued to stare, as if Grey's dark tan complexion were some unspecified transgression that demanded a further explanation.

"It's true. I'm Perceval Grey." When that failed to appease Euripides, Grey added, "I was requested."

"Not by me. It's the old man that wants to see you. Damned if I know why." Euripides brushed past, heading for the front door.

"Mr. Grey, I'm Jason Webster." The first speaker had emerged from the side room, his plaintive voice now amiable. The slender, light-haired man held out his hand. Grey estimated him to be about fifty years old.

"And that whirling dervish of indignation was my older brother." Jason dismissed the butler with a nod. "I'll take him up."

While Jason led Grey upstairs, he said, "I admit I'm equally in the dark about why our father wishes to see you. But, having witnessed how annoyed it makes Euripides, let me just say a thousand welcomes to you, good sir."

They arrived at a room that held a settee and two separate chairs. On the opposite wall was another door, which opened just as Jason was about to speak. An older man with thick spectacles and a head crowned by only a few meticulously placed strands of hair emerged. The man's hands were full, but he managed to ease the door closed behind him. In one hand he held a lit taper in a candlestick, which he now blew out.

"How is he, Dr. Thayer?" Jason asked.

"I've just given him a sedative." The doctor held up a syringe as proof of the statement. He set it down on a sterile cloth laid out on a side table next to his leather medical bag. Grey noted the single, pathetic-looking bit of blood, not enough to form a drop, that lingered indecisively at the tip of the needle.

"You should have a minute or two to speak with him, if you wish. Phebe's inside, trying to get him to eat a little something." The physician gathered up his belongings, then moved toward the hall. "As I told her, send word if there are any changes. Otherwise I'll check back tomorrow morning."

"If you don't mind, Mr. Grey, I'll let you enter alone. I don't like seeing him in this state." Jason lit the candle again and handed it to Grey, who received it with a puzzled look.

"Sorry, but bright lights bother his eyes," Jason explained.

Horace Webster's modest bedroom was dimly lit. Curtains shielded two close-set windows. Apart from Grey's candle, the only other light in the room was a stub on the bedside table. Horace Webster's meager form occupied a narrow bed in the corner. Seated beside it was Phebe Webster, who looked up and watched Grey approach. The dark-haired woman held a porcelain bowl of soup on a silver platter, which she now set aside. As Grey neared, he caught hints of chicken broth mingled among the scents of various medicines, most notably camphor. None of these, however, could overcome the stale odor of the old man's dying body in the poorly ventilated space.

"Miss Webster, I'm Perceval Grey." He kept his voice to a whisper, since the old man in the bed appeared to be sleeping. The man looked ancient in the candlelight, the shadows accentuating the deep wrinkles on his face.

Phebe held out her hand from where she was sitting. "Yes, Grandfather was asking for you a while ago."

Grey took the offered hand and gave a short bow of his head. "Has the sedative taken effect already?"

Phebe shook her head no. She leaned close to the bedridden man, rubbing his left arm while she whispered into his ear. Grey studied Phebe. He put her in her mid- to late twenties. Now that he was closer, he could see that her hair was actually auburn, with streaks of red highlighted by the candle's glow. She would not likely be thought a classical beauty by most; her form was somewhat lanky, and her facial features were slightly sharp and angular. Still, there was a depth and surety in her gaze that Grey found arresting.

Phebe leaned back, and Grey saw that Horace's eyes were now open and focused on him. One eye anyway; the left looked cloudy, and the flesh on that side of his face sagged as if he'd suffered some form of palsy. The old man gave a barely perceptible nod.

"Come closer, please," Phebe said. "His voice is weak."

The bed was not tall, so Grey kneeled down in order to get within eight inches of Horace's face. Quarters were tight by the bedside, and he apologized to Phebe for brushing against her crossed leg. She accepted this with an understanding smile. Grey focused on Horace Webster, and long seconds passed with only thin sighs of breath passing from the old man's lips.

A slight croak escaped Horace's throat, followed by his rasping voice, quiet but desperate to be heard. "Help her. Dig deeper."

The man's gaze remained locked on Grey. He felt Phebe's hand come to rest lightly on his shoulder, but Grey wasn't sure if the gesture was for his benefit or for hers. He glanced sideways and watched a passing cloud of distress float across Phebe's features. Horace's breathing eased, and Grey saw that the man's eyes had closed. He and Phebe made their way softly across to the door and out into the sitting room, where Grey repeated the old man's message.

"That's all?" Jason's face held a mixture of amusement and disappointment. "This big to-do about summoning the renowned detective—and the old codger manages a grand total of four words." Jason released a curt laugh, almost a cackle. "How fitting. He graces the family with another riddle. The perfect ending to an imperfect life."

"Really, Jason. I don't think this is the time for one of your . . . commentaries."

"You're right, dear, how untoward of me. Please excuse my disappointment, Mr. Grey, though I'm sure yours must be running quite high at the moment as well. I'm not certain what there is for you to do from here, but good luck to you." Jason smiled and nodded to the pair of them before he slipped out the door.

"I truly must apologize for both my uncles, Mr. Grey. I heard Euripides bellowing downstairs earlier. My grandfather's condition has frazzled all our nerves."

"There's no need for you to apologize, Miss Webster. A man's character is only what he chooses to make of what he's been given. Your uncles' characters would have been firmly set long before they ever had the opportunity to benefit from your acquaintance."

"You're most kind. I suppose we all know what it's like to deal with an odd assortment of family members."

Grey said nothing at first, but Phebe's eyes called for an agreement, and he answered, "I can imagine."

"Well, I suppose I ought to check in on my grandfather again. If you don't mind?"

"Not at all. But before I go, and I hope you don't mind my asking, when he said 'Help her,' do you suppose your grandfather was referring to you?"

Phebe seemed happy to have a reason to smile. "I can assure you, Mr. Grey, I am not in need of your assistance. Thank you all the same."

She seemed genuinely amused by him, which was not a sentiment that Grey was particularly used to. He was more accustomed to initial encounters where people reacted with some level of discomfort. They weren't always sure what to make of him. His mannerisms, tailoring, and choices of phrase were not what white people would let themselves expect from a man with his deeper skin tone.

"I'm sorry you've used up your morning for a mere four words," Phebe said. "Seems rather a pointless errand for you after all."

"Perhaps. I'll reserve judgment for the time being. Four words could prove to be quite telling. Countless men have used far greater numbers to say far less."

"You have a fascinating way of seeing things, Mr. Grey."

"It's been my experience that there's no limit to what you can see if you're willing to look close enough." Grey's eyes were fixed on hers.

"Words to make any woman nervous." She gave a small chuckle. "I'll have to remember to keep you at arm's length. Life's a bit more comfortable for all of us if you men let us have our little secrets."

Phebe bade him good day and slipped back into her grandfather's room. Grey made his way down to the front hall, where the butler handed over his hat and walking stick. Once on the sidewalk, Grey slid his hand into his pocket to recover the letter left for him from Horace Webster's attorney. He broke the seal and pulled out a single handwritten page on letterhead from the firm of Dyer & Fogg, Counselors-at-Law.

Mr. Grey,

My apologies for not being present to shepherd you through your meeting with the Webster family. I trust you survived relatively unscathed. I am sure you have questions that remain unanswered, and I am afraid they will remain so for a short while. I do have additional information to provide you regarding the business arrange-

ment that Mr. Webster is proposing. However, I request a further bit of patience from you. Given Mr. Webster's uncertain condition, I am understandably preoccupied with various legal matters that require prompt attention while my client is still of sound mind. Please indulge me a few days longer, and I'll contact you again at the first practicable opportunity.

Regards,

Albert Dyer

Grey glanced back at the house, and his eyes were drawn to a slight motion in one of the two central windows on the second floor. He made the mental calculation and determined that these were the pair of close-set windows in Horace's bedroom. The curtain on his right was fully drawn. The left, however, was pulled aside about six inches. He saw a woman's figure; Phebe Webster was watching him. His eyes settled onto hers for a second, but the distance between them was too great for him to read anything in her gaze. A moment more and she stepped away, letting the curtain drop back into place.

[Chapter 5]

DEPUTY LEAN STOOD JUST INSIDE THE MORGUE AT THE Maine General Hospital. The space was built mostly underground, which helped keep the room cool. Still, rather than being refreshing, the quality of the air was dulled by the heavy scent of chemicals that, in Lean's mind anyway, couldn't fully mask the underlying currents of dead bodies.

The paunchy, gray-haired surgeon, Dr. Sullivan, was across the room rinsing his hands in a washbasin. In the space between the two men, a table held the laid-out body of Frank Cosgrove. A crisp white sheet covered everything but the man's charred face.

"I'm really not certain my services were required to review Mr. Cosgrove's body yet again. He was already murdered last Sunday. Not as if you can add a second murder charge for digging him back up." Sullivan dried his hands and threw the towel aside.

"I do appreciate your indulging me."

"That's it, isn't it? An indulgence. Not my business at all. Not as if I'm paid any extra for repeating an examination on the likes of this petty thief."

"Yes, the examination," Lean said, trying to steer the surgeon away from whatever was distressing him and back to the business at hand.

"Well, even without the burns he's in worse shape than the last time I saw him. He wasn't embalmed." He added the last bit with contempt, as if it were a personal failing of the deceased.

"Is that unusual?"

"I'm the city physician," Dr. Sullivan declared with a shrug, annoyed to be bothered with such a question. "Ask the undertaker. The burn marks are posthumous. Common lamp oil, I suspect. There's a scent of it around his collar and his cuffs."

"What about his fingernails?"

Dr. Sullivan shook his head. "What about them?"

"Cracked? Any dirt beneath? Signs he'd been digging?"

Dr. Sullivan's expression went from inconvenienced to downright exasperated.

"No, I'm not mad, and I don't think he crawled from his grave, Doctor. Rather I'm wondering about the people who perpetrated this hoax. How elaborate and detailed were they in their efforts?"

"No. No signs of dirt under the nails. However, there was dirt all through his hair, in his pockets, and in the cuffs of his trousers. "

Lean moved closer to the body. "Gathered as he was pulled up out of the burial plot."

"It would appear so. By means of a rope, most likely." Dr. Sullivan took hold of the sheet and lowered it from Cosgrove's neck down to his waist. He moved the dead man's arms away from his sides. "See here. Marks around the chest and in the armpits. Inflicted after death."

Lean bent in for a look at the discolorations. There were faint scuff marks, signs of stress on the skin, but no actual rope burns. No direct contact. They'd somehow managed to tie a rope around him after he was in his funeral coat, then later dug down to the coffin and pulled him to the surface.

"Anything else, Doctor?"

"I have nothing further to add."

"Meaning that the body reveals nothing further or that there is something else and you just don't care to say it?"

"There is nothing further. I consider my involvement in the matter concluded."

Lean continued to stare at the man.

"Let's be clear, Deputy. I'm not Virgil Steig. I won't be sharing his degree of involvement in any of your cases. Nor his fate."

"I'm not certain what you're referring to."

"Dr. Steig reviewed a peculiar homicide victim for you shortly before his death."

"Dr. Steig suffered a heart attack in his study." Lean recited the lie in good conscience and with a casual fluidity. He'd repeated it many times in the past year. The doctor's niece, Helen Prescott, had insisted on it in order not to cast a shadow on the legacy of the late doctor's work with some of his mentally troubled patients.

"I've heard rumors otherwise."

"Then you've been misled. You're correct about one thing, however."

"Which is?"

"You are not Dr. Steig. He was a consummate professional and a good man." Lean tipped his hat and exited the morgue.

The memory of Dr. Steig's unhappy end was painful in its own right. More so because of Lean's insistence on second-guessing what he and Grey could have done differently last summer. Their misplaced certainty over the identity of the killer they were pursuing had allowed the true madman to claim a final victim. Lean forced himself to at least realize that it could have been worse. After the doctor's death, they had managed to save Helen Prescott and her young daughter, Delia. The whole grisly ordeal had left Helen and the girl shaken, of course. Helen had taken a sabbatical from her post at the historical society and gone to stay with some distant relations in Connecticut. She'd been planning to return to Portland eventually, but Lean hadn't heard anything recently, and so he could only wonder and hope that the woman and her sweet child were doing well.

He shook his head, trying to sweep away the cobwebs of last summer's tragic events. This was a new case; he needed to focus on his next step and figure out who could have tampered with the dead man's coffin.

⊱ ⊰

"WHEN I WAS YOUNG, it was cabinetmakers who used to make coffins," said the undertaker, Harry Rich. "The old boxes with six sides, narrow at the foot. Even when I first started, after the war, coffins were still made by hand, good and solid."

"Last a lifetime?" Lean suggested. He didn't think the undertaker would mind. The man was far more animated than Lean had expected. He couldn't shake the foolish preconception that all undertakers should be tall, gaunt men with serious expressions and voices as quiet and somber as the turning of the pages in a Bible.

"So to speak," Rich said with a chuckle that shook his rotund belly. "They'd last a lot of years anyways. But there's no undertakers left in town who make their own coffins anymore. The manufacturing of them's a business of its own these days. In most of the large manufactories, they're done with machinery."

The man led the way from the funeral parlor's vestibule into the chapel. Rows of chairs faced a casket surrounded by a generous selection of floral arrangements. Lean paused at the sight.

"So the coffin that Frank Cosgrove was buried in was . . ."

"The least expensive that we had on hand. Eleven dollars. Coffins can cost up to fifty. Though we don't sell as many these days. Cloth-covered caskets is what most folks want. Some of those can go for hundreds."

"Honestly?"

The undertaker wiped his small, round glasses with a handkerchief. "It all depends on the inside trimmings: a good satin or velvet or even silk. Of course, there's always been a range of costs. It used to be that even rich folk would be buried in regular coffins, only they'd be made of San Domingo mahogany. Try laying your hands on that anymore."

"I thought Cosgrove's thin pine box was a thing of the past. I mean, they even have metallic ones now."

"Yes, but they'll never take the place of good chestnut, oak, or walnut. The iron generally corrodes, so they're not used much anywhere in New England. I hear they do better in the South—better suited to the climate, I suppose. Besides, they're terribly heavy just to move about properly."

"You handle all the bodies yourself?" Lean asked.

"Me or my son. Unless it's a female who's died. We have a woman who'll go round the house, prepare the body, and get everything ready so that we can come by with the carriage and place the body in the icebox."

"The icebox. That reminds me, Cosgrove's body wasn't embalmed. Why not?"

The undertaker showed a bit of surprise at Lean's knowledge on that point. "Embalming a body costs another fifteen. Even when folks can afford it, it's not always done. People aren't always educated up to it. Many relatives have an idea that the body has to be cut open or mutilated for the embalming to work. A body that has been embalmed presents a more natural appearance than if it were placed on ice. Even so, it works best in winter. A hot spell in the summer . . . well, there's no guarantee the embalming will last."

"I thought embalming was more or less permanent? Like mummies and all."

"Proper old-time embalming is a lost art. Today's process is very simple, just an injection of a prepared fluid. But the chemical's action isn't permanent. A New York doctor, name of Lowell, has made improvements, however." The man's eyes' lit up as he launched into a monologue on the technicalities of his work.

Lean strolled up the aisle, ignoring all the talk of arteries, chloride of zinc, and albumenoids or some such. He reached the casket that patiently awaited its visitors and laid a hand on the polished wood.

"Eleven dollars isn't much of a payment for a coffin, is it? Not enough to keep you in business for long."

"On the bright side, it came without a struggle. More than I can say if his friends were paying for a richer casket." The undertaker gestured toward the dark, handsome casket beside them. "Likely only get five dollars at the front, on the installment plan. Practically the twentieth century, but folks are still superstitious about paying a man's funeral costs right off. Afraid it might mean another death will follow quick after the first."

Mr. Rich noticed that Lean was watching him closely. "You know, Deputy, you never actually said just why it is that the police are still interested in Mr. Cosgrove. Even after he's dead and buried."

"It's not exactly Frank Cosgrove I'm interested in. Rather I'm curious about who might have paid you to make any unusual arrangements with the body or the casket? While it was here, in your possession."

"Well, he didn't have any immediate family, if that's what you mean. We were paid from the funds found on him at the time of his death. Enough to replace the shirt he was wearing, covered in blood. But we had to bury him in the same suit he was killed in. There weren't any unusual arrangements to be made. I can't say that I'm comfortable discussing such private matters."

"I suggest you make yourself comfortable, Mr. Rich. You see, certain things have come to light. Some irregularities with the contents of Mr. Cosgrove's coffin." Lean rapped on the nearby casket. "And since, as the undertaker, you were the only one handling Mr. Cosgrove's body . . ."

"What sort of . . . irregularities?"

"Serious ones. So if no one else had access to the body and the opportunity to take any liberties with the arrangements of his coffin, then I'm afraid you're going to have to come down to the patrol station and answer some rather unpleasant questions."

"Well, now. Wait just a minute. There was a visitor—a cousin. Came the night before the burial after the viewing was over. He was rather beside himself, asked if he could have a few minutes alone with Mr. Cosgrove."

"Describe the man."

"Average height, dark hair, I think. A regular-looking fellow. Wore a long, heavy coat."

"In this weather?"

"He said he was in from out of town. Just come from the train. He was carrying a small suitcase."

"And you showed him the body?"

"Yes, right back here."

The undertaker hurried forward, eager to leave behind the spot where accusations of misconduct had been suggested. He led Lean to an inconspicuous door at the back of the chapel. Inside was a small, windowless room, undecorated except for a crucifix hanging on one wall with a sepia-toned portrait of Jesus opposite. A pewlike bench was set beside the doorway.

"We sometimes keep the caskets in here before the next visitation."

"How long was this cousin in the heavy coat alone with the body?"

"He came out maybe thirty minutes later. Asked that we seal the coffin right then and there. Couldn't bear the thought of seeing his cousin again, because of the violent nature of his death. He stood by silently while my son and I nailed it shut."

"I was at the church and the graveside." Lean worked his hands together, cracking a few knuckles. "Trying to recall the scene. Not sure I remember any such person."

"That's the odd thing, isn't it?" Rich's eyes were wide within the circular lenses of his spectacles. "After all that to-do, the cousin didn't even bother showing up for the burial."

Chapter 6

LEAN WALKED DOWN THE WINDING, ALLEYLIKE SPACE BE-hind a row of tenements. Ahead was what looked like a short, windowless barn. At one point it may have served as a large shed or maybe a small stable. Now it pretended to be a sort of saloon, the kind that served rum so cheap that even the men drinking at this hour could afford it. Lean pushed open the plank-board door. Two tiny windows and a hanging oil lamp provided a bare minimum of light. A wide beam atop two standing barrels formed the bar. To Lean's surprise the place actually held a billiards table, though its legs had all been replaced by crates and the felt was barely hanging together.

Only half a dozen souls, or what passed for souls, occupied the place. They all glanced up. Lean recognized most of the men. A couple that weren't familiar figured out who he was quick enough from the looks and body language of the regulars. Lean scanned the faces and settled on the man with a cue stick in hand.

"Barney Welch, you're going to tell me what you know about Frankie the Foot."

Lean stepped farther into the room, leaving the door for those who suddenly had someplace else to be. He kept his eyes on Welch, who stood straight up and clutched his pool stick in both hands. Welch was of medium height and thin, but not weak. He sometimes picked up work on the docks when he was sober enough. When he wasn't, he made his rum money by stealing whatever he could. The man's bloodshot eyes darted around the room. Lean had the sense the man was scared, more than he ought to be just over getting questioned. And his panicked looks hadn't been directed at Lean but at the others in the place, men who were now slipping out the door. Within seconds only the stocky, bearded bar-keep remained with them in the room.

Lean gave the man a glare. "Catch a five-minute break, why don't you."

As soon as they were alone, Welch muttered, "I don't know nothing 'bout Frankie."

"You know enough. You've worked with the man. Thick as thieves, as they say."

"The man's dead. Can't you leave his name in peace?"

"Someone else wouldn't let him lie, so now I can't either," said Lean. "I need to know who that someone is. Who did it to him?"

"Swear to God I ain't heard nothing." Welch's grumbled words held little conviction.

Lean almost smiled. "You know, some people swear an oath like that and you know they mean it. You, on the other hand . . ."

He rounded the edge of the ramshackle pool table. With his hands closer to the tip, Welch hauled off and swung his cue back over his shoulder. He meant to settle matters with one blow, but the big windup gave Lean plenty of time to react. The deputy raised his left arm to block and stepped in close enough that when the stick hit his forearm, it was only the thin end. It snapped, and the fat handle flew harmlessly across the room.

Welch wobbled, drunk and off balance from the effort. Lean drove his right fist into the man's side, below his ribs. The punch knocked the air from Welch. Lean followed with a left hook to the side of the face that sent the man staggering back into the wall.

Desperate gasps filled the air, and Lean gave the man a second to soak in the meaning of the hits he'd just taken. That should pretty much be the end of the matter. Lean stepped forward, thinking to take the man by the front of the shirt.

Welch's right arm flashed forward in a wide arc. Even in the dim light, Lean saw the glint from a metallic edge. He jerked back, feeling no pain as the razor whipped close under his chin. He heard cloth rip. Welch had committed too much to the attack, throwing himself wildly off balance again. Lean grabbed the man's arm, spun him around, and then wrenched Welch's wrist down against the edge of the pool table. The razor skidded across the felt.

Lean drove his fist into Welch's face, and the man collapsed on the floor.

"What the hell were you thinking—assaulting an officer of the law? Tell me what I want to know or it's going to go hard with you."

"I can't," Welch mumbled.

"Trying to protect someone? Whoever it is can't protect you—not from me. And right now I'm the only one you've got to worry about," Lean said. "Frankie the Foot's dead, so out with it."

"I heard about him over to Vine Street."

"Heard what?"

"Hellfire got him." Welch stared up, fear set deep in his eyes. "Hellfire."

"That's a load of horseshit," Lean said.

"It ain't," Welch said as he started to rise.

There was a mix of defiance and desperation in Welch's voice, and Lean didn't care for either. He gave the man a kick in the ribs that sent Welch back against the wall once more. The deputy snatched the razor off the pool table. He crouched down and pressed the blade into Welch's cheek, the tip close to the man's eye.

"You're worried about hellfire, that's simple: Stay alive. And that starts by telling me about Frankie."

"I can't talk. Them others know you're at me about Frankie. They'll know I cracked."

"Life's all about hard choices, Barney." Lean edged the blade's point ever so slightly closer to Welch's eyeball.

"Frankie's old partner, Sears."

"Chester Sears?"

Welch had to restrain himself from nodding with the blade so close. "Aye, he's been back in town. Heard he's flopping down at Darragh's. He'd know anything worth knowing."

Lean stood up and stepped back. "See, that wasn't so hard."

He stuck the razor tip-first into the worn wood on the side of the pool table and jerked the handle, snapping the blade in two. As Lean took a step toward the door, he heard Welch's pained voice.

"Hold on. I helped you. You gotta do the same." Welch stood up and wandered to the scantily stocked bar.

Lean gave him an incredulous look. "Just tried to slice me, and now you're asking for favors."

"They know what you were after. You leave me here with just a few bruises, they'll know I talked." Welch grabbed a near-empty bottle from behind the bar, took a swig, and then held it in Lean's direction. "Finish the job on me. When they come back in, I can't still be in any shape to talk or they'll know I did."

"You're mad." Lean stared at the man, wondering if he'd already taken too strong a blow to the head. Welch's eyes were clear, at least by the standards of the drunks in this place. "What the hell's got you so messed up in the head?"

"Hellfire, Deputy. There's the devil in the air. And I don't want no trouble with him." His arm still stuck out; he gave the bottle a shake as if he were luring Lean in.

Lean took two steps closer and seized the bottle.

Welch turned his back. "Do it right the first time."

Lean judged the weight of the bottle and was glad to see that the glass wasn't thick. "Good luck."

He swung at Welch's head, trying to angle it just a bit, to take some of the edge off the blow. The glass shattered, and the man fell in a heap. Lean bent down to make sure he was breathing. A trickle of blood appeared on his scalp where a lump was already swelling. Lean stood and straightened his coat. He reached up to fix his bow tie and felt one end ripped clear through. He remembered the tearing sound when Welch had cut at him.

"Damn it." He was tempted to go through the man's pockets and find the fifty cents it would cost to replace the tie. Then again, Welch had paid his share many times over today. Lean hoped that the man's friends, when they found him unconscious, would leave him enough change to at least buy a drink when he came to.

Chapter 7

ARCHIE LEAN TOSSED THE FOLDER ASIDE ON HIS DESK. IT didn't hold the answer he was looking for. The thought had occurred to him that he was reading too much into the removal of Cosgrove's body from its plot in Evergreen Cemetery. The explanation could be a simpler one than the occult imagery at the scene tried to indicate. Digging up bodies wasn't unheard-of. The crimes of so-called resurrection men, who sold freshly buried corpses to hospitals or anatomists, were largely a thing of decades past. Still, it happened once in a while. Maybe someone had gotten hold of the body, run into trouble, and decided to simply ditch it at Vine Street and cover his tracks. The folder held the details on all such cases in the last five years. There had been a string of incidents at Evergreen three summers ago. The two men responsible were caught and were both currently in jail on other charges. There'd been another incident last fall in the Eastern Cemetery. No one was ever arrested in that case, but the two disturbed graves there were very old and the bodies, useless to any medical practitioner, had been left in the coffins. The whole thing was put down to a lot of work by criminals hoping to find a bit of interred gold or jewelry.

In any event, those records showed no promise of any connection to the current inquiry. Lean pushed those thoughts aside, gathered his hat, and exited the police station from its basement home in City Hall, emerging from the side doors onto Myrtle Street. He rounded one of the building's square corner towers and crossed Congress Street, then strolled down Market amid a light stream of foot traffic. The lower section of the block was occupied by an elegant building of white Vermont marble that housed Portland's post office on the ground floor and various court offices above. The sight of Perceval Grey leaning against a carriage with a newspaper in front of his face surprised Lean. As he approached, he realized that Grey wasn't actually reading the paper. His eyes were aimed just over the top edge, focused on something inside one of the tall, arched windows that lined the entire side of the post office.

Lean threw an inconspicuous glance inside. There were a few people milling about at a bank of small post-office boxes. He surmised that Grey was studying a middle-aged man in a tan coat and matching gloves. The man held a cane, with which he was casually tapping several of the doors to the wooden boxes.

"I thought we were meeting at Mitchell's Restaurant."

"You're early," Grey said, without looking at Lean.

"Are you watching out of mere curiosity, or is it a professional interest?"

"Professional."

"What's the man doing?" Lean asked.

"Sending a signal, I believe. What it is and to whom, I cannot yet say." Grey folded his newspaper and turned away from the window.

Lean glanced over his shoulder and saw the man with the cane was walking toward the front of the post office. "Well, I won't delay you. I assume you mean to follow the man."

"Unnecessary. He's revealed all that he will on this day." Grey finally looked Lean in the face. His eyes dropped for a second to Lean's neck and his shredded bow tie. "I hope you're not trying to start some new bohemian trend in men's neckwear."

Lean shook his head in disgust. "Emma picked this out."

"Obviously. It goes well with your suit. I take it you're still working on the inflammatory matter of Frank Cosgrove?"

"Yes, but all his associates are scared. This business with the burned corpse has them looking over their shoulders. I thought I might be close to a dead end."

"A dead end? A bit ironic, given the circumstances."

Lean chuckled. "But I've just recently come across some news. A former accomplice of Cosgrove's has been back in town recently. He's boarding down on Fore."

"So much for Mitchell's Restaurant. On to Fore Street it is," Grey said.

They walked on, passing by the front of the post office, where three round-arched entryways led into a narrow portico. Above this, fronting the second and third stories, a series of Corinthian columns supported a low-pitched triangular pediment that completed the look of a Greek temple. The white marble glistened in the sun, giving the building a formal, aloof air and setting it off from the familiar, ruddy brick that dominated the other buildings nearby.

Lean summarized his findings from the second postmortem and the undertaker as the two men proceeded along, soon turning in to the narrow confines of a side street where the three-story brick buildings were enough to cast them in shadows as they passed over the uneven paving stones. Farther down they entered into sunlight again by the Silver Street Market. In a futile attempt to escape the din of the haggling voices that surrounded the dozen stalls of provisioners, fishmongers, and purveyors of pork and mutton, they crossed the street. The smell of corn cakes enveloped them as they passed Goudy & Kent's steam bakery.

"What's this man's name?" Grey asked.

"Chester Sears, an old partner of the dead man. He was around a few days ago, staying at Darragh's boardinghouse."

"He's not local?"

"From Boston originally and headed back there a couple years ago, after they pulled one of their bigger heists."

They entered the boardinghouse's front room, which barely had enough space for the reception desk. The manager sat smoking a thin cigar with his head tilted back, reading the paper through dusty glasses.

"Help you?" he said with the briefest of glances at Lean and Grey.

"Chester Sears in?" Lean asked.

"I'd say you missed him." The cigar, wedged in place of a missing bottom canine, trembled when the man spoke. Ashes tumbled down onto the faded black vest he wore over a dingy shirt.

"What time's he usually get back in, then?"

The corners of the man's mouth turned down, and he shook his head the merest fraction. "Nah. Mean I think you missed him for good."

"What—he's checked out?"

"Nope. Paid through the month. But he left in a hurry yesterday."

"What time?" Grey asked

Lean glanced at Grey, then waited for the answer while the boardinghouse owner gummed his cigar in thought.

"Came rushing in the door early. Not long after seven. So I s'pose he was out all night. Often was. Only queer 'cause that means he'd usually sleep the day through. Not Friday, though. Couldn't have been more than three minutes before he came tearing back downstairs. Bag in hand, looking like he's seen the Ghost of Christmas Yet to Come."

"Maybe he had," said Lean as he showed his badge to the man. "I need the spare key."

"Sorry. I'll lose business if I start letting coppers go looking about in guests' rooms."

"We'll be discreet. Or else I'll start announcing how we'll be back to search every room. See how much business you keep then."

"All right." The man retrieved a key from under the front desk, made sure no one was approaching from the inside stairs or the front door, and slid it across to Lean. "But be quick about it. One floor up, Room G."

The detectives climbed the spongy, cracked stairs and entered a thin hall unlit except for a lone, grime-covered window at the far end.

"So did Sears put Cosgrove's body in the house at Vine Street?" Lean wondered aloud.

"Or did he only flee when he heard about it?" Grey countered.

They passed several doors, including one that, from the odors emanating, must have been the common toilet. Lean found G and unlocked the door. The room was sparse and cheerless. Faded wallpaper blended into a wooden floor that hadn't seen polish or even soap in many decades and a ceiling that could no longer lay claim to any true shade of white. A frayed curtain hung in the thin window frame. The only furniture in the room was a small, unmade single bed, a dresser with each drawer partly open, a wobbly side table, and a wastebasket. A quick search of the room revealed a comb, a lone sock in one of the drawers, and a bit of loose change along with an almost empty packet of cigarettes on the side table.

"I see why he doesn't spend much time here. Not much bigger than a prison cell."

"Then he should feel right at home," Grey said as he picked up the waste bin.

"Lived sparely," Lean said, "almost monastic."

"Hardly," Grey said as he drew out one liquor bottle, then another from the bin.

"Can't blame him all that much. Even you'd take a nip or two confined within these filthy walls."

"A remarkably charitable assessment coming from you," Grey said after regarding Lean for a moment. "It leads me to conclude that congratulations are in order. I take it you've been blessed with your second child and finally managed to purchase the new home you wanted."

"Yes. Thanks for asking—in your own peculiar way. Don't suppose you care to elaborate on just how you figured that."

"You used to worry about the impending birth and whether you could afford to move from your apartment to a house of your own. Nothing in your manner indicates that you're still dealing with grief, or your lovely wife's grief, over the loss of a child. So the birth occurred without incident. And now, seeing Sears's squalid quarters, you exhibit only pity, not commiseration, meaning he's less fortunate than you. Thus you are no longer in the similar position of being forced to make do in a cramped residence."

Grey pulled a newspaper from the bin and handed it to Lean. It was Thursday's morning edition. Next Grey retrieved a crumpled bit of paper, which he smoothed out and studied in the dusky light from the window.

"What's that?" Lean asked.

Grey didn't respond, so the deputy peered in.

The paper was a three-by-five-inch sheet with the words TREMONT HOUSE imprinted across the top. Written in neat block letters in ink was HORSFORD—BRATTLE ST. CAMBRIDGE. Below, in pencil, a messier hand had scribbled *"Tues. 7–11"* and then a series of random words and numbers: *"boy 22 horse 78 dog ink sun."*

"Three days from now," Lean said. "And Tremont House—that's in Boston?"

"Yes. Curious why Sears would have this stationery. One of the most expensive hotels in the city." Grey motioned about at their current meager surroundings before returning his attention to the paper.

"This code is most peculiar." After a moment Grey added, "I'll telephone ahead to Walt McCutcheon in Boston. Have him check the guest registry at the Tremont House and look into the identity of this Horsford of Brattle Street. We need to know the connection to Cosgrove."

Lean smiled. He hadn't heard the name of Grey's old colleague in a while. McCutcheon, a Pinkerton detective who was memorable for his carefree manner and oversize appetites, had helped them on their investigation a year earlier. Lean's smile faded as he recognized Grey's meaning.

"I appreciate the offer, but I can't impose. This is strictly a police matter. You've got your own business to attend to." Lean reached out for the handwritten note. "I can't expect you to volunteer your time and energies—"

Grey's eyes flicked from the note to Lean's hand, then up to his face. He made no movement to turn the paper over. "I can certainly spare a day or so. Besides, I've been meaning to get down to the city. Take in a concert or some such."

Lean didn't believe that last bit, but he didn't want to object too strenuously. Grey's familiarity with Boston, and his connections there, would surely be useful.

"I'll need time to make arrangements at the station, get the marshal's approval," Lean said.

Chapter 8

LEAN WAITED AT THE BASE OF THE MAIN STEPS OF CITY Hall. Word had been passed down that he was to meet Mayor Baxter there at half past six. As he watched the doors, his eyes drifted up the light yellowish brown Nova Scotia Albert stone to the building's grandiose center dome, which loomed 160 feet above him.

Only a minute later, the mayor appeared, took in the scene from the top steps, and smiled down at Lean. The mayor was in his early sixties, and his bowler hid a severely receding hairline. His rounded face and slightly bulging midsection reflected his hugely successful business ventures in the canning and packing industry. A thin salt-and-pepper goatee circled down below the jawline to leave his distinctive chin cleft exposed.

"Deputy, walk along with me. I wanted to speak with you about this poor fellow who went and got shot last week or whenever. Cosgrove, I think his name was."

"Oh, of course, Your Honor. Didn't realize you were following the matter."

"As mayor, my time is put to better use working on the broad issues and efforts at civic improvement. So while my approach to police work in the city may be rather hands-off, that doesn't mean I keep my ears closed."

Baxter's reputation for a keen intellect, along with his sharp eyebrows, lent a certain gravitas to the man's comments.

"Every Monday morning I have a chat with the marshal about various goings-on. He told me about this murder you're investigating. And someone went and dug the poor fellow up. Very disturbing. I understand you've requested permission to go to Boston to seek out his murderer."

"Just a known accomplice, but he may well be aware of what happened."

"And you've involved an outside investigator, Perceval Grey."

Lean considered a response as they passed a wide flight of stone steps leading up to the First Parish Church. It was a solid, elegant structure, old enough to have a spacious lot around it despite its location in the heart of the city. He glanced up at the clock face set in the church's front tower of undressed granite and realized he couldn't delay his response any longer.

"I wouldn't say 'involved,'" Lean answered. "Not in any official capacity by any means."

"Don't worry yourself, son, I haven't called you here to drag you or this Grey over the coals. Quite the opposite. You see, I received the queerest package a few months back, shortly after I took office. Sent to me with a letter from a Mrs. Helen Prescott. I knew her from her position at the historical society."

"Of course." Lean was well aware of Baxter's many philanthropic efforts in and around Portland. Not the least of these was his funding the construction, several years earlier, of the city's new building to house the public library and historical society.

"I also knew her uncle, Virgil Steig. The package she sent contained a journal that he'd started last summer. It detailed his work on the body of a murder victim by the name of Maggie Keene. Not the sort of thing a city surgeon would normally devote an entire journal to. But, as you well know, the investigation took some rather bizarre turns."

Two gentlemen standing outside a handsome block of brick stores that included the entrance to the Odd Fellows Hall tipped their hats and bade the mayor a good evening. Baxter was very popular; Lean had noticed other passersby smiling or waving at the mayor as they walked. Baxter possessed an uncanny ability to graciously acknowledge his well-wishers with a nod, a wave, or a return tip of his hat without so much as a pause in his conversation with Lean.

"An additional murder out of state," Baxter continued. "A missing woman reported in the city, not so peculiar, until Dr. Steig mentions her body being inexplicably found in one of the city tombs. Entrance to which was apparently gained without any legal authorization. The suspicion of the murder falling upon the son of one of our city's prominent citizens despite the young man's being locked up in an insane asylum in

Massachusetts. The journal ended prematurely, of course, when Virgil died. Natural causes was how I heard it."

They started to cut across Congress Street heading for Monument Square. While other pedestrians retreated back to the sidewalk or else quickened their steps to dodge an oncoming horse-drawn railcar, the mayor just kept on at his same steady pace. Lean had to restrain his urge to grab hold and rush the man forward. It wasn't with any arrogance that the mayor forced the trolley to slow and yield to him, just a sense of surety, a purpose in his stride that would not be deflected or delayed.

"Mrs. Prescott's letter picks up the tale there," Baxter said. "It rather shocked and saddened me to learn that he was, in fact, murdered. Along with others—a priest, even. Adultery and blackmail, poison and black magic. And to top it all off, Mrs. Prescott herself and her young daughter kidnapped and planned to be murdered in some occult ritual. Only to be saved at the last moment by you and this Perceval Grey." Baxter gave Lean an appreciative nudge with the back of his hand as they walked.

"It's all a bit hard to fathom," the mayor said. "I wouldn't have believed any of it if I didn't know Mrs. Prescott and her uncle. She wanted to impress upon me just how much you and this Grey fellow had done to bring the true murderer to justice, that you deserved to remain a deputy marshal when I made my official appointments."

Lean nodded. His original appointment to deputy under the prior mayor had been unexpected. The increase in salary had allowed him and Emma to purchase their modest home. He'd been incredibly relieved earlier this year to learn that Mayor Baxter hadn't chosen to replace him. "Very considerate of her."

"Suppose it was the least she could do for the man she credits with saving her daughter."

"I'm only thankful we arrived in time," Lean said. "Of course, I should be quite clear on just how much Helen Prescott assisted in the investigation. She displayed bravery and insight far beyond that which we could have expected from someone in her position. A position I'm hopeful she will soon return to."

"Of course, I'll see to that. Whenever she wishes to return, the historical society will be waiting. Her story did have a few gaps in it that interest me. If I understand correctly, the man behind those murders was obsessed with the occult and was assisted by others, including a woman. And—is this true—she tried to burn Mrs. Prescott's daughter alive?"

Lean nodded.

"A woman! What kind of monster could attempt such a thing?"

"We never did learn that, Your Honor. She set herself aflame and fell into the ocean. The body was never recovered. She seemed to be similarly obsessed with occult ideas. Obviously, she was very disturbed, not in her right mind."

The mayor nodded and sighed, accepting the explanation as the only one that could ever possibly make sense in the world. "I understand that the fellow behind the murders also died in the . . . attempt to arrest him. Though the death was never officially reported."

"It seemed a full report would have prompted a slew of questions that might have been hard to explain, and perhaps quite damaging to other people and interests," Lean said.

"Mayor Ingraham's feelings on the subject, no doubt."

"Yes, sir."

"And the killer's body was disposed of how?"

"Perceval Grey saw to that in a matter he thought fitting."

A look of morbid curiosity dawned on the mayor's face. "Which was what, exactly?"

Lean considered how to phrase his answer and drew in a deep breath. It proved to be poor timing. They were passing Horp Lung's shop. Bright red letters painted on the window declared "Hand Laundry." A vent leading out from a small basement window sent waves of hot, steamy air onto the sidewalk. A less-than-pleasant odor of human life enveloped them for a moment, the heavy scent of laundry being pressed by hot irons. Lean's mind recoiled to the midnight visit to the Western Cemetery and the wall of stuffy, rancid air that had washed over him and Grey as they'd unsealed a heavy metal door.

"He put the body in the same tomb where we'd earlier discovered that the missing woman's corpse was being hidden."

"The Marsh family tomb?" Baxter's normally calm eyes widened. "That brings me to my final question: What exactly was the role of Dr. Jotham Marsh in all this?"

As they rounded the corner and entered the bustle of Monument Square, Lean tried to gauge what the nature of Mayor Baxter's interest was in the subject of Jotham Marsh, but the man's voice and expression were completely neutral.

"I can't honestly say. He had some connection to the murderer through that mystical order he runs. He was a kind of teacher in occult matters. But he denied any knowledge of the man's activities or murderous interests. He, or at least his followers, did hide that earlier victim's body, but it seemed less to aid the murderer and more to avoid any scandal."

They paused before the entrance to the United States Hotel, where Baxter was meeting business associates for dinner. Baxter raised one of his sharp eyebrows and asked, "And your friend Grey thought that action warranted having a murderer's body dumped in the family's tomb?"

"Grey suspected that Marsh was more involved than it outwardly appeared. That he had a sort of sinister hand in all of it."

As the mayor weighed that information, Lean glanced past him to survey the open plaza and its surrounding avenues. Apart from the elegant United States Hotel, Monument Square was also home to the grand Preble House, along with dozens of other restaurants, theater halls, offices, and shops providing the full gamut of products and services. The square had been reconfigured two years prior when the center of the plaza yielded to the erection of a massive Civil War monument. *Our Lady of Victories*, a bronze, laurel-helmeted Athena, towered over the plaza from atop a large pedestal bearing reliefs of soldiers and sailors.

"I've met the man a few times," the mayor finally conceded. "He's becoming something of a fixture in certain social circles."

"Well, like I said, Grey had his suspicions. There was no hard evidence of wrongdoing."

"Don't worry, Lean. Marsh is not a friend of mine. In fact, I find there's something about the man that isn't quite square." The mayor chuckled. "Mrs. Prescott, on the other hand, strikes me as a person who makes quite a bit of sense. She spoke highly of you and your unofficial colleague Mr. Grey. So go ahead with your hunting expedition to Boston. Utilize Grey's talents as you see fit. Of course, if you can apprehend the murderer this time, rather than tossing him off the side of a building, all the better."

"Understood, sir. Thank you."

⌘ ⌘

LEAN RAN THROUGH the dark, not knowing exactly where he was going, just rushing straight ahead beneath a cloudy, troubled night sky. His trouser legs snagged on the tangled brush as he raced over the uneven ground. Then ahead he saw a flickering flame. He ran harder, closing the distance, watching the flame grow larger as he neared. He reached a rock ledge, a craggy outcropping jutting into dark, empty air. To the sides he saw whitecaps raging on the black water. The flame, a burning torch, was close now. A woman in a white dress held it above her head as she pressed forward, farther out along the rise of the ledge.

Lean bounded up the slope of small, sharply angled rocks. The ocean grew louder; lightning flashed beyond the fleeing woman's outline. She reached the point and turned to face him. In the light of the torch, Lean saw her teeth bared in a twisted, furious snarl. Her red hair was pulled back, and her eyes were lit with sheer hatred. He knew that face now. He raised the pistol, aiming directly at her chest. Then, remembering the futility of it, he lowered his gun. Her snarl eased into a menacing grin.

"It's already over," Lean heard himself say.

"Fool," the woman hissed. "The Master is rising even now. You can't stop him. And the stronger the spirit offered up, the brighter the flame calling him back to us."

The woman's right arm, the one holding the firebrand, dropped to her side.

"Don't!" he cried.

The flame touched the bottom of the woman's dress and blazed upward. Lean stepped forward, his coat in his hand to smother the fire, but her hair was already burning. The woman's arms shot skyward like two fiery pillars. Lean tried to move in, but the heat of the flames was unbearable, and his nostrils filled with the overpowering stench of oil and burned flesh. He was about to attempt a tackle when she turned and ran headlong off the rocks. She dropped down into the ocean, leaving a sickening hiss in her wake.

The world flashed. Lean's body convulsed, and he heard his own voice. He wasn't sure what he'd said. A sweaty film coated his body. He felt all tangled and worked his legs free before sitting up in his bed.

"What's wrong?" Emma said.

Lean stared at his wife before reality settled back into his mind.

"Nothing," he said. "Just a dream."

Emma was silent for a moment then asked, "Not that same one from before?"

A bothered, whimpering sound erupted from beyond his wife's side of the bed, saving Lean from having to answer.

"Oh, she's awake," Emma whispered as she rose and moved to the crib against the wall.

"Sorry," Lean whispered back.

Emma gave him a tired smile and turned her full attention to their ten-month-old daughter, Amelia. Lean wandered out of the room and downstairs to use the water closet before finding a cigarette in a coat pocket. He eased his way out the back door and walked across their small, fenced-in yard. They'd bought the little house only that spring, and Lean was still getting used to the place. The grass, where it hadn't yet gone brown or bare, felt refreshing beneath his feet. His thoughts began to wander as he returned to sit on the steps and finish his smoke.

In a few hours, he'd be up and on his way. A train ride to Massachusetts with Grey to track down a man connected to a strange, gruesome murder. He tried to shake the dreams and his thoughts of that former case from his head and focus instead on tomorrow's task. Just find Chester Sears and they'd find out what Cosgrove was up to. Lean wondered if everyone upstairs was back to sleep yet. Emma would likely forget everything by morning. He wouldn't have to lie about having the same dream again. He drew in a final breath of smoke. The last bit of paper glowed in the darkness before he dropped the butt on the ground and watched it die.

[Chapter 9]

THE NEXT MORNING LEAN ARRIVED AT GREY'S BUILDING ON High Street and instructed the cabdriver to wait. He knocked and stood there until the door creaked open just far enough for the landlady's face to reluctantly make its appearance.

"Why, Deputy Lean, you're a welcome sight." Mrs. Philbrick actually smiled.

Lean tried to remember if he'd ever seen her do that before. He removed his hat and stepped into the hallway.

"You wouldn't believe the assortment of characters he has parading through here at all hours. More than a few of the criminal element, I'd say." Mrs. Philbrick rolled her eyes to the heavens.

"Have you seen Mr. Grey this morning?"

"Seen him? No. Heard him enough. Up there pacing back and forth all night long. In one of his confounded moods."

Lean headed up the stairs, then paused in the short hallway just long enough to rap on Grey's door before entering. The main room served as a parlor, library, laboratory, and office. The space usually held some degree of organization and tidiness, but not this morning. Flat sheets of discarded paper competed with those of the balled-up and tossed-aside variety for dominion of the floor, desktop, and every other horizontal surface in the room.

Grey stood near the windows, writing on a chalkboard that must have been a new addition to the room. After noticing Lean, he glanced at his pocket watch. "You're early."

"I had a feeling you might need a reminder of our schedule." Lean saw that Grey was still wearing the suit he'd had on yesterday. The jacket was slung over a chair, and the sleeves of his shirt, from wrist to elbow, were covered in chalk from wiping the board clean. "Just in case you were preoccupied."

Lean picked up a sheet of paper and saw *"boy 22 horse 78 dog ink sun"* written across the top. Columns of what looked like random letters and numbers were arranged below. On Grey's desk Lean noticed an atlas opened to a map of Portland along with the city directory half buried beneath sheets of scribbled notes.

"Have you been at this all night? Trying to decipher the words on Sears's note. You should've gotten some sleep. We'll have four hours on the train to Boston to consider the code."

Grey looked at Lean, finally accepting the truth of his presence. "Easier for me to work . . . here."

Lean grinned, amused rather than offended by the effort it must have taken for Grey to end that sentence with something other than "alone."

"I'll see if Mrs. Philbrick can manage some toast or something while you get dressed and pack."

⊱   ⊰

THEIR TRAIN PULLED IN, and the two detectives stepped off into a scene of total anarchy. The B&M depot was the fourth in a row of terminals, behind the Fitchburg, the B&L, and the Eastern, all of which were in the process of being shut down and demolished to make way for Boston's massive new North Union Station. Grey led the way down to the corner of Portland and Traverse, where a covered four-wheeled carriage awaited.

Walt McCutcheon stepped down from the cab. His bright blue plaid suit was visible from a distance. He'd forgone the custom of matching vest to suit, selecting one of dazzling gold silk instead. He completed the mismatched combination with a green necktie. He touched his fingers to the brim of his bowler in salute, while his dark handlebar mustache danced above a wide grin.

"Good to see you, Grey. As always, you're looking fit as a fiddle and brown as a nut, long kept and dried."

Grey extended his hand for a collegial shake.

"Lean!" McCutcheon gripped the deputy's hand and clamped his shoulder. It was not a greeting of old friends, one of deeply felt joy at a reunion too long in coming. Instead it held the exuberance of two men who didn't truly know much of each other but who had faced down a common danger. Now the sight of the other would always remind each man of a frozen moment, amid the swirling sea of life's tedious days, when they'd felt keenly what it was to remain alive.

"You made a full recovery from our escapade last summer, I take it?" Lean asked.

McCutcheon laid a hand on his slightly bulging side. "Good as new."

The men settled into the shaded seats of the carriage.

McCutcheon lit a cigar, then asked, "So, Grey, gotten bored of Portland yet? Could always come back to the city."

The question hadn't occurred to Lean before, but now that it was in the air, he found he was anxious to hear the response.

"I keep myself occupied," Grey said.

The answer was hardly informative, but it satisfied McCutcheon. The man launched into a series of updates on the activities and well-being of several common acquaintances from the days when Grey had worked alongside McCutcheon in the Boston office of the Pinkerton Detective Agency.

As the carriage rumbled over the West Boston Bridge, crossing the Charles into Cambridge, McCutcheon finally rounded the corner into the business at hand.

"No Sears or Cosgrove registered at Tremont House in the past two weeks."

"Not surprising. He'd stand out like a wolf among the fold. What about the other bit?" Lean asked.

"The infamous Horsford of Brattle Street. Eben Norton Horsford. Former professor of chemistry at Harvard. Was also a part owner in the Rumford Chemical Works. Apparently he made a fortune from his re-formulation of baking powder."

Lean nodded as he made the connection with the familiar one-pound red can that was always present whenever Emma was baking bread or whatnot. The carriage continued up Broadway.

"Have you been in contact with the man?" Grey asked. "We need to determine what he knows of Sears and Cosgrove. And if our strange coded letters mean anything to him."

"I'm good at my job, but not that good. This Professor Horsford passed away on New Year's Day. Don't worry, though—natural causes. Lived a full, long life."

"Married?" Lean asked.

"She's out of town, but I did manage to find a daughter, *Miss* Cornelia Horsford. She was a bit alarmed when I explained myself and the situation, but she's graciously agreed to meet us at the house and show us around."

Grey allowed a hint of a smirk as he studied McCutcheon's features. "Miss Horsford, is it? And you're thinking this lonely baking-powder heiress has been waiting all her life for a certain type of man to come along. A larger-than-life sort of fellow with a taste for loud waistcoats, potent cigars, and off-color anecdotes."

"Well, the professor was an old man. She can't be too young herself anymore." McCutcheon drew the chewed-up cigar from his mouth and brandished it at the passing scenery: large, tidy brick buildings and the occasional small, manicured lawn. "Obviously, she hasn't found anything she likes among all these namby-pamby Harvard types."

"No doubt she'll find you to be a breath of fresh air," Grey said as he waved away a blast of rancid cigar smoke.

The carriage rounded the northern edge of Harvard's campus and skirted the bustle of Harvard Square before arriving onto Brattle Street. They soon entered the 100 block, and the carriage pulled over.

"High-class neighborhood," Lean said.

"That's the truth." McCutcheon pointed across a wide lawn to a large Colonial house painted a pale yellow with white trim. "The Longfellow house there. Until he died anyway. Back before that the place served as Washington's headquarters during the Siege of Boston."

McCutcheon nodded in self-congratulation at having such a notable historic fact at his disposal. A dark look had settled on Lean's face.

"What's the matter, Deputy? Something against George Washington?" McCutcheon asked.

"Don't mind Lean, it's just his territorial nature," Grey said as they disembarked. "He objects to any other city staking even a bit of claim to Portland's poet laureate."

"The true Longfellow House sits on Congress Street in Portland. That's where he was born," Lean said.

"Maybe, but you can't choose where you're born. The man elected to make his family's home here the last decades of his life. Speaks volumes, if you ask me," McCutcheon said.

"You can choose anywhere in the world to work and rest your old feet, but there's only one place where you were raised. One place that shapes a man's view of the world, gives him his poetry."

"Here we go again," Grey said, and then walked with a purpose toward the front door of the Horsford house.

Lean placed one hand upon his breast, the other held out toward the sky. " 'Often I think of the beautiful town / That is seated by the sea; / Often in thought go up and down / The pleasant streets of that dear old town, / And my youth comes back to me.' "

McCutcheon stood speechless, regarding Lean with a queer look.

"He wasn't talking about Cambridge," Lean announced before proceeding up the walk.

A maid led the way to the front parlor, where Miss Cornelia Horsford greeted them. Her hair was pulled back into a tight bun, making her anxious face look even more stern. She wore a plain-skirted walking costume of deep purple, and Lean wondered if she was observing some old-fashioned state of half mourning for her late father.

McCutcheon introduced himself, then the others. Miss Horsford wondered aloud about a thief having this address and whether she ought to call the police directly.

"It's never harmful to be overly vigilant," Grey commented. "Though you don't actually live here, I understand. Is the house currently occupied?"

"A minimal staff has stayed on while Mother's away. She's gone to Europe for the spring and summer. A desperately needed change in scenery after Father's death. She'll be gone until September. Couldn't bear missing New England in the autumn."

"And the staff hasn't had anyone unusual calling at, or lurking about, the house?" Lean asked.

"Nothing the slightest bit out of the ordinary. I telephoned as soon as I heard from Mr. McCutcheon. I had Harriet, the maid, and the others comb the house. Not a thing missing or out of place."

"The entire house?"

"Every inch except Father's study. I have the only key."

"Would you mind?" Lean asked.

"Not at all. This way, gentlemen." She led them into the hall and up a staircase.

"Is there some particular reason you have the sole key to the study?" Grey asked.

"It was too much for Mother. She asked me to make arrangements for his things, since I knew the most about his work. I've even been pursuing some of his archaeological interests. Mother and my sisters found it all terribly dull, I'm afraid."

They came to a closed door, which Cornelia Horsford unlocked. Upon entering the room, Lean felt a bit as if he were stepping into a photograph, only real and in color. The air was stale and heavy with the scent of books and old paper, like a dead-end aisle in the bowels of a library. Everything in the room, from the grand desk to the portraits and framed maps on the walls, had the look of being set in place, permanent and immovable.

"A bit stuffy, isn't it?" Cornelia said as she crossed the room to open a window.

"Was your father working on anything new? An advance in some chemical formulation, perhaps. Something the competitors of the Rumford Chemical Works might be interested in?" Grey asked.

"No, Father hadn't really been doing any of that kind of work for years now. In fact, he'd been rather single-mindedly devoted to his historical research. And I can't imagine why anyone would want to steal any of those papers. After all, history already belongs to every one of us. Certainly no money in it. To be frank, my mother would get quite annoyed at Father for how much he spent on his history projects. But then money isn't everything, is it?"

"Not when you have plenty of it." McCutcheon offered a grin that struck everyone else as rather ham-handed.

"True . . . I suppose," Cornelia answered haltingly. "But for Father history was a passion. And I have to say, I found it quite interesting as well."

"What sort of history was he studying, exactly?" Lean asked.

"The Norsemen."

"The Norsemen?" Lean gave her a blank look.

"Yes. Oh, you know, Leif Eriksson and his discovery and settlement in North America."

"Ah, yes, the Vikings. The Vine Land sagas," Lean said.

"Vinland. Now the so-called experts might say otherwise, but Father had proof that—"

"Sorry to interrupt, Miss Horsford"—Grey had wandered to a tall bookcase with glass doors—"but could you tell me if anything is missing from this case? The shelves are only half filled. Books on geology and archaeology, some atlases and such. Markings along the frame here show that the lock may have been forced. The glass door was open."

The others all approached. Lean watched as Grey drew out a clean white handkerchief, wrapped it over a finger, and swiped the outside of the glass.

"Father probably lost his key and pried it open at some point. He was always misplacing his keys. He used to keep his own notes and historical research materials in there."

Grey repeated the process, taking a sample of the dust on the inside of the glass, then compared the two specimens. "I'd say this door was only opened in the past two weeks or so."

"It probably wasn't closed properly. I assure you, there's no cause for alarm. Father's papers haven't been stolen. All of his Norsemen material was donated to the Athenaeum after his death. Per his instructions."

"The Athenaeum's a museum, isn't it?" Lean asked.

"A library," Grey said.

McCutcheon raised his eyebrows in a look of mock snobbery. "For private members only. All very hoity-toity."

"You say that about any place with more than two books in it," Grey said.

McCutcheon offered a shrug in his defense. "What do you need with more than two? The city directory and—"

"The Bible?" Cornelia Horsford offered.

"Why not? Thank you, Miss Horsford," McCutcheon said with a smile, as if her contribution had somehow won the day for him.

"We did a bit of work at the Athenaeum a few years back." A mischievous smile appeared on McCutcheon's face. "Grey, do you recall that fellow who—"

"Yes. Though it's not really the most opportune time for reminiscing." Grey had made his way to the room's windows, where he completed his examination of the latches before opening one and sticking his head out to survey the outer sill and the side of the house.

"Is there a problem, Mr. Grey?" Miss Horsford asked.

"Not at all, Miss Horsford. Nothing you need to fret about in the slightest."

"Thank goodness. You worried me."

Grey gave her a smile, then snapped his fingers as if he'd just remembered something. "Miss Horsford, could I impose upon you to use the telephone? Rather urgent, I'm afraid."

She led the men downstairs and showed Grey to the telephone before retreating to the well-appointed parlor with McCutcheon and Lean.

McCutcheon glanced about the room, settling his attention on a finely crafted Chinese vase that appeared to be a valuable antique.

"It befuddles the mind—all this out of working on household supplies. I'd say you can toss out every cake, bread loaf, and pastry across the land. It's no contest: Your father clearly got the biggest rise out of baking powder the world's ever witnessed."

McCutcheon guffawed at his own effort, while Cornelia Horsford smiled politely. Lean, embarrassed at his colleague's attempt at cheerful banter, casually strolled from the room. He stepped across the hall. Grey was in a side room with the telephone receiver to his ear. Lean didn't mind eavesdropping, since he was sure Grey wasn't making a personal call. He couldn't imagine whom Grey would seek out for a personal conversation even on an ordinary day, let alone in the middle of an investigation. Lean's brow creased in confusion when he heard Grey's request to the operator.

"Yes, could you please connect me to the Suffolk County Courthouse switchboard?"

[Chapter 10]

PHEBE WEBSTER STOOD IN HER GRANDFATHER'S DIM ROOM with her arms crossed, trying not to watch as Dr. Thayer made another unsuccessful attempt to administer the opiate-filled syringe.

"His veins are much contracted due to his weakened condition and recent lack of adequate food and water. Almost impossible to find one." The doctor proceeded to tie a cord around Horace Webster's shriveled biceps.

"Miss Webster, would you be so kind as to hold that candle closer so I might have a better look?"

Phebe stepped nearer to the narrow bed tucked into the corner. She took the candle from its perch on the side table and crouched down. The doctor readied another effort with the syringe, so Phebe looked away, finding her grandfather's thin face. He'd been old as long as she could remember, but the flesh was so much reduced now that she barely recognized the man who'd been the closest thing to a father she'd ever known. As she met her grandfather's eyes, different now, cloudy and distant, she knew that his spirit was still there, still with her. His weak gaze fell upon her like a foggy morning sky where the sun, though watery and indistinct, still makes its presence known.

The old man's face pinched for a moment.

"There we go. That ought to help his pain." Dr. Thayer replaced his material into his black leather case. "Rest now, Horace."

The doctor motioned for Phebe to accompany him to the door.

"I really don't think it will be much longer now," Dr. Thayer said in a quiet voice. He laid a reassuring hand on her forearm with a concerned yet resigned smile that would have done the most stoic undertaker proud.

"Thank you, Doctor. On your way out, could you see if my uncles have arrived yet? And let them know."

The doctor eased out of the room, and Phebe returned to the bedside to resume her vigil. She wet a cloth in the porcelain bowl on the bedstand and dabbed her grandfather's brow. His eyes searched her out, and a look of relief crept across his features.

"There you are. I was worried . . ." His eyes fluttered, and his faint voice paused as if he were marshaling the remnants of his strength. " . . . that I'd lost you. But you're back."

Phebe smiled at him, and her eyes welled up. "I'm right here with you, Grandfather. Don't you worry. I'll stay right here."

Her left hand moved forward to take his. He was too weak to match her grip. His eyes tried to focus on her once more, but Phebe could tell that confusion was settling over him.

"Will you be . . . ?" he whispered, then was silent for a moment. "When . . . ?"

"Yes, Grandfather, I'll be right here with you. It will be soon now. You'll see." She laid her right hand against the side of his face. "Everything will be just fine. It will all be right again. Rest now."

A while later, when she heard stirring downstairs and footsteps coming up to this floor, Phebe rose from the bedside, where her grandfather's body had lain silent and motionless for at least five minutes. She moved to the outer room and awaited the appearance of her two uncles.

When they entered, she didn't need to speak the news. Her expression and her red-rimmed eyes were clear enough. Phebe's two uncles went to the bedroom door and looked in on the thin frame of their father. Phebe had already crossed Horace's arms and raised the sheet over his head.

"How long ago?" asked Euripides.

"A few minutes," Phebe answered.

"Damn. Sorry, it's just . . ."

"I don't think it would have made much difference to him, Uncle. He was somewhat muddled."

"Was he at peace?" Jason asked. "Toward the end, I mean."

"He was not in pain," Phebe answered.

"Should have come sooner. Still, you were here, did your duty,"

Euripides said before heading back toward the doorway. "I'd better start making arrangements."

A shred of anger flashed through Phebe's mind. How typical of her uncle to treat the passing of his own father as if it were some routine engagement to be faced in the grand military campaign of life. In Euripides' eyes she'd done her duty. Horace's final moments on earth were the equivalent of a high piece of ground to be secured. Being by his side through his final breaths, she'd held the flank until her uncle could come to the rescue and bring his artillery to bear, save the day, and move on to the next conflict. She wanted to scream at him, shock him out of his ignorance, but she held back. Not now, not at this moment. This was to be a time of gratitude and treasuring the memory of her grandfather. She would not let Euripides' narrow feelings and careless tongue mar this moment forever.

"It was not my duty, Uncle," Phebe said calmly.

"What now?" Euripides turned back from where he'd just stepped out into the hallway.

"It was my honor, my deepest pleasure—not a duty."

"Ahh," was all that Euripides could be troubled to offer in return before he moved away down the hall.

"Oh, don't waste your thoughts on him," Jason said. "This is one of the few times we can look on his rigid and methodical nature as a blessing. You can set your mind at ease and dwell on whatever brings you solace now. He'll manage all the morbid details and see to it that the funeral goes off without a bump, in an efficient and proper manner."

"Is that supposed to bring me solace? A true and fitting farewell for someone you love ought to be more than efficient and proper. A hell of a lot more, if you don't mind my saying so."

Jason nodded. "I don't think I mind one bit."

[Chapter 11]

After crossing back into Boston, the detectives paused for a light snack at a café near the Public Gardens. Grey explained that they were not scheduled to arrive at their stop, the intersection of Commonwealth Avenue and West Chester Park, for another hour yet. During the leisurely break, the three men discussed a plan of action to investigate the possible presence of Chester Sears at the Tremont House either today or in the recent past. All three of them would monitor the hotel lobby and rear entrances that evening. McCutcheon, who would be in charge of procuring whatever information could be purchased from the desk clerks or bellhops, was eager to begin his efforts.

"Shouldn't at least one of us monitor the Horsford residence?" Lean asked. "That address was on the note along with today's date."

Grey shook his head. "Those two items of information were written in different hands. It would be a mistake to read them in unison. Besides, the window to Professor Horsford's study had been forced. I suspect that Sears has already been there. It's just not clear what he was searching for and whether he found it. No, our best chance of catching the man is at the Tremont House."

Upon stuffing one final morsel into his mouth, thus completing his successful conquest of the lion's share of the food at the table, McCutcheon bade them adieu and good hunting. Grey entered into a contemplative mood, which only amplified Lean's restlessness. He suspected that Grey was secretly enjoying the impatience he caused by not revealing who or what awaited them at their next appointment. Rather than give him any further enjoyment in the matter, Lean turned his attention to the picturesque view of the gardens' ornamental flower beds.

As the time neared, the two men made their way to the western edge of the gardens, where the central pathway met the Arlington Street entrance. At the eastern terminus of Commonwealth Avenue, they engaged a four-wheeler to transport them the mile length to their destination at the Back Bay Park. The driver of the carriage, an older fellow with rosy cheeks and a glint in his eye that hinted at an affection for a midday nip or two, welcomed them aboard.

"Down to the fens, is it? You know for just a slight bit on top, I'd gladly brighten your trip with a mention of all the wonderful points of interest along the route."

Just as Grey was preparing to decline the offer, Lean handed over twenty-five cents, garnering a somewhat toothless smile from the driver.

"Small price to pay to better acquaint myself with my surroundings," Lean said in answer to Grey's disapproving looks.

A tree-lined mall bisected the entire length of Commonwealth Avenue, giving it the appearance of two parallel thoroughfares. Almost immediately following their launch into the heavy traffic, the driver pointed out the granite statue of Alexander Hamilton. Lean puzzled over the less-than-obvious connection between Boston and Hamilton, other than the city's overt fondness for all things relating to the Revolution.

"By filling in the swampy Back Bay lands, hundreds of acres of terra firma were added to the city proper—and some of the city's most fashionable acres, I might add," the driver announced. "Many of the city's finest churches have relocated to the Back Bay over the years, following their parishioners—and their purses—out of the older parts of the city."

As evidence of this assertion, the driver pointed out the First Baptist, on the corner of Commonwealth and Clarendon. The eighty-foot-tall stone church was so massive and unyielding in its appearance that if not for the rose windows Lean would have half suspected that the building was solid rock the whole way through. As they passed the next few blocks, the driver waved his hand to the left, where one or two blocks away were such notable enterprises as the Massachusetts Institute of Technology and, opposite that, the new building of the Young Men's Christian Association, the oldest such organization in the country.

"Down Clarendon at Copley Square, you have the Second Church. Before relocating there, it was the Old North Church. Known in the seventeenth century as the 'Church of the Mathers.' Reverends Samuel, Increase, and Cotton each held the pulpit in turn for its first six decades. You know, even Ralph Waldo Emerson was minister at one time."

"Not that it would impress you much, Lean," Grey said. "After all, you had Longfellow in his youth."

Along the avenue Lean noticed very little in the way of commercial interests, apart from the numerous fine hotels such as the eight-story marble-faced Vendome. The driver boasted of its more than three hundred rooms and the latest improvements in plumbing, ventilation, electricity, and steam-powered elevators. Opposite stood another in the seemingly endless array of statues, this one honoring the famed abolitionist William Lloyd Garrison.

After traveling a final long, rectangular block, the driver pulled over by the intersection with West Chester Park, where Commonwealth Avenue ended its straight, mile-long stretch from the Public Gardens before it angled off to the west. The passengers stepped down onto the central mall area. A tall bronze statue resembling some stylized opera-stage Viking stood overlooking the narrow point where the Back Bay Park approached the Charles River. Lean thought that calling it a park was a bit generous. The lush green space was landscape architect Frederick Law Olmsted's valiant effort to transform the murky, sewage-flooded Back Bay fens into something resembling the original pristine saltwater marsh.

"Our distinguished contact awaits."

Grey motioned toward the statue, by the base of which stood a tall man of fifty or so whose erect bearing and well-tailored suit gave him an air of earnest importance. Lean could see that the man was regarding them closely from a pair of deep-set eyes. Beneath a prominent nose resided a splendidly overgrown white handlebar mustache. They approached the man, who smiled and stretched out his hand in welcome.

"Perceval Grey. Glad to see you again, and doubly so that it is on business not directly involving me."

"Deputy Marshal Archie Lean of the Portland police," Grey said, "allow me to introduce the Honorable Oliver Wendell Holmes Jr., justice of the Massachusetts Supreme Judicial Court."

"Ah, so this is some manner of criminal investigation. I'm not at all surprised, though I must say I'm pleased to see you working alongside an authorized representative of the law." A glint of humor had appeared in Holmes's eyes.

Lean's own eyes lit up as he extended his hand. "A pleasure, Your Honor. I'm a firm admirer of your father's literary works."

"Thank you, Deputy. Most kind. Well, gentlemen, I for one have something of a timetable that must be met. So let us forgo further pleasantries and direct our attention toward that very item which conspicuously demands it."

Justice Holmes turned and took a step in the direction of the tall bronze statue that dominated the mall near the intersection. "The renowned Viking explorer Leif Eriksson."

The statue was not the barbaric seafaring raider that Lean would have expected. Instead a classical figure rose before them, an athletic, clean-shaven Viking with flowing locks, calling to mind some Nordic version of Apollo. One hand cupped a horn behind his back while he held the other to his forehead, shielding his eyes as he scanned the western horizon. An inscription of Nordic runes appeared on the broad stone pedestal that at its base was carved to resemble a Viking longship complete with dragon-headed prow.

Justice Holmes cleared his throat. "I must apologize for making you come this far out just to see this statue for yourself, Grey. But then you did ask me what I knew about Eben Horsford, his recent work on the Norsemen, and the purchase of his papers by the Athenaeum. After a little thought, it became clear to me that even a brief vision of the statue would provide the required moment of insight. It would impart the true essence of the matter, the nature and extent of Eben Horsford's preoccupation with the Norse explorers, his obsession with convincing the world that they actually landed here. That's something which, even after hours of effort, I might not be capable of conveying to you in words."

"Brings one word to my mind." Lean paused to light a cigarette. "Preposterous. A city full of sculptures dedicated to statesmen, generals, and Founding Fathers—and then this. Leif Eriksson certainly looks out of place on the banks of the Charles River."

"As much today as he would have been nine hundred years ago, if he'd ever actually made it this far," Justice Holmes said.

"Can we assume that the statue's presence here has some connection to Professor Horsford?" Grey asked.

"The idea of erecting a monument to Leif Eriksson in the city was first suggested in the seventies. The inspiration came from Ole Bull, the great Norwegian violinist and ambassador of Scandinavian culture. He settled for some time in Cambridge and became close friends with Longfellow. Bull had heard the theory that the ancient Vinland of the Viking sagas was located in New England. If that were true, Leif Eriksson would have been the first European to land on our shores, in 1000 A.D. Longfellow also came to put his faith in this theory. Even wrote some poems about it, as I recall."

" 'The Skeleton in Armor,' " Lean interjected.

Grey gave him cautioning look and said, "Let's not interrupt the tale now."

"In any event," Justice Holmes continued, "Longfellow, my father, and their circle grew quite enthused with the subject and came up with the idea to commemorate the supposed event with a statue. They recruited a committee stacked with prominent citizens, including the mayor, the governor, the president of Harvard, along with, of course, Professor Eben Horsford. The project wasn't brought to fruition at the time due to resistance from saner organizations, which argued that there was no firm evidence to support the claim of the Norse discovery of America. Then, with the deaths of Bull and Longfellow in the next few years, the project floundered."

"And yet . . ." Lean rolled his eyes at the statue that loomed over them.

"The effort returned to life years later under Horsford's sponsorship. He'd become enraptured with the Leif Eriksson story. Since he was retired, time and money were no object. Horsford turned his full attention to the Viking explorations and, in particular, the idea that the Vikings were the founders of the legendary lost city of Norumbega."

"Norumbega?" Lean asked.

Justice Holmes gave a subtle tilt of his head, enough to convey he was only reciting facts of the case, not declaring them to be credible. "It's something of an odd tale. Perhaps it would help if you told me exactly what it is you're searching for."

Chapter 12

I N SHORT," GREY ANSWERED THE JUSTICE'S QUERY, "WE HAVE
reason to believe that a criminal element may have taken an interest in some aspect of the late professor's more recent research. The
exact nature of that interest remains a mystery. So anything you could
tell us about Professor Horsford's scholarly endeavors might help resolve the question."

"Eben Norton Horsford's archaeological research sought by some
nefarious criminals. Wouldn't he be terribly excited? And even more
puzzled to hear it than I am." Justice Holmes tapped the fingertips of
both hands together as he contemplated a starting point.

"I shall do my best to provide a thorough assessment of the topic. Despite what schoolchildren might hear, the coast of North America was
already well known to European sailors long before the Pilgrims landed
at Plymouth Rock in 1620. In the French and Spanish maps of the 1500s,
the name of Norumbega appears frequently, under a multitude of spell-
ings. It's not so famous now, but in its day it ranked alongside El Dorado
as a fabled lost city of gold. This one was reputedly located somewhere
in the Northeast. Verrazano designated the whole area as Norumbega
and sailed up the Hudson in 1524, looking for the supposed capital city.

"The stories gained new life in the late sixteenth century after publication of the tale of an Englishman, one of three who'd been marooned
along the coast of Mexico. He claimed to have crossed the eastern half of
the United States on foot, along with two other men, before being rescued by French traders in Nova Scotia. Among other fanciful claims, the
sailor reported visiting the city of Norumbega, somewhere near present-
day Boston Harbor. He told of kings decorated with giant rubies and
borne aloft on silver thrones. Pearls strewn about as common as pebbles.
Streets wider than those of London and houses with pillars of crystal."

"So you do come from old family money after all," Lean whispered to Grey.

Grey stifled a chuckle. "Pardon the interruption, Your Honor. You were describing European efforts to locate Norumbega."

Justice Holmes had a smile on his face as he continued. "Yes. Champlain searched thirty or forty miles up the Penobscot River in Maine in the early 1600s but discovered no indications of a city or of civilization, just an old moss-grown cross in the woods. Perhaps it was a marker left by those three sailors. If so, it was the most concrete element of that fantastic story. Over time even the most hopeful of travelers finally came to accept that no such fabled city ever existed.

"Leap ahead to the nineteenth century and bear with me a moment. In the 1830s the Danish historian Carl Christian Rafn published his theory that the old Norse sagas were not mere legends. He argued that some of these were factually based accounts showing that the Viking explorer Leif Eriksson had completed a voyage to North America in 1000 A.D. In those ancient Norse sagas of the discovery of Vinland, Leif Eriksson first sailed up a river that broadened into a lake. Crossing that, he headed up another river as far as his ship could float. Don't think Eben Horsford was alone in such fanciful ideas of Viking visitors in his backyard. The saga's description is vague enough that after Rafn's theory came out, folks up and down the coast proposed dozens of locales as Eriksson's landing place.

"Decades later, after poring over old maps and Viking sagas and whatnot, Horsford became convinced that the last part of Leif Eriksson's description of his journey matched the Charles River. But, placing validity in the old tale of the wayward sailor, the professor took his hypothesis a step further. He argued that not only was Vinland located along the Charles but that it was this same Norse settlement that would prosper and become the historical basis for what would later be known as the fabled lost city of Norumbega."

Grey had been quietly absorbing the information but now interrupted. "I assume that Horsford's rather inventive theories were refuted by other, more established scholars."

"Thoroughly. But he persisted in his search for proof of a Viking presence here."

"Why would Vikings give their settlement that name?" Lean looked to Grey. "Isn't Norumbega an Indian word?"

Grey nodded. "The generally accepted origin of the name Norumbega is from the Algonquin term meaning 'a quiet place between the rapids.'"

"And Eben Horsford certainly knew about the Indian origin of the name," Justice Holmes added. "He was the son of a missionary among the Indians and acquainted with various dialects and vocabulary. But he was nothing if not imaginative. He interpreted the name of Norumbega as being an Indian corruption of the word 'Norvege'—that is, Norway."

Lean cleared his throat. "Not meaning to brazenly announce my confusion on the subject, but could there be any validity at all to the professor's idea of a Viking settlement in these parts?"

"While it's not outside the realm of possibility, there is no evidence to support the event. Consider the matter for yourself," Holmes said. "As Horsford envisioned it, a thousand Norsemen settled along the lower reaches of the Charles River over a few hundred years, building forts, canals, and churches. Surely there would be vestiges of this sizable settlement that we could still recognize. Now, Horsford conducted small excavations in Cambridge and did succeed in finding stone house foundations, but the only artifacts to be found in the area were from the Colonial age. Rather than taking this for proof that the foundations were those of English colonists, he dismissed those artifacts as simply having being left during a later period. He ignored the evidence and concluded that he had unearthed Leif's house.

"Three years ago Horsford claimed that he'd found Norumbega up the Charles, close by Weston. What Horsford in fact found was a somewhat orderly scattering of rocks in what is generally rocky terrain. You can argue many points, but the deciding question really is this: Where are the artifacts and remains? The tools, animal bones, building timbers, charcoal residue in the old soil from cooking fires and forges?"

Justice Holmes paused briefly, as if either of the detectives might actually possess information with which to refute his rhetorical challenge.

"The indisputable truth is that when a group of people occupy a place, they simply do not leave it in a pristine condition. Even transitory Indian tribes left traces—arrowheads, bones, shell heaps, and whatnot.

There's no proof found of any Norse settlement, let alone the extensive, centuries-long sort of colony that Horsford propounded. Still, he insisted that he'd uncovered a Viking settlement and the fabled city of Norumbega all in one. He built a massive stone tower upriver to commemorate the site. Must have cost him tens of thousands of dollars."

"Surely people pointed out to the man the flaws in his reasoning," Lean said.

"I have spent enough years among lawyers to assure you that otherwise reasonable men will cling with all their life's blood to a solitary piece of evidence if it supports their claim, regardless of a mountain of facts to the contrary," Justice Holmes said.

"Clearly, the professor was never dissuaded, as indicated by our large bronze friend here," Grey said.

"The man's fervent beliefs persisted, and despite the renewed rebuttals the idea caught on. With Horsford's financial backing and a growing interest in the Vinland theory, the distinguished sculptress Miss Anne Whitney was commissioned and the Leif Eriksson statue was finally dedicated in 1887."

Lean shook his head. "So he's nothing more than a misled soul who squandered years and a fortune on this crackpot theory?"

Holmes paused for a moment before adding, "No, Horsford was definitely not just some deluded old fool. The Vikings weren't his only passion in life. Apart from his contributions to science and chemistry, he was a philanthropic soul. Extremely generous when it came to issues of public health and education, especially higher education for women. This particular theory may amount to a wild-goose chase, but it shouldn't sully the name of a great and kind man."

Justice Holmes checked his pocket watch. "I'm sorry, gentlemen, that I wasn't able to be of much use in illuminating any dark criminal secrets in the research of Eben Horsford. Though if I have whetted your appetite for further historical discourse, I recommend you visit the Athenaeum tonight. There's a reading of a new paper by an up-and-coming historian, Frederick Jackson Turner, on the American frontier and its defining role in our history. I've heard it's quite a fascinating work, though maybe a touch dry."

"Perhaps a dry recitation of the facts is best for historical discussions," Grey said. "Otherwise you risk blurring the line between history and fiction. The effort to add bold color and allure to the facts of the past can too easily cause one to stumble and produce mere illusions. Then what are we left with, other than bronze statues of Vikings on innocent city streets?"

Holmes weighed this and squinted at Grey. "A valid concern, perhaps, when you consider that history has always been, and by necessity will always be, only what the men who come after make of it. Yet I for one will rue the day when history ceases to be anything more than empty words on a page."

The justice leaned forward just a few inches, ready to impart some wisdom. "The danger is not in seeking to give inspiration to events. Rather, men court futility and peril when they allow the desire for history as they wish it had been to overpower the truth."

"But why?" Lean wondered aloud. "What in the world would possess an otherwise sensible, scientific man to do something like this?"

"It strikes me as an instance of that phenomenon where a mind once stretched by a new, alien idea can never again manage to recapture its original dimension," Justice Holmes said.

"When one looks at the image chosen to represent the Viking settler, the reasons start to become apparent," Grey said. "This figure never actually existed as he appears before us. We don't see the rough, fur-clad pillager that would be recognized in 1000 A.D. He looks more like some overgrown Northern European altar boy, and believe me, that altar would be located in a Protestant church. Leif Eriksson might not be Anglo-Saxon, but he could certainly pass for it with greater ease than could the likes of Columbus, who sailed under the flag of papist monarchs."

"You're looking for shadows on a cloudy day, Grey," Lean said.

"It was less than a decade ago that Boston elected its first Irish mayor," Grey said. "I'd be skeptical to hear that the Protestant elite of the old city on the hill haven't watched the rising numbers of Irish and Italian immigrants without a certain measure of alarm."

"We are all tattooed in our cradles with the beliefs of our tribe, and for better or for worse it is a basic human reaction to battle for the survival and primacy of one's own band," Justice Holmes said. "Sadly, you cannot educate a man wholly out of superstitious hopes and fears that have been ingrained in his imagination and so often prove to be indelible marks, no matter how strongly reason may strive to reject them."

The judge waved toward the bronze statue of the Norseman. "To the victors go the spoils. It applies to the writing or rewriting of history as much as it does to gold or land. It may be what drove Horsford."

Lean took his hat in his hand and shook his head. "Despite all we've learned of Professor Horsford, we haven't gained any real clue as to just why Chester Sears was interested in the man. If we can't lay our hands on the fellow tonight at the Tremont House, I fear the trail will be lost. Frank Cosgrove's murderer may well go free."

Justice Holmes stepped forward and clapped a hand onto Lean's shoulder. "I can't speak to that, Deputy, but don't lose heart. While our acquaintance has been brief, I find comfort in your clear determination to see the villain brought to justice. If this should prove our farewell, then I would speak these few final words to you: Have faith and pursue the unknown end."

"Thank you, Your Honor."

"And, Grey, it would sadden me to have our latest endeavor together be so brief. You really should join me tonight for that reading on the American frontier. It's supposed to be quite good."

"Unfortunately, I think I shall have to . . ." Grey paused and stared for a moment at the bronze Viking looming over them. "You know, I may do that. It could prove to be just the sort of welcome distraction that I need."

"Very good. I shall see you tonight then."

Lean waited until Justice Holmes departed before speaking. "Something Justice Holmes said made you give up on the Tremont House? Do you think the Athenaeum is a better lead?"

"No, you and McCutcheon should still go ahead at the Tremont," Grey said in a distracted voice. He began to pace back and forth beside the tall statue of Leif Eriksson. "Nothing about Professor Horsford has given me any insight into Sears's interest in the man, or anyone's motivation for shooting Frank Cosgrove. I don't see any firm link to the

Boston Athenaeum either. But there might be something there, and if not at least I have the chance to further extend our gratitude to Justice Holmes for his valiant efforts to assist our inquiry."

"We don't even know for certain that Chester Sears was after Professor Horsford's work on Leif Eriksson and ancient Indian cities of gold. Maybe he was having a secret love affair with one of the scullery maids or something? That would make more sense."

Grey shook his head. "I sincerely doubt that a man would need to write down the address of the woman with whom he's having romantic dalliances, as well as noting the name of her employer. Not to mention some coded message. He had the name and address because he was unfamiliar with the location. Nothing in the house was disturbed except for the window to the professor's locked study and the glass bookcase therein."

Grey stopped pacing with his back to Leif Eriksson and bowed his head in thought. "We cannot ignore the connection merely because its true nature eludes us. Rather we must pursue it with renewed vigor."

" 'Have faith and pursue the unknown end,' " Lean said glumly.

[Chapter 13]

GREY MANEUVERED AND PARDONED HIMSELF THROUGH THE clusters of well-dressed proprietors, as the members of the private Boston Athenaeum were known. The doors on the left side of the vestibule, housing the American Academy of Arts and Sciences, were shut, and the milling crowd was slowly moving toward the right. Grey instinctively mirrored the progress through the hall of his host, Justice Holmes, pausing whenever that man stopped to engage in short bursts of animated discussion with one of his innumerable acquaintances. Although he recognized a few faces among the crowd, Grey avoided eye contact, refusing to convey any hint that he would welcome even the briefest bit of conversation. His mind was still snared by thoughts of Chester Sears and the man's coded note, which bore today's date.

Once more he felt a flash of doubt over his decision not to accompany Lean and McCutcheon. There was nothing overtly rational in his election to spend the evening at the Athenaeum. That the professor's esoteric and unconvincing writings had ended up here after his death seemed a tenuous connection to the case at best. All he could manage by way of consoling himself was the knowledge that his two colleagues should be perfectly able to locate and handle Sears.

Despite the tangle of thoughts that twisted through Grey's mind, he couldn't resist a glance toward the end of the hall and the glaring absence there of the grandiose Sumner staircase. The magnificent structure, which had formerly dominated the interior of the building, had been regrettably sacrificed four years earlier to accommodate the library's ever-expanding collections. Grey had spent many hours within these walls, one of the favored places of his youthful school days. Memories pressed against the outposts of his mind, but his defenses held, repelling the sentimental notions, denying them every possible inch of ground within his thoughts.

The electric lights flickered, signaling the approach of the night's main event. The crowd began moving in earnest now, and Grey heard several references to the long room, meaning the first-floor sculpture gallery, which had been converted to a lecture hall for the evening. Though the Athenaeum numbered women among its list of proprietors, it still had the feel of a gentlemen's private social club. The crowd reflected this, being made up of primarily male members of Boston's cultural elite, a few of whom cast questioning glances at the copper-toned face of Perceval Grey.

Inside the sculpture room, hundreds of wooden folding chairs had been arranged in neat rows among the central space as well as in the room's alcoves, which were separated by various classical figures in marble and carved busts resting on pedestals. Grey and Justice Holmes found seats not far from the windows that faced south, looking onto the open expanse of the Granary Burying Ground. Two hundred or so attendees, still greeting one another with self-pleased aplomb, settled into place with all the order and muted grace of a human landslide. Grey's eyes sought out the peaceful contrast on the far side of the south windows. There, pale shapes, squared off or round-topped, gently faded into the night's gloom.

One of Boston's earliest graveyards, the Granary housed the earthly remains of such Colonial and Revolutionary luminaries as Samuel Adams, John Hancock, Crispus Attucks, and Samuel Sewall, whom Grey recalled as having presided at the Salem witch trials. Two hundred tombs and upwards of two thousand stones crowded into the two-acre graveyard, though it was home to more than three times that many souls. Most of the names had been lost to history through poor record keeping, alterations to the cemetery, the moving of stones, and the reusing of lots. Space was so tight in the Granary and its immediate environs that the Athenaeum ran right onto the burying ground. The library's rear wall actually contained a short arch that maintained the building's straight back line by carrying it over several old headstones.

The din in the room began to die away as the Athenaeum's head librarian, Mr. Lane, who'd recently been given the task of living up to his renowned predecessor, Charles Cutter, began to speak. After brief opening remarks, the librarian introduced a nervous-looking young man who'd earned the honorable position of reader this evening.

With little ado the man launched into the subject. His voice fluctuated over the first few sentences as he became acclimated to the acoustics of the full, and not-quite-silent, hall.

" 'The Frontier in American History,' a paper by Frederick Jackson Turner.

" 'Chapter One: In a recent bulletin of the Superintendent of the Census for 1890 appear these significant words: "Up to and including 1880 the country had a frontier of settlement, but at present the unsettled area has been so broken into by isolated bodies of settlement that there can hardly be said to be a frontier line." This brief official statement marks the closing of a great historic movement. Up to our own day American history has been in a large degree the history of the colonization of the Great West.' "

Grey could bring little of his attention to bear on the subject of the speech. His mind insisted on the criminal matter of Cosgrove's death and Sears's mysterious note. He desperately longed for his rooms in Portland, curtains drawn, blocking out the calls and clatters, all the distractions of a world both doomed and eager to pursue an endless slate of minute and ultimately trivial obligations. Intense concentration was denied him, so his mind prowled back and forth, caged in by the continuous assault of nearby noises. Whispered comments mingled with the scraping of chairs on the floor as occupants shifted their weight. The hacking coughs of elderly men, or those old enough to have smoked for far too many years, split the air. Struggling to overcome his annoyance at the sundry noises from the audience, Grey tried instead to focus solely on the monotonous voice of the speaker.

" 'In the settlement of America we have to observe how European life entered the continent, and how America modified and developed that life and reacted on Europe. The frontier is the outer edge of the wave—the meeting point between savagery and civilization. The wilderness masters the colonist. It finds him a European in dress, tools, modes of travel, and thought. But he must accept the conditions which the frontier furnishes, or perish, and so he fits himself into the Indian clearings and follows the Indian trails. Before long he has gone to plant-ing Indian corn and plowing with a sharp stick; he shouts the war cry and takes the scalp in orthodox Indian fashion. Little by little he trans-forms the wilderness, but the outcome is not the old Europe but a new product that is American.' "

As the room settled into the methodical rhythms of the speech, Grey's thoughts fell into place, like the needle of a compass settling on magnetic north after having been spun about. He returned to the first el-ement of the inquiry: the death of Frank Cosgrove. The motive was un-knowable at present, meaning that the dead man's old partner, Chester Sears, could not be eliminated as a suspect. Grey doubted that possibil-ity. Sears's hasty flight from Portland could indicate guilt, but the man hadn't fled immediately after the murder—only after Cosgrove's corpse had been disinterred and burned. There was another party involved in the goings-on in Portland.

What to make of the Boston connection? The note with Horsford's name and Cambridge address, along with the apparent code, was found in Sears's room. He hadn't written the note for his own benefit; notes meant to be seen by only the writer's own eyes didn't require the use of a code. Cosgrove wouldn't have written it, since it was on Tremont House stationery and referenced people living near Boston. Cosgrove worked exclusively in the Portland area. Besides all that, there was no discern-ible reason for the criminal partnership of Cosgrove and Sears to be interested in scholarly information or items such as would be present in the late Professor Horsford's study. The only obvious motive for trying to steal something from the professor's study would belong to a com-mercial competitor of his. The idea seemed logical given the fortune that Horsford had made from his various chemical inventions. But then his daughter had indicated that his recent studies were not at all commercial in nature. They amounted to little more than hypothetical musings, re-ceiving scant notice in academic circles.

Something was missing, some connection, and Grey couldn't shake the feeling that it had to do with the coded reference on Sears's note: *"boy 22 horse 78 dog ink sun."* He ran the numbers and words through his head again and again. There was something oddly familiar about them. The frustration at his inability to recognize the code gnawed at him. He was barely able to subdue the urge to rise and begin pacing. He noticed that Justice Holmes was glancing at him, a keen worry in the older man's eyes.

"Feeling well, Grey?"

Grey nodded. He could only imagine the look of concentration on his own face that had prompted the judge's concern. Needing to calm his thoughts once more, he stared ahead at the man reading Frederick Turner's paper on the role of the frontier in American history.

" 'The story of the border warfare between Canada and the colonial frontier towns furnishes ample material for studying frontier life and institutions. The palisaded meeting-house square, the fortified isolated garrison houses, the massacres and captivities are familiar features of New England's history. The Indian was a very real influence upon the mind and morals as well as upon the institutions of frontier New England. The occasional instances of Puritans returning from captivity to visit the frontier towns, Catholic in religion, painted and garbed as Indians and speaking the Indian tongue, and the half-breed children of captive Puritan mothers, tell a sensational part of the story; but even in the normal relations of the frontier townsmen to the Indians, there are clear evidences of the transforming influence of the Indian frontier upon the Puritan type of English colonist.'

" 'For example, Connecticut in 1704 ordered her frontier towns that for the encouragement of our forces going against the enemy, the public treasury will allow the sum of five pounds for every man's scalp of the enemy killed. Massachusetts offered varying bounties for scalps, according to whether the scalp was of men, or women and youths. One of the most striking phases of frontier adjustment, was the proposal of the Reverend Solomon Stoddard in 1703, urging the use of dogs "to hunt Indians as they do Bears." The argument was that it would not be thought inhuman; for the Indians "act like wolves and are to be dealt with as wolves." Thus we come to familiar ground: the Massachusetts frontiersman like his western successor hated the Indians; the "tawney serpents," of the Reverend Cotton Mather's phrase, were to be hunted down and scalped in accordance with law.' "

A grotesquely absurd image stuck in Grey's mind: various-size scalps hanging in a line befuddling some powder-haired Colonial treasury clerk whose job it was to measure and classify the scalps according to gender or age and pay the proper bounty. The Cotton Mather Human Scalp Gradation scale. He would have chuckled to himself in spite of the historical horror of the idea if another, even more painful, thought hadn't struck him at that same moment: a system of classification. Frustration and disappointment bordering on self-loathing began to well up from the lowest point of Grey's stomach. He felt a pain in his knee and looked down to see his own fingers digging into his pant leg. He forced his hand to release. The brutal obviousness of the answer threatened to overwhelm Grey's mind, and for several seconds he couldn't harness his thoughts.

The speaker droned on. " 'This is one of the most significant things about New England's frontier in these years. That long blood-stained line of the eastern frontier which skirted the Maine coast was of great importance, for it imparted a western tone to the life and characteristics of the Maine people which endures to this day. Within the area bounded by the frontier line, were the broken fragments of Indians defeated in the era of King Philip's War, restrained within reservations, drunken and degenerate survivors, among whom the missionaries worked with small results, a vexation to the border towns.' "

The words and numbers on Sears's note were not a code at all, not technically, but rather an entry in a classification system. A system Grey was familiar with, one that had been invented in this very building.

"Damnable fool!"

Grey uttered the condemnation louder than he'd intended as he bolted up from his seat. Edging past his neighbors to the central aisle, he incurred disapproving glares and murmurs the whole way. The ire of the crowd was only partly mollified by the reader plodding on valiantly and by the presence of Justice Holmes, who followed close behind Grey.

The door to the hall was ajar, and a plump, middle-aged lady standing just outside, listening to the lecture, had to quickly step aside as Grey exited. Grey paused, and Justice Holmes laid a hand on his shoulder.

"You ought not to get so vexed over the language, Grey. It's an historical assessment of the character of the Indians after a brutally contested war, not a current indictment of the people. And certainly no need to curse the poor man reading."

"What?" Grey faced Holmes with a look of utter confusion that took several long seconds to fade away. "No, I was cursing myself. I've been utterly blind when the answer was right before me."

Now it was Justice Holmes's turn to be perplexed.

"The man whom Deputy Lean and I have pursued from Portland, the one with Professor's Horsford's address and a coded note. It's not a code at all. It's a call number in the Cutter Expansive Classification system. It's a book somewhere here in the Athenaeum!"

[Chapter 14]

LEAN STOOD ON BEACON STREET ACROSS FROM THE SIDE entrance to the Tremont House. Though the hotel had been thoroughly modernized, it maintained an air of stolid old-time respectability with its plain face of granite blocks and the simple Greek columns. He'd been waiting for Chester Sears for over an hour and was beyond the point where he could honestly say he still felt inconspicuous. He made frequent trips to the corner to inspect the foot traffic there as well as the passengers on the horse-drawn trolley cars that stopped just in front of the hotel's entrance. Lean didn't spend more than a few seconds at the corner, since Walt McCutcheon was in the lobby and responsible for the main entrance. A rumble passed through Lean's empty stomach, causing him to imagine that McCutcheon had by now somehow figured a way to fulfill his monitoring duties while also sampling the hotel's famously delightful cuisine.

Lean headed back closer to the side entrance. A fair number of patrons had entered and exited over the past hour, but there was yet to be any sign of Chester Sears. In the fading daylight, Lean contemplated crossing over the street to more closely inspect the faces of the comers and goers. The move would make Lean himself easier to spot. On the bright side, it had been years since he'd had dealings with Sears back in Portland. He trusted that time and the lack of any expectation of seeing a Portland deputy in Boston would dull the man's ability to recognize him.

Another minute passed before a man in a dark sack suit carrying a leather case came out of the side door. The man glanced about, and Lean averted his gaze. He thought the man was not so much looking for anyone but instead trying to see if anyone was looking for him. Peering sideways, Lean watched the man move toward the intersection with Tremont Street and decided that it just might be Chester Sears. Staying on the opposite side of the street for a block and a half, he made a vain effort to confirm the man's identity. Rows of multistoried buildings dropped a veil of shadows over the man, and even when they passed into open spaces, the low glare of the setting sun hit Lean in the face. He crossed over, wanting to stay close enough that if his man hailed a cab, he could quickly land another one passing in the same direction.

Maintaining a distance of twenty paces, Lean kept up through several turns before emerging on another major avenue that he didn't recognize. Without warning, the man halted by the curb and waited for an approaching railcar. Lean hesitated, then hurried on, reaching the man just as the horses pulling the trolley eased to a stop in front of them.

Lean reached out for the man's shoulder and announced, "Chester Sears."

The man flinched in surprise, and his head jerked around. Lean suddenly realized he'd been pursuing a man who was clearly a decade older than Chester Sears.

"I beg your pardon," the man said with a look of mild contempt.

"Terribly sorry, sir. Mistook you for someone else." Lean tipped his hat to the startled man and turned on his heel. Frustration yielded instantly to the desperate need to get back to his post at the Tremont. He glanced about, trying to get his bearings in the somewhat unfamiliar city. The failing light didn't aid his efforts. He'd mostly head straight on from the Tremont, though they had moved two or three blocks to the right during the walk.

After hurrying through a few turns, Lean came to an intersection and saw the green space of the Boston Common. Grateful to have his bearings back, he walked in that direction until he reached Tremont Street again. The tall spire of the Park Street Church shot up directly opposite. He crossed over, knowing that just down the block, past the old Granary Burying Ground, he'd be back at Tremont House. There was still hope. Even if he'd missed Sears in the past ten minutes, McCutcheon still might have spotted him.

Once past the towering church, he came even with the start of the cemetery's tall wrought-iron fence that ran the length of its Tremont Street side. Along with a several other solitary pedestrians and strolling couples, Lean made his way beneath the canopies of a series of massivetrunked elms that lined the sidewalk. He approached the cemetery's tall stone entrance, shaped almost like the Greek letter pi but styled in a manner reminiscent of ancient Egyptian carvings. He noticed that an approaching couple had slowed under the lintel of the entranceway, beneath a pair of hawklike stone wings surmounted by an orb carved in stark relief.

"Look, darling, across the way," the woman said to her husband. "I think I see a man atop the roof there. What is that?"

"The Athenaeum, I believe. Queer time for roof maintenance," the man said in a dismissive voice. Unfazed by the strange sight, he picked up the pace again, his wife in tow.

Lean's thoughts instantly fixed on Grey's presence in that building. He stepped into the entrance to the burial ground, his gaze fixed on the distant rooftop. Then came a shout from up high. The words, unmistakably urgent in their origin, acquired a distant, ghostly tenor as they drifted down to Lean across two hundred feet of headstones.

"Chester Sears! Stop!"

Chapter 15

THE PLUMP WOMAN WHO'D NEARLY BEEN BOWLED OVER BY Grey at the doorway had been listening and now stepped closer. "I'm Mrs. Holden, assistant librarian. Can I be of assistance, Justice Holmes?"

Holmes paused to consider the question as he watched Grey rush to the front desk nearby to retrieve a pencil and a scrap of paper.

Grey returned, holding the scrap in his left palm and writing on it as he muttered, "Boy, two, two, horse, seven, eight, dog, ink, sun."

"I certainly hope so." Justice Holmes offered a bemused smile as he answered the woman.

She reached out to take the paper that Grey handed over. On it was printed "B22H78DIS."

"This would be up in our second-floor reading room—on the left, about a quarter of the way along," she said. "If you care to follow me?"

Without waiting for her to take the lead, Grey turned and strode ahead to the alabaster-hued statue of Washington that stood guard at the base of the stairs. He pulled aside a velvet rope meant to deny access to the upper floors. The second floor was dominated by the large reading room, built like the rest of the interior in the alcove style. Grey swiped at a series of switches, and several overhead electric lights flickered to life. He moved past the alcoves on the left-hand side of the room, his eyes sweeping along the nearest books until he reached the vicinity of his target. He began a closer inspection of the spines, passing over a variety of volumes, interspersed with occasional thin blocks of wood that were used as placeholders for borrowed books. His fingers slid along the titles until he came to call number B22 H78 D, *The Defences of Norumbega*. Where B22 H78 DIS should have stood was a gaping space that skipped ahead to B22 H78 L, *The Landfall of Leif Erikson*, A.D. *1000*. Both of those volumes had been written by Eben Norton Horsford.

Grey turned at the sound of Justice Holmes and Mrs. Holden catching up to him.

"Shouldn't there be a wooden space holder here as well?" Grey asked the assistant librarian.

"Indeed." She looked around, confused. Grey did the same, and his gaze landed on the long, thin reading table toward the center of the room. A book rested there.

"How'd that get there?" Mrs. Holden mused. "We go through and reshelve all the books each evening. It couldn't have been overlooked in plain sight on the table."

Grey rushed over and read the title: *The Discovery of the Ancient City of Norumbega*, by Eben Norton Horsford.

"He's been here sometime in the past hour or two." Grey said before he glanced at the spine. " 'B22 H78 DI.' The call number is wrong. Ends with only 'DI' not 'DIS.' "

Grey brought the book back into the alcove and slid it into place on the shelf. It took up only half the empty space.

"There's still a volume missing. He mistook this book for his target and left it on the table after realizing his error. He collected the next and has stolen it. That's why today's date was important. All the commotion of the reading produced an opportunity to gain access to the building unnoticed and then slip upstairs."

"Impossible," said Mrs. Holden. "No one came through the front doors after closing time. The entire staff was milling about, setting up chairs and all. And we've been greeting the members as they came in tonight. No perfect stranger could have just waltzed on by."

"During the reading, then?" Grey offered.

"I've been standing at the doorway. Listening in, I'll grant you, but I'd have noticed anyone coming in late and creeping by on the way upstairs. That I assure you. And then again on his way back down."

"What if whoever took the book is not the same fellow you've been trailing, Grey?" Justice Holmes asked. "Perhaps it was taken by one of the proprietors."

Grey shook his head. "A member could have taken the book at any time. He wouldn't have needed to do it on this day, during this distraction. No, he's here surreptitiously. And if he didn't come through the front door, then where? Other means of access? There's a door above, in the picture gallery."

Hearing it phrased like an accusation, Mrs. Holden began to justify the existence of the door on the third floor. "Yes, there is the exit out to the small roof area overlooking the cemetery."

Grey started back toward the stairs with Justice Holmes right on his heels. Mrs. Holden was obliged to follow after them as she completed her explanation. "But there are two bolts on the door. I locked them myself this evening at closing time."

The stairs led to a small picture gallery on the third floor. Inside that chamber, wooden handrails kept visitors away from the portraits and landscapes that hung thick upon the walls inside wide, elaborately embossed and gilded frames. Grey stopped and scanned the nearby wall for light switches but saw none. When Justice Holmes and Mrs. Holden arrived, he motioned them to stand still. The sound of paper being torn came to them from one of the other galleries on this level. With his eyes still not fully accustomed to the dark, Grey hurried forward through a ten-foot-tall entranceway leading into the next picture gallery.

This room was much larger. Dim light filtered down from a large rectangular opening cut into the tall ceiling that led up to a skylight. A series of unlit electrical bulbs hung below on a frame that matched the ample size of the skylight. The only artificial light in the room came from a small oil lamp sitting on a viewing bench positioned in the middle of the room. Crouching by the side of that bench was a dark figure. The man's head shot up at Grey's arrival.

"Stop where you are!" Grey shouted.

The dark figure made a violent motion, tearing another page from a book that lay upon the bench. The others followed Grey into the room, and Mrs. Holden let out a piercing shriek at the sight of the dimly visible man lurking thirty feet ahead of them.

The man frantically shoved the ripped page into his breast pocket, jumped atop the bench, and vaulted into the air. Impossibly, he stopped in midflight and hung there, arms raised over his head. It took Grey another second to catch sight of a thin rope rising from just above the bench and disappearing up into the wide shaft leading to the skylight.

"Summon the police," urged Justice Holmes, who'd grasped Mrs. Holden's shoulders in an effort to calm the shocked woman.

Grey sprinted ahead and leaped onto the bench. Pausing only long enough to ensure that his feet were under him, he launched himself again, trying to capitalize on his momentum. He clutched the rope as it wavered in the air. Seeing a series of knots tied every two feet, Grey wrapped his feet around the cord and pressed down onto the closest knot for support.

One hand shot out for the next knot, and he hauled himself upward, pushing with his legs as the other hand reached past the first. His eyes were locked onto the thief, who was scurrying up the rope with what seemed like inhuman speed. The man was already approaching the skylight.

"This is madness! Come down!" Justice Holmes called out below, but Grey focused solely on climbing faster.

Above him Grey saw the man pause briefly to grab hold of one of the skylight's edges. A wide, slanted pane had been removed, and the thief twisted his thin body and pulled himself through the narrow opening. Grey's left hand slipped several inches, and he felt the rope burn in his palm. Ignoring it, he forced himself farther up the rope, hand over hand. His feet twisted and locked together around the rope, coiling against the next knot in the line, then springing, pushing him along.

The thief's face appeared in the frame of the skylight looking down at Grey, who was still one body length shy of the goal. Grey pulled even more desperately, spurred on by the thought that the man might cut the cord. Instead the thief vanished from view. A few seconds more and Grey reached out for the ledge of the skylight. With his other hand braced against the wooden frame of the missing pane, he hauled up and got his torso through the gap. He spun his head around, making sure the thief wasn't close by, ready to ambush him. The man was fleeing along with one foot just to each side of the peak of the building's pitched roof. Grey stood up near the middle of the Athenaeum's 114-foot length, by the third of four raised skylights. Ahead of him the thief reached the last skylight and began inching his way around it.

Grey steadied himself before continuing the pursuit. To his left the roof sloped away toward Beacon Street and the building's front entrance, sixty feet below him now. On his right the roof sloped down toward a lower addition, then the wide, dark expanse of the Granary Burying Ground. He followed the thief's example: one foot on either side of the peak, sliding each forward more than actually lifting his feet to take steps. By the time Grey reached the next skylight, his quarry had disappeared from view. Grey turned sideways with his weight leaning in above the slanted glass panes for balance as he shimmied along the edge of the raised skylight.

The thief had shimmied down a short slope at the end of the Athenaeum. He'd made the descent and was now inching along a stone ledge that jutted out just below the edge of the roof. Grey could see only his head and shoulders.

"Chester Sears! Stop!"

Grey saw the man's silhouette stop and wobble in surprise at the sound of his name. The pause in the thief's flight was only momentary. Sears moved on, reaching the end of the ledge, where he was able to drop a few feet to a flatter section of roof. Grey recalled seeing a narrow alleyway on that side of the building, separating the library from its neighbor. The thief now stood on an addendum to the Athenaeum where a circular bulge jutted into the alleyway. It would allow Sears to get close enough for a leap to the neighboring rooftop, one story lower.

Seeing that he was in danger of losing the man, Grey sat down on the side of the roof that faced the rear and the burying ground. Although steeper, it offered a direct route to the lower, flat section where Sears now stood. Grey quit bracing himself with his hands and slid on his backside down the pitched roof. He tried, with little success, to slow himself as he approached the rim, but he wound up falling onto the flat section of roof at full speed and tumbled roughly several times before coming to a stop.

Grey looked up and saw Sears fifteen feet away, standing at the edge of the roof. The thief glanced back at Grey. There was moonlight enough for Grey to see the last ripped page from the book still jutting out of Sears's breast pocket like some ridiculously oversize kerchief. There was also a look of panic on the man's face.

"You've reached the end, Sears. Don't try it. You'll end up like your friend Cosgrove."

"No. You won't do me like you done him. You won't get my soul!"

Sears turned to face the alley again and backed up two steps.

"Don't jump!" Grey cried as he bolted to his feet and rushed toward the man.

Sears took two quick steps, launched himself off the roof, and dropped out of sight. Grey skidded to a stop a foot short of the edge. Sears cleared the alleyway to reach the neighboring rooftop, which was steeply pitched with its peak running away from him. He landed awkwardly, his momentum carrying him forward, out of control. He tumbled head over feet and made one flailing grab for the peak of the roof. He missed—and continued to topple down the roof slope, picking up speed as he went. The thief let out a scream as he careened off the roof and fell thirty-odd feet toward the Granary Burying Ground.

Grey watched in horror as the man dropped toward the old black wrought-iron fence that bound in the city's ancient cemetery. Sears missed the fence's spikes but landed inside the burying ground with a sickening crack, as if he'd hit a stone rather than just the grassy earth. Grey stared down but couldn't make out any movement there in the dark. Even the moonlight was cut off by the shadows of nearby buildings and the cemetery's scattered trees. What he could see was the solitary white page that Sears had stuffed into his breast pocket. The paper floated down, carried by gentle evening breezes, to land fifty yards off amid the headstones.

[Chapter 16]

FTER A MOMENT LEAN RECOGNIZED THE VOICE CALLING out for Chester Sears to stop. He saw the second figure, Grey, on the rooftop. Lean's legs moved faster, though he dared not run. He had to heed the stones, some of which were short and darkened with age. In the gloomy space of the burying ground, these lurked like treacherous reefs ready to doom a passing ship. During one of his glances down to the ground and back up again, both the shadowy figures above slipped from view. He paused at a small raised square of earth surrounding a tall obelisk and caught sight of a man close to the edge of the roof.

"Don't jump!" Grey shouted.

Sears flew through the air, briefly visible in the sky between the Athenaeum and the neighboring building. Lean watched the man crash down and tumble along the slanting roof. Quick scratching, scrambling sounds were followed close behind by a shriek. The figure plummeted off the side of the building and landed with a crack on the dark ground below.

Lean raced forward to the site of the horrible landing and stopped several feet shy of the crumpled body. Chester Sears was alive; Lean heard ragged, desperate breaths. The man lay on his side, and Lean guessed that some part of him had struck a headstone standing just feet away. Lean knelt and eased Sears onto his back.

"Is anything broken? Where does it hurt?" Lean asked.

In the faint moonlight, Sears's dazed, stunned eyes met Lean's. A look of confusion rose up through Sears's pain as he regarded the deputy's face staring down at his own.

"Father Leadbetter," the injured man muttered.

"No—you're going to live, just hang in there, man. We'll get you a doctor."

"No," Sears said.

What at first appeared to be a wild grin Lean now understood to be a grimace of pain mixed with a sliver of relief.

"You've failed." Sears's breath was fading. He glanced sideways at the grave marker and then said in a gurgling whisper, "Hallowed ground."

"What?" Lean bent in closer, not sure he was hearing the man correctly.

"My soul's safe now."

Lean stood as he heard the sound of feet on pavement nearby. Help would be there any moment now, but he glanced down again at the limp body of Chester Sears and knew it was too late.

⊨ ⊣

"And that's it, then, Your Honor?" Inspector Greeley asked.

"In sum and total, Inspector," Justice Holmes said to the investigator from the Boston police.

They'd returned to the scene of the attempted theft, the top-floor painting gallery, and had been going over the details for the past hour. Lean, Grey, Mrs. Holden, and Justice Holmes had each recounted events as they knew them, minus the more gruesome and confusing details of the digging up and burning of Frank Cosgrove in Portland. Inspector Greeley, a stout bulldog of a man, had enough time on the job to be very concerned about the details of Lean and Grey's interest in the recently deceased Chester Sears. Fortunately for the Portland detectives, the inspector was also wise enough not to spend too much energy questioning the straightforward account given by Oliver Wendell Holmes Jr., a justice on the state supreme court.

"It all seems to fit. Mr. Grey came back down this rope." He glanced at the assistant librarian, Mrs. Holden, who nodded, confirming that she'd returned to the third floor in time to witness that. "So he never left this roof. And from where this fellow Sears landed, he clearly fell from the roof next door. Too far to possibly have been pushed. He must have jumped to his own death." The stocky, round-faced inspector scratched his head, where the thinning strands of hair offered little resistance.

"Certainly queer, though, isn't it?" Greeley said.

"Yes, that he would risk death to avoid capture after such an elaborate break-in and all for a dozen pages from some obscure book on Viking settlements," Grey answered.

"It's madness. And I daresay it might be catching, Mr. Grey. Climbing that rope and chasing him across a slanted roof—must be fifty feet up, in the dark. You're lucky the meat wagon collected only one set of shattered bones tonight."

"Exactly," Justice Holmes agreed. "I called out the same when he started after the man."

"Caught up in the moment, I suppose," Grey said, and held up his hand. A handkerchief was bound about the rope burn on his palm. "I suppose I'll have a little souvenir to remind me to think twice in the future."

Lean fought back a smile, knowing full well that Grey would commit the same reckless pursuit a hundred times over and was now trying to play the part of naïve bystander to assuage the inspector's doubts about the whole situation.

Justice Holmes might have been sharing Lean's thoughts, since he immediately returned the focus to the burglar. "Though as Deputy Lean said, that Sears chap may recently have murdered an old accomplice in Portland. May well be that the man was some sort of lunatic. Who's to say?"

"Not me," Greeley said with a shrug. "I've got work enough for me in writing up this mess as it is. I think I'll do well if I can get it all down just with the facts as they stand. Gentlemen, Your Honor." The inspector set his bowler atop his head and touched his fingers to the brim in Justice Holmes's direction. "I should make sure that all's been set to rights out back in the burying ground. Good evening to you."

He picked up the torn-out pages, which he tapped into line before handing them over to a uniformed officer. He looked about on the table for Professor Horsford's book. His frown deepened as the sound of a turning page led to the sight of Grey skimming through the damaged book. Inspector Greeley held his hand out for the book and cleared his throat like a broadside from a man-of-war.

"Says here that these symbols were originally found etched into a rock ledge just north of Portland in the early 1830s," Grey declared.

"Inspector, will it be necessary for you to remove the book and pages from the Athenaeum?" Lean asked. "I am a bit curious to get a closer look at them. See if there's any possible connection between them and the murder back home."

"Sorry, Deputy. As these pages amount to the property being stolen at the time of the death, I'll need to withhold them until the coroner's inquest is completed. Send them back here as soon as that's done with, however. Best I can do. You understand."

"Of course. I appreciate your help," Lean said.

"What I'd appreciate is if next time you're snooping around Boston for a possible murder arrest, you maybe give us local boys a tip of the hat first. Maybe we avoid another situation like this." Greeley shot him a sharp look.

"Agreed," Lean said. "Just meant to ask the man a few questions. Certainly wasn't expecting all this."

"I reckon I could come here every night until I die at a ripe old age and I'd never expect to see what I've seen here tonight," the inspector said.

"True enough. Remarkable turn of events, to say the least. All the more reason perhaps to at least let Deputy Lean have a quick look at the pages," Justice Holmes suggested. "A bit of that professional courtesy you referenced earlier."

The inspector's frown lasted only an instant; he could hardly deny a direct request from Justice Holmes about sharing knowledge of a crime with another police inspector, even if the man in question was from Maine.

"Fair enough." Greeley motioned to the patrolman, who placed the book and ripped pages back on one of the benches.

Lean spread out the dozen separate, double-sided pages, which held reproductions of sketches of various strange symbols. Justice Holmes leaned in for a better look, while Grey opened the book and flipped back through the pages of the manuscript. Upon finding what he was looking for, he jotted a few details in his notebook.

"What have you found?" Inspector Greeley asked him.

"Dastine LaVallee. The name of the woman reported as originally finding these carved markings."

"When was that?"

"In 1834."

"Damn near sixty years ago," Greeley scoffed, then turned away as if he wanted to physically distance himself from such an obviously futile line of pursuit.

Grey finished his notes and turned his attention to Lean's perusal of the symbols.

"I have to give it to old Horsford," Justice Holmes said. "Wherever he supposedly found these images, some of them do certainly have the flavor of Viking runes."

"But then some look familiar, don't they?" Lean asked. "Greek?"

"There are limited similarities, but I might actually classify some of these as older than Greek. Phoenician, perhaps" Grey said.

"Ah, yes," Lean muttered with a roll of his eyes, "how foolish of me. Definitely Phoenician."

"Others I don't recognize at all," Grey continued, ignoring Lean's last comment.

"One thing's for sure," Inspector Greeley said. "Whatever they look like to you, in the end they're just drawings on paper. And to me they don't look anything like the real reason a man goes jumping to his death."

⚶ ⚶

AFTER SAYING THEIR farewells to Justice Holmes, Grey and Lean walked along the sidewalk away from the Athenaeum.

"That bit you mentioned inside about the woman who found those symbols," Lean said.

"Dastine LaVallee."

"In 1834, though? She must be dead by now."

"The newspaper article cited by Horsford referred to her as a young woman out for an afternoon stroll with her beau. So she may still be in her late seventies," Grey said.

"Even if she is still alive, she likely goes by her married name. And no sure thing that she's even lived in Portland for the past fifty or sixty years."

"Granted, it's not the most promising lead, but the best link we had to Cosgrove's murder was Sears, and the best link we have to him is these curious symbols. We must learn whatever we can about them."

"That'll need to wait until Greeley decides he's done with the book," Lean said.

"I'll ask Justice Holmes to check in with the librarian and monitor the book's return. I'd also like to find the original newspaper story and learn the location of the ledge where the symbols appear. But in the meantime we can start with this."

The two men paused by themselves beneath a streetlight as Grey drew a folded piece of paper from his pocket and handed it over. Several paragraphs of close-set type covered the outer side of the paper. Lean unfolded the page to reveal a large diagram on the other side. It was a rough circle resting upon a cross. A short arc, almost like a pair of horns or a thin crescent-moon shape, sat atop the circle.

"An extra page from Horsford's book. Did you tear it out?"

Grey shook his head. "This was the last page Sears ripped from the book and shoved into his pocket. It drifted out during his fall. I managed to slip aside and retrieve it."

"Well done, though I'm not sure it provides much in the way of assistance at this point."

"Perhaps not," Grey said as he accepted the paper again. "According to the limited text here, Professor Horsford attached particular import to this page. He viewed the image as a Viking head. The arc here represents his horned helmet. Horsford took it as definitive proof that the entire set of symbols was produced by the Norsemen."

Lean shrugged and began walking again. "Maybe. If it's not a Viking rune, what is it?"

"I can't say. Though it does strike me as vaguely familiar."

"Well and good, Grey, but I fear it will take a sight more than vague familiarity to breathe any life back into this case."

The pair had only just rounded the corner from the Athenaeum, passing along the final bend in Beacon Street, when Walt McCutcheon came striding up behind them.

"Evening, gents. Was that the sound of defeat I heard in your voice, Lean?"

"There you are, McCutcheon," Grey said, without breaking stride. "So I take it you didn't have any luck tracking down Chester Sears?"

"Not while he was alive, no." McCutcheon chuckled as he paused to light his cigar, then hurried to catch up. "Saw him lying dead in the old boneyard. Heard the commotion earlier around the back, but Inspector Greeley was already arriving so I steered clear."

"Had some trouble with the man, have you?" Lean asked.

"Let's just say the fellow lacks a certain appreciation for some of my more . . . imaginative investigational tactics."

They crossed to the corner of School and Tremont and paused near a vacant and blemished lot. McCutcheon identified it as the site of the Tremont Temple before its fiery destruction months earlier. The charred space looked darker and more desolate than Lean could have imagined possible for a space in the heart of Boston. Several doors ahead stood the Parker House, where Grey and Lean would each stay for the night. McCutcheon meant to part ways there.

"Is that it, then? The end of the line for you along with Sears?" McCutcheon asked as a trolley passed by them.

Grey turned and stared down street where, a stone's throw away, stood the Tremont House. He nodded toward the hotel.

"We could try to gain entry to his room, see if he's left any evidence behind," Lean suggested.

"I'm one step ahead of you, Lean. After seeing the scene at the burying ground, I came back here directly, paid for his room number, and conveniently found his door not entirely locked. All for naught, though. Room looked like he hadn't even set foot in it."

"He checked in alone?" Grey asked.

"Alone and under the name of Leadbetter," McCutcheon said.

Lean's surprise blossomed into a grin as he turned to Grey.

Chapter 17

INQUIRIES THE NEXT MORNING TO THE ARCHDIOCESE OF Boston revealed no Catholic priest in the city or the surrounding towns with the name of Leadbetter. However, the voice on the other end of the telephone line did mention, with a certain tone of disapproval, remembering an Episcopal rector by that name some years ago.

Not long after ten o'clock, Lean and Grey descended the short flight of stairs from the sidewalk down to the door of the basement apartment on a nondescript side street in the North End. After finding no name or number posted, Lean shrugged and banged on the door. Annoyed barking and several muffled words came in reply before the detectives heard the latch release. The door split open a crack from its frame to reveal a cautious face surrounded by an unkempt white beard and matching shock of hair.

"Father Leadbetter? I'm Deputy Marshal Lean."

The man gave an unsure shrug. "Again? I've already answered your colleague's questions. I really don't know what else I can tell you."

"So I take it you've heard the news about Chester Sears."

"Horrible. Such an unnecessary tragedy."

"I'm not actually with the Boston police. I'm from up the coast—Portland."

Confusion registered on Leadbetter's face as he worked through that bit of information. "Oh, a Down-Easter. I always enjoyed a trip up that way whenever I had the chance. Been a while, though. Well, you've had yourselves a journey—why don't you come in?"

Leadbetter's slippered feet shuffled forward into his cramped apartment. A grizzled old dog, white around the eyes and whiskers, started to rise from his place on a low-lying sofa. Leadbetter made some reassuring sounds, and the dog flopped back into position, though it continued to watch the visitors through clouded eyes. The L-shaped room was a decent size for a single human resident, but so stuffed with books that it felt cramped.

"Thank you, Father," Lean said once they were inside. "That's correct, isn't it—'Father'? Or do you prefer 'Rector'?"

"I'm no longer a part of the ministry, actually. So you can just call me William. After all, we don't stand on formality around here, do we, Rufus?" The dog made a halfhearted effort to respond but produced nothing more than a deep sigh.

"Yes, I understand you were defrocked." Lean lowered his voice a notch, as if the lessened volume would ease the accusatorial sting of the question.

"Deposed," Leadbetter corrected. The look in the older man's eyes spoke of regret, but a hint of defiance lingered there as well. "If you've heard that much, I can only assume you've heard the whole bit. Don't you believe it. I left the ministry for professional reasons. A difference of opinion with others in the ministry regarding fundamental matters of belief and learning. There were those on the periphery of the matter who came to despise me, and they were not above smearing my name with every manner of inappropriate and distasteful rumors regarding my personal conduct. All lies."

"I didn't mean to rankle you. We're not here for anything to do with your past, except as far as it relates to Chester Sears."

Leadbetter puttered about the room, picking up small items of trash and making attempts to straighten up the place. In his long brown robe, with its faded pattern and threadbare cuffs and collar, he reminded Lean of some old hermit living away his quiet days in a cave or a shack deep in the woods. Only here the background of stalagmites or trees had been replaced along the perimeter of the room by waist-high stacks of books.

"Can I offer you something to drink?" the old man asked, though his heart was really not in the offer.

Leadbetter's outfit was rather slovenly, and he carried his shoulders in a hunch that would have done Atlas proud, but Lean hadn't detected anything in the man's behavior or physical appearance to suggest insobriety. Lean glanced about. There was a sink against the far wall with a few paltry cups and dishes set out to dry. He saw a teakettle, but few other signs that Leadbetter was equipped to extend much in the way of sustenance. The man himself was rail thin. Grey denied any thirst, and Lean followed suit.

"Have a seat, please," their host said.

Apart from a chair pushed away from the writing desk, the sofa was the only seat available. Leadbetter's hound stretched over half the cushions. A small throw pillow and a decorative but worn tartan quilt cast over the back gave Lean the impression that this was likely the older man's bed. He preferred to remain standing but felt obliged to accept the only offer of hospitality that Leadbetter appeared able to provide. Lean sat down on the edge of the sofa, and the old mutt immediately jostled and wiggled his way around to rest his head by Lean's leg. Grey remained standing and wandered by to casually inspect a full bookshelf.

"As I mentioned, the city police were here earlier—an Inspector Greeley, I believe. Rather gruff fellow. He said Chester was in the midst of some sort of theft at the time he died. He mentioned something about further trouble up your way. I suppose that's why you're here."

"Mr. Sears was in Portland recently," Lean said. "And yes, we have reason to believe that he was somehow mixed up with some trouble there. A close friend of his was shot and killed."

Leadbetter's head recoiled, shocking his spine fully upright for the first time since the detectives had entered. "Chester had his faults, serious ones, I won't dispute that. But he was not a killer."

"We agree," Grey said. "And we were hoping he might know who actually did shoot his friend. But we weren't able to get to him in time. Now we're left to grope about, rather in the dark, I'm afraid. Chester Sears wasn't able to tell us much before he passed."

"Except my name." Leadbetter plopped down into the desk chair as if he'd suffered a sudden loss of air. "Yes, the police mentioned that. Asked if I had any information about why he was trying to steal something from the Athenaeum."

"And do you?" Lean asked.

"He came to see me recently. Seemed rather upset—frightened, even. I asked him what was the matter, but he wouldn't say. He only asked that I say some prayers for him."

"Even though you're no longer in the ministry."

"He assumed I was. A reflection on Chester's absence from services as much as my own. I hadn't seen him in years—the last time I was still a rector at his family's church. The one he attended in his youth. I explained the situation, but he didn't care. To him I was still Father Leadbetter. So I prayed for him, and it seemed to put him at ease."

"And that was the extent of it? He didn't say anything more about who or what had frightened him?"

"Nothing particular—he wouldn't say. Just that he feared for his soul."

"In the sense of dying in a state of sin? Or was it more than that? Did he think that somehow someone out there was a threat to his soul?" Lean asked.

There was a long pause. Lean guessed Leadbetter was weighing whether to speak and how much to say. Lean scratched the lolling dog's neck and casually said, "The reason we're interested is that we're trying to figure just why Chester might bother to steal the material he was after at the Athenaeum. Not the kind of stuff you might expect him to risk life and limb for."

Grey drew the stolen page from his pocket, unfolded it, and set it on Leadbetter's desk for the man to see the circle with the short, upward-facing arc set atop. "This is one of the pages he was attempting to take from a book. Did he mention anything to do with books or symbols such as this one?"

Leadbetter stared at the page for a moment, and then his eyes darted back and forth between the two detectives.

"What is it, Mr. Leadbetter?" Lean asked. "Do you recognize this symbol?"

Leadbetter went to a stack of books. Grey stepped back to make room for the man but caught sight of the book title that mentioned Rosicrucian secrets.

"The Rosicrucians," he said.

"What are Rosicrucians?" Lean asked.

Leadbetter flipped through the pages of the book as he spoke. "That's not a straightforward question to answer, seeing as historically they were a secret hermetic society. Many scholars doubt that they ever actually existed. Think that it was all a hoax of sorts. There has been a renewed interest in the Rosicrucians in recent times, but it's not clear how much of a similarity, if any, these modern organizations have to the original group. The Rosicrucians first became publicly known in the early seventeenth century when three anonymous manifestos appeared in Germany. Supposedly the founder of the order, Christian Rosenkreuz, was born three hundred years earlier, but his name never appears until the final of the three pamphlets appears, *The Chymical Wedding of Christian Rosenkreuz*."

"Chymical?" Lean repeated.

" 'Chymical' is just a variation of 'alchemical.' The wedding story is an allegory, a sacred wedding, the joining of opposites to create a new, unified element."

"Are the Rosicrucians heathens of some sort?" Lean asked.

"No, just look at his name—Christian Rosenkreuz. The symbol of the order, the Rosy Cross. They were definitely proponents of Christianity, but with a belief in ancient esoteric truths that over the ages have become lost to mankind. They thought that if they could decipher these ancient teachings, through the kabbalah and other means, they would bring about a reformation in human understanding of the physical and the spiritual aspects of the universe."

"Rather grandiose ambitions," Grey said.

"The early seventeenth century was a period of religious warfare, with terrible suffering and instability in Europe. People were entranced by the thought of an elite group: scholars, philosophers, and alchemists who claimed to be ready to usher in a new era of enlightenment."

"We're still waiting," Lean said.

"Which is why, in time, other groups took inspiration from the Rosicrucians," Leadbetter said. "The movement influenced the practices of the Freemasons and the evolving Scottish Rite. In recent years new hermetic societies have claimed to be the true heirs to the secret learning of the Rosicrucians."

"Even though it all may have been a hoax, you said, and this Rosenkreuz may have existed on only a few anonymous pamphlets," Grey said.

"Perhaps. Though some oral accounts claim to support the truth of Rosenkreuz's life. They say that as a young boy Rosenkreuz was the last descendant of a doomed noble family all put to death as heretics by the German Inquisition. He was spirited away to the safety of a monastery, where he was educated in the beliefs of the Cathars. According to legend, Rosenkreuz went along on a pilgrimage to the Holy Land, where he discovered esoteric wisdom from a variety of Arabian and Persian mystics and sages."

"Seems I've heard a story along those lines before." Lean cast an uneasy glance toward Grey, who ignored him.

"He created the secret Fraternity of the Rose Cross upon his return to Europe, spreading his teachings to an elect group during his lifetime. It is said that one hundred twenty years after his death his body was discovered by one of the Rosicrucian brothers in a sarcophagus hidden in a secret underground chamber. The body was still perfectly preserved. He'd had the interior of the stone door to his tomb engraved with the very year that his hidden chamber was to be discovered."

"According to unsubstantiated reports, of course," Grey said.

"Of course," Leadbetter agreed. "Most scholars dismiss such tales and assume that the anonymous authors of the manifestos were actually prominent historical figures, such as Francis Bacon, wishing to espouse certain doctrines without fear of retribution.

"Yet others, including the modern occultists, take the more fantastical position that not only did Rosenkreuz truly live, he later reappeared in various guises. Most notably these folks point to the Count de St. Germain. A nobleman, adventurer, and alchemist, he appeared in the royal courts of Europe throughout the 1700s, never aging, always decked out in gold and jewels, speaking with firsthand knowledge of events from centuries earlier. He was rumored to have achieved the ultimate alchemical goal of producing the philosopher's stone."

"Which is what, exactly?" Lean asked.

"The one true goal of alchemy, the supreme achievement. The azoth, the alpha and the omega unified, the substance that grants mastery over the ability to turn base metals to gold. The elixir of life."

Leadbetter continued to turn pages as he spoke. "Here we go— Rosicrucian symbols. Not strictly speaking, since most of these are old alchemical designs and not specific to the Rosicrucians. The symbol you have there is that of mercury, one of the most important alchemical symbols. The ideal of transformation, mercury is both the one thing while containing all things. A dual nature unified in one element."

Leadbetter's finger landed on a small image that looked exactly like the one on Grey's paper. "So there's your answer, though I'm not sure why Chester would ever be interested in that page."

"We think someone else put him up to it. Either for pay or by threat. Likely the same person who's responsible for the murder of his old friend up in Portland," Lean explained.

"In that murder some rather ominous occult markings were left in conjunction with the dead body, and Chester Sears knew that. It could explain why he was nervous when he came to you. Occult markings would seem to be within the realm of your academic interests, Mr. Leadbetter." Grey motioned to the nearby stack of books. "Rather a surprising number of titles among your collection relating to spiritualism, ancient religions, and the occult."

"I told you I was removed from the ministry over a matter of fundamental disagreements with my superiors in the church. Show too much interest in a topic, dare to believe there might be some questions worth asking instead of dismissing everything out of hand, and you're deemed some sort of heretic."

Grey drew a pencil and a small notebook from his pocket. He sketched quickly, then presented the drawing to Leadbetter.

"How about this figure?"

Lean recognized it as the charcoal face marked outside the room where Frank Cosgrove's burned body had been deposited. "The devil?" he suggested.

"A common misconception. No, that's not Satan. It's Baphomet."

"Beg your pardon?" Lean said.

"Baphomet. Don't be surprised never to have heard of him. He's essentially a fabricated pagan deity."

"As opposed to what?" Grey asked. "A genuine pagan deity?"

"Point taken," Leadbetter said with a chuckle. "I suppose it's all a matter of pedigree. The name didn't appear until the eleventh century. The Crusaders mention the Saracens calling upon Baphomet before battle. It's not difficult to recognize the origin of the term as European ears mistaking the name of the Muslim prophet Mahomet.

"Two hundred years later, King Philip IV of France wanted to break the power of the Templar Knights. He ordered their simultaneous arrest, without warning, throughout the country on October thirteenth, 1307. The original Friday the thirteenth, just so you know. Most of the accusations against the Templars were the same sketchy charges routinely made against Philip's political enemies: heresy, idolatry, spitting on the cross, and sodomy. The name Baphomet comes up, under severe torture, in several of the Templar confessions. It becomes one of the primary accusations—that they worshipped a pagan idol in the form of a preserved head or skull they called Baphomet. The name would have remained as something of a historical footnote if not for Éliphas Lévi."

"The occult author," Grey said aside to Lean.

Leadbetter nodded. "Yes, one of the most prominent of the modern ceremonial magicians. Helped spur on the revitalized interest in magic and the occult this past half century. Around 1850 or so, he wrote his first of many books on the occult, *Dogma and Ritual of High Magic*."

The former minister selected that same book title from his top shelf and opened to the frontispiece. "This is his drawing where he pictured Baphomet as a Sabbatic Goat."

The picture in the book showed a winged human body topped with a bearded goat head. Between the two great horns, a torch emerged from the head. A five-pointed star was emblazoned upon the being's forehead. The body displayed a pair of breasts, while a rod entwined by two snakes rose from beneath a robe that covered the figure's pelvis.

"That's not supposed to be a picture of the devil?" Lean asked again.

The older man shook his head. "Certainly some similarities to what you might see of the devil in places such as tarot cards. But Lévi actually saw the image not necessarily as a religious one but rather a symbolic depiction of the absolute. Male and female, light and dark, justice and mercy. All in unity and harmony. The pentagram points up as a symbol of light toward the torch, the flame of enlightenment. The flame of the soul rising above the base matter of the body, the one hand points up toward a light moon, the other one down toward a dark moon, in equilibrium and universal balance. Quite a bit of symbolism here, really."

Lean had been studying the picture while Leadbetter spoke. Of all the peculiar and unsettling elements in the image, one baffled him the most. "That rod, rising out of his . . . loins, what is that?"

"Mercury's staff, the caduceus. Mercury, or Hermes, is considered the symbolic male. Also, as I mentioned, mercury is the fluid metal, very important in terms of occult or alchemical thinking as the primary transformative element. Other alchemical symbols are present in the figure as well. See the words tattooed on his inner arms: *solve* and *coagula*—'dissolve' and 'congeal,' two of the vital transformative processes in alchemy."

Lean clapped his hands together. "There's a possible link, then, between this picture of Baphomet and Sears's stolen image. They both relate to alchemy—mercury in particular."

Grey held up a cautionary finger. "That's not certain. Whoever drew the image in Portland may not even have known exactly what he was drawing. He attached the words 'Hell Awaits.' He's mixing his symbolic metaphors. It's amateurish. He may have meant to draw the devil and produced an image of Baphomet by chance, without understanding the distinction. He may have had no inkling whatsoever of any connection to alchemical imagery."

"It wouldn't be a major surprise for someone not an expert to make the mistake," Leadbetter noted. "Much of the modern work on ancient occult wisdom has become something of a mishmash of ideas. But anyone familiar with Éliphas Lévi's work would know of the man's fascination with alchemy."

"Understandable," Lean muttered. "Who wouldn't want to be able to spin straw into gold?"

"Lead into gold, not straw," Grey corrected him. "You're thinking of Rumpelstiltskin."

Leadbetter chuckled, then said, "Actually, in his defense, Lévi followed a more philosophical view of the subject. He viewed the Great Work of alchemy as much more of a spiritual endeavor rather than a physical, metallurgical one."

"So if he's not after gold, what then?" Lean asked. "What you said before, something about the elixir of life? The goal's immortality, is it?"

"The Great Work, the philosopher's stone, the elixir of life, the highest level of enlightenment. Perfection." Leadbetter flipped ahead in the pages of Éliphas Lévi's book of magic.

"Elixir? Is it a drink?" Lean asked. "I thought it was a stone."

"Your confusion is understandable. It's called a stone, but descriptions of its appearance vary. It may be best to think of the word 'stone' as a metaphor. It is, after all, meant to be a mercurial, transformative substance embodying opposite properties, including solid and liquid."

Leadbetter regarded Lean's still-perplexed face for a moment. "Maybe the author's own definition will help. Here it is: 'The Great Work is, before all things, the creation of man by himself, that is to say, the full conquest of his faculties and his future, the perfect emancipation of his will.' "

Lean gave an unsatisfied nod. "I'll just settle for its being a metaphor."

"The Great Work," Grey said quietly, recalling something. "Would I be correct in expecting that someone like yourself, deeply interested in such arcane studies, would have occasion to meet and converse with a variety of others interested in the same matters?"

Leadbetter nodded. "There are various groups and societies who study spiritualism and whatnot. There's even an actual church of sorts, the First Spiritual Temple here in the city."

"Have you ever come across a man by the name of Dr. Jotham Marsh?" Grey asked.

Leadbetter flinched. "Why do you ask? Are you a friend of his?" The older man's voice went up in pitch as if he were physically uncomfortable.

Grey offered a sarcastic smile. "More of an acquaintance, you might say. I've heard him use that phrase—the Great Work."

The older man regarded Grey closely. "Not a man you want to be overly familiar with, if you want my advice."

"Why do you say that?" Grey asked.

"He's a man of great . . . ambitions. And perseverance. Not the sort you want to cross swords with, so to speak."

Leadbetter was visibly agitated at the turn in the conversation, and Lean was sensitive to the older man's feelings. Lean felt the prolonged confinement in the cramped, musty basement apartment overcoming him. Furthermore, the realization was dawning on him that Leadbetter could ramble on for hours and not tell them anything firmly related to their inquiry into the deaths of two thieves.

Grey retrieved his paper from the desk before the detectives thanked the deposed minister for his time and made their way out onto the street.

A horse-drawn railcar passed by at the corner, and Lean glanced up at the telephone wires that ran along the street poles. The images helped his mind vault forward by centuries, from an age of secret societies and alchemical manifestos to the comfort and certainty of the present day.

"A lot of information to digest, but I'm not sure it gets us any closer to who pulled the trigger on Frank Cosgrove or who scared Sears enough that he'd risk a deadly jump off a building."

"You're partly right," Grey said. "We've gained no decisive information on the meaning of those images Chester Sears was attempting to steal. Leadbetter's ideas about alchemical symbols aren't much more convincing than Professor Horsford's accounts of Viking runes."

They paused to hail a hansom cab as Lean lit a cigarette.

"However," Grey continued, "his identification of the ashen face from the house on Vine Street is interesting. The name of Baphomet is not exactly common knowledge among Portland's criminal practitioners. But we do know one expert to call on when the subject of occult ritual intersects with murder."

Chapter 18

GREY LET HIMSELF INTO HIS FRONT HALLWAY, WITH LEAN close behind. The door to Mrs. Philbrick's rooms on the first floor popped open, and the landlady appeared in the frame.

"Back again, Mr. Grey? With no prior notice, but just in time for afternoon tea. I suppose you'd want me to fix something right up?"

"Wouldn't think of putting you out, Mrs. Philbrick. You already do so much to ease the daily burdens of the world. Just the papers and my mail."

Grey held out his hand. Mrs. Philbrick ducked back into her door and emerged seconds later with a short stack of newspapers and envelopes. She reached into an apron pocket and withdrew another letter.

"Had to sign for this one yesterday. From a lawyer's office." She fixed a suspicious eye on Grey, who took the envelope and set it atop the others.

Mrs. Philbrick produced another envelope, this one smaller, and waggled it. "This looks important as well."

Grey snatched the smaller envelope and glanced at the face of it. Lean noticed an element of surprise on Grey's face as he slipped the envelope into a coat pocket.

"Anything else of interest lurking there in the recesses?" Grey gave a general wave toward Mrs. Philbrick's outfit.

"Nothing that need concern you." The older woman began to retreat toward her rooms but paused and laid a hand on Lean's arm. "I have some coffee on, if you'd like, Deputy?"

"That would be splendid, Mrs. Philbrick," he answered as he headed for the staircase.

Once in his apartment, Grey deposited his papers and several articles of mail on his desk. He retrieved the smaller envelope from his pocket and tossed it onto the others before focusing his attention on the legal post. Lean hung his hat by the door and began to amble about the perimeter of the large parlor, reacquainting himself with Grey's professional materials and equipment. He saw Grey's brow furrow.

"Trouble?" Lean asked. "Something you said?"

"Notice from the firm of Dyer & Fogg. Horace Webster died yesterday. The funeral is tomorrow morning."

"Friend of yours?"

Grey spared Lean a glance just long enough to confirm that they both recognized the inherent improbability of that statement. "An invalid who wished to confer with me on a matter. Tomorrow is the reading of the will for the man's considerable estate. The attorney requests my attendance immediately after, at four o'clock, to discuss the still-extant business requested by his late client."

"What's it about?"

Grey held up the letter, as if waving a white flag. "I suppose I'll find out tomorrow."

Lean had now circled to Grey's desk, where he glanced at the small envelope that Mrs. Philbrick had set aside as important but which Grey seemed intent on ignoring. He recognized the delicate, finely formed handwriting. He turned it over and saw the return address in Connecticut.

"Grey, is that a letter from Helen Prescott? Have you been in correspondence with her all this time?"

"No." Grey found a pad of paper and tore off a sheet. "Not regularly, by any means."

Lean wondered if Helen had written to say she was returning soon. Lean hoped so; it would be a delight to see the woman and her daughter again. Apart from the genuinely warm feelings he'd developed for the pair during last summer's inquiry, he couldn't deny a new and selfish reason for hoping she'd return to Portland soon. He viewed Helen's historical-research skills as nothing short of miraculous. The thought of having her available to assist with any necessary perusals of treatises on ancient runes, Vikings, and archaeology was comforting.

"Well, aren't you going to read it?" Lean asked.

"Later, perhaps."

"Perhaps?" Lean grinned at the man's stubborn reticence. "I'm to believe you might actually not read it. I'd have thought you'd be more excited to receive a letter from Helen."

"I'm sure it's not of pressing importance," Grey said. "I shall attend to Mrs. Prescott's news or whatnot later, along with the rest of my correspondence."

Grey finished tracing the symbol that Sears had held at the time of his death. He stood and handed the original piece of evidence over to Lean, who was staring at him.

"Just another bit of dull old correspondence, is it?" Lean asked.

"Don't you have pressing matters of your own? Your family to attend to, at your own home, where people presumably enjoy your bemused ramblings?"

"True enough." Lean smiled. "And a far more enjoyable bit of company they are than what awaits you. A dead man's lawyer. Not much joy there—unless the man happened to be a wealthy and childless uncle. And what about our old friend Jotham Marsh? You still mean to see him about that occult symbol in the house on Vine Street?"

"In the morning, I think. I'd prefer to be rested before dealing with Marsh. Even then I don't expect to get from him much of what he likely knows about Vine Street, Cosgrove, and Sears."

"I agree the man's dealings are somewhat dubious, but I'm still not entirely certain that Jotham Marsh has fully earned the animosity you bear." Lean meandered toward the door to the hallway. "I'm glad you haven't conjured up some deep, suspicious grievance against me."

"As always, I must remind you of the dangers of making presumptions. But in any event, I don't have reason to suspect you of secretly orchestrating a string of gruesome murders."

"Yes, that's one of my strongest virtues. The reason Emma agreed to marry me, actually."

"Another mystery solved," Grey said.

Lean chuckled as he closed the door behind him.

PART II

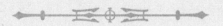

July 13, 1893

When the Investigating Officer has taken care to employ upon every imaginable clue which promises to bring forth some discovery the men most fitted to each, he is then free to direct all his efforts to the point where in his own opinion the correct clue is to be found.

—HANS GROSS, *Criminal Investigation*

Chapter 19

THE FOLLOWING MORNING A SILENT WOMAN LED GREY UP the staircase from the foyer where he'd been kept waiting since his request to see Dr. Jotham Marsh. The entranceway had been plain and unremarkable, giving no hint as to the purpose of the building that housed Marsh's thaumaturgic society. The Order of the Silver Lance was its formal name. As best Grey could tell, the members—adepts, they called themselves—considered it a bastion of enlightenment, a place that promised initiation into the esoteric, hermetic teachings of ancient mystics. In other words, Marsh had gathered to himself a group of deluded hopefuls clutching at the past because the present had failed them and the future promised nothing more.

The woman glanced back at him as they reached the second floor. She had dark eyes in a face that was strikingly pale given the apparent absence of any of the cosmetic powders or creams in common usage. Her fingernails made up for the lack of color in her face. They were painted a dull black, all except for the index finger of her left hand, which was a glossy crimson. Grey wondered if she stood under some bond of silence related to her progress through the magical order's ranks. Either way he was grateful.

They moved past several tall, south-facing windows that lit the narrow hall. The silent woman wore a trim, floor-length silk dress that seemed out of place given the morning hour. It appeared almost black when she passed through shade, but glimmering reflections of scarlet revealed themselves in the material whenever the sunlight caught her. Opposite the windows were a series of doors set close enough that together they could hold only large closets or cell-like rooms. Grey thought perhaps the building had once been a boardinghouse.

They came to a door farther removed from the others, and the woman admitted Grey, then departed. He stepped into a somewhat spacious study with paneled walls of dark-stained wood, decorated with a few paintings. Dr. Jotham Marsh slowly came around from a standing podium-like desk. A heavy open volume sat on the surface, and Marsh looked to have been working in inks, copying something. His sleeves had been up, but now he smoothed them down and fixed the cuffs.

In his middle forties, Marsh looked, as he often did, to be on the edge of smiling. In contrast—and Grey suspected that this was intentional— Marsh cultivated a grave and worldly look in his eyes that hinted at a history of wondrous sights. Grey had never been able to ascertain exactly what species of doctorate the man supposedly held. He was tempted to ask but assumed that the answer would be intentionally opaque, the sort of nonsensical parlor talk, hinting at danger and intrigue, designed to captivate a circle of onlookers over cocktails.

"Don't think me unwelcoming, Mr. Grey. But I agreed to make time for you only because I'm positively brimming over with curiosity as to the purpose of your visit."

"Frank Cosgrove."

"Is that name supposed to mean something to me?"

"He was shot dead a short while back, apparently after the robbery of an unusual item."

"Then it's hardly a surprise. It's a violent world, especially when one chooses that sort of life," Marsh said with a benevolent shrug.

"True. The surprising element came when his body was stolen from its fresh grave, his hands and face were burned, and his corpse was planted in an abandoned house with this figure sketched nearby." Grey presented a sheet of paper with his rendition of the horned, demonic-looking head that had been drawn in charcoal where Cosgrove's body was located.

Marsh's eyes barely moved toward the diagram. "Yes, I can see how that would be received as rather shocking. So just what is it I can help you with, Mr. Grey?"

"You are the local expert on things related to esoteric or occult studies. I wished to hear your interpretation of this figure."

"A common enough portrait of the devil, I should say," Marsh declared after another passing glance. "Someone had an ax to grind with the fellow and wanted the world to know his opinion of the fate that awaited Cosgrove. I suppose a man doesn't last long in that profession without making at least a few dear enemies." He raised his eyebrows at Grey as he finished that sentiment.

"So you don't take this figure to be a representation of Lévi's version of Baphomet?"

The brief spark of surprise that replaced Marsh's previous look of boredom was genuine, and Grey took that as a small opening victory.

"Baphomet? I have to applaud such an arcane reference from a layman. Yes, I suppose that Baphomet would be a more fitting model. Was the picture labeled?"

"No. But another expert on the subject, in Boston, was kind enough to enlighten me."

Grey watched Jotham Marsh's face, knowing that the man was silently running through his head the possible identities of those who could have so informed Grey. The pause was short. He sensed that Marsh wanted to ask for the unspoken man's name, or even guess it, but that he didn't want to be wrong or to appear desperate to gain information from Grey.

The older man merely nodded. "I see."

"Odd that you wouldn't make the connection at once."

"I was viewing it through the prism of what someone like you would see or what the likely culprit intended. Even if someone had ever seen Éliphas Lévi's figure of Baphomet, the common man has had his mind so greatly indoctrinated throughout modern times that he is incapable of grasping the crucial distinction between that vital symbolic figure and the devil so popularized in Christian mythos."

"I don't believe I take your meaning, Dr. Marsh," Grey said absentmindedly as he allowed himself to be distracted by one of the more macabre paintings on the wall.

The work was a copy, smaller than the original, showing the devil in the profiled form of a black-robed he-goat lording over a coven of fearful witches. They cowered before him with contorted faces and poorly formed bodies. Grey had seen the painting in the course of his varied studies as a younger man and recalled it as an early-nineteenth-century work by the Spanish master Goya. He remembered a museum lecturer speaking of it as the artist mocking the fearful irrationality of the masses, welcoming their own captivity at the hands of kings and priestly inquisitions.

"The devil, as he is conceived of in the popular imagination, does not exist," Marsh said. "Satan is a false name invented by the church to imply a unity in its ignorant muddle of beliefs. A devil who possessed a unity would be a god. And he is not, but neither is he the true enemy of Man. He is only painted as such to satisfy the needs of the church, a symbol of fear to oppress and control the ignorant. Even within such a flawed framework, we ought to thank this so-called devil. He who gave Mankind the potential to themselves become gods. For it is only with the knowledge of good and evil that Man can ever truly know himself and receive initiation."

"An interesting take on Man's fall from grace," Grey said.

"What else would you have Mankind be—a race of drones at work and play in the garden, never questioning, never seeking the truth, just existing in ignorant bliss? Despicable creatures, never yearning to attain the fullness of spiritual being that God meant for us?"

"But you say this Baphomet represents something different from the Christian devil. So why is he painted with the same brush?" Grey asked.

"He needn't be, but any power perceived as different from your own god is always perceived as evil. Simple men have always viewed the world thus. Baphomet's true identity is far removed from the idea of the devil. He is the hieroglyphic figure of arcane perfection. He represents Life and Love. He is the Eye that allows us to see, and he is the Light; Baphomet represents the Union of Opposites. The uniting of the soul with God, of the microcosm with the macrocosm, of the female with the male. All of it is the stuff of the Great Work."

Marsh paused for a moment. He ran his fingers over his forehead, pushing the mostly dark hair back from his sharp widow's peak.

"The quest for the Holy Grail, or the Golden Fleece, or the philosopher's stone—by whatever symbolic name we choose, whatever mythical parable we tell, the Great Work is an endless pursuit. Success would only reveal even greater possibilities, rendering the entire universe the mere plaything of the newly crowned and all-conquering child that is Man."

"I see," Grey replied in a flat tone. He searched his memory for the details shared by Father Leadbetter. "So this work, it's never been obtained or perfected. Not even by the notorious Count de St. Germain?"

Marsh chuckled, though his eyes remained stony, seldom even blinking. "A controversial figure, to say the least. The subject of many tales and rumors. Though if he had perfected the philosopher's stone, whatever became of him? Why don't the masses in the street know his name today? Maybe he's dead, or else his attainment of cosmic understanding made him retire from the world. Or perhaps he simply forgot that he was not supposed to die." Marsh gave a resigned shrug. "I think we both have better things to do than spend our time debating the ultimate fate of such a fantastical character as that."

"Yes, in fact I do have one other item for consideration. What about this symbol?" Grey again took out the sheet showing his drawing of Baphomet but turned it over to reveal the symbol of a circle topped with an arc, sketched from the one he'd recovered after Chester Sears's deadly fall.

"Is that meant to be a child's version of the Baphomet figure? Did your policeman friend sketch that one for you?" Marsh said with a dismissive smile.

"I thought it might be an attempt at the alchemical symbol for mercury. What can you tell me about it?"

Marsh tilted his head. "It signifies azoth, which was originally a term for an occult formula, the universal solvent, sought by alchemists. Over time azoth became a more poetic word for the element mercury."

"The key transformative element," Grey said.

"Yes, mercury or azoth is the essential agent of transmutation in alchemy. As the universal force of life in the cosmos and within each of us, the azoth is that divine, mysterious force responsible for the relentless drive toward physical and spiritual perfection."

"Whatever in the world would simple men, the likes of Cosgrove and Chester Sears, be doing, risking their lives over alchemical symbols?" Grey watched Marsh for a reaction to the latter name, but the man didn't take the bait.

"Another name you assume has some meaning for me."

"Sears. Before he died, he made a comment about fearing for his soul. Implying that someone was actually threatening his very soul. As if someone—a living, breathing person—had the power to accomplish such an inconceivable act." He stared into Marsh's cold, somber eyes.

"I must say, Grey, I find your attitudes perplexing. You seem to think the worst of me, that I'm some sort of monster. And all because of what? One student, who took my teachings, warped them about in his obviously unstable mind, and committed a horrible act. Would you blame the shopkeeper for murder because he sold a man a fishing rod? Only because later that fisherman, in his misguided fervor, comes to fatal blows with another over a favored fishing spot?"

"Of course not. But what of the shopkeeper who fills a young man's head with tales of a magical fish who swims in a mystical pond and will grant wishes to any angler who catches it. 'Oh, and by the way,' whispers the shopkeeper, 'the only bait that works is human flesh.'"

"You seem a reasonable man, Mr. Grey, but I think you have an overly active imagination. It can be quite a worrisome thing, to let such fanciful ideas get the better of you."

"The danger of fanciful ideas—at least we agree on that much. Quite worrisome indeed."

The two men regarded each other for a long moment.

"It would be for the best if you didn't feel the need to come here again, to speak of things you cannot understand," Marsh said.

"A shame. I've so enjoyed our little talks."

Marsh moved across the study and opened the door. Grey followed him out of the room.

"Farewell, Mr. Grey." Marsh looked past him and called out, "Jerome!"

A door along the hall opened immediately. A slender man with dark, slicked-back hair and wearing checked suit pants with a matching vest came into the sunlit hallway. Grey recognized Marsh's youthful lackey as Jerome Morse. The pale young man regarded Grey with a cool indifference. He motioned with a sweep of his arm for Grey to follow him back down the staircase.

Grey folded his paper and slipped it back into his pocket. He gave Marsh a slight tip of the head. "Another day."

"Perhaps," Marsh answered in an unconvinced tone.

Grey strode down the hall and past Jerome, not bothering to wait for the pale-faced man to show him the way out. He heard the thin, sickly-looking fellow's footsteps hurrying down the stairs to keep up with him.

Grey reached the front door first, opened it, and stepped out.

"Be sure to give my regards to your friend Deputy Lean," Jerome said.

Grey paused and turned; he hadn't expected any parting comments from Jerome, who had never struck Grey as more than a spineless minion who warranted little regard. He studied the man's face. He had the same sly, weaseling look about him as always, but now there was a self-satisfied edge to the man's pointed smile. He looked rather like a stupid man who thinks he's about to do something cunning.

"We haven't forgotten him," Jerome said as he laid a finger to the side of his nose, "or you."

It was a prominent nose that hadn't fully recovered its original line in the year since Archie Lean had broken it and put Jerome on the floor with a single punch.

Grey didn't reward Jerome with any response other than a dismissive flick of the eyes before he turned his back and walked away.

Chapter 20

G REY SAT ON A PADDED BENCH IN THE OFFICES OF DYER &
Fogg. For the fifth time in the past five minutes, his eyes settled
on a grandfather clock on the far side of the room. Two rolltop
desks against the walls were manned by smartly dressed law clerks,
eager men of twenty years or so. The clerk who had welcomed Grey ten
minutes earlier noted his glances.

"Mr. Dyer shouldn't be much longer." The young man looked
down the hallway leading off to the firm's offices, but no evidence
emerged to support the veracity of his claims. Instead he offered an
overly toothy smile and held it for an undue length of time, inviting
a return effort from Grey that would implicitly grant forgiveness for
being kept waiting.

Grey remained stone-faced and returned his attention to the grandfather clock. Its faint ticking fell into rhythm with the far-off but constant clacking of a typewriter. Grey imagined its operator to be some
humorless woman, a modern-day galley slave, hidden away in some
windowless closet that held no distractions from her tedious work. Albert Dyer's voice seeped down the hall to reach Grey, a muffled droning
from which no distinct words could be rescued. The voice paused, and
a door opened.

"Emery!" Dyer called from down the hall.

The young clerk's eyes lit up. He checked the knot of his tie before
scurrying off to answer his employer's summons. When the clerk came
back, he had a key in hand, which he used to open a solid-looking door
in the corner of the firm's front room. Grey listened to the tinny clanks
and scrapes of Emery fumbling around out of view. The clerk returned
carrying a long metal lockbox in both hands. He began an awkward
attempt to secure the box under one arm while battling the door's stub-

born lock. Grey stepped forward and offered to hold the lockbox, which Emery gratefully handed over. As he did, the white, heavily starched cuffs jutted farther out from his coat sleeves. Grey noticed pencil marks, notations, scribbled on the inside left cuff, a short list of various numbers followed by combinations of *w, p,* and *s.* Emery finished locking up and took the box back.

"The final bit of business," he assured Grey before hurrying down to Mr. Dyer's office.

By the time Grey renewed his vigil on the bench, the lawyer's drone resumed for a mercifully brief announcement. This was followed by a loud, unintelligible interjection by another male voice, which Grey suspected belonged to Horace Webster's eldest son, Euripides. Grey assumed that the entire family was inside, and he'd made out multiple voices since his arrival but hadn't yet detected Phebe's, although it was possible that hers simply didn't carry far enough. At the very moment he was recalling the pleasant tenor of Phebe's voice, a sudden eruption of noise came rolling out of Mr. Dyer's office in a jarring blend of shock, dismay, and recriminations.

"Please, please, everyone. A moment!" called out Mr. Dyer. The lawyer's voice descended back to its usual subdued tone, though a new urgency flowed through the words.

Grey made out a series of plaintive denials and assurances in the higher voice of young Emery. The door to Dyer's office opened just enough to spit out the clerk. He came down the hall with an uncertain, shuffling gait, like a man not yet accustomed to his newly fitted leg irons. The clerk made no attempt to meet Grey's gaze. He found his way to his desk and took out a sheet of paper. Rather than write anything, Emery could manage only to hold his head aloft with one hand while the fingers of the other tapped the desktop at a furiously nervous pace.

The office door opened again, revealing the thin, suave form of Jason Webster, wearing a dark suit with a golden check pattern. Behind him stood his older brother, Euripides, in a simple black suit more appropriate to the occasion.

"I want to hear from you the moment you've rectified this situation," Euripides barked into the office.

"I understand your frustration, Euripides. However, legally speaking, the only aggrieved party here is Miss Phebe. I will of course notify her the second it's found so that she may collect the item."

"Don't try to hide behind legal technicalities, Albert. This is a gross display of negligence in handling the family's affairs, and I for one am certainly questioning the wisdom of allowing your firm to continue on in its current capacity."

Grey stood as the two middle-aged Webster men approached in the hallway. Jason had a cheery glint in his eye that was at odds with his having just concluded the business of his father's earthly wishes. His expression seemed less a matter of how well he'd come off in the will and more like a deep-seated pleasure at the degree of annoyance currently vexing his older brother.

"We meet again, Mr. Grey. I suppose that's a danger of life in a small city," Jason said.

"City's large enough, judging from all the idlers and flimflammers about." Euripides spoke loud enough for the lawyer to hear him, but he had his sights fixed on Grey as he stormed past.

Back in the doorway, Attorney Dyer held the hand of Phebe Webster and assured her in heartfelt, consolatory tones, well suited to her long black funerary dress, that he was greatly sorry for the misunderstanding and any inconvenience it caused. However, he was sure to have matters sorted out in no time at all.

Phebe nodded wholeheartedly before taking her leave.

"Mr. Perceval Grey, what an unexpected surprise," she said.

"Miss Webster. Please accept my condolences, for your grandfather."

"Thank you. It's very trying, of course, though for the best." She was about to say something further on the matter when a puzzled look came across her face. "Mr. Dyer didn't call for you ahead of time on account of the . . ." she gestured back toward the scene of the recent commotion.

"No. That is, Mr. Dyer didn't mention any specifics to me. Here on a different matter, I believe."

"I see. That other business of Grandfather's. Well, your being here is quite fortuitous. Perhaps you can assist Mr. Dyer in tracking down the missing artifact." Phebe's eyes remained moored to Grey a moment longer. "Good day, Mr. Grey."

"Good day. And, again, my deepest condolences."

"Mr. Grey, sorry about all the bother. Please come on through." Albert Dyer waved him forward with one hand while the other dug around for a handkerchief to wipe at his face, which had gone a bit red with the recent fuss. He didn't close the door, preferring to allow a meager sea breeze to pass through an open window that looked out over the bustle of Exchange Street.

On his way over to one of the four chairs arranged before Dyer's desk, Grey glanced into the empty metal lockbox. "Something amiss, I take it."

"We have a vault of sorts where we keep clients' valuables, documents, or other items. Apparently our incompetent clerks have spent the past weeks bungling matters. I'll be here late into the evening now sorting out which lockbox is which." Dyer's fingers seemed unwilling to do his brain's bidding. It took him several attempts to light his cigar. He began to pace without any awareness that he was doing so.

"My father and his father before him have served as attorneys and counselors to the Webster family. And now, at the most solemn and trying of times, a family heirloom entrusted to our care is misplaced. Damned embarrassing." His eyes lingered on the lockbox.

"Speaking of the unfortunate Horace Webster, you've been quite diligent about keeping me in suspense as to his request for my assistance," Grey said.

A smile edged its way onto Dyer's uneasy face as he continued to pace behind the desk. "Let you in on a little secret, Mr. Grey: The practice of law is at least fifty percent showmanship, making people so anxious to hear what you will say next that they don't even mind paying for the privilege of listening."

"No offense to you and your illustrious brethren, but the fact that attorneys insist on behaving as if their every utterance is a grand address to the Roman Senate, one that we are privileged to hear, seems to the rest of us less a trade secret and more a necessary evil."

Dyer let out a dry chuckle. "You're here, aren't you? Don't pretend that you're not curious as to Mr. Webster's dying wish."

"The exact request may hold some unanticipated detail, but I already know that you're going to ask me to locate a woman. The one who was meant to occupy the fourth chair set out here for those members of Horace's family mentioned in his will."

"Very good, Mr. Grey. Maybe there's a glimmer of hope for this endeavor after all. Yes, Madeline Webster is the woman in question. Left home two years ago. Hasn't been heard from in over a year."

"Do you have cause to believe she's met with some ill fortune?"

Dyer fidgeted with his cigar and struggled to keep his eyes off the conspicuously empty lockbox as he pondered how best to respond. He opted for a frustrated shrug.

"For all I know, she's gallivanting through the capitals of Europe. She was always an impetuous one. Her parents, Horace's youngest son and his wife, both died at an early age. The two daughters were raised in Horace's house, and he doted on them. They didn't always receive the firm and guiding hand that the youth of today require. Madeline in particular always struck me as a restless spirit."

Grey shifted his chair noisily, preparing to interject, but Dyer stopped his pacing and held up a slim leather case as if it were a piece of damning evidence to be considered by a jury.

"This firm has certain fiduciary obligations to the Webster estate. Of course, we made our own inquiries of her friends and associates. All our notes are in here." Dyer pulled out a photograph and handed it over.

Grey looked at the photograph of Madeline Webster. He could see some resemblance to Phebe.

"Perhaps you can make more sense of it than I have," Dyer said. "Horace was desperate to see the girl again before he passed. To make sure she was safe, that he could take care of her—financially, at least. And while it's too late for him to find any peace in this matter, his instructions remain in effect. Information on Madeline's current whereabouts would be rewarded with five hundred dollars."

"You wish me to find a missing woman who's in no obvious danger and who seems perfectly content not to be found. And to illuminate the issue, you offer a briefcase full of notes from unsuccessful conversations. It doesn't sound promising or, to be honest, particularly interesting."

"Please, Mr. Grey, Horace Webster was a good man. This was his dying wish. Look over the material. Then talk to Phebe Webster. I'd wager that five hundred dollars she has some inkling of where her sister ran off to. They used to be inseparable. Damned if she was going to reveal Madeline's secrets to me, though." A bit of Dyer's earlier frustration crept back into his voice. "Please just consider the matter. And if you decide there's nothing to be done, then so be it. I'll pay you for your time."

"Mr. Dyer—"

The attorney crushed out his cigar and stared at Grey in earnest desperation. "Yes, you can easily dismiss my entreaties. I'm just a lawyer, and one who likes to keep you waiting. But a dying wish? A lost woman who could be in who knows what manner of trouble, and perhaps not another soul in all the world who could help her, or even cares to try? Those things shouldn't be so easy to ignore."

A half dozen reasons to turn the matter down jockeyed for position in Grey's mind. Most of them related to the probability that there would be no meaningful venue of inquiry to pursue here and that the search for Madeline Webster would prove fruitless until such time as the young woman's whims carried her home at last. She was a woman of means with more privileges in the world than most would ever know. Objectively, it was difficult to justify feeling any undue concern on her behalf. Still, Grey knew well enough from his own experience the deep veins of unhappiness that could run just below the surface of even the most privileged and proper families. He stood and approached the desk.

"I'll review the material and speak with Miss Webster. But I wouldn't recommend that you entertain much hope of a successful resolution."

"Thank you, Mr. Grey."

Grey took the black leather bag and started for the door. Before exiting, he turned back to see Dyer pressing his knuckles into his desktop and staring at the metal box.

"As for the object missing from that lockbox," Grey said, "if it should happen not to turn up in your vault, you may want to look into your clerk Emery's gambling habits. He's been wagering on horse races— keeps his notes on his sleeve. It's an easy way for a young man to get in trouble quickly with an unforgiving class of debtors. Purloining the contents of a lockbox, which might not be missed for years, might seem like an easy way out of trouble to a young man in dire straits."

"Well, I suppose I'm happy to say that you're wrong on this matter.

First off, Emery doesn't know a thing about racing. He keeps those notes on his cuff to remember which bets I've told him to place. *I'm* the one who enjoys horses, and I'm not in any trouble on that account." The lawyer managed a weak smile. "Secondly, if he were going to help himself to the contents of one of our boxes, it certainly wouldn't be that of Horace Webster. Emery was well aware that the poor state of Webster's health guaranteed that the contents would be needed sooner rather than later. And furthermore, he was with me when we checked on the box just two weeks ago—getting everything in order. He knew what was inside. Not the sort of thing like cash or jewelry that a man could easily convert to his own profit."

"Good to know." Grey nodded at the attorney before leaving.

Chapter 21

LEAN KNELT DOWN IN THE CENTER OF THE CRAMPED ROOM. Large racks of colored fabrics lined the walls, looking like oversize spools of thread tipped on their sides. A rug had been pulled up to reveal a trapdoor set in the floor of the storage space of Ezra Grosstack's tailor and drapery shop. The small padlock had been removed from the rusted iron clasp that secured the door to the neighboring floorboards.

Mrs. Louisa Grosstack stood looking over Lean's shoulder. In her late forties, the woman had enough substance that her own dress looked as if it might be made from an entire spool of fabric. Behind her was a uniformed police officer.

"It's a cellar, but you've never used it?" Lean asked.

"No use to me. Or Ezra, of course. Too damp and dirty for storing any material down there. If it weren't for that lock setting a bump in the rug, I'd have plumb forgot that door was even there," she said.

"But then you smelled lamp oil burning this morning?"

"Not me—Ezra did. Soon as he came through the door. He's got the keenest sense of smell. And a bit of a worrier as well. Terrified of overturned lamps or whatnot. Afraid for all this inventory. It's the life of the business. He's collecting another shipment down at Brown's Wharf at this moment."

"Well, let's have a look." Lean worked his fingers under the door and lifted it up. The officer came around the other side to take the hand-off and set the door down, exposing a three-by-four hole in the floor. Wooden stairs descended into the musty darkness. Lean lit a lamp and dangled it down into the entry. The light wasn't enough to reveal the entire space, but he could see it was a dirt-floor cellar, not particularly high. The far reaches of the space remained hidden. He moved the lamp about and peered more closely; the ground below looked odd, as if it were spotted. Finally the situation at the tailor shop on Exchange Street was beginning to bear out the report he'd received at the patrol station, passed on to him with only the vague description of "suspicious behavior."

"Do you have a second lamp we could use?"

Mrs. Grosstack gave a quick nod, then bustled away. Despite her size, Lean got the impression that she was a woman of action. When she returned a minute later, she had a lamp in one hand and a black iron fireplace shovel in the other. Lean gave her a quizzical look.

"Who knows what manner of critters are scurrying around down there?" she said.

"I suppose," Lean said with a shrug as he reached out to accept the small shovel.

Mrs. Grosstack took a defensive step back. "You've got a pistol. This here's mine, young fellow."

"Right." Lean turned toward the trapdoor again and, with his lamp in hand, began a slow descent of the stairs. Creaks of protest met each cautious footfall. The entire staircase felt as if it were sinking just a bit into the dirt under Lean's weight. He was halfway down the steps when the staircase gave a noticeable shudder. He looked up to see Mrs. Grosstack coming after him. True concern showed itself on the face of the officer still standing in the lit storage room above.

"There's really no need for you to come down here, Mrs. Grosstack."

"This is my property. Ezra's, too, of course. If someone's been tampering right under my feet, then I ought to know about it firsthand."

Lean reached the bottom, looked around to ensure that there was nothing immediately pressing, then reached up to take Mrs. Grosstack's elbow as she maneuvered down the last steps. Once she was clear of the rickety wooden stairway, the officer followed.

The room was more or less rectangular, about twenty by thirty-five feet, with walls of mortared stone that were cool to the touch. Near one dark corner of the room, a sort of brick chimney jutted out several feet from the wall. At one point it had had an opening for a stove, but that appeared to have been blocked up some time ago.

"How long have you owned this property?" Lean asked.

"My father bought it in the late sixties, when it was rebuilt after the Great Fire."

"But the cellar would be original," Lean mumbled to himself.

"He retired in '75 and passed it all down to me. And Ezra, of course. He'd been working under my father for a decade before that."

Lean crouched down to inspect the ground. Old bits of trash and junk lined the base of the walls, but almost the entire central area was crisscrossed with a regular pattern of holes spaced out, six inches apart, in an even grid. Each perfectly circular hole was about an inch in diameter and surrounded by a short mound of dirt, giving the appearance of a symmetrical pattern of large anthills.

"Someone's been drilling holes down here," Lean said.

"There must be hundreds of them. What on earth for?" said the officer.

Lean palmed a clump of damp earth from atop one of the holes. The edge of the hole looked smooth, and inside he noted a spiral, ridged pattern.

"This is freshly turned earth. Someone's been boring in with an auger."

"No claim jumping, gents. If there's oil struck, it belongs to me," Mrs. Grosstack said.

"And Ezra, of course," Lean completed the woman's customary phrasing for her.

"Ezra who?" Mrs. Grosstack barked out a laugh that sounded as much like she was officially declaring her amusement as she was actually being amused.

Lean found a piece of thin wooden dowel among the junk by the wall and slid it into two different holes. "About two feet. They were certainly drilling for something. But if this is meant as some sort of burglary attempt, it's about the strangest I've ever seen."

A harsh thwack combined with an abbreviated squeal sounded behind him. Lean's head shot around, and he saw Mrs. Grosstack scooping up a dead rat with her fireplace shovel. The newly deceased creature was too big for the implement; its head hung limply off one side of the shovel while its long, tendinous tail drooped off the other end. Mrs. Grosstack expertly cast the newly crumpled body into a far corner, near the old brick chimney. Her look of repugnance shifted to one of confusion.

"I don't understand. Nothing upstairs was touched. Do you really think someone broke in to our store without leaving a trace and without robbing it, just to sneak into the cellar and drill holes?"

"What else could it be?" the uniformed officer asked.

Lean stood and held his lamp high as he looked over the nearest stone wall. He scanned the room, and his gaze landed on the sealed-up chimney. As he walked to that corner, his eyes seemed to play a trick on him. The shadow cast into the dark corner behind the protruding chimney did not vanish, even as the position of his burning lamp dictated that it must. He stepped closer and leaned in toward the corner. Now the shadows vanished, giving way to a further darkness receding down a long, thin passageway. A series of short boards that had once covered the opening now lay scattered about inside the passage.

"There's a tunnel cut through here."

Mrs. Grosstack shouldered the officer aside as she hurried to the corner. Lean saw only surprise on the woman's face when he looked to her for an explanation.

"Don't ask me—I didn't build it." Mrs. Grosstack held her hands out to her sides, palms up, inviting Lean to actually look and compare her ample frame to the narrow passageway.

By lamplight Lean inspected the old wooden supports that lined the walls and ceiling of the two-foot-wide tunnel cut through the earth.

"It's been here a while. Seems sturdy enough," he said, though he wished he were more convinced. He turned to the officer. "Stay here with Mrs. Grosstack, in case I run into any trouble."

He turned sideways and started into the passage but halted, glanced back, and reached out his hand. "Shovel, please."

Mrs. Grosstack presented the implement with as much solemnity as if she were passing a battlefield standard. Her face was screwed up tight, pitying the deputy's claustrophobic situation and plainly unwilling to even contemplate the thought of trading places with him.

With weapon in hand, Lean began edging his way along the dank tunnel. He used the shovel like a machete, cutting a swath through the cobwebs hanging from the ceiling. He heard several rats scurrying off before him. The flickering lamplight revealed the silent movements of centipedes and other small crawly things. Beneath his feet the ground was uneven, and he tried to step over the low spots where murky puddles had collected. Lean glanced back occasionally to see the shrinking light held up by Mrs. Grosstack, but after about fifty yards the gradual curve of the tunnel blocked that sight. There was no sign of light ahead of him, and after another minute he discovered why.

The tunnel ended in a wall of three vertical boards haphazardly cobbled together. Just to the side, two thin metal augers were leaning against the earthen wall, seemingly abandoned there. Lean set the lamp down, then slid the head of the shovel between two ill-fitted boards. Just a small tug popped one board out of place. After that, Lean easily pushed the other two out of the way with his hands. The lamp revealed what looked like a storage closet, filled with small wooden crates and casks. Lean could see a door a few feet beyond. He stepped past several stacked crates and pushed on the door. It budged but wouldn't open. He leaned back, then threw his shoulder into the door. The cheap wood splintered, and the door crashed open.

His lamplight revealed another dirt basement, but this one showed evidence of regular use. Lean peered into one of many open-topped crates and saw empty liquor bottles. Above him, through the floorboards, he heard several people talking and a strange cracking sound that it took him a few seconds to identify as pool balls being struck. Lean tried to reckon his location, but he'd lost track of his bearings in the tailor's cellar and then the winding tunnel.

The mystery was solved when a door to the ground floor opened, casting a shaft of light into the basement from above.

"That better not be you down there, Murphy. If you're busting into any of my casks, I'll split your damn fool skull open."

Lean recognized the gruff voice as belonging to John Foden, the proprietor of a billiard hall and saloon on Fore Street, near the corner of Market. The man's bulging midsection made its appearance on the staircase, followed shortly by the thick white mustache and goatee that dominated his otherwise hairless head. Foden marched down with a purpose, a sturdy wooden truncheon in hand. Lean held his lamp up and waited for Foden. The sight of the deputy caused the air to go out of the stout proprietor, who stuck his weapon into his back pocket.

"Deputy Lean, how'd you? I mean . . ." Foden paused and glanced about at the stacked boxes of liquor and casks of beer.

While it was generally given little more than lip service, the state of Maine did have a liquor law on the books prohibiting the sale of alcohol except by authorized agents, and that generally for medicinal or commercial and manufacturing purposes. Foden managed only a shrug as he decided to meet the potentially awkward situation head-on.

"Is this going to be much of a problem?" he asked, nodding toward the copious evidence of his violations of the liquor law.

Lean weighed the situation. The augers had been left on the tunnel side of Foden's beer closet. Whoever had brought them in through this side in the first place didn't want them to be seen on the way out. If Foden was involved, or even knew what was going on, he wouldn't bother to hide the tools from himself. Still, it was the only lead, and Lean needed it to pay off.

"No, not much. So long as you tell me who's been coming through your cellar to reach this tunnel back here."

A look flickered in Foden's eyes. In the dim light, Lean couldn't tell whether it was confusion or fear.

"Sorry, Lean, but I guess this is going to be a problem."

"You'd be looking at a very big fine."

Foden shook his head and spit on the ground. "There's things far worse in this world than that," he muttered, then crossed himself.

Chapter 22

Y OUR GRANDFATHER WILL BE WITH YOU IN JUST A MOMENT,
sir." Cyrus Grey's butler, Herrick, took Perceval Grey's hat and
walking stick. "Where would you care to wait for him? The
attic? The gardening shed? The rest of the staff and I always like to
place a small wager." He couldn't resist a dry smile.

"The study will do."

"Excellent, sir. Yet disappointing."

Though the majority of his time had actually been spent away at
various schools, Grey had been raised in his grandfather's house from
the age of seven through his teenage years. When Grey was at home,
Herrick had often been cast in the role of his avuncular caretaker. Now,
however, he was formally a guest, and so Herrick felt obliged to show
him to the study. An immaculately organized cherry writing desk stood
before windows that looked out over the back garden. Stocked book-
shelves lined the walls.

"Can I bring you anything, sir?"

Grey shook his head and asked in return, "How's the old man faring
these days?"

"Well and good, sir."

"You're normally a very convincing liar, Herrick. So I can only assume that despite your perceived duty to him, you actually desire to tell
me some less optimistic news."

"I take exception to that, sir." The stout, middle-aged butler's round
face retracted a bit, forcing his jowls into sharp relief.

"Which bit?"

"That I occasionally engage in deception—even when needed as
part of my household duties."

"But not the other part? That you are well skilled in the art?"

"No, not so very much, in truth," Herrick said.

"Out with it, then."

"Nothing particular, sir. He's just becoming a bit more . . . shall we say, deliberate in his movements. And this heat hasn't done much for his spirits."

"Has his physician been around recently?" Grey asked.

"Saw him for that cough he had in April."

"Maybe you could telephone, see if the man's willing to stop by for an unscheduled social call of some sort."

"I think that would be wise, sir."

"That is, if you don't object to a bit of deception."

"I think I can make a small allowance, just this once," Herrick said.

"Right. Thank you, Herrick."

Once alone among the books, Grey moved along the right-hand wall, then knelt down at the far end to see the spines on the second-bottommost shelf. There, tucked deep among thicker volumes, was his late mother's family Bible, right where he'd placed it years earlier. He slipped the volume from its spot, cradling it in his hands. The book was old and hadn't always been treated with the greatest of care during his mother's travels. It carried the musty scent of stale, yellowed pages. He opened the cracked, stained cover and saw the name of Eliza Grey penned in the studied yet graceful hand of a girl. Below this, in a more forced and rigid hand, he saw the final message she'd left for him. Although it had been two decades since he'd last seen the words, he didn't need to read them. He'd done that countless times in his youth, and the few delicate lines were ingrained in his memory. Still, he let his eyes run over the page.

Dearest Perceval, my good, strong, lovely boy, I pray that in time you will come to understand and forgive me. There are truths this life will show you that are beautiful beyond description, yet others that are beyond bearing. It is my final hope for you that you'll have the courage to see fully all the truths that are to be seen in this life, and the greater courage still to carry on—always.

Know that your father loved you, that I love you.

Grey folded the book once more and felt the stiff cover beneath his fingers, as if he could draw something further out of it. His grandfather's muffled voice and the slow procession of feet down the staircase reached his ears. He carefully replaced the Bible and walked out the door and a short way down the hall.

"Yes, Perceval, come out of the library. I can't believe there's anything left in there that you haven't already conquered." A thin smile crept onto Cyrus Grey's pale, arid face as he spoke, revealing long, yellowish teeth.

Perceval guessed that the welcome was intended as a feint, an effort by his grandfather to make his descent down the stairs seem effortless. Even though thick carpet runners lined the steps and made a slip unlikely, Herrick followed at his master's elbow ready to lend assistance. Grey studied his grandfather's appearance. The stark white light beaming down from the electric chandelier made Cyrus's fair skin seem almost translucent. There was barely a difference in hue between the eighty-year-old man's bald pate, stretched taut across his cranium, and the strip of ghostly white hair that circled from temple to temple, dropping down at each end point to form long, scraggly sideburns. The dark sheen of the railing beneath Cyrus's hand only highlighted the pallor of the man's meager flesh.

Grey's eyes darted aside, finding another image of Cyrus, this one decades younger, staring down from its place among the formal portraits that lined the wall above the staircase. Men and women, most of them past the prime of their lives, stood shoulder to elbow, in a rising cavalcade of close-set gilded frames. Perceval knew most of that pantheon of somber-looking Greys by name only. Apart from his own mother's portrait, Cyrus's was the only one that he recognized by sight, though the artist's brush had been kind and there was little resemblance left to the man now before him.

Cyrus's hand grazed across Grey's arm as he motioned toward the living room.

"We have a few minutes until dinner." Cyrus made his way into the large room and across to a side table set before a series of tall windows. Grey meandered over to the room's grand piano and sat on its bench.

"Had it tuned again, at long last," said the old man.

Grey watched, though he tried not to blatantly stare, as his grandfather poured himself a glass of brandy. The cut-crystal decanter shook in the old man's hand and sent diamond-shaped reflections shimmering across the ceiling.

"Doctor's orders?" Grey asked.

Cyrus made a short scoffing sound. "Has Herrick been in your ear? That man gets at me worse than your grandmother ever did."

Before he replaced the crystal stopper, Cyrus glanced at his grandson. "Care for a bit, Perceval?"

"No, thank you."

"As my own father used to say, you don't always have to be quite so proper to be a proper gentleman. Though I'm not sure that animal still exists: the proper gentleman."

Cyrus dropped the stopper into place with a clatter and then, tumbler in hand, took his customary seat in a tall chair near the brick-faced fireplace that dominated the end of the spacious living room.

"Whatever it is that passes for proper these days, some of us have to work harder to be seen as measuring up," Grey said.

"Is that it? Don't want to show any weakness, eh?" There was a note of approval in the old man's voice.

"At least not that one. You're doubly damned if you show any sign of the flaw they expect to see in you. Even a simple toast to good health: One man's social grace is evidence of another man's, an Indian man's, weak nature."

"Ah, a teetotaler out of spite for all those who doubt your character at first glance."

"Not spite." Grey shifted about on the bench, bringing his legs under the keyboard and flipping open the fallboard. As he studied the keys, he explained, "I just never cared to give them the pleasure of thinking their ignorant opinions were justified."

"That's you, Perceval. Always having to prove yourself right by proving everyone else wrong."

"I'd be more than happy to quit my end of that equation, if only everyone else would give up the annoying habit of being wrong so much of the time."

Grey's fingers deliberated over the keys before touching down and working into the low, solitary notes of the opening of Liszt's Sonata in B Minor.

"Horace Webster passed away the other day," Grey said.

"Yes. The service was well attended, though mostly in connection with the younger generations. Not many left now who knew him in his greener years."

"You did. What can you tell me about him and his family?" Grey asked.

"Why the sudden interest?"

"He asked me to perform a service before he died."

Cyrus paused a second. Then, seeing that his grandson was not volunteering any further details, he said, "I suppose it's not the sort of thing I'd wish to hear about anyway."

With slow, stiff movements, the man rose from his chair and strolled closer to the piano, forcing the blood to move and stir what recollections his mind could muster.

"A longtime widower, same as me. The oldest son works in munitions; he's done well with it. Started that up when he came back north after the war. The other has never given much account of himself, from what I understand."

Close to a minute into his playing, Grey's fingers suddenly sprang into action as the piece exploded to life. He played another thirty seconds, then stopped.

"There was a third son, wasn't there?"

"Oh, yes." A glint of remembrance came into Cyrus's dull eyes. "Of course, young Alexander. Horace's favorite. He loved that boy—his loss was such a blow. After Alexander's funeral was one of the last times I really talked with Horace."

"What happened?"

"Nothing, no falling-out or any such. We were each just busy. And he was always an eccentric sort. Only got worse as he got older."

"I meant with the third son," Grey said.

"Tragic. The sorry fool blew his brains out with his service revolver. Was wearing his old Union officer's uniform when he did it. Horace had been so proud of him, enlisting just like his oldest brother. The middle son avoided it with health complaints or something. Bought his way out of it. But Alexander did his duty. Horace said he was never quite right in the head after: moody, forlorn. Left two daughters behind that Horace then raised up, as I recall."

The two men exchanged a wary look, each cautious to avoid prompting the other into expanding that topic beyond its current range. They silently agreed to leave the matter where it was, pinned safely to some other family.

Cyrus coughed and lurched back into the conversation, "But, as I said, the whole lot of them are a bit on the eccentric side. Runs in the family."

"How so?" Grey asked.

"The older ones were a bookish lot. I don't recall how they made their money. Horace's father was an inventor of some kind. Always dabbling about in science treatises and chemicals. A violent temper on him, though. He almost killed Horace once, when we were young men, just coming into our own." Cyrus took a sip, then added, "Over a girl."

Grey leaned forward. "Horace Webster and his father quarreled over the same woman?"

"No, not like that." Cyrus shook his head. "You always get the queerest ideas flying through your brain. His father disapproved of her. She was a pretty servant girl, a young Negro. What was her name? Something odd or fanciful, and French-sounding: Destiny, perhaps."

"Could it have been Dastine?"

Cyrus's head tilted as a faint memory rattled down from one side of his brain. "It might have been." He looked at his grandson with surprise.

Grey quickly asked, "What were you saying about her and Horace?"

Cyrus wavered between a demand for how his grandson knew that detail and his own memories, finally opting for the latter. "Horace's grandfather had come to Maine from England, by way of the West Indies. Brought a family of servants from there. Obviously, none of us, his friends, approved when we found out."

"Obviously."

Cyrus ignored his grandson's sarcasm. "The girl had her charms, to be sure, but still. When his father discovered what was going on, he beat the tar out of the girl, drove her from the house. Put a pistol to Horace's head. Said he'd kill him if he ever saw the girl again."

"Did he? See her again, that is?"

"No. He was a fool in love—I suppose."

Grey noted Cyrus's discomfort as the old man tacked on the last two words, as if he couldn't bring himself to wholly endorse the concept of actual love existing between his white friend Horace and a woman of Caribbean descent.

"But not a complete fool," Cyrus continued. "It put a bit of a rip in his sails, I think. He was withdrawn after, slowly drifted away from the rest of us. I suspect he bore a grudge against his father until the day the man died."

"Hard to find fault with him if he did," Grey said.

"His father's methods may have been rather blunt. Too forceful, perhaps."

"Perhaps?" Grey raised an eyebrow at the word. "You said he beat the tar out of the girl."

"I suppose. An overreaction, but sometimes that's what's needed to see that things are taken care of. A mere warning would never have forced Horace's hand. It could have been disastrous if left unchecked."

"Yes, who can say what horrors would have resulted?"

Cyrus gave a half sneer at Grey's sardonic and self-referential comment. "Very droll, Perceval. But the man had the best wishes at heart for his child. The same as any parent, wanting to protect his child, see right done for him."

"'Best wishes.' An oddly turned phrase, given the results that so often follow."

"Easy for you to say with no child of your own to fret over. You do what you can, all that you can, but still, ultimately, you come down to nothing left to offer but wishes for your child."

"Is that so?"

"Yes, now let's see if dinner's ready and put our mouths to better use than this."

"What do you have left for me, in terms of wishes?" Grey asked with a grin.

"Nothing. Except maybe a wish that you'd let an old man be and not rake him over the coals with such glee."

Chapter 23

PHEBE SAT AT A DESK IN THE STARKLY APPOINTED FRONT room of her Uncle Euripides' corporate office on Cross Street in Portland. Pages laid out in neat rows showed various production orders, bills of lading, and inventory reports. She stared at the paper in front of her, failing to focus on the array of figures that held no meaning for her at that moment. She'd come into the office that morning desperate to escape the sorrow that draped the house she'd shared with her grandfather. Instead she found herself painfully distracted from the menial paperwork that Euripides handed her.

Vague thoughts and memories of Horace Webster meandered through her mind, each one colliding with or fading into another. Phebe ignored the vision of the man as he'd been in the past month, feebly lying in bed. Her images were pulled from the prior twenty years, when her grandfather, though old, still carried himself with an inner strength and dignity. She longed for those happier days and his solid, reassuring presence.

Goose bumps trickled up her arms, and a tingling sensation flashed across the back of her neck, like the reach of fingertips just a hairsbreadth from her skin. Though her head was bowed over the desk, she caught sight of something along the upper reaches of her vision. Phebe saw a man's body, darkly dressed, standing several feet in front of her desk. Her eyes shot up to meet a serious, wrinkled face interrupted by a long, grizzled mustache and topped by a large, wide-brimmed hat. There was no real resemblance to her grandfather, but the sudden, silent appearance of an older man right before her eyes was still enough to force a curtailed yelp from Phebe.

"Terribly sorry, miss. I didn't mean to startle you." The man doffed his hat briefly, revealing long gray hair brushed back from the front. "I sometimes forget to walk loudly enough for white folk to hear me coming."

Phebe wasn't sure what the man meant, but she did glance toward his feet, where he wore thick-heeled boots. His heavy trousers and dark tan frock coat also looked suited to an active outdoor life. Apart from having a face so weathered that she couldn't hazard a guess as to his precise age, the man himself looked white. Still agitated from the surprise, Phebe let the man's apology pass without any other thoughts. She forced a smile.

"Can I help you?"

"That's what I'm hoping. I've got to speak with your boss, Mr. 'Ripides Webster."

"You mean my uncle."

"Ah, forgive me." The man froze for a second. Then he removed his hat a second time and held it to his breast. "My condolences, miss, on your grandfather's passing. May the Great Spirit bless him and smile upon him."

"Thank you." At something of a loss, Phebe glanced down at the papers on her desk, futilely seeking guidance from a collection of sheets that had absolutely no relevance to her uncle's daily schedule. "I wasn't aware he had any appointments today."

"I 'spect he wouldn't grant me an audience. Except maybe on the first Friday after never. But yet, I assure you, it's a matter of the utmost importance that I speak with him."

"I see," Phebe said with a glance back at the closed door to Euripides' office, which offered no hint that her uncle was on the verge of appearing to remedy the unexpected arrival of this stranger.

"Let me just check with him and see if . . ." She edged toward the door, then glanced back at the man. "I'm sorry, I didn't catch your name."

"Chief Jefferson."

She offered another set smile as she reached for the door handle. "One moment, please."

"*Kchi oliwni*—great thanks," the chief said.

Phebe slipped into the office and eased the door closed behind her.

Euripides spared a glance but continued writing at his large maple desk. "Did I hear some bit of commotion out there?"

"There's a man here to see you. Says it's rather important." The last part was framed as almost a question. When Euripides stared at her with a crooked eyebrow, she added, "He says his name is *Chief* Jefferson."

Euripides bolted upright, dropping his pen, which splattered ink droplets across the page he'd been working on.

"That damned arrogant son of a—" Euripides caught his tongue.

Phebe rushed over to remedy the mess. She set the pen back in its holder and cradled the spotted page in her hands.

Euripides leaned forward and planted two angry fists upon his desk. "Father's barely even in the ground and here he is, back again—worse than a bloody vulture."

"I'll ask him to leave," Phebe said, "and see if I can salvage this page." She turned toward the door and gasped. Chief Jefferson was standing there, just inside the room. She took a step back and to the side, allowing Euripides to see the uninvited arrival.

Chief Jefferson gave a solemn nod in greeting. "No disrespect, and I don't mean to rile you, coming so soon after your father's death. But you know what I'm after, and I couldn't risk waiting. In case you had thoughts of selling the item to any other interested parties. Course, I'd be willing to match any other offer for the Stone of Pamola."

"It's not the bloody Stone of Pamola, and it's not for sale. Even if it were, I'd sell it to someone else for half what you'd offer. Better that than lower my family's name by taking money from the likes of you: some filthy fake Indian!"

Phebe watched in alarm as the veins bulged in Euripides' neck. She looked toward the door, hoping for a sign that the chief would accept this rebuke and leave, but the man didn't move an inch.

"I understand this is a hard time for you, and you can keep on bullyragging me all you like. But that don't change the truth." Chief Jefferson kept his voice level. "What you're hiding belongs to the Abenaki. It was stolen from our people."

"From *your* people, is it? A traitor to your own race is what you are. Nothing but a two-bit fraud and liar. Stolen from you! I see it now—this visit is just a ruse, a dirty trick learned from 'your people' to cover your tracks. You're the one who stole the thunderstone!"

The accusation caught Phebe completely off guard. Chief Jefferson looked even more perplexed.

"What do you mean—I stole it?" The chief took a step toward Euripides, the display of civility that he'd maintained since his arrival finally cracked. "What's happened to the stone?"

"Listen to him, pretending he doesn't know!" Euripides declared.

"This is some ruse of yours to keep the stone from its true owners," Chief Jefferson answered back, his voice rising.

Phebe stepped in front of the man, trying to create a buffer between him and Euripides. Her hands still cradled the inky page before her, giving her the appearance of pleading.

"Please leave, before matters get worse. I shouldn't like to have to summon the police."

Chief Jefferson turned his attention to her, a hint of disgust upon his cheerless face. "More men with guns, along with badges so that others will think what they're doing's right. When all it amounts to is more of the white man's habit of beating skulls and thievery."

She paused a second, unsure of how to respond to the man's sweeping accusation. Scraping sounds from behind grabbed her attention. Euripides pushed his chair aside and ripped open a desk drawer. He came around the desk, a pistol in hand. Phebe barely had time to react, stepping aside as he rushed forward like a charging bull. Euripides grabbed Chief Jefferson by the shirt front and shoved him back into the wall. He didn't aim the pistol, only held it before the chief's face.

"I don't need the police. If you harass me again, or my niece, or any of my family, so help me God—I won't need the police. I'll shoot you down myself."

Euripides' furious grimace went still. A look of fear shot into his eyes. Phebe saw a knife in Chief Jefferson's hand, seemingly conjured from thin air, the razor-sharp point pressed against her uncle's neck.

"I don't wish for violence," the chief said in a low voice. His free hand went up to remove the pistol from Euripides' grasp. "That's not why I came. I only want what was taken from my people. Nothing but a curious stone to you, but a sacred relic to us."

"I'll see us both dead before I ever let you have that stone," Euripides hissed through clenched teeth.

Chief Jefferson tossed the pistol to the floor, then felt for the door handle. With the knife still in place, he moved Euripides back a step, creating a space between them.

"I'm terribly sorry for all this thrashing around, miss," the chief said to Phebe, without taking his eyes from her uncle. "My sincere apologies."

With that, the chief escaped out the door, closing it behind him. Euripides stood fuming in the center of the room for a moment before retrieving his pistol from the floor. Phebe peeked into the outer room to be sure Chief Jefferson was safely gone.

Chapter 24

M Y SISTER, MADDY? REALLY, MR. GREY, DIDN'T YOUR mother ever teach you that it was poor form to ask a lady to tea only to bring up the subject of a younger woman?" Phebe Webster gave him a look of mock indignation.

"Actually, no. The subject never came up."

"Pity for you," she said with a sympathetic smile, "and now for me as well."

A bit of color came into Phebe's cheeks after the last comment. Grey wondered if she felt embarrassed at having spoken a touch too openly with a man she hardly knew. He smiled, and, to give her a moment, he glanced out the window of the restaurant. They were on the second floor overlooking Fore Street. A gap in the buildings down toward the waterfront afforded them an obstructed view of Portland Harbor, where tall-masted sailing ships mingled with steam-powered boats coming in and out from the dozens of wharves there.

"I can honestly say, Mr. Grey, that Maddy does not need to be found by you. I'm sure she's in no danger or distress, so you can put your mind at ease. In fact, you should march right down to Mr. Dyer and report that there is nothing here that needs looking into and move on to matters that actually require some investigating."

"So you've heard from her recently, then, and she's well?"

"No. I didn't say that."

"Just what are you saying, Miss Webster? I don't mean to sound presumptuous, but it strikes me as a bit peculiar that you don't display the least concern over your sister's whereabouts and well-being. I'd have thought you'd be anxious to see her again."

A hint of melancholy touched Phebe's face. "Believe me, Mr. Grey, nothing would bring me greater happiness than to have Maddy at my side this very minute. But I'm not about to sit by wasting away and waiting for that to happen."

Phebe took another sip of her tea as Grey's silent waiting became more and more awkward.

"My sister was full of life. A bit too full, some would say. She wasn't exactly satisfied with what she could find here in Portland. She wanted more."

"More of what, exactly?"

"Everything. She wanted to see the world, to drink it all in, to experience life on a grand scale and understand all its wonders."

"And it doesn't bother you in the least that she hasn't contacted you. Not a telegram or even a postcard?"

This time the look of sadness lingered a moment longer about Phebe's eyes. "My sister loves me. That I know. She always did. Since we were young, we were everything to each other. And I cherish that. But, in truth, Maddy wasn't always the happiest child. Our parents both passed when we were young."

Phebe regarded Grey intently, and he wondered if the look was meant to communicate some underlying connection or sympathy. It was plausible that the attorney, Dyer, had thoroughly looked into Grey's own history before recommending his services to the ailing Horace Webster. The fates of Grey's parents were certainly no secret among Portland's upper classes. Nor was it hard to surmise that Dyer likely had shared his information with Miss Webster.

"It was especially hard for her," Phebe continued. "Home was not a place where she knew true joy. For her there was always an emptiness here. And so, while her actions do pain me, I don't take her leaving as a slight directed at me. It's just the circumstance she found herself in. I pray that makes sense."

Grey found himself pleasantly surprised by Phebe's stoic approach to the issue. He had originally thought her to be of an emotional nature, based on her manner at Horace Webster's bedside. Perhaps that situation was simply an overwhelming one and the current outlook marked her true character. He realized he might need to reassess Phebe Webster; it might turn out that she was cut from sturdier cloth after all.

He nodded his agreement and said, "I suppose it makes good sense. And so you don't want me to find her?"

"No good would come of it. She'll be with me again when the time is right."

"And there's nothing more you can say on the matter?" Grey asked.

"There's nothing more I care to say on the matter, at present."

Grey studied her face, gauging the intent of those final words. "Meaning you may yet have a change of heart?"

"It's always a woman's prerogative to *have* a change of heart. The difficulty is in *wanting* to change it."

Grey tilted his head slightly to the side as if dodging that idea. "Merely the matter of making a conscious decision, an exercise of one's reason and free will."

Phebe sipped her tea and thought a moment before setting her cup down. "I think the philosopher David Hume said it best when he noted, 'Reason is, and ought only to be the slave of the passions and can never pretend to any other office than to serve and obey them.'"

Grey had to pause a moment to appreciate the unexpectedly erudite comment. "For the sake of argument, I will defer to Hume. He was, after all, an eminently *reasonable* man."

His gaze drifted out the windows and settled on the distant movements of the vessels entering and departing Portland Harbor. "And to the extent that his observation may be true and applicable to the great majority of mankind, I am glad for it. It makes men, and particularly those who give in to their passions, more easily understood and thus more easily found out. One who could employ reason to hide his avarice, rage, or whichever other passions drive him would indeed be a most dangerous person."

Phebe gave him a doubtful look. "My theory is that you only believe yourself to be governed by reason over passion because deep in your heart you wish it were the truth."

"Just as easily I could theoretically argue that you believe me, along with everyone else, to be governed by passions, not reason, because deep in your mind you wish *that* were the truth."

"Let's not theoretically argue in public. We don't wish to cause a hypothetical scene."

"A truce," Grey said with an amused smile.

He filled their cups from the small silver teapot at their table. Phebe added cream and a sugar cube while Grey kept his black.

"So, then, what passions in your heart could change and convince you to help me locate your sister?" he asked.

"Perhaps we could strike a deal. It turns out that I could use that reasonable mind of yours, which I heard Mr. Dyer praise to my grandfather. I've come into a little mystery of my own and am at something of a loss."

Grey arched an eyebrow and waited for her to continue.

"I suspect that you heard the commotion the other day at Mr. Dyer's office. An object has gone missing from my grandfather's lockbox that was supposedly being safeguarded by the attorneys."

"Mr. Dyer mentioned something about a mistake, that the item would turn up in another box," Grey recalled.

"Unfortunately, he now assures me he's been through every box in their vault and my grandfather's stone is not there. Somehow it's been stolen."

"Stone?" The extent of the consternation displayed by the attorney and his clerk now became evident to Grey. "A diamond or rare gem?"

"No, as I understand it, it was actually a stone. I'm not sure exactly, in terms of a geological classification, but some sort of rock."

"But of enough value to place in a lockbox? I'm sorry, Miss Webster, some detail is evading me. Please, describe this stone."

"I'm afraid I can't. I've never actually seen it. It's been locked up in the offices of Dyer & Fogg for"—she paused to do the quick calculation in her head—"twenty-three years. Uncle Jason saw it when he was much younger. Said it was smooth all around and rather egg-shaped. About so." She cupped her hands approximately eight inches apart. "He says it had several etchings on the face of it."

"I see." Grey's brow wrinkled at the bizarre and seemingly pointless turn that the conversation had taken. "Have you reported this to the police? I'd recommend that you speak with a Deputy Lean. It was, after all, bequeathed to you, correct?"

"Surprisingly, yes. Everyone assumed it would go to Euripides. I feel rather odd about it. He hasn't said so, but I'm certain he's quite insulted that Grandfather passed him over. So it's for me to say, and I've decided not to file a formal complaint. I'd prefer to deal with the matter privately, and quietly."

"Is that wise? Surely the authorities should be notified. If the item was of such value, I assume there would be an insurance claim at stake," Grey said.

"The value of the stone itself is not . . . readily ascertainable. And I believe that publicity is what caused this problem in the first place." Phebe raised her cup to take a sip.

"Yes, the discovery of an egg-shaped rock must have caused quite a frenzy at the newspapers," Grey said with an entirely straight face.

Phebe, who had her cup at her lips, was unable to stifle her laughter. Her hand shook, and a spot of tea splashed down on her dress. She dabbed at it with her napkin.

"One small benefit of having to wear black," she said.

"Please accept my apologies. For making you laugh."

"Oh, don't apologize for that. I can't quite remember the last time I had a good laugh. Weeks ago, probably, before Grandfather worsened. Besides, it's not entirely your fault. I must have sounded daft, the way I'm explaining myself."

Phebe set her napkin on the table and folded her hands as she gathered her thoughts. "My great-great-grandfather discovered the stone. He called it a thunderstone. It was unearthed while he was digging out a root cellar. He was fascinated by its shape and the strange etchings. Maybe more than fascinated. He was supposedly consumed with the thing and with protecting it. Claimed it was worth a thousand times its weight in gold. In his will he left strict, and shall we say odd, instructions for its custody and protection."

"Such as?"

"I can't recall the exact wording, but Mr. Dyer went over the original decree the other day, at the reading of my grandfather's will. For example, it's not to be displayed in the presence of anyone outside the family, nor are the markings to be reproduced. That's why it's been at Dyer & Fogg for so long. My grandfather allowed it to be photographed at an exhibition of Maine history commemorating the fiftieth anniversary of our statehood. The executor of the estate at that time, the current Attorney Dyer's father, deemed it a violation of the terms of the bequest and revoked possession of the thunderstone."

"And you believe the publicity from that 1870 exhibition, twenty-three years ago, is behind the current trouble and disappearance of the stone?" Grey didn't bother trying to hide his skepticism.

"Not just me. Uncle Euripides and Uncle Jason think so, too. You see, once the existence of the stone became known at the exhibit, a man named Chief Jefferson began to make quite a fuss about it. He's an Indian. Well, as it turns out not a real Indian at all. Not even . . ."

"Of mixed heritage," Grey didn't mind offering Miss Webster a hand in the awkward attempt to politely describe his racial classification. Her uncertainty seemed strictly linguistic, lacking the masked discomfort or even blatant contempt that so often characterized others' approach to the subject.

"Yes, as it seems he's actually a full-blooded white man, though you wouldn't know it to look at him. Plays the part of a chief very convincingly."

Grey smiled a bit, wondering how on earth Miss Phebe Webster would know that the portrayal of an Indian chief was accurate. Grey could see by her expression that she'd noted his reaction, so he quickly launched into the matter.

"I recall reading an article about him. Supposedly a lost child found and raised by some roving Indians, passing his youth among various families and groups throughout Maine and Canada. A popular speaker and attraction at the traveling Indian shows and demonstrations. A shrewd businessman."

Phebe said, "All I've heard of him is that he turns up every so often, asking—demanding, really—that our family hand over the thunderstone. He claims it's really an old Indian stone of some sort and that by rights we should give it back."

"He believes this thunderstone is an Indian artifact? Because of the symbols on it?"

"Precisely. Over the years he's made several verbal and written demands to Dyer & Fogg to hand the object over. He's even offered to purchase it from my grandfather. But, of course, that was never considered."

"Of course," Grey said with only the faintest hint of irony. "After all, it's said to be worth a thousand times its weight in gold. Why, exactly?"

Phebe leaned in, forcing Grey to do likewise, and in a conspiratorial tone she whispered, "According to family lore, the stone is somehow supposed to reveal a priceless treasure."

Grey's eyebrows shot up. He would not have guessed that such an absurd statement would issue from a woman who just minutes earlier had struck him as notably levelheaded.

"You say that in all seriousness?" Grey's embarrassment at the feeling that he'd misjudged Miss Webster's character was assuaged by the sudden grin that lit up her face.

"Me? No, not particularly. I know it sounds fantastic—childish, even—but family lore is very earnest on that point."

"Enough so that your eagerness to recover the thunderstone exceeds that same feeling with regard to your sister."

"Of course not. Two different kettles of fish entirely, Mr. Grey. As I've explained, Maddy's made her choices. Unlike the thunderstone, my sister wasn't stolen from me. Regardless of the improbable rumor attached to the stone, it is nevertheless a Webster family heirloom. One that was important to my recently deceased grandfather. If he'd been aware of its disappearance, I think those four little words he whispered to you at his bedside would have been different."

Grey took a moment to absorb the information, sorting out the relevant facts from the thread of familial eccentricity that had emerged in the telling of Phebe Webster's story.

"In any event, you were saying about this Chief Jefferson . . ."

"Yes. Just yesterday the man made an offer to Uncle Euripides directly. No doubt also assuming that he would be the new owner when Grandfather passed."

"I take it Euripides did not respond kindly to the man's financial overtures."

"Not kindly," Phebe repeated. "That's putting it rather mildly. My uncle threatened to kill the man if he ever approached the family again." Her nose wrinkled at the unpleasant admission of her uncle's fiery temper.

Grey considered this for a moment. "But Chief Jefferson's offer came after the stone was already stolen."

"Uncle Euripides thinks that's a clever attempt to throw suspicion off himself."

"A valid concern," Grey said. "Another valid concern is that Euripides falls solidly on the side of David Hume's assessment of reason and the overriding passions. Could your uncle have had prior knowledge that this thunderstone wouldn't pass to him in your grandfather's will?"

"What are you suggesting—that Uncle Euripides himself could have stolen it?" Phebe let out an uncomfortable chuckle. Seeing Grey's cool, analytical expression, she added, "He's passionate, surely. That doesn't mean criminal. Besides, I doubt there's any way he could have learned the contents of the will from Mr. Dyer beforehand. Dealings between the two of them are strictly business."

"I see." Grey leaned forward a bit in his seat and stared at his interlocked fingers, contemplating the information gathered over the lunch. Finally he leaned back and turned his attention once more to Phebe, who regarded him with a look of intense curiosity.

"It's agreed, then, Miss Webster. Our own business dealing: I will find this thunderstone, if it is to be found. And you, in turn, will tell me everything you know, or believe, with regard to your sister's whereabouts."

Chapter 25

L EAN STOOD IN DEERING OAKS WITH HIS SHOULDER AGAINST one of the park's trees. His eyes moved over the crowd of pedestrians meandering beneath the tall canopy of the ancient oaks, seeking shelter from the July sun. Soon enough he caught sight of Tom Doran. The man was hard to miss. He stood well over six feet, and when the massive Irishman came face-to-face with him, his broad chest and arms seemed to occupy an equal amount of horizontal space.

Earlier that day, when Lean had tracked down Tom Doran, it had been in an alley behind one of the unlicensed saloons that Jimmy Farrell operated. Farrell, along with his counterpart, McGrath, headed the two rival Irish gangs that controlled much of the flow of illegal liquor into Portland. The Maine Liquor Law was mostly enforced when it had to be, when the flouting of it became too public, too visible in the city's commercial heart or in respectable neighborhoods. Doran hadn't flinched at the sight of a deputy catching him unloading barrels of illegal beer. His boss paid people higher up than Lean to let him do business, so long as it was done quietly.

Three hours later the deputy noted that the big man had changed out of his grubby work clothes. He was smartly dressed, with a brushed bowler squatting atop rusty hair that had been freshly slicked back. Even his regularly bushy mustache had been trimmed since that morning.

"Shouldn't have come around earlier," Doran said. "Don't look good for either of us."

"An act of desperation, I suppose. Need a bit of help," Lean said. Then he smiled and added, "You know I asked to meet strictly for business?"

"Course. Let's keep walking." Doran moved along, circling the park's duck pond, while Lean struggled to match his long strides. "What'd you mean about strictly business?"

"You've gotten all dapper-looking. I thought you might have it in mind to ask me to go for a paddle." Lean nodded toward several short rowboats available to let, often to aspiring couples, for a trip past the pond's water fountain and elaborately modeled Victorian duck house.

"Funny."

Most men would have thought twice about attempting such a joke with the somber-faced behemoth. But then even Doran wouldn't be so bold as to drive one of his massive mitts into a deputy's nose in broad daylight. Also, there was a shared history; a year earlier the two men had risked their lives together in the daring rescue of Helen Prescott's eight-year-old daughter. Most important, the big man was grateful for Lean's role in avenging the murder of Dr. Virgil Steig, who'd been a father figure to Tom Doran.

Doran stopped walking and positioned himself with his back toward the acres of tall oaks, facing the fingers of land that poked into the irregularly shaped duck pond. A look approaching deep contemplation clouded his face. "What do you want anyway?"

"Information."

Doran's brows creased at the request.

"Frank Cosgrove." Lean paused to gauge Doran's reaction, which amounted to a hint of a shrug. "Buried with a hole in his chest, but then . . ."

"Yeah, everyone knows about that."

"But they're all scared to death to talk. Not much happens in Portland that your boss doesn't know about. You must've heard something."

"Heard all sorts of things," Doran said.

"Right. Any of those things involve who dragged the poor bastard out of his grave, burned him up, and stashed him over on Vine Street?"

"Sure. Devil did it. Took his black soul down to hell, then spit it out again. Wasn't done with his business on earth. A score to settle. The man was cursed, and so's any that gets involved in his business."

"Is that so?" Lean asked.

"That's what they're saying."

"Someone's got to know better. Who has a reason to do this? Who could pull it off if they even wanted to?"

"It's always been if something big happened round here, it was 'cause

Jimmy gave orders for it to happen, or else McGrath put the word out. And if there's a problem between the two of 'em, it would come down to who's got more muscle or money. Now maybe there's someone else having a say on things, and there's more on the table than muscle or money. Even Jimmy seems a bit shaken."

"Heard any names?" Lean asked.

"Not a whisper."

Lean was about to press the issue further when he noticed Doran staring past him. The Irishman seemed fixated on a young woman in a pale green dress, strolling arm in arm with another woman, probably her mother. Doran pulled a golden locket from within his vest and worked it over in his thick, callused palm.

The true nature of the encounter rushed into Lean's brain, though Doran's current reaction threw him off.

"Is that her?" Lean wanted to ask more, but he'd forgotten the young woman's name.

Doran nodded. "My daughter, Katie. Mullen now. She were married in the fall."

"Congratulations." Lean was unsure of what else to say. "Did you go to the wedding?"

Doran's head shook. "Never spoken to her."

Lean stared at the man who struck instant fear into the hearts of many of Portland's rougher elements. The massive figure looked utterly cowed by a pretty young woman strolling fifty yards away. He stood amazed at the sight of Doran, all washed, buffed, and tucked on the off chance that his daughter would happen to glance over. All so that she might not be offended, even at a distance, by the appearance of a man to whom she couldn't fathom the slightest connection. Lean wondered how many times this scene had played out in the year since Perceval Grey, in a bit of emotional blackmail, had handed over the identity of Doran's long-lost daughter.

"You've never talked to the girl? Told her who you are?"

Doran stayed silent until the two women came to a stop by the edge of the pond.

"Your wife's had kids, Lean. Tell me, do you think Katie might be with child?"

Lean craned his neck a bit, trying to get a better angle at the young woman's profile. There was a slight bulge there, in a spot normally constricted by the various machinations typically hidden among the many layers of modern female apparel.

"You know," he said in a slow, studied voice, "I think she may well be."

The two men kept a quiet vigil until the women continued moving away along the path.

"You go to church regular?" Doran finally asked.

"Mostly."

"What if, next Sunday, you were walking out and they handed you a note. Inside it says one way or the other whether your soul's going to heaven or hell. Would you open it?"

"Yeah, I suppose," Lean said. "You?"

Doran's hefty shoulders raised and dipped. Lean sensed that the man had thought this through, probably over many long, trying hours, but still he needed to search out the right words.

"Sometimes when you think you'll never really know the truth of something, you get used to it. You sit yourself down in a spot where you think you ought to be. After a while that spot just feels right. Then one day some smart fellow comes along and says he's got the answer you were waiting on. And you think you're glad for it. But then what if you were wrong all along? That spot that seemed good was all wrong, and you can't stay there no more?"

As the words sputtered forth from Tom Doran, Lean stared after the departing young woman. She probably carried another whole lifetime inside her, while a troubled soul, all that was left of those who'd given her life and first loved her, stood close by, fearfully watching. She walked along, blissfully unaware of how the past, present, and future tangled together around her in an unknown, unknowable knot.

"Don't know what to say, Tom. You can't always know what you're supposed to do. You'll go mad thinking over it too much. Maybe someday you'll just feel in your gut the time's come to say something to her."

Doran gave a noncommittal nod and walked in the opposite direction from his daughter.

"Frank Cosgrove." Doran's voice was flat, and Lean could tell he was simply desperate to change the subject. "I don't know what happened to put him on Vine Street. Whatever secrets that house is holding from that night, it can keep them. And if it's the devil's business, you should just let it lie."

[Chapter 26]

THE SHARP CLATTER OF IRON HORSESHOES ON CONGRESS Street's paving stones made Lean look up from the brick sidewalk. One of the city's horsecars passed, carrying a load of people who'd wisely elected to ride the trolley rather than walk in the sweltering heat. The deputy threw his cigarette into the street and cursed the midday sun. As he did every summer, he vowed never again to complain about the depth of Maine winters, a promise that he would likely keep until the first week in January, at which time he would vow never again to complain about the humidity of Maine summers. He felt drops of sweat pooling at the small of his back where his shirt was collected and tucked into his waist. Suddenly aware of the moisture in his clenched right palm, he switched the large manila folder he was carrying to his other hand, fearful of dampening the two gruesome pictures that Grey had requested he bring along.

He walked by a long stream of shops and doctors' offices before reaching the entrance to the Baxter Building, which housed the Portland Public Library and the Maine Historical Society. The Romanesque Revival building, opened only four years earlier, featured elaborate ornamentation on its central façade of brown freestone accented over the arched doorway and windows with pale Ohio sandstone. Lean glanced up as he approached the double doors. Three figures, representing Art, Literature, and History, topped the roof, one at each front corner of the building's buttressing side sections and the third atop the sixty-foot-high central gable. Once inside, he was glad to be spared the direct sunlight. The interior walls, hard-plastered and tinted, set off by ash trim work and hardwood doors, gave a relaxed, fresh feel to the library, but the lack of circulation did nothing to relieve the heavy air.

The wide entrance corridor extended back into the building and held the reception desk as well as a section of wall lined with rows of stacked drawers that made up the card catalog. Lean crossed the black and white floor tiles to the library's well-appointed reading room on the right side of the corridor. He peeked in and scanned the various occupants. At one end of the room, enclosed by a gilded rail, he spied Benjamin Paul Akers's famed sculpture *The Dead Pearl Diver*. The white marble figure lay stretched upon a large rock. In search of a far livelier, and less alabaster-toned figure, Lean headed back into the wide hallway. As he moved toward the stack room at the rear of the building, Lean glanced up the broad flight of cast-iron stairs leading to the great Baxter Hall on the second floor. There was no sign of Perceval Grey, only the high, Gothic-styled, open-timbered ceiling with its chamfered, varnished beams.

The spacious stack room held a desk at its center that was often used by the library clerks but now sat empty. Solid sets of shelves stood out from the walls, forming book-lined alcoves that held more than thirty thousand volumes. A railed upper level of shelves was topped with a series of marble busts looking down over the stacks. Tall windows filled the room with light during the day, while incandescent electric light fixtures hung overhead to illuminate the evenings. Lean wasn't overly familiar with the classification used by the library to sort its books, nor did he have any idea what Grey was researching, so he resorted to glancing down each row as he passed.

"There you are," Lean said after spotting Grey's slender, neatly dressed form in one of the last aisles.

Grey gave him a nod and approached with a thin book tucked under one arm. He slipped by and headed for the vacant clerk's desk.

"They've reorganized, made some changes to the place," Lean noted.

Grey looked at him queerly. "Yes, some time ago. When was the last time you came to the library? Please tell me it wasn't last summer."

"I've been busy. Work, the new house, another child at home. We don't all live a life of casual luxury. It's nice." Lean looked around. "Still, it's just not the same without Helen Prescott. Has she told you if she's returning anytime soon? I'd have thought she'd have come home already."

"At the end of the summer," Grey said absentmindedly. "In time for her daughter to begin the school year, I think."

Lean started to ask another question, but Grey cut him off with an impatient look.

"If we've covered the social niceties, could we proceed with the actual business at hand?"

"I suppose, though I should warn you about the cavalier attitude you're displaying toward Helen. If you're not careful, you're going to end up on your own, sitting in a dark room, blind from peering through microscopes and whatnot. You'll have to hire an assistant and resort to having descriptions of crime scenes read aloud and dictating your conclusions. A sad end, if you ask me."

"Well, then remind me not to ask. You seem to have given the idea quite a bit of thought. If it's the promise of future employment you're angling at, then I have to warn you: You'll need to improve your atrocious handwriting before I allow you to take dictation from me. Now, again, the business at hand."

Lean nodded his consent. "Which is what, exactly? Don't know what you need with these murder-scene photographs at the library."

"That will come later. But first let me tell you something of Horace Webster. You'll recall I had word of the ailing man's passing that day we returned from our inquiries in Boston. I'll spare you all but the most necessary details for the time being. This Webster was in possession of an unusual family heirloom called a thunderstone, which had apparently been unearthed several generations ago. Due to what I can only describe as family peculiarities, the item was kept guarded from the public eye. The sole existing image or description of it is from the state of Maine's fiftieth-anniversary exhibition, which took place in 1870. Various historical items and curiosities were displayed, including the thunderstone."

"Fascinating." Lean pretended to stifle a yawn.

Grey almost grinned but otherwise managed to ignore Lean's sarcasm. "At the reading of Horace Webster's will, this thunderstone, contained in a lockbox in possession of his attorneys and executors for the past two decades, was found to have been stolen."

"A theft from an attorney's office? I don't recall hearing anything."

"The property was left to Miss Phebe Webster. She's elected not to file a formal complaint. She's requested that I locate the thunderstone for her."

Lean frowned. Though he held Grey's abilities in the highest regard, he still took it as something of an insult to his professional dignity that the Websters hadn't even thought it worthwhile to notify the police of the crime.

"The attorney last viewed the items about two weeks prior. The thing that makes this thunderstone such a curiosity is the presence of several unusual etchings carved into its otherwise smooth surface. Look here, closely."

Grey set down the cloth-backed book he was holding, one whose title bore reference to Maine's statehood. He angled the book toward Lean and opened it to a photograph of a thin, proud-looking man standing next to a short, rectangular glass case. Inside the case, set on a padded box, was an oval-shaped stone. Lean bent his head toward the picture on the table.

"This will help." Grey handed him a magnifying glass that he'd taken from his leather equipment satchel. Lean moved in with the glass just above the paper, finding the optimal magnification. It took him a moment to make out the small, faint image. He pulled his head back a touch and then refocused, starting from scratch, wanting to make sure he saw the item clearly before he jumped to what seemed an impossible coincidence.

"It's blurry."

"Granted," Grey said, "but . . ."

"But it certainly looks like . . ."

Grey placed a white page on the desk, next to the book on Maine history. It was the image stolen from the Boston Athenaeum, a circle topped with an upward-facing arc and with a cross extending from below.

"That same symbol. So this . . . what do you call it? Thunderstone? It was stolen in the past two weeks. And since then Chester Sears flees Portland and dies in Boston with an identical image in his pocket. And scared out of his wits that some diabolical fate will befall him, the same as his partner, Cosgrove."

Lean paused as his train of thought splintered in various directions. Grey picked up the thread for him.

"Cosgrove was shot dead two weeks ago, possibly in the same time frame that the thunderstone disappeared from its lockbox."

"So just a minute while I sort this out. Old partners Cosgrove and Sears are working together and steal the stone. Someone kills Cosgrove, maybe even Sears himself—got greedy, perhaps. In any event, someone's angry about the situation, digs Cosgrove up and burns him, leaves threats around the body as a message. To hear Tom Doran tell it, that bit of handiwork has every criminal in the city spooked, but maybe it was intended specifically for Sears. He flees for his life down to Boston."

"Or does he? Perhaps he's still at work. Trying to appease whoever killed Cosgrove. After all, it seems he still had work to do. He managed to break in to the home of the late Professor Horsford, only to find the book containing the strange symbols already gone. Then he pressed on in his endeavor, breaking in to the Athenaeum on a night when the commotion from the gathering downstairs would provide cover for his attempt to gain the pictures from that book."

"But where is the thunderstone now? If Sears took it for himself, it could be anywhere."

"I don't think Sears is at the heart of this. This wasn't a priceless gemstone or a fortune in gold, the kind of thing you go and shoot your old friend over. It's just a stone with strange markings. Though, in the interests of full disclosure, according to Miss Phebe Webster, the stone is supposed to be the key to some hidden treasure."

Lean greeted Grey's ridiculous statement with a dismissive snort. "I know that people are getting desperate these days," Lean said, thinking of the numerous bankruptcies that had struck many overextended railroad companies around the country and the disastrous results that had rippled through the rest of the nation's economy, "but a hidden treasure. I know you don't put any stock in that."

"Don't be absurd. The fact that it sounds so preposterous makes it all the more unlikely that Sears would have shot his old friend Cosgrove over it. But then there he is at the Athenaeum, looking into a book containing similar symbols."

"How would he have known that the book was at the Athenaeum? Or that Horsford had even written such a book? It was never actually published. This doesn't add up at all."

"Agreed," Grey said. "The whole business is far too grand in terms of imagination and planning for a common thief like Sears. Especially when you consider the most glaring omission among the facts at our disposal. How could Cosgrove or Sears have known where to find the thunderstone in the first place? It hasn't been seen publicly in twenty-three years, and very few people knew that the stone was in the possession of the Websters' attorneys other than the family members."

"An inside job, then?" Lean suggested.

"It stands to reason. Someone within a limited circle of the family or their attorneys likely played some part. Though something as innocent as a simple slip of the tongue, while in the wrong company, can't yet be ruled out. And here's one last item to consider, if we can trust my own grandfather's admittedly foggy memory. He was a youthful acquaintance of Horace Webster and recalls that Horace had a somewhat tragic dalliance with a young woman by the name of Destiny or perhaps Dastine."

. "Why's that name sound familiar?" Lean asked.

"The woman who found the symbols in Horsford's book, the ones carved into a ledge north of Portland," Grey said.

Lean rapped his knuckles on the table as he thought this all through. "Have you had any luck finding the woman?"

"No. The original newspaper from that time's been lost. Perhaps you'd have more success with locating any City Hall records."

Lean nodded, then held aloft the envelope containing the crime-scene photographs. "Well, perhaps Miss Webster didn't care to alert the police as to the theft of this thunderstone, but now it's linked to the murder of Frank Cosgrove. So I guess I'll have the pleasure of making her acquaintance after all."

"Which brings us to our next appointment," Grey said. "The offices of Dyer & Fogg, where the thunderstone was being held. I've requested that Miss Webster meet us there."

Chapter 27

B UT, MR. GREY, I THOUGHT WE UNDERSTOOD EACH OTHER. I meant to rely on you, not the police, to aid me in recovering the thunderstone." Phebe took a step away from Grey in the direction of her attorney's desk.

Albert Dyer rose from his seat and came around to join her.

"Yes, Grey, my client expressly informed you of her wishes. The presence of the good deputy here is an utter breach of trust. Need I remind you—"

"Please be aware, Mr. Dyer, if you would, that three out of the four of us present are not being paid by the hour. Now, Miss Webster, rest assured that it was my first and honest intention to act independently in this inquiry. However, circumstances have come to light that render the involvement of Deputy Lean unavoidable. I apologize, but I'm certain within a few minutes' time you will understand completely."

"And for what it's worth, miss," Lean added, "I have no interest in your thunderstone per se and even less interest in intruding upon private matters. There is, however, a more grievous crime at issue that now appears related to the theft of your property."

"What sort of crime?" Dyer insisted, trying once again to take charge of the conversation's rudder.

Grey motioned to the large envelope in Lean's hand. The deputy drew out the photograph depicting Frank Cosgrove from the chest up, taken at the scene of his murder.

"Has either of you ever seen this man?"

Dyer looked down his nose, through his spectacles at the photograph, while Phebe leaned in close for a better look.

"Never," said Dyer.

Phebe shook her head. "Who is he?"

"Frank Cosgrove," Grey said. "A habitual criminal, mostly burglary. He was very adept at picking locks."

"How did he die?" Phebe asked Lean.

"It's not important, miss." He withdrew the photograph.

"You may call me 'miss,' but that doesn't mean I'm some fragile little girl who'll collapse at the mention of blood, Deputy Lean."

Lean glanced at Grey, who nodded and looked impressed with Miss Webster's cool, self-assured demeanor.

"He was shot."

Attorney Dyer butted in. "What's this got to do with Miss Webster? Is this miscreant the one who stole the thunderstone?"

"It's a possibility." Lean left the photograph on Dyer's desk and drew out the second picture. This one, obtained from the Boston police, showed the face of Chester Sears, lying on the ground inside the Granary Burying Ground.

"How about this unfortunate fellow?"

Again Phebe and Mr. Dyer both failed to recognize the man.

"Chester Sears. A known accomplice of Cosgrove's. He fell to his death last week in Boston while clutching this image in his hand." Grey set his sketched symbol on the desk.

Phebe gave him a puzzled, almost comical look. "He died trying to steal a piece of paper? With a drawing on it?"

In lieu of reasserting the facts he'd just laid out, Grey turned to the attorney. "Mr. Dyer?"

"Yes, I recognize the image. It's one of the signs etched into the thunderstone."

Phebe's jaw dropped open. Her eyes went from Dyer to Lean and then settled on Grey. Lean noticed that during the discussion Phebe Webster had abandoned her place by the side of the attorney's desk and drifted closer to Grey.

"Whatever does this mean?" she asked.

"It means, Miss Webster, that while firm proof is not yet in the offing, it would appear that the theft of your thunderstone has, for some reason, led to the murder of one burglar and the accidental death of another. This little matter of your curious family heirloom has now taken a decidedly grave turn."

"I see." She studied her hands, clasped before her, for a moment. "I'm sorry I objected to your presence earlier, Deputy Lean. This is certainly a distressing development, and I will assist in any way possible, regardless of any concerns for my family's privacy. But, Mr. Grey, what of the other matter we discussed?"

"The details of that are, and shall remain, strictly private, I assure you," Grey answered.

A bit of ease returned to the woman's troubled expression, and she rewarded Grey with an appreciative smile. Lean, however, gave Grey what he intended as a blatantly suspicious glare.

Grey walked to the window overlooking Exchange Street, then turned back to face the attorney.

"At present the only obvious motive for the theft of the thunderstone is the one mentioned by Miss Webster—namely, that family lore states the thunderstone will reveal the hidden location of some priceless treasure. I understand, Mr. Dyer, that your family—that is to say, your firm—has served as legal counsel to the Websters for several generations. Surely you can shed some light on this suggestion."

"I know nothing at all about that." Dyer looked embarrassed by the implication that he was somehow involved with such a fanciful concept, but, recognizing that he'd been careless in shading his incredulity, he offered Miss Webster an apologetic smile. "All I can speak to is the terms of Thomas Webster's original will from 1814."

"It's perfectly all right to speak freely on the matter, Mr. Dyer. If you've something to say about the issue—or my family, even—I can assure you I've heard such comments before."

"Well, obviously I have no firsthand knowledge on the subject, but it's my understanding that your ancestor, Thomas Webster, was remarkably far along in years at the time of his death. He was even known as 'Old Tom.' I think perhaps it is not outside the realm of possibility that, from the point of his mental acuity, Old Tom may have been pushing past that side of the pasture where the grass is still green."

Dyer approached Phebe and laid a sympathetic hand upon her arm. "As you recall from the reading of your own grandfather's will, the original instructions left by Old Tom regarding the thunderstone are indicative of a certain . . ." he searched for a polite turn of phrase. "eccentricity that can come with old age."

"Is that the document you mentioned, Miss Webster? The one placing certain safeguards on the item, requiring it to be maintained strictly within the family, et cetera?" Grey asked.

She nodded.

"Would it be possible to——"

"Certainly, if you think it would be of assistance in retrieving the item." Mr. Dyer called out for his clerk. The eagerness in his voice betrayed the acute desperation he felt to remedy his firm's failure to secure the thunderstone, as well as to validate his characterization of the mental status of Phebe Webster's ancestor.

The young clerk, Emery, stuck his head in the door. Grey noticed that his face appeared thinner than it had days earlier when the lockbox was discovered to have been looted. He could only assume that since that time the atmosphere in the law office had grown even tenser than usual. Mr. Dyer ordered the fellow to fetch the paperwork for the Webster estate. The clerk dashed off and returned less than a minute later. The attorney searched briefly through the contents of the folder before producing a yellowed, fragile-looking page, which he carefully placed upon his desktop.

"Here we are. This is from the original will and testament of Old Tom Webster. Written in his own hand. You'll understand if I ask you not to handle the page. Instructions were left that this document was to be read at the time of his own passing and then again in conjunction with the reading of the will of whichever family member in subsequent generations had been chosen as sole heir to the thunderstone." Directing his attention to Lean, he added, "Obviously, most recently that was Horace Webster, Miss Phebe's grandfather."

Dyer wiped his spectacles clean on a handkerchief before proceeding. "Since I'm familiar with the script and the ink is somewhat faded, allow me to do the honors."

"Vary you not from these instructions or else the keepers appointed by me shall reclaim the thunderstone for as

many of the earths revelation about the Sun as shall be appointed you and until such time as you shall pass into the earth and then the next generation shall have the right to claim the stone. In no company other than mine own blood shall you let the thunderstone be seen, nor shall its markings be presented in any form to others. To gather in the stone's meaning will won a soul a treasure beyond conception. Read what has been writ in the earth before you and do not be verse to the teachings of the Lord. I alone should appear true and clear to you, and know my meaning is not to enumerate for you, each time I am seen among other fallacies. One can only find the measure of a man at the ends of his days, and understand that his true nature cannot be the base materials of his bodily wants, the needs of the flesh, what he shall drink and ate, but only what he has stood for. Look not to letters or words other than those of the thunderstone, but heed my voice, only then shall you be rewarded, not in my name, nor truly in any human form."

Dyer stood back, slipped his glasses into his breast pocket, and looked as though he'd proved an indisputable point of law. The clerk began to carefully collect the Webster documents.

"Oddly worded, to say the least," Lean said.

"To be expected," Grey said. "Education, and thus any given man's particular spelling and grammar usage, was far from uniform a hundred years ago. Besides which, it's often the case that for one unaccustomed to formal, legal documents, the attempt to set down one's intentions in writing can produce an especially stilted and antiquated phrasing."

As he finished speaking, Grey watched the clerk, whose attention was locked onto the desktop. The young man's head tilted slowly to the side like a clock's second hand sweeping past twelve. Emery finished aligning his view with the crime-scene photographs still displayed on the desk. His eyes grew wide, and his lips eased open as if of their own accord, knowing that they would be called upon to speak even before the man himself consciously realized it.

Still wearing a look of surprise, Emery glanced up and caught sight of Grey observing him. "What on earth has happened to Mr. Robbins?"

"Who the hell is Mr. Robbins?" demanded Dyer. Then, remembering the presence of his client, he added, "Beg your pardon, Miss Webster."

Phebe lifted a hand in dismissal of the offending language. Like the others, she was now staring, perplexed, at the pale-faced clerk.

"You recognize this man?" Grey laid a finger on the image, the modern-day photographic death mask of Frank Cosgrove.

Emery's head swiveled back and forth, taking in the stares directed at him as a series of noncommittal stammers bubbled forth. The young man was now even more startled, having figured himself as late to the conversation, not starting a new and inflammatory one.

"Explain yourself, man!" barked his employer.

"Sorry, Mr. Dyer. Mr. Robbins came around a while back. Remember I mentioned a potential client stopping in? Said he'd come into some money and was looking to maybe set up some trusts. Asked about our services. Neither you nor Mr. Fogg was in, so I spoke with him briefly, showed him about."

"What precisely did you show him?" Grey asked.

"The offices, our library, the vault room," Emery said.

"You let him into our vault room?" Disbelief dripped from Mr. Dyer's voice.

"He asked about it. Said he might need to store some valuable documents. He was worried. Said he never had to do anything of this sort before. Sorry, sir. Like I said, neither you nor Mr. Fogg was available, else I'd have left it to you, of course."

"I ought to sack you on the spot," Dyer said in an exaggerated tone that could have rivaled Caesar's when addressing the knife-wielding Brutus.

"Please, Mr. Dyer, it's evident that Mr. Emery's mistake was an honest one," Phebe said.

"Besides," Lean said, "an old hand like Cosgrove would only want to see the locks he'd be up against in order to make his preparations all the easier. He'd still have been able to commit the burglary even if he'd never been let into your vault room."

A bit of color began to reappear in the clerk's face as his immediate termination seemed to grow less probable with each passing moment.

"The more pressing concern about the intelligence that the thief, Cosgrove, was able to obtain is how he ever learned of the thunderstone's presence in your vault room to begin with."

Grey turned toward Albert Dyer, who, sensing an implied criticism, straightened his back.

"Neither I nor any others in this office ever discuss our clients' confidential business matters outside the firm. I can assure you no improper sharing of information can be attributed to anyone here. And I stand by that point absolutely and unequivocally."

"Miss Webster, do you have any ideas of who, outside your immediate family, would have knowledge of the thunderstone?" Grey asked.

Phebe's lips pursed, and concern rose into her face. Finally she announced, "I can't truly say. That is, we didn't often discuss the thunderstone. But then neither did we treat it as some vital state secret. It was something peculiar and slightly mysterious. I suppose it did come up once in a while, in social conversation. I can't think with any certainty how many people, guests or friends of our family, might have heard of it at some point."

After assurances that Phebe shouldn't blame her own casual mentions of the thunderstone for causing the unforeseeable theft of the item and further promises to her and Attorney Dyer that Grey would keep them apprised of any developments, the two detectives showed themselves out.

"We're still left in the dark a bit as to who might have set this all in motion," Lean said as he paused on the sidewalk to light a cigarette.

"True, but at least we do now have affirmative evidence for our prior assumption that Cosgrove's murder is in fact linked to the thunderstone."

"Though you're no closer to the stone's location, and I'm no closer to the identity of the man who pulled the trigger on Cosgrove. Or to figuring out why he went through all the trouble to dig the corpse up and burn it." Lean resumed walking, thinking and puffing away as they moved up the slight incline of Exchange Street. "I suppose that last bit, the burning, was aimed at Sears. To get him to turn the thunderstone over if he had it, or maybe to get him to hurry up and steal Professor Horsford's papers with the symbols, for whatever reason. What do you think?"

They reached the intersection with Middle Street. Lean would continue on toward City Hall. Grey paused and seemed to consider which direction to take.

"We are not yet arrived at that exact instant when a definite opinion can be reached on this affair as a whole. The solution will not be obtained in one swift motion, but rather step by step. We shall have to subsist upon whatever isolated conclusions can be drawn from the adduction of proof about separate facts and events along the way. Until such time as the grand scheme can be known."

"One thing that's not known, by me, is that other business Miss Webster mentioned. You and the young lady keeping secrets?" Lean asked.

"A distinct and unrelated inquiry into a private family matter."

"I see. An interesting woman, that Phebe Webster. She reminds me of someone. Can't shake the feeling." Lean took a long drag on his cigarette while he pondered the matter. "Intelligent, forthright. Not unlike Helen Prescott."

Grey paused, took in the sky, then the stones under their feet, before addressing his colleague. "That reminds me. We likely have a decent amount of ground left to cover in this inquiry."

"Probably so, but what's that got to do with Helen?"

"Nothing at all, which is exactly my point. And it's strikingly early in the course of this investigation for you to have already become so repetitive and tiresome in your comments." Grey reached a decision and turned left on Middle Street.

"Hmm." Lean was silent as he contemplated the point, then smiled and shook his head. "No. No, I don't think so," he called out after Grey. "Seems about the right time to me."

Chapter 28

THE TAILOR SHOP OF EZRA AND LOUISA GROSSTACK WAS now behind Lean. It was his last bit of work for the evening, checking in to make sure no further curious incidents had occurred below the store. The Grosstacks had seen to that by having a mason come around in short order and brick up the tunnel entrance to their basement. Lean wandered east along Fore Street as the sunlight faded. He removed his derby and ran his fingers through his sandy hair. The breeze coming up from the harbor cooled him. The business of the city's day was winding down, but the streets were still active as people took advantage of the fine summer evening. Gulls circled overhead, adding their shrill, repetitive calls to those of a newsboy hawking the late edition.

Lean strolled on, unsure of why he was heading this way instead of making for home. Within a minute he approached Silver Street and glanced at Darragh's boardinghouse, where Chester Sears had stayed during his trip up from Boston, apparently to assist his old partner Cosgrove in the theft of the Webster family's thunderstone.

As the daylight faded, Lean's mind meandered along its own winding path of dark streets and alleyways, trying to make sense of the two dead thieves and their connection to the thunderstone with its strange symbols.

Lean realized he'd reached Vine Street. Then a new thought came to him, another image: the horned, demonic face drawn in ashes on the wall near the burned, desecrated body of Frank Cosgrove. He turned up the unevenly cobbled street and made his way to the short alley that led to the house. It was a sorry sight, with its sagging roof beam and dark, vacant windows. The decrepit hulk looked like it wouldn't last more than a couple years at this rate. Lean approached the door. As he reached for the knob, two high, sharp notes came whistling out from behind him. He took it as an attempt to get attention poorly disguised as a birdcall.

Twenty paces away, another narrow alley sank into deep shadow between two wooden buildings. Lean peered toward the source of the sound, thinking he could make out a dark form there and a slight movement. A hushed, urgent whisper slipped out of the black space, and Lean took a half step forward. He was about to call out when he heard the violent creak of the house's door being yanked open behind him. Even as he whirled about, bringing one defensive fist up before his face, a body slammed into him. Already off balance, Lean went sprawling on the unpaved ground before the doorstep.

He leaped to his feet and caught sight of a slender figure fleeing toward the alleyway.

"Stop! Police!" Lean called as he launched into pursuit.

The answer, from the original source inside the dark alley, was a panicked "Run!"

Lean charged into the alley at full speed, hands raised to brace himself and push off against the wall. Rushing through the litter-strewn passage, he emerged onto Deer Street and darted left. Ahead of him a few pedestrians stood aside as two men raced past. Lean sprinted after them. The figure in front turned left upon reaching the corner, while the man who'd bolted out of the house cut diagonally right, dodging a two-wheeler cab as he crossed Middle Street. Lean followed the second man across the street, also sidestepping traffic and giving one horse a fright. Although he'd been making up some ground in the pursuit, he felt his lungs starting to labor as he rounded one corner, then another, before bolting across Newbury Street. The green space of Lincoln Park opened up before them, with the stone structures of the First Baptist and Second Parish churches looming across Congress Street on the far side of the park.

The fleeing man made a slight detour to one of the rectangular park's corner entrances, marked by two massive granite posts. The runner easily slipped through the series of short bollards that blocked carriages from entering onto the park's gently curving concrete walks. Seeing the wide-open space of the maple-lined park, Lean knew that this was his best chance to catch the man. He didn't make for the corner entrance, instead rushing forward to the pointed wrought-iron fencing that circled the park. His momentum carried him up so that he could find a foothold between the narrow spikes and launch himself over the rail to land on the soft grass.

Lean made a beeline for the man, who finally seemed to be slowing as the chase wore on. The deputy forced himself onward, summoning every last bit of energy for a final desperate sprint. As the gap closed to a mere few feet, Lean's quarry made several halfhearted feints at veering right, then left, but he stuck to the concrete path. They raced into the park's shaded, bench-lined center, where the walkway encircled a large fountain.

Lean reached out and snagged the man's dark jacket, causing him to stumble forward. The runner landed in a heap just short of the wide, water-filled basin from which rose a pedestal ringed with stone cherubs supporting a three-tiered fountain.

"Police," Lean gasped as he clamped down on the suspect's arm and turned him over to get a look at him.

In the faint light beneath the maples that surrounded the central area, Lean could still make out a youthful face.

"What's your name?" Lean asked.

"Kiss my ass!"

A couple, who'd been enjoying a romantic moment on one of the nearby benches, now rose at the commotion and hurried away. Lean raised two fingers, giving a tip of his hat in their direction.

"Let me repeat myself. Police. Now tell me what you were doing inside that house on Vine Street."

"Let go of me, you prick eater!"

Lean cuffed the young man on the side of the head. "How old are you?"

"Sixteen, what's it to you?"

"Old enough to know better."

Lean dragged the young man closer to the basin, lifted him by the scruff of the neck, and shoved his face into the shallow water. Several seconds of splashing startled the pigeons from their perch atop the now-dormant fountain.

When Lean released him, the young man gasped for air and sputtered, "Christ! Birds shit in this water, you know!"

"Yeah, they do, don't they?" Lean agreed. "Ready to have another
go-round with this, then?"

It took another dunking and the threat of a night in jail for the young
man to come clean. He'd been in the house on a dare. Ever since Cosgrove's burned corpse had turned up there, everyone had been avoiding
the place like the plague. But then people began hearing things, strange
noises, thuds and clanking coming from the house in the dead of night.
So the young man's friend had bet him a half-dollar he wouldn't set foot
in the house and remain inside for five minutes.

"I take it you didn't see anything inside that would be making such
a racket?" Lean asked.

"There's nothing in there, upstairs or down, except a few rats. Nothing to hear."

Sure that the young man's story was true, Lean released his grip and
told him to get lost.

The youth scurried away, making it to a corner exit before he looked
back at Lean and unleashed a roar: "Prick!"

Lean raised a hand as if to wave off an old friend. He stumbled over
to a bench, where he continued to catch his breath. After wiping his
brow, he began to think hard about what the young man had said. People heard noises coming from inside the house, but there was no sign of
anything that would make loud noises. Not upstairs or down.

The answer was like a slap across the face, and Lean smacked his
hands together, half in excitement over the realization that had just come
to him and half in annoyance at himself for not thinking of it sooner: the
basement. He hadn't seen a cellar door in the house on Vine Street, but it
only made sense that there'd be one somewhere. Most of the old houses
in the city had at least a dirt-floored root cellar built at some point.

Lean looked around and thought he really should be getting home
But he was not yet willing to reject the urge to conduct an immediate
search of the house, even though the setting sun now made that idea
difficult. Half a minute later, the solution to his dilemma presented itself in the guise of a uniformed patrolman carrying a bull's-eye lamp.
No doubt alerted to trouble in the park by the displaced lovebirds, the

patrolman was relieved to find Lean sitting on the bench. The two men marched over to Vine Street, where Lean inspected every inch of the floorboards until he arrived at the door to the small closet in the back room. There was no visible trapdoor in the floor, so Lean got down on his hands and knees to inspect the boards all along the edge of the walls.

"Hah! I think the whole damn floor in here is actually a door," he said.

He borrowed a non-standard-issue knife that the patrolman carried and wedged it into a gap along the baseboard. Though the area within the closet was cramped, Lean and the officer managed to pry up the trapdoor enough to get their fingers under the edge, then tilt it up. Cold, dank air came wafting up from belowground. The two men maneuvered the trapdoor out of the closet space and set it aside. Lean took the lamp and held it down into the cellar space. The floor was only about six feet below them. A collection of old scraps of wood below the trapdoor showed that some form of steps had once existed but had rotted away.

The earthen floor was dug up in four different areas to reveal a wide rock ledge just inches below the dirt. The remainder of the floor was dotted with uniformly spaced holes, identical to the ones he'd seen in the cellar beneath the tailor shop.

"Someone's been digging down there. What in the hell for?" asked the patrolman, who was craning his neck to see past Lean.

"Whatever they were digging for, they didn't find it here. Nothing but solid ledge the whole space through."

Chapter 29

THE FOLLOWING MORNING LEAN WATCHED PERCEVAL GREY crouch down close to the dirt floor in the basement beneath the house on Vine Street. He'd assured Grey that no one had entered the space since the pattern of auger holes was discovered. This was followed by a lengthy and detailed study of the footprints left in the cool, damp earth. Grey replaced his tape measure into the dark leather case that he wore strapped over one shoulder and across his chest. He jotted down several notes into a small pad, then retrieved a magnifying glass. With a lantern close by, he began inspecting several different samples of footprints.

Lean had been through this process before and knew enough to simply stand by and wait should Grey have a question. Another minute crept by before Grey motioned Lean over.

"This is the best section of earth for detailed samples of the men's footprints," Grey said. "The slight slope in the ground funnels moisture here."

"Men? I'd have said a solitary man was involved. The prints all look identical."

"At first glance," Grey said. "Which is why I'd recommend you develop a habit of always taking more than a single glance. No, the men wore the same size work boots. Identical pairs, in fact. Likely purchased together and recently."

"What gives you that idea?"

"It's not an idea. Look closely at the imprint. The edges on both sets of prints are very sharp. The boots haven't been worn long enough to even begin to wear down or develop identifying nicks or marks in the soles."

Lean bent for a closer look in the lamplight and saw that Grey was correct. He glanced at Grey's footwear, fine black leather shoes that were splattered with fresh grass clippings. The cuffs of his pants were likewise sullied.

"Looks like you'd have been better off with a pair of work boots yourself. What have you been up to so early this morning?"

Grey followed Lean's stare down to his shoes, then waved off the question, a touch of annoyance in his voice. "A foolish errand. Not worth talking about."

Lean didn't press the issue, returning to the matter at hand. "So then what makes you so sure these prints are two different pairs?"

"Compare where the men set their feet while each manned his auger. This fellow set his squarely, shoulder width apart." Grey took several steps away and motioned to the ground again. "Whereas this fellow planted his right foot forward, closer to the auger, while keeping his left back half a step for greater leverage. He likely possesses less physical strength than the first man. He also smokes cigarettes—traces of ash accompany his prints on several occasions."

"Seems odd to think they might have bought new boots, specifically to hide their number or identity."

"Very odd, given that the entrance to the basement was so well hidden and none of the neighbors dare to even set foot in the building anymore. It's likely their footprints could have remained undiscovered for a long, long time." Grey began to pace, making quick turns in the confined area.

"In fact," he continued, "it's such an odd thought that we can comfortably dispense with it as the true motive for the recent purchase of these identical work boots. We can instead replace that idea with one that is far simpler and, therefore, much likelier to prove true: Upon determining that they'd need to be mucking about in dirt cellars, each man realized he didn't own any serviceable footwear. In all likelihood this type of physical, dirty work is foreign to them and they have been pressed into service by sheer necessity."

"So our mysterious pair of burrowers will not to be found among Portland's common laborers." Lean gave his mustache a few strokes while he ruminated. "Yet it's not exactly the type of thing you can look up in the city directory and hire out: 'Clandestine hand-auger operators needed to sneak into basements around town to perform tedious wall-to-wall search for missing object. No questions asked.'" Lean chuckled at the thought while Grey stood by in silent contemplation.

"I suppose it makes sense for there to be a pair of diggers," Lean added. "After all, they left two augers at the end of the tunnel they used to get into the tailor's basement. No tunnels into this place."

Grey nodded. "In that instance they left their tools belowground so as not to be noticed leaving the place. But here, with the overhead building abandoned, they could come and go under cover of darkness without having to worry about being seen."

"Only vagrants and neighborhood kids ever came here anyway, and not even them since Cosgrove's ashy corpse was found above. Do you suppose that's it? Putting the corpse here was a means to scare people off? So these fellows could go about their digging unseen?"

Grey stared at the ground beneath his feet while he pondered this. "It stands as the only clear motive for selecting this particular location to dump Cosgrove's disinterred corpse. But, more important, why this location? What is it that they're looking for underground here, and at the tailor shop?"

"There's no connection to be seen between the two spots," Lean said.

"Precisely: none to be seen. Each of the two sites is hidden underground." Grey started pacing again. Now that he'd gleaned what information the earth would reveal about the men who'd left the footprints, there was no need for the cautious placing of his own steps such as when he'd first entered the cellar.

"What have you learned about the site of the tailor shop? The history of that property—what used to occupy that space?"

Lean gritted his teeth and scratched at his forehead with a thumbnail.

"You mean to say you haven't pursued that glaringly obvious avenue?" Grey asked.

Lean could tell that Grey was struggling to limit the amount of disdain that came through in his voice. The truth of it was that he knew he should look into that very question but just hadn't gotten around to it yet.

"I've been busy with matters other than the seemingly pointless break-in to a dirt basement, one that resulted in nothing actually being stolen. Cosgrove's murder, for example. Besides, before seeing the digging repeated here, there was nothing to say that the tailor's basement was particularly significant. Could have just been some bored kids with nothing better to do." He regretted the last bit as soon as he said it.

Grey's face took on an incredulous look. "Kids with nothing better to do than systematically drill holes throughout a dark rat hole of a cellar? Just how bored do you think this pair of anonymous scamps is, Lean?"

The deputy put on a straight face, as if seriously considering Grey's barb. "Just so you know, the neighborhood boys and I would often pass a fine summer's day, shovels in hand, crouched low in some root cellar, digging holes for no good reason. Great, wholesome fun, as I remember it."

A short chuckle escaped Grey before he regained his composure. "What I'd prefer you to remember is that the exact site of a crime, the ground upon which it is actually committed, can inform the motive for the crime. As you certainly know from personal experience."

"Just because that was true in one instance doesn't mean I'm to assume it'll be true in another case entirely." Lean saw that Grey was about to say something further when a memory of one of Grey's earlier, and slightly patronizing, lectures on criminal investigation flashed into Lean's mind. The deputy raised a finger, punctuating the air.

"After all," Lean added, "aren't you the man who once warned me not to allow myself to be ruled by preconceived notions? Careless comments or even memories of similar crimes can infiltrate the mind and plant seeds of what you expect the solution to be. They take hold and strangle out other, newer, better theories."

"Yes, preconceived notions are to be guarded against—when *the evidence* provides no support for the presence of such a notion." Grey spoke more slowly than usual, as if addressing a novice rather than one of Portland's higher-ranked policemen. "However, that premise is not intended to blind you to the relevant evidence in a current investigation. Past experience will be a guide, not a distraction, if one always maintains a strict adherence to the evidence. And in the case of the tailor's shop, the evidence shows that the trespassers went out of their way to avoid the location above street level. They had no interest in the current building. It stands to reason they were there because of what used to be in that location. What did that ground hold in the past, before the Great Fire?"

"Fine, fine, you've made your point," Lean said, then added in a low voice that was still meant to be heard, "After the fact, of course, when the discovery of a second, identical occurrence makes it all seem obvious."

Chapter 30

A T THE END OF THE THIRTY-ODD-MINUTE RIDE NORTH FROM Portland, Rasmus Hansen pulled the horse up to a stop at the edge of the dirt road. Other carriages were parked there, near the path that led off toward two buildings that made up the office and the cutting house of the Webster Granite Quarry. Grey stepped down from his seat and took in the scene. Off to one side was the quarry, where a thin haze of stone dust hovered above the massive pit. Apart from the dust, occasional shouts and the constant chiming clangs of metal on granite also littered the air.

"If you closed your eyes, you might think you were being called to church," Rasmus said.

"You would be very much mistaken, I'm afraid," Grey answered.

Grey moved ahead, following the path toward the building that served as the operation's headquarters. He passed by several wagons hitched to teams of powerful draft horses. The loads consisted of rectangular slabs of granite longer than the men who'd cut them. Each one with wooden planks strapped on at the top and the upper sides, like a makeshift box cover, to prevent any unsightly chipping of edges during transport. Drivers and lumpers in dust-covered overalls and shirts milled about making various preparations for hauling and loading the blocks. Though it was not yet noon, the workers' shirts were already wet through by the heat. Their broad-brimmed hats, worn to fend off the sun, showed old white salt stains across the foreheads.

Before Grey reached the building, the door opened and Jason Webster emerged and greeted him with a raised hand. Jason looked as if he should have been stepping out of a salon in the city. His slicked blond hair was topped by a white hat tilted at a rakish angle. He wore a tan linen frock coat and light checked pants, as well as buttoned suede gloves.

"There you are, Grey. Nice to see you again. Though I wish it could have been under more pleasant circumstances." Jason wrinkled his nose at the thick air and drew out a silk handkerchief, into which he offered a small, forced cough.

"Your brother seems to be a very busy man. He let me know how fortunate I should feel even to get a few minutes of his time here."

"Oh, yes, he's a terribly important person," Jason announced in a lilting tone. "As he'll no doubt remind you."

As they talked, Grey became aware that the clanging had stopped. Several workers readying to go down into the quarry had paused in their tracks near the lip of the pit. One carried a hand plug drill, while others set down or even leaned on a variety of striking or bushing hammers, as if waiting for something.

"Fire in the hole!" shouted a distant voice. Seconds later a small explosion in the quarry sent a shudder through the ground that Grey felt up through his legs. A plume of brownish smoke rose from the pit.

"You and I could have met in the city, in a more relaxed location," Grey said.

"Perhaps some other time, but for business Euripides insisted I meet you here. I don't believe he trusts me to discuss the family's personal or business matters outside of his earshot." Jason chuckled, as if his elder brother's low estimation of his tact and propriety didn't offend him in the least.

"Besides," the man continued, "the documents for the operating structure of the quarry require that, as a partner, I attend and oversee the works at least once a month. This visit of yours satisfies the bill."

"The quarry's a joint family business, then?" Grey asked.

Jason nodded. "Euripides is the operating partner; handles the day-to-day matters and whatnot. But yes, we all own the thing. Even Alex's daughters have minor stakes in the quarry part."

"It looks like quite a production you have here."

"Oh, yes, our granite is used in buildings and roads from Boston all the way down to New Orleans," Jason said. "This other bit, with the explosive charges, that's strictly Euripides' work, thank you. He started his gunpowder mill and munitions factory a few years after the war. Always fiddling about and testing his new detonation materials here at the quarry. Killing two birds with one stone, as they say."

"A noble practice," Grey said, "for those who enjoy killing twice as many fowl, that is."

"Speak of the devil."

Jason nodded toward the edge of the quarry where a rickety-looking set of stairs led down into the pit. Euripides climbed up to the rim and swatted at himself with his hat, sending quick bursts of dust swirling into the air. The robust middle-aged man marched to a nearby water barrel. Two workers—stone cutters, judging by the points and chippers they carried—made room for him there. One handed over the ladle that hung from the barrel by a piece of twine. Euripides downed two helpings of water, then dragged a dirty sleeve across his mouth.

"Not paying you two dollars a day to stare at a thirsty man!" he declared to the workers.

Euripides saw his brother and Grey standing twenty paces off. With the look of a man who was about to have a tooth yanked, the older Webster waved the men over. Grey approached and got a better view of the quarry operation. Below them, terraced ledges cut into the earth left an impression like an inverted, misshapen Mayan temple dug into the ground. A series of tall telegraph poles dotted the location. Secondary poles angled out from the bases at forty-five degrees and were topped with pulleys for shifting the massive granite blocks. The posts were set into round, gearlike platforms that could rotate to move the rough slabs into position or load them onto sledges to be hauled out by the oxen teams.

Euripides held up a blasting cap and declared, "Needs replacing."

He drew a stick of dynamite from his back pocket and tossed it to the unprepared Jason. The stick bobbled about in Jason's hands for several seconds before the wide-eyed man corralled it and clutched it to his chest.

"Are you mad?" he growled at Euripides. "All that jostling could have set it off."

"You're thinking of liquid nitroglycerin, Jason."

"Dynamite is composed of a roughly three-to-one mixture of the liquid with diatomite, a particularly absorbent and soft variety of soil material that stabilizes the otherwise extremely volatile nitroglycerin," Grey said.

"Quite right, Grey. There may be a sliver of hope for you yet," Euripides said. "I haven't got all day—what is it you want, exactly?"

Grey handed over the photographs of the dead men, Frank Cosgrove and Chester Sears.

The Webster brothers examined the images. Jason glanced at Euripides to see if his older brother had any inkling as to who these men were, but that man's face remained as flat and impassive as the granite being dug out of the quarry.

After the excitement of the explosion, the clanging work had started up again. Grey looked over the edge and briefly watched two men below as they finished setting wedges into a series of holes drilled into a massive slab of granite. Then they took up their hammers to drive iron half rounds between those wedges, sending splits along the line of holes that would break the granite into blocks.

"Don't know them," Euripides said. "You?"

Jason shook his head and looked to Grey for an explanation.

"Those two men may be involved in the theft of the thunderstone from the law office of Mr. Dyer." Grey saw a look of disdain pass over Euripides' face. "I'm investigating this at the request of your niece, Phebe."

Euripides relaxed just a touch. "Sometimes that girl gives me fits. I'll have to speak to her when I get back to the office."

"She does some sort of work for you—correct?—in your munitions-related business, but not here?" Grey asked.

Euripides waved toward the torn, barren-looking surroundings. "Certainly no place for a woman."

"You've let her come through here on occasion," Jason said, "once or twice."

Euripides didn't appear eager to admit the correction, but he nodded. "Well, yes, she has shown some curiosity. Only natural, I suppose, when she sees the items on paper so often, to wonder about the real-world use of the material. And it is rather impressive to behold, you must admit. The force of the stuff and the ability to control that, to direct it to one's own purposes for progress and profit."

"That blast now," Grey said. "Sizable, but didn't seem extraordinary."

"That's the key. I could blow out an entire wall of the pit if I so desired. But that would shatter every usable bit of granite in the place. The key is to set a series of smaller, accurately placed charges. You can't fall victim to the siren call of raw power. Like many other things in this world, it's a matter of knowing just where to exert pressure. Lesser force, deftly used, will gain you your end. It's an amazing exercise. I never tire of it."

Grey nodded, then turned the subject back to Phebe Webster. "If I may be so bold, it surprises me that you would employ a woman, even if in only a clerical function."

"No more surprised than *I* was at first. Truth be told, though, Phebe has an astonishingly sound head on her shoulders for a young woman. Damnedest thing, but she really has a certain expertise with numbers."

"Always very sharp in her studies as a child," Jason said. "A natural with patterns and calculations."

"Besides, she's family," Euripides said. "She can be trusted. This is a competitive business, Mr. Grey. You'd be surprised to know to what lengths firms will go to learn one another's secrets. Vieille, working in Paris in 1884, managed to change guncotton into a smokeless powder three times as strong as black powder. How long do you think it took firms in every other European nation to get their hands on that?"

"Maxim got the U.S. patent in '90," Grey noted.

Euripides raised an eyebrow, once again impressed by Grey's knowledge on the subject.

"DuPont is experimenting with new materials and will patent an improved version soon enough, you watch. Now, I can't claim to be in competition with the likes of them, of course. We're not nearly on that scale, but you take my meaning."

"A cutthroat business," Jason said, "as all business tends to be."

"Yes, but worth it. Even with a small fraction of the market in this country, there'll be a fortune to be made in the next war," Euripides said.

"The next war?" Grey asked.

"Of course." Euripides almost smiled. "There's always a next war,

Mr. Grey. Since the Declaration of Independence, this nation has never gone more than thirty years or so without a major war. Even bucking the averages, we're certainly due for one before the decade's out."

"Sooner, with any luck," Grey added, keeping a straight face.

"In those times of crisis, the government doesn't haggle over much as to the price of gunpowder and munitions, and I will be ready to capitalize. But I won't get there standing around all day jawing back and forth about some dead souls who got what they deserved. If, in fact, they were the ones who stole the thunderstone."

"You don't think they were responsible?" Grey asked.

Euripides shrugged. "Maybe they were hired to do the dirty work, but I know full well who was responsible. And if it were my business, I'd have both eyes on that scoundrel Chief Jefferson. Not that it's any matter of my concern." Euripides' eyes flashed with bitterness.

"It is a Webster family heirloom," Grey prodded him.

"My father in his endless wisdom saw fit to pass that damn stone to Phebe. And so it seems I'm to be done with it."

"It's just a rock, Rip. An artifact, perhaps, but a mere curiosity for the mantelpiece when all's said and done," Jason said.

"Easy enough for you to say. But I was raised to be my father's son and give a damn about the Webster name and traditions."

"There's still time. You may yet get over such things," Jason answered flatly.

Euripides took a step forward, looking very much as though he would actually strike his younger brother. Jason didn't back away or appear in the least bit perturbed by the aggressive stance.

Grey edged closer to the brothers. "Gentlemen, as pleasant as this little get-together obviously is for each of us, I have no desire to prolong it unnecessarily. If you could just assist me on one final matter, I'll be on my way."

"Final matter? I mean to hold you to that, Grey." The words seemed to catch in Euripides' dusty throat. He snorted and spit on the ground. "Let's have it, then."

"It concerns your niece."

"Phebe? Go and ask her yourself. She's the one wasting good money to have you nosing about."

"No, her sister, Madeline."

The comment caught Euripides off guard, but he recovered in one breath.

"What do you care to know about that one?" He threw a disgusted look at Jason. "Another without the faintest ideas of responsibility and duty. At least she had the good sense to go off and let us be rid of her immature escapades."

Jason responded with an unimpressed shrug. He seemed to hold a more forgiving opinion of his absent niece.

"When was the last time either of you heard from the girl?" Grey asked.

"Year ago winter, perhaps," Euripides said.

Jason nodded. "That sounds about right. Maybe early spring."

"Did Madeline have any identifying characteristics?"

Euripides was staring down at the work progressing in the pit but turned to face Grey for a moment. "Does a reckless disregard and disdain for her family count as an identifying characteristic?"

"I was thinking something more visually recognizable. A limp, a nervous tic, anything along the lines of a scar, a mark—a tattoo, even," Grey said.

Euripides' face recoiled, and he barked out a dismissive grunt. "I don't know what type of woman you commonly associate with, Grey, but for all her faults Maddy was still a Webster. Not some brawling seaman's harlot. A tattoo indeed!"

"Not even a birthmark?" Grey asked, undeterred by Euripides' rankled outburst.

Jason began with one pensive finger raised, "I don't recall any childhood accidents that would have left a scar or anything of that sort. And there was nothing else visibly noticeable. Not on her hands or face anyway. Perhaps you should ask her sister. If there was any identifiable mark elsewhere . . . well, she'd certainly be more familiar with Maddy."

Euripides let out a satisfied chortle. "Not going to be much use to you in terms of anyone having seen it in passing, recognizing her by it. Hah! Desperation—that's what it's come to, your search for my niece. My father's dying wish being thoroughly bungled. Dyer recommended you—there's something else to thank that useless dung heap for."

He started back toward the steps down into the quarry. "I've got further charges to set, so good day to you both."

Grey and Jason moved toward the dirt road where, the horses having already been watered, their hansom cabs waited.

"I suppose that's that," Jason said. "Probably went as well as could be expected, truthfully. Sorry you didn't learn much apart from my brother's rather callous hopes for a war in the near future."

"Not at all. There were questions that needed to be asked, and every answer provides some bit of information." Grey climbed into his seat. "Learning that you didn't recognize either of the dead men fills in the picture, albeit more slowly than I would prefer. Still an informative morning's work." He tipped his hat to Jason Webster as the cab started off for Portland.

[Chapter 31]

THE SEAMEN'S BETHEL AND READING ROOM, A CHAPEL AND benevolent society for mariners and others, was set back from Fore Street. Two short wooden fences stretched between it and the buildings on either side, blocking passage around to the back of the building. A shop stood on one side of the Bethel. On the other, at the corner of Deer Street, stood the Curtis & Son factory, where innovations in the production of spruce gum had made Portland the original chewing-gum capital of the world forty years earlier. That was the most interesting thought that came to Perceval Grey as he paced the length of the block in front of the Bethel yet again. Beneath a streetlamp he checked his pocket watch and saw it was five minutes past midnight.

The Bethel was built in the Neoclassical design, the triangular peak facing the street. The front entryway jutted out a few feet from the building and was capped with another, smaller triangle that echoed the shape of the main roof. Faint flickers of candlelight were still visible through the tall, rounded windows set on either side of the front door. If there was a congregation in the city that needed ministering in the hours after dark, it was certainly the population of local and transient mariners. The doors were still unlocked; earlier Grey had ventured in to see if his mysterious contact was there, but the place had been silent. Besides, the note he'd received that evening had been specific. He slipped it from his pocket and glanced at the typed words again.

CHESTER SEARS? OUTSIDE THE SEAMEN'S BETHEL.
MIDNIGHT. ALONE.
—AN INTERESTED PARTY

Grey shoved the note back into his pocket, then moved away from the narrow cone of light beneath the lamppost. Obscured behind thickening clouds, the moon lent only marginal visibility. A few pedestrians passed in the next ten minutes, moving along Fore Street, which had remained somewhat lively during most of his vigil. Grey had arrived a half hour before the appointed time in order to survey the scene. The crowds had dissipated as the minutes slid past midnight, and the threat of a powerful thunderstorm loomed from the southwest. A tipsy couple passed by, hand in hand, wobbling along the street.

"Hurry," the man urged his drunken companion, "it's gonna be a real ripsnorter."

Grey glanced skyward where distant flashes of lightning could be seen. He refocused his attention on the street, studying every person who came by, particularly lone men. There had been several over the last fifteen minutes, but none had slowed or shown the slightest interest in Grey or the Seamen's Bethel.

He walked to the corner of Deer Street and trudged uphill. His eyes darted to the side as he passed doorways and alleys between houses. A block up, he turned and retraced his steps. He passed by his own cab, and the horse gave a gentle snort in his direction. He assumed that the animal could sense the impending storm and expected Grey to take some action in that regard. Grey had given his driver, Rasmus Hansen, leave to go to a saloon two blocks away, from which Grey would fetch him when this business was done. He hadn't wanted Rasmus's presence to scare his contact into abandoning their secretive meeting.

Several more minutes passed, and Grey glanced at the door of the Bethel, thinking he might soon need to take shelter there from the elements. A voice down the block caught his attention. A woman lingered there, most likely a prostitute, a short distance from the nearest streetlamp. A man in a dark frock coat moved away from her, heading toward Grey. His hat was pulled low, and Grey couldn't make out the man's face as he approached. Grey's hand closed around the pistol he'd slipped into his pocket before leaving home. As the man came within steps of Grey, he didn't slow, but he did touch his hat as he passed.

"Evening, Mr. Grey."

"Good evening," Grey responded. He stared after the man, thinking that the voice was faintly familiar. Grey expected the man to pause and turn back when he reached the corner, but the dark figure only hurried on across to the next block. With his focus set on the departing man, Grey barely noticed the sound of the four-wheeled cab coming toward him, pulled by a pair of horses. The clattering of the iron shoes slowed on the paving stones. Grey glanced up in time to see the driver pull a revolver from inside his dark coat.

Grey sprang forward, trying to get past the gunman before the man could aim. The driver twisted awkwardly in his raised seat, rushing to fire off three rapid shots. One bullet clanged off the metal lamppost as Grey dashed past; the others ricocheted off the sidewalk, sending up small fragments of brick. The shots startled the four-wheeler's horses. They tried to bolt forward, forcing the gunman to reach for the reins. The momentary pause was enough—several more strides and Grey took cover behind his own carriage.

He drew his pistol and readied himself to return fire, but the would-be assassin was already spurring his horses forward, fleeing the scene. Grey cast about for any sign of Rasmus Hansen. With his driver nowhere in sight, Grey scrambled up into the seat. He flicked the reins and started the horse forward. Keeping the whip active, Grey raced up Fore Street past a series of tenements and boardinghouses to where it crossed Franklin Street at an angle.

Mirroring the events on the ground, the dark, towering clouds released a long, booming peal of thunder. Grey sped along Fore as it angled to the right. His attacker was a hundred yards in front of him. Farther ahead, rising up several stories was the massive Grand Trunk Railway's roundhouse, its circular roof slanting in to where a dome rose up topped with yet another cupola. Before reaching the roundhouse, Grey's attacker turned right onto India Street. The man's current course would put him on the waterfront at Commercial Street, where he'd be forced to turn again. To his left would be the Grand Trunk's rail yard and beyond that the Portland Company was more or less a dead end.

Sensing the opportunity to cut his attacker off, Grey yanked on the reins, forcing his horse to veer to the right into a dark passageway that could easily have been overlooked. Bradbury Court was a street in name only, and its quaint title belied the winding reality of its 250 feet of tenement back doors and coal sheds. Barrels and stacked boxes at some narrow parts of the passage, along with several scavenging dogs, slowed Grey's pursuit through the unlit side street. Halfway along, another thunderclap and a blinding flash of lightning heralded the start of the long-simmering storm. Grey lowered his head, tipping the brim of his hat forward to protect his vision as best he could from the hard rain.

He pulled out into Commercial Street, where blackened storefronts of merchants, grocers, and restaurants lined the shore side of the street. Coal storehouses and fish markets stood sentry at the entrances to the many wharves that commanded the waterfront. All were made darker and more distant by the torrent of rain. Whatever pedestrians and loiterers usually remained at this hour had sought shelter, leaving the hundred-foot-wide avenue virtually empty of life. The street had been filled in decades earlier to link the city's northern and southern rail depots and facilitate the movement of goods through the city. At that very moment, a freight train, fresh from the Grand Trunk depot and only slowly picking up any speed, moved past from Grey's left. It rumbled along its tracks like background accompaniment to the heavenly roars and cracks that now assaulted the atmosphere.

Grey spied his attacker's cab dashing forward, as if in a fierce race with the freight train.

He spurred his own carriage on, trying to intercept the other, but the unknown gunman had built up enough speed that he slipped past Grey by a few yards. His horse was rattled by the storm, but Grey urged it on mercilessly, trying to pull even with his quarry, who now edged past the slow-moving freight train.

Ahead of him Grey saw his target swerve sharply to the left cutting across the rails just in front of the train. He noticed the freight train starting to inch ahead as it gradually built up speed. His assailant was slowing to turn around and escape back the way he'd come. Grey urged his carriage on in one last frenzied attempt to keep up the pursuit. A few seconds more and he pulled forward of the freight engine. Sensing that his horse couldn't maintain the pace for long, Grey veered to his left.

The rain, puddling everywhere, made the sharp turn less precise than it needed to be. He instantly felt the shudder of the freight train nudging into the left rear section of the carriage, just below his driver's seat.

Reacting on instinct, Grey vaulted off to the side. He landed and tumbled ahead in a bruising roll across the wet paving stones. Grey's eyes darted around to locate the horse. It was still alive, running away down the street in panic and trailing the shattered remains of the cab's front portion. The rear of the carriage lay in pieces just to the side of the rails, having flipped over several times after the force of the engine overtook it.

Grey raised himself up on one knee, then paused as his body became suddenly familiar with its new pain. His left elbow felt swollen, his right pant leg had a short tear, and he could see blood running down from his knee. He ran his tongue across the backs of his upper and lower teeth, making sure they were all in place. The rain made it hard to tell, but he thought he might also be bleeding from his forehead; when he sucked in a deep breath of air, droplets of water came over his open lips carrying a salty, coppery taste.

Grey looked east in the direction that his attacker had fled. A hundred yards distant, he saw the cab. The man was no longer fleeing but had circled the carriage around so that it was now aimed at Grey and picking up speed. Grey looked about for something to defend himself. His gaze lit on the wreckage of his own carriage. He rushed over, ignoring the pain in his right knee and the sudden stiffness in his hip. With several yanks and twists, he dislodged a solid, four-foot section of the axle.

The carriage was fast approaching, and Grey took several steps out from the wreckage to face the new assault. The gunman now aimed to run him down, or at least knock him aside and then finish him off. Grey gripped the axle as if it were an overly thick fighting staff. He bent his right knee, testing the strength that he would need from that leg. The carriage bore down on him, closing to within yards before Grey pushed off. He sprang to his right as he twisted his upper body back toward the passing carriage. He aimed for the large rear wheel and thrust his axle forward like an ancient spearman running an enemy through.

The wooden pole passed between two wheel spokes and spun up

until it smashed into the underside of the carriage and lodged there. The whole vehicle gave a violent shudder, and the driver was forced to rein in the horses, which pulled to the left as the stuck wheel forced the carriage into a quarter spin. As the carriage slid to a halt, facing perpendicular to its original path, one of the spokes finally snapped and the axle came free from where it had lodged in the wheel.

With the driver distracted, Grey seized his opportunity and rushed toward the carriage. He reached for his gun as he ran, but the driver saw him and cracked the whip at the horses again. The carriage started forward. Grey abandoned the attempt to draw his pistol and instead reached for the cab with both hands. He got one foot onto the side board and managed to haul himself partway into the cab as the horses picked up speed. The driver was trying to turn them when Grey stretched up far enough to land a fist on the man's jaw.

The driver dropped the reins as he fell backward halfway into the passengers' seat. The horses were still aimed at the side of Commercial Street and ran forward, heading down the wharf that stretched away in front of them. The driving rain, the swerving motion of the carriage, and his own injured leg cost Grey precious seconds as he climbed into the carriage. The driver had recovered by then and grabbed hold of Grey. They exchanged quick jabs to the body as they grappled for control.

Grey knew that the wharf didn't go on forever. This fight had to end soon so the horses could be brought under control. His left arm had taken a rough blow when he'd jumped from his own carriage and was rapidly weakening. He had to act now. In desperation he broke off from the driver and tried to reach his pistol. The move left him open, and the driver delivered a quick uppercut. Grey fell back, sprawling over the driver's seat. The driver pulled his gun and aimed. Grey lashed out with a kick, knocking the man's arm up as he pulled the trigger. The errant shot flew over the horses' heads, and the animals rushed forward even faster. The carriage swayed side to side behind the animals' frantic sprint.

Grey sat up and grabbed the driver's arm. The cab drifted close to the edge of the wharf, and the left wheel struck one of the thick posts set there for tying up boat lines. The force of the collision lifted the right side of the carriage up, launching Grey and the driver. After flipping over through the air, Grey splashed down in the water of Portland Harbor. When he broke the surface again, he was met by rain and the sight of wharves on either side of him. He trod water and shielded his eyes against the downpour until he spotted a series of wooden rungs leading up out of the harbor to the topside of the pier.

As he climbed up, making slow progress with his injured left arm, he glanced back toward the water. He couldn't see the driver. Once he gained the top of the wharf again, he looked around. The horses had come to a stop short of the wharf's end. There was no sign of the gunman. Grey stood and studied the water below. The surface bubbled and spattered beneath the downpour, but no sign of life appeared.

Chapter 32

LEAN STOOD FACING THE DOOR OF THE SAME RUN-DOWN house on Vine Street where he'd examined the charred body of Frank Cosgrove. Events seemed to insist that he keep returning to this spot. Now he waited in silent contemplation of the door, a good portion of which was covered by a woolen blanket that a patrolman had nailed up.

At the sound of steps approaching on the uneven stones, Lean turned to face Perceval Grey. There had been other times when he'd seen Grey after a sleepless night devoted to some intriguing point of a case. But this morning was different; Grey looked exhausted—battered, even. Lean noticed him limping and saw the edge of a small bandage sneaking out from below the man's hat, near his eye.

"You look like death, Grey. Rough night?"

"You could say that."

"Well, sorry to rouse you so early in the morning, but I thought it best you see this immediately. It seems that someone has taken issue with your involvement in this case."

Lean stepped up to the door and lifted the blanket. He exposed a painted figure: a rounded face, traced in dark red, topped with horns and staring back with vacant yet menacing eyes. Beneath the grim visage, also in red, was an inscription that Lean now announced.

" 'The Vengeance of Hell awaits you Percival Gray.' "

"It's always rewarding to have one's efforts noticed and appreciated. Spelled my name wrong in two places, however."

"I don't think you should take this lightly. This is a threat at the very least, maybe even a bounty of sorts. I've told you how badly Cosgrove's dug-up and burned body rattled the city's criminal circles. Who's to say what ideas some of them are going to get when they hear about this?"

"Have it painted over and be done with it," Grey said.

"If only it were so easy. Similar images were painted on Munjoy Hill, outside of Jimmy Farrell's place, and another at Gorham's Corner on a brick wall facing McGrath's. Every miscreant in the city with a violent streak and an itch has already seen this or will hear about it soon enough."

"When were the images first reported?"

"Patrolmen noticed the others between two and three this morning," Lean said. "This one wasn't found until five a.m."

"You needn't worry, then. This isn't any sort of order for my head after all. It's merely a diversion, an attempt to widen the pool of suspects to include the entire city."

"Pool of suspects? For what?" Lean dropped the blanket back into place.

"An unidentified man tried to shoot me, then run me down last night—"

"What?" Lean's voice was almost loud enough to further loosen the old building's peeling paint. "Are you all right?"

"Nicks and bumps." Grey flapped his left arm a bit. "But it happened shortly after midnight—hours ahead of these advertisements. Despite your opinion of my appearance this morning, the man failed. I suspect that these dire threats were then created in order to confuse the issue of the would-be assassin's motive and identity."

"Just a moment. Let me see if I'm understanding you correctly. My fears for your safety are unfounded . . . because somebody already tried to kill you before these threats were posted?"

"In a manner of speaking. That is, I'm in no more danger now than I was this time yesterday, before these ridiculous paintings appeared."

"You have the oddest way of looking at life," Lean said.

"You'd have little use for me otherwise," Grey said.

"Well, thank heavens you were able to escape real injury and evade the man."

"On the contrary, my assailant was able to avoid me. Apparently by drowning."

"I haven't heard anything about a body!" Lean declared.

"That's why I said 'apparently.' No sign of him this morning either. But a body in the water will surface, sooner or later."

Lean waited to see if Grey would add any further details, but the man suddenly seemed caught up in some new thought.

"Run you down. So he was in a hansom? Anything in there to say who he was? Grey?"

It took Grey several seconds to realize he was being addressed and needed to respond. "Belonged to Soule's Hack Stables. Stolen from one of their drivers at gunpoint an hour before my encounter."

"Where'd this all happen?"

"Started at the Seamen's Bethel. I had a note promising information."

"The Bethel, that's close to Darragh's boardinghouse. The same old locations keep popping their noses up."

"Old locations," Grey repeated. "That reminds me—whatever became of your efforts to identify the use of the former building at the tailor shop's location? Anything of interest turn up?"

"I've gone to the historical society and asked our old friend Meserve to lend his researching expertise," Lean said.

"Excellent."

"Underground passages, unexplained drilling holes, stolen rocks, dead thieves. This case seems to keep circling around back onto itself in the strangest fashion. And now death threats against you. Are you at least carrying a gun?"

"Since our return from Boston," Grey answered. "Whoever put a bullet in Frank Cosgrove is still active. Chester Sears was plainly in fear for his own life. So whatever as-yet-unseen hand is in play here is perfectly willing to commit murder to further his own ends."

"I'll put a man on you, in street clothes. In case there's another attempt on your life."

Grey waved off the suggestion. "I don't think that's necessary. If someone is already watching me, I'd prefer not to frighten off whoever it is. I'd rather have the chance to flush him out on my own, see who's behind this."

Lean paced across the dingy alleyway, kicking at loose bits of rock as he turned and wandered back. "I don't like your cavalier attitude. You act as if this is all just some private challenge of yours that doesn't affect anyone else."

"Well, it is a grand old game after all, isn't it? But I do take your point about the recent raising of the stakes. Which is why I suggest that the two of us limit our future collaborations. Openly, I mean. We can meet covertly to exchange information as needed."

"What are you driving at?" Lean asked.

Grey motioned toward the now-concealed threat painted on the ramshackle door. "Someone objects to the pursuit of this inquiry, and he seems to have singled me out. If I can keep his attention focused on me, there'll be no need to make yourself a target as well."

The color rose in Lean's face as he absorbed Grey's meaning. "You seem set on overlooking that I'm the one wearing the badge. I'm not about to leave off finding Cosgrove's killer."

"I was suggesting no such thing. But if our unseen villain's watchful eye is focused on me while you conduct your investigation unimpeded, so much the better." Grey stepped a pace closer and spoke in a lower tone. "Yes, you are the one with the badge. But I shouldn't have to remind you that you are also the one with the wife and two young children."

"Ah, that's it, is it? You're thinking about last year and the murder of Dr. Steig. The kidnapping of Helen Prescott and her daughter. All the more reason not to try going about this on your own." Lean fought to keep his voice free of the urgency he felt. "If there's danger here, then we'll beat the bastards by watching each other's back. We're in this together, eh?"

"A fine sentiment, Lean, and I appreciate the intent. But if Dr. Steig's death taught me anything, it's that the unavoidable truth of the matter, whether you care to admit it or not, is that each of us is in this very much alone."

Grey reached out his right hand. A look of annoyed uncertainty grew on Lean's face, but he shook the offered hand.

"Send word to me if necessary. I shall do the same." Grey nodded, turned, and walked off across the uneven alleyway.

[Chapter 33]

GREY WATCHED THE MAN APPROACH DOWN QUEBEC STREET, where modest inquiries had revealed he was staying with friends during his time in Portland. Though Chief Jefferson clearly outfitted himself with an air of rough living, it was a relief to Grey to see the man dressed in appropriate street clothing. He'd been prepared for an ostentatious costume designed to highlight this white man's claim to his adopted Indian heritage. That wasn't the case at all. Chief Jefferson even sported a long mustache such as would have looked foreign upon a full-blooded Indian.

"Chief Jefferson, thank you for agreeing to meet me."

The chief tipped his tall, broad-brimmed hat. "Perceval Grey. Always willing to help one of our kind, even if he is doing the bidding of a wealthy white man whose greatest pleasure in life seems to be pissing in my porridge."

"My client is Miss Phebe Webster. My services have in no way been engaged by Euripides Webster."

"Well, that puts a better shine on things. Explains why you were sent instead of some ruffian. The young lady did seem less intent on seeing me dead."

The two men headed toward the midpoint of the Eastern Promenade, strolling slowly to accommodate Grey's lingering limp.

"Yet you were still willing to talk, even when you believed that Euripides had hired me. Explains your choice of a public venue," Grey said with a wave toward the passing wagons and carriages.

"I was a bit worried. But curious, too," the chief added. "Heard the rumors about you all those years back, the Abenaki boy taken and raised by rich Portlanders. Besides, you aren't the only one looking for information."

"I'll provide what answers I'm able," Grey said.

"I came to Portland soon as I heard old Horace Webster finally slipped off the boat. He was never willing to give a thought to selling what he calls his thunderstone. I was foolishly hoping the son might be open to reason. Though I knew from before that he's as stubborn as a deaf mule. With a temper on him, too. When I saw him the other day, 'Ripides said the stone had been stolen. He telling the truth for once?"

"Do you mean to say you don't trust such a fine, upstanding citizen?" Grey asked.

"Hah! The whole family's so damn crooked the neighbors bring their stone walls indoors at night. When did it get stolen?"

"The last two weeks, maybe three."

"Any idea where it is now?" Chief Jefferson asked.

"I'm talking to you, aren't I?"

"He said the same. That I only came round at all so I'd look innocent. I hear you got more sense than the average fool on the street. You truly reckon me as the thief?"

Grey shrugged. "The matter remains unclear at this point. But the Websters certainly view you with suspicion."

"I suppose that figures easy enough to them."

"You're the only one who has ever shown an overt interest in possessing the stone."

"The only one apart from them, that is." The chief spit on the ground, then regarded Grey with an earnest look. "I give you my word: I do not have the Stone of Pamola. I've never had the honor of holding it in my hands. And you can bet, if I was lying now and had the stone, I wouldn't be here talking to you."

"You could merely be keeping up your charade of innocence."

"I wouldn't bother doing a dance about it for the benefit of that lot. And I wouldn't care if you thought me guilty neither. I'd be gone already."

"And where, for the sake of argument, would you be gone to?" Grey asked.

"Back to its home, where it belongs. Pamola."

Grey scrutinized the older man, like a sort of palm reader trying to glean hidden meaning from the crisscrossing lines and wrinkles of the chief's weathered face.

Chief Jefferson cracked a smile. "There's more than a little something to be said for finding your way home. You ought to think a long while on that."

"Sorry? I don't follow," Grey said.

"Your spirit has wandered far from the paths it was meant to travel. Soon perhaps you will come to know that your time has arrived. The time for you to go home as well."

"I'm as home as I choose to be. And I suspect that your comments are meant to take me down a path other than the one I'm interested in."

"A man's free to choose as he may, of course"—Chief Jefferson tapped the side of his head first, then his breast—"but a man's true home is where his heart tells him he belongs."

Grey recognized this as mere distraction but was unable to ignore the hypocrisy in the chief's position. "Odd words coming from a man who's spent his life other than where he belongs."

"The blood and the heart can sometimes be of two minds. I weren't long off my mother's pap when I went missing from my white home. I suppose I must have known I was lost at first, but at that age it didn't take long for memories of my first family to fade. I spent five or six years with that Abenaki couple that first found me. Makes them about as close as I can ever remember of having parents. How old were you when you left the Abenaki?"

"Seven," Grey said curtly. He was slightly irritated at the man's digression but held his tongue, hoping the dialogue might come around to something more relevant to his inquiry.

"Ha, aren't we just heads and tails on a strange old coin? So you were old enough to recall going from our people to a fancy house, being raised among Portland's tippybobs. You must have missed it."

"After a manner, I suppose." Grey kept a straight face and clear eyes, not wanting to reveal any hint of the strain of those early years that might encourage the chief in his verbal meandering.

"Oh, 'after a manner,' he says. How could you not? Going from that life—freedom, movement, living in the round of the year. And trading it in for a white childhood. Barely a childhood at all. Nothing but primers and teachers' rules. Keeping your knees clean and your ears scrubbed. You missed out on something precious."

Grey looked out over the open, sloping expanse of green park. It was nearly half a mile wide and five hundred feet deep. A short, level space by the Promenade gave way to a sharp slope that dropped down to where it leveled again at the rocky shoreline of Casco Bay. A train chugged slowly along the Portland & Rochester line, the tracks laid out along the outer rim of the Neck. For a moment the engine's smoke mingled with that of the Portland Smelting Works, the sole commercial endeavor located along the base of the eastern end of the city's neck. The wafting smoke dissipated in the air before it could ruin the pristine sight of the bay dotted with its dozens of islands and hundreds of boats of various sizes and purposes.

"There was nothing left for me in that life," Grey said.

"You're wrong. Take it from me, one who's lived long enough to know."

"I'll judge for myself. Don't mistake me for one of those who lazily assume that age brings wisdom to every man. Years bring experience but also give a man time to stake out a spot and dig himself in so deep he can no longer see five feet past where he's standing."

"I tell you, Grey. Once it's inside you . . . well, the pull of that life stays with you, always. I was seventeen when I came traveling back south with some Penobscot families. Some fellow in Arundel caught sight of me and recognized something." Chief Jefferson lifted his left hand. The top knuckle of his little finger was missing, and an old scar still showed across his other three fingers.

"Childhood accident. It wasn't long before the police had a hold of me. The next day an elderly white fellow and two younger women came to the jail. They stood there gawking at me for a good ten minutes, comparing me to an old photo, before they decided I was the little boy they'd known as John Jefferson. I thought they were all mad. Weren't until what turned out to be my elder sister hummed an old bedtime ditty— one my mother used to sing me—that the memories began to stir."

"That's touching," Grey said, "but what I'd like to hear about—"

"I was glad to know the truth," Jefferson blurted out, ignoring Grey's attempt to divert the conversation to the present once more. "There was a queer sort of joy in coming back to a home I'd forgotten. But still, finding out I'd been meant to live another life could never erase the one I'd actually lived. They wanted me to put my past behind me, pretend it never happened. That's what this whole country wants the Indians to do. But I could never shake it out of me. Whenever I heard that a group of Abenakis had come within ten miles, I'd run off to join them."

A faraway look had settled into Chief Jefferson's eyes, and he chuckled. "It got to the point my father hired armed men. They'd stash me away at a hotel in Biddeford. Sometimes it worked, other times I still got loose. Eventually my father learned he had to let me be who my heart said I was."

"Why are you telling me all this?" Grey asked.

"You want to know why I'm so interested in this thunderstone? That's why. Learning I was born a white man, that I didn't truly have Abenaki blood . . . well, it was like a piece of me got hollowed out. Never could quite fill it up all the way again after that."

"And you think recovering this thunderstone is somehow going to make you whole once more. That this is really an ancient Indian artifact that will make a true Abenaki of you."

"When I first saw that stone, it hit me like a flash of lightning. I knew what it was. I felt its spirit calling to me. So yes, I do believe I was meant to take the stone back. And when I do, maybe in some small way that will help the rest of our people, be a small reminder of the people they truly are in their hearts."

Chief Jefferson stopped along the sidewalk, opposite from where the city's grandest thoroughfare, Congress Street, reached its eastern terminus. A tall granite pillar stood on that spot, along the seaward side of the Promenade. The Cleeves and Tucker Memorial honored the first two English settlers to stake a permanent claim on the area of Portland Neck in the year 1632. Above the square base, each of the four sides was engraved with one of the names the city had held in its history.

"Portland," recited Chief Jefferson as he began a slow walk about the pedestal. "Before that they called it Falmouth. Earlier still, the English ears heard an Abenaki word describing the place as Casco." The chief stopped in front of the last panel. "And the original Abenaki name:

Machigonne, 'the Great Neck.' Call it what you like. This was all the land of the Abenaki: The Dawnland."

The chief's arms fanned out wide. "The white men came and ripped it from them. It was here in Machigonne, or Casco, that Thomas Webster uncovered the Stone of Pamola. He was a wealthy man. Over time he'd bought property all over the Neck. And at one of these sites, his workers dug up the stone. Of course it's an Abenaki artifact. What other possible explanation is there under the sky or, more precisely, under the earth?"

"The most logical explanation, especially when you're considering the words and actions of someone you obviously think of as such a devious white man: He lied. He didn't dig it up at all. It's a hoax. The stone is too perfectly shaped to be natural," Grey said.

"Natural. You mistake nature for only what you can see and understand with your eyes. But that is not all there is in the world. There are forces and spirits beyond what man can see."

"Old Thomas Webster made that stone," Grey said.

"Why? Tell me where your logical explanation goes from there." Chief Jefferson started to become flustered by his own urgency to make his point. "Why would a man commit a hoax only to never let anyone know about it? If it was fake, why hide it from public view all his life? Why bind his heirs from ever showing off the fruit of his grand jest?"

"I could ask the same of you, if what you say is true. Why would a white man hide away an Indian artifact?"

"For the same reason the family is still dead set against it coming into my hands. Because a man like me would know what it truly is."

"Please, enlighten me." Grey let the sarcasm show on his face, challenging the chief to reveal whatever he knew of the true origin of the thunderstone.

"Because even a hundred years ago, Thomas Webster was smart enough to recognize that this is the Stone of Pamola, that it holds a sacred power. Pamola is the Abenaki god of thunder. The Websters acknowledge that themselves—that's why they call it the thunderstone."

"An idea not unique to the Indians. Other cultures, even European ones, have placed superstitious value in the idea of formed stones that appear from lightning bolts or fall from the sky. Gifts from the gods, or weather spirits, or whatever nonsense rules the day in that particular time and place."

Chief Jefferson's eyes were set as hard as rocks, and Grey momentarily relented before the full brunt of the man's stubborn insistence on the impossible.

"Fine, let's have it, then," Grey said. "What awesome power does this Stone of Pamola hold? In your hands it will call to life some Great Spirit who will swoop down and drive the white men back into the sea?"

"I'm not fool enough to think that we'll ever have our country back. That war has already been lost. But that doesn't mean there aren't battles yet to be won. And maybe, at first, the only victories to take are symbolic ones. But there's power in that, even—the power of a full heart. That's what I want—to do what I'm meant to do and to feel the Great Spirit in me. And maybe by doing that I'll help our people remember who they truly are."

Playful shrieks wafted up the hill, carried on a pleasant afternoon sea breeze. Grey let his eyes drift down to the shore. He expected to witness women in long, light dresses and straw hats sitting or strolling about, paying some mind to the boys and girls in full-length bathing outfits who splashed away in the shallow surf. Instead the land made a short, final dip. The East End Beach's bathing house and the brief stretch of rock-strewn sand were hidden by thin birches and a scattering of other scraggly hardwoods.

"Look here." Chief Jefferson drew a folded paper from inside his coat. "This is the news article—the photograph of the so-called thunderstone taken at Maine's statehood anniversary. It's grainy, but look at the stone." He produced a small magnifying glass and offered it to Grey.

"I've seen this photograph before."

"Then you have no doubt seen the symbol there." Chief Jefferson pointed to the circle topped with a small arc.

"What do you say this proves?"

"Are you familiar with Pamola?" the chief asked.

"Not intimately, no."

"Pamola was the thunder god who lived atop the great mountain,

Katahdin. Though he had the body of a man, he had the talons and wings of an eagle and the head of a moose. This symbol, the circle with horns on top: It's the head of Pamola."

"The human mind wants to recognize what it sees. It wants the world to hold a unique and personal meaning," Grey said. "And so you see what you wish to see, much the same as other men have."

"That's what I'm counting on. The Stone of Pamola is, after all, a symbol. It's a symbol I believe in. One for our people to see again, to remember." Chief Jefferson folded up his picture.

"And bringing this stone back to its home will make of you what you've always believed yourself to be?" Grey asked.

"Returning the stone is what I've been called upon to do. It's a sacred duty. Something I feel in my heart. Maybe you're not familiar with that feeling, can't understand what it is I'm saying. I know you aren't yet convinced, Grey. But later, when you've had time to think on this, you may yet see."

Chief Jefferson looked Grey over once more and extended his hand.

Grey shook the man's hand and said, "You've certainly given me some thoughts to consider, but as for my coming around to your way of seeing this symbol—I doubt that very much."

Chapter 34

ND THAT IS HOW ULYSSES ESCAPED THE CYCLOPS," LEAN
said as he closed the tattered copy of Bulfinch's *The Age of Fable*.
He saw the disappointment in Owen's eyes as the boy looked
up from his pillow. Before any pleas for another chapter could start,
Lean announced, "That's enough for tonight. Tomorrow we'll do his
adventure among the Laestrygonians." He had to flip the book open
again to make sure he'd gotten that last name right.

"The who?"

"A tribe of giant cannibals," Lean said. "We'll just call them the giants."

Owen nodded at the wisdom of that decision. Lean stood up from the
edge of the bed and extinguished the light.

They said good night, and Lean made it almost to the door before the
boy's voice caught up to him.

"I don't think Ulysses should have told the Cyclops his real name.
He was smart to trick him before and say he was Noman. Now that the
Cyclops knows it's him, he might try to find him again."

"He doesn't. But the Cyclops's father, Neptune—or Poseidon—
does take revenge on Ulysses."

"I knew he shouldn't have told him. I wouldn't have told him my
name."

"Usually it's best to own up to your actions. But once in a while I
suppose it's better to be Noman," Lean said as he eased toward the hallway. "Like when you took that extra cookie from the tin and Mom asked
who stole the last cookie. Maybe you should have said Noman did it."

A quiet giggling emerged from the darkness as Lean said a final
good night.

He made his way downstairs and out the back of the house. He drew in a long, slow breath through his nostrils, savoring the smell of their little backyard garden like a parting kiss before striking a match. He lit a cigarette, drank in the smoke, and sighed. The tiny flame mesmerized him, that briefest spark, so alive yet so doomed. The match burned down toward his fingertips, and he dropped it. The flame evaporated into smoke even before it reached the bare patch of earth between his feet, leaving nothing but a charred, broken remnant.

He heard the screen door to the kitchen close behind him and Emma's soft steps across the creaky back porch. He kept meaning to grab a few long nails and hammer down those loose boards, but once again that thought passed from him the moment after he had it.

Emma settled in next to him on the step. "Something the matter? Is it work?"

Lean nodded. He knew she was silently waiting for him to spill his guts. He smiled to himself, fully aware that he would do exactly that, and that she knew the same. Sooner or later he'd have to vent the mental steam percolating in his mind over the investigation and what felt like a dismissal of his services by Grey. He decided to get it over with and to reward Emma's patience by doing it as matter-of-factly as he could, sparing her the need to cut through any of his grumbling rants over the situation. He gave a brief summary of the case and his conversation with Grey after discovering the threat marked on the house on Vine Street.

"So he thinks you'll each have more luck if you each take your own tack. Come at the problem separately. After all, your real concern is the murder. His is the robbery from the lawyer's office?"

"He's worried about harm coming to me. To us."

"To us? Whatever for?"

"It's all that business that happened last year. Dr. Steig. Helen Prescott and her daughter." Lean stopped, instantly regretting having raised the subject and fearing that he'd cause Emma unnecessary worry.

"I see." Emma paused and studied her husband's profile. "And what do you think?"

"Well, I don't think we ought to be letting killers into the house—or strange men of any type."

"Oh, well, there's a welcome bit of advice."

Lean stared at the blackened, twisted matchstick lying between his feet. "Strange women neither. Strangers, I mean. Your sister's still welcome."

Emma slapped his shoulder, then whispered, "You should hear what she says about you."

Lean smiled and nodded.

"What do you think, then?" she asked.

Her voice was casual, but Lean heard the concern running beneath it. "I don't see it happening again. Not like that."

She laid her hand atop his. "But you've been having the nightmares again. About that woman, the burning."

Lean gave her an embarrassed look that he tried to lighten with a smile. "The sight of another charred body didn't help. And I can't quit worrying some when Grey goes and resurrects the idea of danger striking home. But this isn't the same. That was murderous insanity. This one, a man was killed all right, and someone's trying to paint it all gruesome and scary, but at its heart it isn't madness. This is more thought out. Colder."

"You've got a good head on your shoulders, Archie, and a good heart, too. I trust it. If you don't think we're in danger, then I don't think so either. We'll just be extra careful, is all. Keep two eyes open instead of just the one."

He held her hand. "I don't believe we're in danger. Like I said, someone's thinking this through, and in his mind I suppose I'm just some run-of-the-mill policeman. It's Perceval Grey they've singled out as a problem. He's the one who needs to watch himself."

"He's your friend, Archie. If he's in trouble, it's you who needs be watching out for him."

"He won't let me."

"Since when do you need permission to do what you think's right?" Emma said.

"He'd spot me spying on him a mile away." Lean dropped his cigarette butt and crushed it out underfoot.

"Then get some patrolmen to do it."

"The marshal would hear of it before a day had passed. Try to explain that one: The men aren't doing their rounds because I've got them spying on a man who hasn't even committed a crime. I just want to know what he's up to, like I'm some schoolboy craning my neck to see what answers Grey's got on his paper. On account of I can't do my own job and I think he'll get a better fix than me on who shot Frank Cosgrove and dug him up."

He took out a second cigarette. Emma wrinkled her nose but stopped herself before chiding her husband about his smoking.

"Isn't there anyone else who could help you?"

Lean struck another match, and his breath drew smoldering life into the cigarette. He watched the paper burn.

"Yeah, maybe so."

⛵ ⛴

FROM INSIDE PORTLAND'S Western Cemetery, Grey glanced up the gentle slope toward the arched stone gateway that led out to Vaughan Street. He watched an enclosed carriage slow and park across the street. He'd observed the same vehicle earlier in the neighboring town of Deering. His excursion into various sections of the much larger Evergreen Cemetery had consumed most of the day. Though the carriage seemed to be casually traversing that parklike cemetery's winding pathways, Grey had noted its nearly constant presence on the periphery of his examinations.

He continued his meandering course through the burial ground. A few pedestals were present, but the graveyard was dominated by mostly small, rounded tombstones from the middle portion of the 1800s. Some markers bore slightly elaborate designs featuring urns, shrouds, or willows, but absent were the winged death's-heads and other more macabre symbols that could be found in the older grounds of Portland's Eastern Cemetery.

The faint approach of footsteps drew Grey's attention. A short figure had entered under the archway and was now passing the practically defunct receiving house. The Western Cemetery, packed into just over a dozen acres along the crest of Bramhall's Hill at the western edge of Portland Neck, had reached its fill. New interments were now the exception and limited to deceased persons with existing family plots that could still accommodate new arrivals. That thought sent Grey's eyes searching off to the side of the front gate. A series of eleven granite tombs were set into the side of a brush-covered hill. Short metal doors stood in the narrow stone faces that were no more than seven feet high at their gabled peaks. In his mind he heard the clang of one of those doors swinging open, and the ghostly smell of rotting flesh tore through his nostrils, then vanished.

Grey placed a hand upon the stone where he'd paused. He closed his eyes and awaited the voice of the young man who would soon approach him. A soft breeze brushed his face. A sense of calm settled onto him, and he felt some of the exhaustion of the past weeks drain away, like dark water flowing out from some well deep inside him.

"'Eliza Grey, 1837 to 1869, Beloved Daughter and Mother.' That your mom?" said the youth in a cracking voice.

"Yes." Grey opened his eyes and took in the unkempt form of Dennis "Ducky" Leonard. A crooked smile lurked beneath a pug nose on the young man's pimple-ridden face. Greasy, unshorn hair jutted out from beneath a beaten cap. An unseemly gap between his trouser hems and his shoes spoke of a recent growth spurt. Despite the new inch or two in size, Grey predicted that a chronic lack of proper nutrition would keep Ducky, like many of his ilk, at a below-average height. All in all, he liked the young man. Ducky possessed an uncommon persistence for his age, somewhere around thirteen years. Grey wasn't sure if it was born of a willful stubbornness to see a job through or just the utter lack of social graces and self-awareness that would normally cause a human being to move on from an untenable situation. But in either case, Ducky Leonard managed to persevere in his tasks, usually without attracting too much notice. And that was useful.

"My mom's dead as well," Ducky volunteered.

"These things happen."

"Was she nice?"

"Indeed she was," Grey said.

"My mom was nice, too, mostly. Used to tell me stories 'fore bed. Your mom do that?"

"Indeed she did. You like stories, Ducky?"

"Sure, depending on what it's about and all."

"I like stories, too. I want you to tell me one. It's about an older man, long mustache, he's staying at this address." Grey handed the youth a slip of paper along with a dollar bill. "You'll know him by a close look at his hand—the tip of his little finger's gone. The story's about everything this man does. Where he goes, who he talks to, everything. Also there's a twist to this story, because someone else is probably eavesdropping as well. I want to know who else is enjoying the tale. And if you want to avoid trouble, don't let that other person notice you. Understand?"

"Sounds like I'd use a bit of help on this one."

Grey handed him another dollar.

"Understood, Mr. Grey." He tipped his cap. "If there's nothing else . . ."

"There is, actually. The front gate's being watched. Why don't you exit through the back trees. I'll loiter hereabouts for another ten minutes to make sure whoever it is keeps interested in my doings instead of yours."

The cemetery was shaped like a triangle, but with a rounded bottom. Trees ran along that curved boundary, beyond which a drop of about five feet led to one end of the city's Western Promenade. Another line of trees on the far side of that wide avenue partially obscured the dazzling views of the Fore River and, beyond that, the town of Cape Elizabeth. Grey watched for a moment as Ducky Leonard set off. He smirked, impressed by the young man's self-control in simply heading toward the tree line without a single glance back at the front gate. Once the boy was gone, Grey walked fifty feet to his left, then knelt before a completely random tombstone. He made a show of studying and copying the inscription, just to give his unknown observer something to think about.

[Chapter 35]

L EAN STOOD IN A SHORT ALLEYWAY ON CHAPEL STREET facing two mismatched men who looked uncomfortable to be meeting the deputy just a block or so from police headquarters. Joe McCrink, a scrawny, mouse-faced man, shifted his weight back and forth while inhaling a poorly rolled cigarette. The giant Irish ruffian Tom Doran looked even more massive standing next to his diminutive colleague.

"Okay, McCrink, so you followed Grey all day yesterday. Let's hear it," Lean said.

"I hope to hell this was a one-shot deal," the thin man said. "Don't think I could do 'nother. He spent the whole goddamn day wandering 'bout Evergreen Cemetery."

"Doing what?"

"Just that—wandering. Christ, I nearly stabbed myself in the leg just to keep awake. Finally, thank God, he left there and drove directly to the Western Cemetery. Spent half an hour there, mostly standing still, though. Passed words a minute with some kid, then home again, home again, jiggity-jig. Suppose he had his supper on time, which was more than I can say for myself."

McCrink paused, looking like he was waiting for some sign of gratitude for his personal sacrifices. When no hail of cheers arrived, he continued.

"Then he left again, on foot. I was on him as far as Oak Street. Half block 'head he turned onto Free, and by the time I made the corner, he'd disappeared. Don't ask me how, 'cause I can't figure it. I circled about for twenty minutes but never saw him 'gain."

"Fair enough," Lean said.

"Is that it, then?" Doran asked. "Or you want me to put another man on him?"

Lean's mind raced over possible explanations for Grey's sudden interest in graveyards.

Why would he be visiting more than one? Grey's mother and Dr. Steig were both buried in the Western Cemetery. Maybe the good doctor's murder was weighing more heavily on Grey than Lean realized. But that wouldn't account for a full day rambling through Evergreen Cemetery. He was searching for something—for someone. He was on Free Street. He'd heard it mentioned just that morning inside the station. A patrolman had mentioned that same location. Lean closed his eyes and tried to hear the officer's voice again.

"What the hell's Grey up to?" Lean mumbled.

"Go and ask him if you're so damned curious," Doran said.

Lean looked up at the russet-haired behemoth.

"So—we gonna do this again or not?" Doran's already ruddy face was taking on a more impatient hue.

Lean raised a delaying finger while he returned his attention to the mousy-faced spy. "McCrink, you didn't see anyone else shadowing him, did you?"

"Not a soul," the man said.

Lean nodded, letting that bit of good news settle the matter. "No, I suppose we don't need another go-round."

"Right." Doran jerked a thumb back down the alley in the direction they'd come. The little man turned and started off. Before Doran could follow, Lean stuck out a hand and grabbed the giant's forearm.

Doran stared at it, and the hint of a glare in the big man's eyes was enough to let Lean know that the motion was not appreciated. Lean dropped his hand.

"Someone in the city has Grey in his sights. Someone with resources, who knows damn well what he's doing. If you hear anything . . ."

Doran allowed half a nod and grunted his agreement before he lumbered away down the alley.

$\approx$ $\approx$

IN HIS SMALL OFFICE in the basement of the city building, Lean ran his finger down the Portland directory's listings for Free Street, near its crossing with Brown. The entries were mostly residences, with a few shops and plenty of doctors' offices scattered about. The Convent of Our Lady of Mercy broke up the monotony, but nothing leaped from the page.

"You wanted to see me, Deputy?"

Lean looked up to see the solid form of Officer Kenney in the doorway. Perched above the dark blue uniform was a pink, rounded face that always reminded Lean of an undercooked Christmas ham.

"I hear you went over to Free Street first thing today. A reported break-in."

"Yeah. Doctors' offices." Kenney reached into a back pocket and pulled out a notepad. It took him a moment to find the page and decipher his own handwriting. "Dr. Thayer and Dr. Stowell—95 Free."

"Burglary?"

"More or less. Meaning the lock on the office door was forced clear enough but weren't anything found missing."

"Do the doctors regularly keep any funds at the office or mention any other reason someone might think to try robbing them?"

Kenney shook his head. "Not an idea between them. And like I said, nothing was taken."

Lean stared at the man's blank face, wanting more.

"Told them to get a stronger lock," the patrolman added.

"Right. Good work." The utter lack of enthusiasm in Lean's voice was enough to dismiss Kenney.

It could be a coincidence, Lean thought. His next immediate thought was that Grey would laugh in his face if he voiced that word aloud: coincidence. He was left with his earlier question from when Doran and McCrink had first briefed him on Grey's movements: What the hell was the man up to?

Chapter 36

DUCKY LEONARD STOOD IN THE SHADOWS OF AN APART- ment building on Clark Street, watching the two-story brick house across the way. A lamp above the front steps lit up the entrance there, but no one had come or gone in hours. The mustachioed man with the missing pinkie had arrived just after sunset, and Ducky had seen him pass by an open second-story window several times. He hadn't heard any church bells in a while and guessed it was almost eleven p.m. now. He knew he shouldn't announce his presence, but he lit a cigarette anyway. Despite Mr. Grey's warning, there wasn't any sign of anyone else taking an interest in the actions of the man he'd been hired to watch.

Minutes later Ducky noticed a man across the street moving toward the house. He was notable for having one arm wrapped around a medium-size box covered in brown paper. The man's brisk pace slowed several houses away as he checked the street numbers. Upon identifying the proper address, he launched himself up the stairs that Ducky was watching. He set the parcel down and banged on the door with his fist. The man nearly tripped on the stairs in his haste to get away, then hurried along the sidewalk, moving closer to Ducky's location.

Ducky left the cover of the shadows and made for the street. He had no intention of stopping the man, but he was sure Mr. Grey would pay extra if Ducky could manage a decent description of the fellow seen delivering a mysterious package. In this dark he'd have to pass right before the man to make out his features. Ducky didn't get the chance. He was only halfway across the street when both he and the deliveryman were startled by the sudden appearance of a hansom cab from around a corner twenty yards off. The vehicle raced toward them, the driver whipping the horse.

Losing track of the man he meant to identify, Ducky bolted forward, out of the path of the onrushing cab. He dove aside and tumbled to safety on the sidewalk, not far from the front doorway he'd been watching. It turned out to be an overreaction on his part. The driver of the carriage yanked the horse to a stop several yards short of where Ducky had been standing. From the ground, the young man watched the cabdriver's head swivel back and forth, torn between the package on the steps and the fleeing deliveryman. Taking advantage of the confusion, Ducky bolted for shelter at the corner of the house. He looked down the sidewalk in time to see the deliveryman dash away between two buildings. The cabdriver urged the horse on again and rounded the next corner in pursuit.

Ducky stood and brushed himself off. He'd forgotten about the newly delivered package on the doorstep until he heard the doorknob turn. The young man crouched low to the ground, hiding behind a scraggly bush as he peeked out to observe.

"Who's there?" the figure in the doorway called in a tepid voice. His hand shielded his eyes as he futilely peered from the lit doorstep into the surrounding darkness. The man scooped up the package and slammed the door behind him.

Ducky moved out from his hiding spot. He edged along the front of the house until he was directly beneath the open window on the second floor. He heard someone enter the room, followed by a garble of low, curious voices. Next came the distinct sounds of a package being ripped open. There was the briefest pause, then an explosion of excited shouts from at least three voices. Within half a minute, one man succeeded in quieting the others. Then the mustachioed man stuck his head out the window above Ducky. The man didn't bother looking directly below him. Instead he glanced up and down the dark street, saw nothing to gain his attention, and slammed the window shut.

⊱ ⊰

DUCKY LEONARD FINISHED recounting the incidents of his evening and morning. Grey remained seated behind his desk with his hands folded before his face. He finally turned in his chair and stared out the windows overlooking High Street. In the ensuing silence, the young man gravitated toward the table in the corner that held Grey's microscope along with his burner, various beakers, and racks of chemical compounds.

"Get away from there," Grey ordered without looking up.

He turned back to his desk and flipped through the pages of maps. After a moment he did look up at Ducky.

"Just to be sure of the relevant facts, tell me again: Exactly how big was the package?"

The youth held his hands about a foot apart.

"Think hard, now. A man brings it inside and upstairs. It's opened. Do you recall any details of what the men upstairs said?"

"They was all in an uproar," Ducky said. "Very excited and talking over each other. I think one of them said something like, 'My goodness, this is it!' Another one said he couldn't believe it."

"Would you recognize the deliveryman or the carriage driver if you were to see either one again?"

Ducky's shoulders rose in a prolonged shrug, and his face contorted into a doubtful sneer. "It was awful dark, Mr. Grey. And things happened fast."

"Then what? No activity until the next morning?"

"As far as I saw. I dozed a bit during the late-night hours," Ducky said.

Grey made a sideways swiping motion with his hand, as if absolving the boy for the sin of fatigue. "So then you saw the fellow with the missing pinkie and another man leave together in the morning with their bags packed, and they hailed a cab. They said what, again?"

Ducky held out one finger, then another as he recited the two bits of information he'd overheard. "They told the driver to take them to the Maine Central rail station. Then I passed by close as they got in, and the fellow with the finger and the long mustache said something like, 'Before we reach Tarden, we'll need to—' And that was it. The carriage started off before I could hear the rest."

Grey stood, located several dollar bills in a pocket, and handed them to the youth. "Good work, Ducky. Now I suppose you've some sleep to catch up on."

It took Grey half a minute of searching along one of his wide bookcases before he located the specific atlas he was looking for. He was so intent upon the maps that it wasn't until he retook his seat that he noticed that Ducky Leonard had not yet chosen to depart. The fact surprised and annoyed Grey.

"Awful lot of books here. Have you read 'em all?" Ducky asked.

Grey didn't acknowledge the question. If any offense was intended, none was taken by the young man, who didn't actually need an answer before marching on to his next question.

"The stories your mom used to tell you. Are they in any of these books?"

This new question got more of Grey's attention. The dollars he'd handed over did not appear to be sufficient to ransom himself from the young man's presence. He was going to have to buy his solitude at the price of a few more moments of conversation.

"What was your favorite?" Ducky asked.

Grey ran the question through his head again. What would most easily appeal to the youth about the stories his mother would read him? He remembered himself and his mother in her room. She would sit before her grand mirror, the large makeup kit from her theater days laid out before her. She would make the two of them up for some play they would put on to amuse themselves on dark winter evenings.

"There was a tale about a young man whose noble father died in battle," Grey said.

"Oh, yeah?" Ducky's eyes lit up. He was hooked already.

"The boy's mother feared that the same fate might befall the boy. In a panic she took him away and raised him deep in the woods, far from civilization. Until the day came when he saw a group of knights ride by in their gleaming armor. He thought they must be angels and longed to join them. His mother tried to prevent him from leaving, told him the knights were men of violence and warfare, but she could not stop the young man's yearning to go out after them. Finally she relented, blessed him, and sent him along to the edge of the wood, where he would find a good hermit who had formerly been a knight.

"The boy set off on his valiant steed, a broken-down donkey. He wore an old piece of metal as a breastplate, a bucket upon his head for a helmet, carried a sharpened stick for a lance. Along his journey all those he passed scoffed at him—he looked like such an ignorant rube in his outlandish armor. The old hermit, however, saw that the young man meant well and so agreed to teach him to fight. But the young man also learned how to behave as a knight: to be brave and chivalrous, merciful and generous to those in need, and a respectful guest who did not question his host. Finally he was ready to venture into the world in search of glory and adventure.

"One day the young knight came upon a castle in a desolate land. He was taken inside before the king, who lay forever dying from a wound in his thigh. The knight saw servants carry a procession of treasures through the room: a broken sword, a serving plate, a spear that dripped blood from the tip, and finally a magnificent grail. Having learned that it was impolite to speak too much or to question his host, the knight restrained his curiosity and remained silent. In the morning he awoke to find himself lying again in the barren wasteland. The castle had vanished, no more than a dream. Only later did he learn that if he had asked the right questions, he would have healed the wounded king and restored the barren kingdom. He then spent years searching to find the castle once more. At last, older and wiser, he discovered the castle again, and this time he asked the meaning of the treasures he had seen and how he could help the king. Thus he broke the spell and returned the land to splendor."

"I have a question about the story," Ducky said.

"Good for you, what is it?"

"Whatever became of his mother?"

Grey shook his head. "She fainted when he departed. He looked back and saw her on the ground, but he knew he had to ride on. Soon after, she died of grief from his leaving."

"Shouldn't he have gone back to see if she was all right?"

"I'm sure he wanted to. Or perhaps he never thought to. After all, maybe he couldn't comprehend something so foolish as dying of grief. Besides, this isn't her tale, it's the knight's. He has to go forward. Otherwise there is no story, and that's dreadfully boring for everyone."

"Not for the mom," Ducky pointed out, then shrugged. "Anyway, it'd have been a better story if he fought battles and dragons and such."

"He did. Battles of all sorts: treacherous knights, bloodthirsty giants, evil witches."

"You didn't mention any of them."

"I didn't want to keep you." Grey rose from his desk once more and approached the young man. "Surely you have important matters to attend to elsewhere."

Ducky shrugged again. "I do like when stories have a lot of adventure in them."

"You know what sort of stories my landlady, Mrs. Philbrick, likes? Sad ones." Grey rested a hand upon the young man's shoulder and steered him out the door. "So be sure to tread heavily down the steps. She'll peer out. If you look pathetic enough, which should be no problem whatsoever, she'll take you in for biscuits and tea."

Chapter 37

LEAN SAT ACROSS THE DESK FROM F. W. MESERVE, THE head of the city's historical society. He was a plump fellow in a light coat that was well worn at the elbows and cuffs. Thick glasses perched close to the end of his upturned nose. The sharp tips of a dark, carefully groomed mustache stretched out across his pale and fleshy cheeks. The deputy could see only the man's molelike face, the rest of him hidden behind several mounds of papers and books.

"I have some answers for you, and even a surprise or two." Meserve had a mischievous look in his eye.

Lean supposed that as far as the socially awkward historian was concerned, having some little-known facts stashed away in his pocket was the equivalent of an inside joke, so he smiled at the man and let him enjoy his moment.

"Where to begin?" Meserve mused as he glanced at his stacks. "Ah, the tunnels. That will be easiest, since there's really not a stitch of research to report on the matter."

Lean straightened his back and craned his neck to see what lay atop Meserve's piles, as if by doing so he might actually spot a crucial piece of information the historian had overlooked. Of course, the notion was absurd. Despite the apparent chaos on Meserve's desk, every scrap of information was exactly where the man had placed it according to some elaborate organizational scheme that existed in his head.

"There are no city plans?" Lean asked. "Maps, blueprints, or anything?"

Meserve shook his head and set his jowls wobbling. "No need. The tunnels, such as they are, were never an official city project. And they're not so extensive as to warrant anything of the sort. What they are, essentially, is an overreaction to the Great Fire of 1866."

Lean nodded at the reference. A youngster's careless play with matches had ignited a fire that quickly spread to a store of fireworks intended for that evening's Fourth of July display. The resulting flames had ignited Brown's sugar factory next door, and the massive blaze then cut a catastrophic swath across the center of Portland Neck. Two hundred acres were consumed, destroying two thousand buildings and leaving ten thousand homeless. It had taken several years for the city to rise up again from the ashes.

"When people were rebuilding, they naturally had the possibility of another such disaster in mind. Although only a single soul or two was lost in the fire, the idea was bandied about to build tunnels, escape routes, out of the center of the city toward the safety of the waterfront along the harbor." Meserve pushed his dipping glasses back over the bridge of his nose as he went on.

"Some landowners began the tunnel process, but it soon fell out of favor. The tunnels were difficult to build. Maine is famed for its rocky coast, and Portland Neck is part of that. Besides, when folks did rebuild, as anyone can plainly see, it was done mostly in brick. People took an immense pride in the new look of the city as well as the practical aspects of the construction. The threat of another massive fire spreading so quick as before seemed an impossibility. And the new water lines running in from Sebago Lake provided a sense of security. New fire engines would be supported by the massive reservoirs on the east and west ends. The city would have the water power that had been lacking in '66. People looked ahead with a new hope for prosperity. The lingering fear of the fire faded, and the plan for a network of tunnels withered away and was soon forgotten."

"So how many tunnels do exist?" Lean asked.

Meserve's head tilted to his left, then bounced back to his right, looking like a wobbling top winding down above the stack of paper on his desk. "Of the sort and length you mentioned, I can't really say. If I had to hazard a guess, maybe half a dozen or a dozen at most could still be found and used."

"But without a plan available, how would someone go about gathering a working knowledge of them?" Lean muttered to himself.

Although Meserve hadn't actually been questioned, he still felt that

as the de facto expert on the subject, he was compelled to offer an educated guess.

"They certainly would have had to do their homework. To the extent
that each tunnel's whereabouts are still known, I suspect it would be a
matter of very local knowledge. If multiple distinct tunnels in separate
areas of the city are being put to some nefarious use, then an individual
would need—"

Lean finished the incomplete thought. "To be asking a lot of questions to shady characters all over town. That would take a lot of work. A
lot of criminal connections."

The door opened behind Lean. Before he could turn his head, Lean
saw Meserve's molelike eyes grow big in his thick lenses.

"I did promise you a surprise or two, Deputy," Meserve said.

"Archie Lean!" an excited voice came from the doorway.

He was so astonished that full recognition evaded him until he rose
and turned. Helen Prescott stood there with a wide grin and beaming
blue eyes. Though she wore a rather drab dress, well suited for the library setting, Lean thought she looked smashing. It had been almost a
full year since he'd seen her, but she looked no worse for the time that
had slipped by. They exchanged a quick, warm hug, and Lean gave the
slightly younger woman a familial peck on the cheek.

"It's so good to see you again, Archie."

"And you. I thought you wouldn't arrive until next month. So many
questions—when did you get back? How's Delia getting along?"

"Just two days ago, still settling in. Delia's very well. She's so happy
to be back. Wanting to catch up with her school friends, so many things
to see and do."

"Speaking of which," Meserve interrupted, sheepishly adjusting his
glasses and glancing at his pocket watch, "I myself have an appointment
shortly that I must keep, I'm afraid."

"Of course," Lean said as he offered his seat to Helen. "We can catch
up later. Perhaps you can stop by for a visit. Emma would be thrilled to
have you. She never tires of showing off the new house."

Helen smiled and nodded her acceptance.

"Anyway," Meserve said, "I've got another bit of news. You wanted to know about the history of the two properties: the one on Vine and the tailor's shop on Exchange."

He stood to reach over his desk and handed a thin folder to Lean.

"I've put detailed notes there. But the long and short of it is this: They've had various owners and purposes over the years, but there is indeed a connection between the two properties. I had to go back almost a hundred years to find it. In the early 1800s, each was owned by a man named Thomas Webster."

Lean's body gave an involuntary start.

"Does that name mean something?" Helen asked.

"Yes. Something I've been working on with Perceval Grey. Thomas Webster is more on his side of things. He'll be very interested to hear this."

"Well, there's a bit more," Helen said. "I haven't officially started back to work yet, but when Mr. Meserve mentioned he was assisting you on an issue, I volunteered to help."

"Yes, the name of Thomas Webster rang a bell for me as well," Meserve said. "But I haven't yet been able to uncover just where I remember him from. Quite bothersome, actually. So while I was looking into that, I asked Mrs. Prescott to make a check of title records and see what other properties our good old Mr. Webster may have owned."

"He seems to have been a man of means," Helen said. "In addition to those two properties, he also owned some pasture land on Munjoy Hill, along where Washington Avenue runs up by the reservoir. I'm still working on the exact location. The old deeds and such aren't the easiest to work with. Previous to that, in the late 1700s, before he owned any of the other properties on record, he built a house near the corner of Oak and Free streets."

"So he was here rather early," Lean said.

"I'll say," Helen agreed. "Back in the 1790s, the land above the Oak and Free lot was a potato field. And where the Union Hall now stands was only frog ponds and whortleberry bushes."

Meserve made a sort of high-pitched humming sound. Lean glanced at the man, who had one hand balled up below his chin while the other was on his desk, fingers tapping anxiously. He looked to be on the edge of saying something, but Lean grew tired of waiting. He took the pages that Helen handed him and studied the precise location of that early building. He'd need to check that one as well, to see if it had suffered the same unauthorized digging in its basement as the other two properties.

"Is that house still there?" he asked Helen.

"It's still a residence. I'm not certain if it's the original. And actually, it was just sold four months ago. I put down the new owner's name there in my notes."

"Jerome Morse," Lean read aloud. He felt himself frowning as he struggled with the name. He knew it from somewhere. He'd have to check into it when he got back to the station.

Meserve slapped his hands together, startling Helen and Lean, who stared at him awaiting an explanation.

"I've just had a notion—the 1790s, you said. I think I know why I couldn't get Thomas Webster out of my brain. I'm going to need time to look it all over again. Deputy, might you come back and see me again the morning after tomorrow?"

"Of course, if you think it's important."

"Oh, it is," Meserve assured him. "It will definitely be interesting."

Lean paused for a moment, noticing how Meserve had replaced the criterion of "important" with his own selection of "interesting." This could end up being some sort of historical footnote that would fascinate Meserve but prove of little worth to anyone else. Still, he assured the historian and Helen that he would see them again two mornings from then.

Chapter 38

THE TRAIN NORTH HAD CARRIED GREY AS FAR AS BANGOR, where he disembarked before it would veer east for Canada's Maritime Provinces. From Bangor a decent upland road followed the east branch of the Penobscot River. The first part of the journey was pleasant enough, passing through picturesque landscapes. Grey took note of islands in the Penobscot belonging to the Indian tribe of that name, where he was happy to see some thrifty-looking homes and farms. He traveled under the name of Poulin, his father's name. Formally speaking, his father's people were Abenaki, but the two groups had always been allied, and 250 years of struggles with Europeans had eased the distinction even further. They were all Wabanaki, the People of the Dawnland. The Poulin name and Grey's physical appearance had the desired effect of gaining the trust and help of the local Penobscots he met along the way. A few remembered his father, including the older fellow who agreed to serve as guide to Mount Katahdin. Others were able to confirm that Chief Jefferson and another fellow had passed through no more than a day ahead of Grey.

The last fifty miles of the journey to the base of the mountain more than made up for the ease of the earliest legs. Their cart had to pass over many long stretches of old, poorly maintained tote roads used by loggers, which often resembled roads in name only. They crossed fords and swamplands, where logs laid crosswise formed what his guide called a "corduroy turnpike." All the while the stark, weather-beaten figure of Katahdin loomed before them. The top formed a bare and jagged plateau. Below there its sides rose sharply, dark except where avalanches and slides had left pale scars on the precipitous slopes. Katahdin had no companions, no surrounding foothills to lessen the solitary dignity of its presence. It was a stone kraken, miles wide, thrusting itself up to rule over a wild and coniferous sea for hundreds of miles around.

His guide led Grey to the old Hunt farm, where he could spend one last night in an actual bed. Then three days of steady forest walking brought them to the base of the mountain, where Grey instructed his guide to wait. The solo journey to the top consisted of a grueling trek through stunted pines that gave way to great granite boulders spilled in endless drifts down the mountainside.

Grey kept his head up as he approached the higher ridges of Katahdin. Once there, he found a stretch of ground that was still rocky but fairly level. The past several hours of climbing and scrambling had gained his feet a sort of familiarity with the mountain terrain. Less intense scrutiny was required now when planting his steps. He was well above tree line and no longer shielded from the full force of the winds atop Katahdin. A thick layer of light gray clouds covered the sky, with only occasional patches of sunlight fighting through to the stark landscape. With the strain of the climb behind him, he felt the sweat cooling on his body.

He looked around, taking in the magnificent panoramas that were partly obscured as occasional low clouds swooped by. Two thousand feet below, he saw an endless forest, mostly evergreens with occasional light patches of hardwood growth, all punctuated by lakes and ponds and streams meandering off in the distance.

He marched on, moving up what he took to be the final rocky ascent to the summit. Below him, off to his right, a wide expanse of tableland stretched away, covered in sections by a short but dense growth of piney brush. Much of the great windswept plateau was littered with small boulders that seemed to have fallen from the sky in some ancient hailstorm of granite. The prevalence of lichen, moss, and other pale, fragile plants was enough that a person might be forgiven for thinking he'd somehow wandered into a strangely misplaced stretch of the Arctic tundra.

The summit was more clearly discernible from a distance, but even then it helped if a climber knew exactly what he was looking at. Katahdin was not a classically shaped and peaked mountain. With its bowl-like cirques carved out by glacial movements, it resembled an ancient, blasted volcano, leaving a very roughly crescent configuration. A series of ridges ran along the top, dipping and rising to create more than one peak along the way. But ahead, amid various jagged outcroppings, he spied a small stone cairn that he took to be the work of prior adventurers marking the mountain's official summit.

On his ascent he'd seen Chief Jefferson and his partner far ahead of him, but now they were gone. Grey paused and scanned the space ahead of him. It took only a few seconds for him to spot the regular puffs of smoke rising from behind a midsize boulder. Grey assumed that his approach had been observed at some point during his climb, but in case he had the fortune to still go unnoticed, he took more care with his steps as he approached the peak. He knew he was outnumbered and did not want to announce his presence any sooner than necessary. Chief Jefferson and his accomplice were not simply going to hand over the thunderstone with a smile and best wishes. Grey slipped his hand into his jacket pocket and let his fingers settle into place around the grip of his revolver as he approached the summit.

He rounded a jutting piece of rock and stopped at the sight of Chief Jefferson, smoking a pipe and looking somewhat out of place for the late nineteenth century. The man wore rugged boots and heavy woolen trousers. A traditional Indian deerskin shirt topped the outfit. He was sitting on a flat piece of rock with a small mirror set up before him. His head was bare except for a thin band stretched across his crown. The man's long, graying hair was pulled back in a tail. In one hand he cradled a large clamshell that held a gooey black mixture. Another shell holding red dye sat next to the mirror. Chief Jefferson had already covered his face in a layer of the red and was now using the fingers of his other hand to apply an overlying series of black markings.

The chief set the shell down, removed his lit pipe, and smiled. "I thought that might be you following us. Few others have the poor sense to come all the way up on a day like this."

Jefferson glanced at where Grey's hand rested inside his coat pocket.

"Please, Mr. Grey, there's no need of that. You can see I am not armed. Katahdin is sacred ground. I would not shed blood here."

"Where's your partner?" Grey asked, not yet releasing his grip on his gun.

"About somewhere," Chief Jefferson said with a nonchalant wave, "gathering up certain herbs and whatnot for the ceremony. You may as well have a seat. He's likely to be a while. Good man, but not the speediest fellow."

"I'll stand, thank you. I don't mean to stay long." Grey spotted a blanket folded over a bulging object by the chief's side. He left his gun in his pocket and pointed at the concealed item. "The thunderstone, I presume. It is stolen property. You understand I need to take it back. Now, if you only require the use of the stone for a brief ceremony and are then willing to relinquish it, we needn't have any difficulty."

Chief Jefferson smiled at Grey and puffed some more on his pipe. "That is most kind of you, Mr. Grey, and I certainly agree it is stolen property. But I'm afraid the stone belongs here on the mountain, the home of Pamola, and this is where I mean to see it remain."

A click sounded to Grey's rear right—a hammer being drawn back. He glanced over and saw Chief Jefferson's comrade, a short, skinny, middle-aged Abenaki man. A long face with a prominent nose stared at Grey over the top of a hunting rifle.

"What happened to this being sacred land and not shedding blood?" Grey asked in the chief's direction.

"That would certainly be our preference, Mr. Grey. We have no desire to see you harmed. But if push comes to shove, I'm sure the spirits would see it as the lesser of two evils. Better than letting the Stone of Pamola get stolen a second time," Chief Jefferson answered. "Now, if you don't mind too much, how about dropping that pack you're carrying."

Grey lifted the strap over his neck and, remembering the telescope inside, gently lowered it to the ground.

"And now that gun from your right pocket. Toss it here."

Grey did as he was told. Jefferson relieved his companion of the hunting rifle but kept it aimed at Grey.

"Grab that length of rope you brought, Louis. Tie his hands behind him and find something to set him tight to."

The short man took a long rope from his own pack and proceeded to tie Grey's wrists behind his back, leaving a length of cord free on each end. After that he had Grey sit up against a tall, thin rock jutting out from a ledge. Louis fastened the loose ends of the rope around the back of the rock, securing them tightly below a notch so that Grey couldn't shimmy the rope up over the top and free himself.

"That's not too tight, is it? Not cutting into your skin?"

"No, not too bad." Grey said. The man was still looking at him with a smile, so Grey added, "Well done."

"I've had lots of practice. Sometimes in the traveling shows, I'll tie up a woman, you know, as a hostage when we stage the battle, and the white cowboys ride in to save her and all that. Course, your wrists are a bit larger than a woman's."

"Good to know. I'll take comfort in that while I'm tied up here against my will. Thank you."

"You're welcome," Louis said with a nod before walking over to join Chief Jefferson, who began to apply a series of red and black stripes and dots to the man's face.

Grey was left staring out over the mountain's enormous and roughly cone-shaped basin. Far below him, down thousands of feet of ledges, boulders, and rockslides, sat a pond that had formed over the ages at the bottom of the cirque. From this great height, it seemed little more than a still, dark puddle. On a sunny day, it probably sparkled a brilliant blue, but not under today's overcast sky.

He had to crane his neck to the right to see what Jefferson and Louis were doing. The thunderstone was set on what looked like a naturally occurring perch. Chief Jefferson kindled a small fire on a flat rock that lay in front it.

"I assume you would have killed me already if you meant to?" Grey asked.

"I spoke the truth, Mr. Grey. I mean you no harm."

"But am I to understand that you intend to leave the thunderstone here on the mountain?"

"Yes," the chief said.

"Not to make you reconsider your decision to leave me unharmed, but after this is done and you march me down the mountain at gunpoint, what's to keep me from climbing up again tomorrow to take the stone back? Or even if I never returned, the next person up the mountain, white or Abenaki, is going to see the stone and think it would make a fabulous keepsake."

"I don't mean to leave the stone in plain sight. I will bury it. And in the night Pamola will come and take the offering and carry it back with him into the heart of the mountain."

Grey remained silent for a moment, considering the chief's explanation and waiting to hear if there was any more to the plan. When nothing more was offered, Grey said, "I see. Hide it beneath a few loose rocks and it will remain safe forever. A foolproof plan."

"You have learned the white man's way of closing your eyes and your heart to anything but that which you can see and touch, measure in weights and scales, and put a price on. I won't waste my breath trying to convince you otherwise. I have long since learned that's a fool's chase."

Chief Jefferson finished applying the ceremonial mask of red and black dyes. He stripped off his deerskin shirt, revealing a torso that was still muscular for a man of his age. He began applying the dyes to his body, making several various patterns and animal shapes.

Grey smelled different herb-tinged fragrances wafting past him from the fire. He heard Chief Jefferson's high, clear voice, then the lower rumbling sound of Louis as he joined the chanting. It was a prayer of offering to the Great Spirit and the storm god, Pamola. Grey could follow most of the words, but he tried to put the chanting out of his mind. His two captors were distracted. He tried shifting his tied wrists back and forth in an effort to fray the cord, but there wasn't enough slack in the rope.

While he worked, his eyes scanned to his left, back down his earlier path to the summit. It had the advantage of familiarity if he were able to untie himself and somehow grab the thunderstone before making a dash for freedom. On the other hand, the long downhill stretch would leave him unprotected against any attack coming from above and behind. Plus, unless he could disarm the Abenaki men, an escape in that direction would mean a footrace. He was younger than his captors, but perhaps they were more accustomed to strenuous climbs. Their legs might not be as sore and tired as Grey's were from his ascent. His eyes went right, out past where Chief Jefferson was conducting his incantations. There the ridge led toward a treacherous crossing over the thin, rocky ridge known as the Knife Edge.

The trip north had provided ample time for Grey to read up on various accounts of Katahdin. None of these ever failed to mention, in the most respectful tones, the Knife Edge. A mile long and a mere two or three feet wide in spots, the crossing was not for the faint of heart, or even the brave when strong winds or poor weather kicked up. That direction was unappealing, but it might provide the best chance of escape. The crossing would require each man's full attention. If Grey could get a hold of the thunderstone and reach the Knife Edge, he would have a chance of putting space between himself and his pursuers. The terrain there was treacherous enough that they would be preoccupied with their own safety and unlikely to be firing a rifle at him. Besides which, if they did shoot, Grey would tumble off the side and fall thousands of feet to his death with the thunderstone in his arms. Then the stone truly would remain on the mountain for all time, but Chief Jefferson would never be able to complete his ceremony.

Grey kept his wrists moving back and forth. The rope was snagging on the rock behind him, but he couldn't feel any lessening of the tension. He leaned forward and bowed his head toward his knees, trying to put more pressure on the bindings behind his back.

The sharp report of a gunshot rang out clear in the thin mountain air. He thought it came from his left and slightly behind him, though it was hard to be sure in the open space and with the echoes and reverberations cast by the various rock outcroppings. He looked in the suspected direction. Two hundred yards off, he saw a thin puff of smoke.

Back to his right, he heard a short, inarticulate cry from Chief Jefferson. Grey's head whipped around in time to see Louis crumple to the ground. A faint mist of blood droplets hung in the air where the man's head had been a second earlier. As the short man's limp body sank into place among the uneven rocks, Grey's eyes settled on the ragged bullet hole in his forehead.

Chapter 39

GREY TWISTED HIS BODY, ANGLING AWAY FROM THE DIRECtion of the shot to get the majority of his vital organs behind his rock. His bound wrists held him in check, leaving some of his limbs exposed. Chief Jefferson stared dumbly at the sight of Louis sprawled before him. He stumbled back a step, and a second bullet passed by. The chief flung himself to the ground behind a low wall of granite.

"Untie me, you idiot!" Grey shouted.

Chief Jefferson stared back at him, a blank look of shock on his face. Another bullet rang off the edge of the rock shelf behind which the chief crouched. The noise seemed to stir him back to the moment.

"How do I know he isn't with you?"

"Yes, of course. That's why he let your man sneak up and disarm me. We wanted to lull you into a false sense of security."

"If he's not with you, why's he only shooting at me?" the chief asked.

"Because I'm tied up. He can kill me at his leisure once you're dead."

Chief Jefferson glanced around, looking for anything that might save him. He saw Louis's hunting rifle leaning against the rock and within reach. He snatched it and checked that the weapon was ready to fire. After taking a moment to collect himself, the chief peeked out to get a look at the shooter's location. Another incoming round forced him to duck back.

"Think of it this way—untie me and he'll have two targets to shoot at." Grey tried to keep the urgency in his voice from bubbling over; he needed to keep the chief reasonably calm under the circumstances. "You're only half as likely to get killed on any given shot. Doesn't that sound nice?"

Chief Jefferson ignored Grey and focused on his aim. He stared down the barrel, waiting for what felt like an endless stream of seconds to trail by. Finally he pulled the trigger and his head bobbed to the side, peering past the discharged smoke to see his target.

"Damn," he hissed.

"He had time to choose his spot," Grey explained. "Sheltered and with good visibility. Given the distance, and the hole in Louis's brain, I'd say he's an expert marksman, probably using a telescopic sight. You have a Trapdoor Springfield '73, single-shot. I suspect he's armed himself with a high-grade sniper rifle. He likely has an impressive quantity of ammunition. How many rounds did Louis bother to shove into his shirt pocket today?"

The truth of his ammunition problem landed on the chief's face like a pile of rocks. He threw a desperate glance at his dead friend, as if he'd hoped that somehow his memory from the past two minutes had been false and the body was actually located within arm's reach. Chief Jefferson set his hunting rifle against the ledge that shielded him. He got his feet steady beneath him and leaned forward in his crouch. One more look over the rock at the unknown shooter, a deep breath, and he pounced.

He landed, bounded forward once more, and reached Louis's sprawled body. His hand darted into the breast pocket of the dead man's shirt but came up empty. He didn't have time to search Louis, so he reached across the body, grabbed hold of it by the shoulders, and yanked, trying to draw the body to shelter. The deadweight, angled away from him and draped awkwardly across the jutting rocks, was too much. The chief's own frame remained fixed in place as he struggled with Louis's lifeless husk. The pause was enough for the gunman. A bullet ripped through Jefferson's left arm, just below his shoulder, taking a chunk of flesh with it.

The chief screamed as he fell off to the side and instinctively thrust his body back to the shelter of the rocks. A sheet of blood ran down his arm. He studied the wound a second before glancing back to the thunderstone and the small ceremonial fire he'd lit there. Keeping low, he moved in that direction.

"Where are you going?" Grey asked.

"Got to stop the blood loss," the chief hissed back at him.

He reached the fire and pulled out a burning stick. The chief whacked the stick against the rock to extinguish the small flames and then pressed it lengthwise against the bloody line of exposed flesh left by the bullet. Chief Jefferson gave an impressive display of stoicism, managing to stifle any sounds for upwards of two seconds. When the noise came, it was more of an angry roar than a pained scream. He cast the stick away and fished a handkerchief out from his trouser pocket. Using his teeth and his right hand, he managed to tie it slackly around his wound.

"For the last time—cut me loose! Before you pass out from pain and he moves in for the kill."

To the extent that any internal debate still waged on, it was brief. Chief Jefferson took his knife in hand and readied himself for another leap. Ten feet separated him from the rock that held Grey bound in place. He leaped. A half second later came the report of the sniper's rifle, but the shot never stood a chance. Chief Jefferson hunched down, making himself as narrow as possible behind Grey's rock. Two more shots rang out while the chief slashed at the length of rope that wrapped around the boulder. One bullet sailed overhead, while the other smashed into the rock and sprayed dust over the two men.

Chief Jefferson, a bit too eager to regain cover, leaped back toward his former position without having fully cut through the last few strands of the rope. Grey had to give several forceful jerks of his body to snap the cord. He turned around so that his face was pressed to the rock as he slipped his wrists free and got his legs under him. He'd been tied in an awkward sitting position too long and wanted to get his circulation going again before he made any sudden movements.

The shooter must have sensed the standstill and taken advantage to rush ahead to a new position twenty yards closer.

"He's coming," the chief warned. "We need to do something. Do we split up?"

"No—he has the range to cover us both even if we head in separate directions." Grey said as he glanced behind him. There was the Knife Edge, the only trail leading off the peak that didn't lead toward the shooter. The thin ledge, nearly a mile long and with the look of a serrated razor, was still preferable to a sniper's bullet. A short cloud plume passed above the center of the trail. Several more clouds, low enough to scrape over the Knife Edge, were approaching.

"Put the stone in my sack and toss it to me," Grey ordered.

"You want to trade it for our lives?"

"He's already committed murder. He won't leave two eyewitnesses alive even after he has it. No, we'll make an attempt across the Knife Edge. You've lost blood—I'll carry the weight."

The chief paused but saw the sense in it. Staying low to the ground, he made his way back to the thunderstone, placed it in Grey's satchel, and tossed it over. Grey shoved in the severed length of rope that had previously lashed him to the rock.

"Now my pistol," Grey said.

"My shooting hand's still good."

Grey shook his head, then glanced over his shoulder. The shooter had advanced another twenty-five yards. "He's getting closer—no time to argue. I'll fire off two shots as you head down the trail as fast as you can. Our best hope is to put distance behind us, and soon. If we can get out far enough, those approaching clouds will shroud our movements until we're out of range. The gun."

The chief tossed the revolver to him.

Grey assumed a prone position and fixed his sight on the shooter's current rock. "Go!"

Chief Jefferson rushed off in a hunched-over position. The shooter raised his rifle to aim, and Grey fired. The bullet didn't strike the shooter's rock, and Grey had no idea of how far he'd missed by, but his effort was enough to force the rifleman to duck. A quick glance behind showed that Chief Jefferson was making himself a hard target as he moved over the thin rock trail in a wobbly motion. Grey hoped this was due to the uneven downsloping terrain and not the man's loss of blood. In any event, the chief wasn't gaining distance as quickly as Grey had hoped.

The next time the shooter raised his weapon, Grey rose up off the ground and made a show of firing without actually pulling the trigger. It was enough to cause the shooter to flinch and go for cover, buying the chief a few more precious seconds. The bluff worked only once more before the shooter decided to stay exposed and get a shot off at Grey. After the next shot of his own, Grey turned and bolted ten steps down the trail before dodging behind a granite slab. Rock fragments erupted near him. He made sure the thunderstone was secure in his satchel and the leather strap firm across his chest and over his shoulder. With a final look toward the sniper, Grey leaped from his cover and bounded down the jagged trail as fast as he dared.

A shot struck fifteen feet below him on the exposed rocks leading sharply down into the southern basin. He couldn't detect the exact spot where the bullet had landed. Whatever faint scratch it made paled beside the remnants of countless years of lightning strikes, stark gray scars that had exploded upon the face of the cliffs, leaving shattered rocks. Distracted for a moment, Grey glanced down two thousand feet below, noting the still-bleak appearance of the basin pond reflecting back the grim sky overhead. A gust of wind shifted his weight, and Grey dropped to all fours to steady himself. At least the shooter was facing the same unpredictable buffeting winds while trying to gauge each bullet's course.

Grey got to his feet and scrambled forward. He focused only on each step, the next landing spot, no longer paying any heed to the cliffs built of countless rough slabs and jagged rocks like massive stone fangs rising up to meet him on either side of the Knife Edge. Another minute, and several more rifle shots, passed before he managed to pull up close behind Chief Jefferson. Grey stepped to the side, down from the uppermost layer of rocks. Leaning in sharply to match the angled slope, he negotiated his way past the chief and assumed the lead. He looked back; whoever had been so intent on killing them wasn't following across the Knife Edge to finish the job.

"Good, he's not coming." Grey glanced southwest and watched an approaching cloud. "Another fifty feet on and that cloud will overtake us. As long as we keep moving, we'll be safe."

He looked ahead. The Knife Edge rose and dipped as it made a general descent toward its end. It would take him an hour to get across with the chief. Along the way he knew they would need to cross sections where they had to scramble on hands and feet over loose, uneven rocks and where the trail narrowed to a few meager feet in width. Then, near the end of the Knife Edge, they would face the Chimney Peak, a steep, hand-over-hand vertical ascent that then dropped almost straight back down into a large cleft. He was glad to have brought the length of rope in his satchel; the chief's face had gone pale from exertion and loss of blood. Even after they made it past the Chimney, a challenging descent awaited them, then days of hiking back to the edge of civilization. A weakened Chief Jefferson meant that speed would yield to caution and vigilance against the possibility of another attack. Grey had only three bullets remaining, and he hoped for a quick reunion at the base of the mountain with his old guide and that man's rifle.

The clouds rolled over them like a fog bank, enveloping them in a wall of cool mist. The winds seemed lighter, and the views of an impending, plunging death on either side faded from sight. There was nothing left but to walk on, gingerly and with extreme caution, across the rough, unrelenting trail.

Chapter 40

THE OFFICE OF THE MAINE HISTORICAL SOCIETY, WITH ITS collections of old and irreplaceable manuscripts, seemed an unwelcome setting for cigarette smoking. Instead Lean satisfied himself with a cup of coffee that Helen Prescott had generously procured for him. They both sat before the desk of F. W. Meserve. The chief historian was now more visible than at the prior meeting with Lean. The man had undertaken the herculean task of clearing away the mountains of books and papers that typically decorated his desktop.

Lean set his cup and saucer on a corner of Meserve's desk and then drew out his small notebook and pencil. He felt like a schoolboy readying himself to take lecture notes that he was sure he would never bother to read over. In contrast, Meserve's beady eyes had swelled in the telescope-like lenses of his wire-rimmed spectacles. He regarded the documents in his hands with a ravenous intensity. Lean half expected the man to begin salivating; he had the look of a Thanksgiving Day feaster who'd purposely skipped breakfast.

"Now, what I'm going to give you is a boiled-down version of what William Willis recorded in his *History of Portland from Its First Settlement*. In 1774, in response to England's draconian Stamp Act and all that, our Continental Congress adopted articles designed to keep the colonies from importing and exporting English goods. They hoped it would pressure England into abandoning its oppressive taxation policies and thereby cool the colonists' forceful calls to defend their rights, even by war.

"Apparently not all the members of Parliament were impressed. Some seem to have taken a dim view of the Continental Congress, whom they viewed as a bunch of bumpkins in woolen caps daring to oppose their authority. The English response was to ensure compliance by musket and bayonet, if necessary. In Portland—Falmouth, as it was then called—that response took the form of the English naval officer Captain Mowat.

"Falmouth strictly enforced the nonimportation agreement. Needless to say, tensions ran high with those who still supported the mother country. One of those loyalists was a timber and shipbuilding man who was barred from landing the rigging and sails he'd imported for his newest ship. He called on Captain Mowat to sail to Falmouth and enforce his right to import English goods."

Lean took a sip of coffee and then interrupted the history recital. "Sorry, but are we going to get to Thomas Webster, or his properties, or something in this century before too long?"

Meserve waved a finger at Lean. "Patience, my good fellow. Now, the townspeople were incensed at having a British warship in port. On top of this, late April of '75 brought news of the Battle of Lexington, which they viewed as the commencement of war. That very day, troops marched off from here to aid Boston. The arrival of Mowat's ship particularly agitated some of the rougher country folk from up the coast, who spoke of destroying the vessel. The inhabitants of Portland Neck knew that any attempt would have disastrous consequences. But not all the zealous patriots would listen to reason. A militia colonel called Thompson brought fifty men from Brunswick. Unbeknownst to the Falmouth townspeople, they encamped in the pines on the vacant north side of Munjoy Hill. An opportunity soon arose: They seized Captain Mowat, his surgeon, and a local loyalist pastor, who chanced to be walking upon the hill."

"Seems a rather fortuitous occurrence for the militia," Helen piped in, a less-than-genuine eagerness dripping from her voice.

Lean suspected she was merely trying to heighten the urgency that was otherwise lacking in her boss's tale. The deputy decided to hold his tongue and hope for the best.

Meserve nodded, the keen audience response spurring him on to greater heights of historical detail and insight. "Willis's notes reference a letter from the pastor mentioning that Mowat had sought out a resident on India Street with whom he had business. A confrontation followed that became so heated that the captain's surgeon recommended

Mowat take a walk in order to calm himself. Munjoy Hill was mostly unoccupied in those days. Being the closest spot nearby in which they could avail themselves of peaceful natural surroundings and not risk further rancorous encounters, they elected to go walking on the hill. In hindsight it was obviously a poor selection.

"Mowat's ship, the *Canceaux*, demanded the prisoners be freed or it would lay the town in ashes. At first the militia leader refused, insisting that Providence had thrown them into his hands in a time of war and it was his duty to hold them. Although one prominent townsman suggested that Mowat be executed, the town was generally against holding the prisoners, and the militia eventually freed Captain Mowat. That's the gist of what appears in the history. What Willis didn't include from his original notes is a little bit of scribble on the side of the page identifying that one prominent townsman who wanted to see Captain Mowat executed: Thomas Webster."

Meserve stared at Lean, awaiting a reaction.

"Interesting," Lean offered up in a polite tone.

"There's more," Meserve promised. "Before morning, six hundred militia men from the surrounding towns poured into Falmouth. The rambunctious soldiers, not being under proper command, looted loyalist houses and generally created chaos. During the mayhem a man went to the waterside at the foot of King Street and fired a musket, loaded with two balls, at the deck of the *Canceaux*, where Mowat was standing, which penetrated deep into her side. In the margin of Willis's notes was scribbled the initials 'T.W.?'

"These aggravations prompted a demand for retribution from Mowat. He required that the man who fired at him should be given up and that the country mob dispel or he would fire upon the town. Eventually calmer heads prevailed, amends were made, and Mowat departed, without Webster. There was no further trouble in Falmouth until October of 1775. Captain Mowat again arrived at the mouth of the harbor with the *Canceaux* and four other ships. The townspeople assumed that Mowat merely wished to get hold of cattle and provisions, and they sent their militia out to guard the bay islands, which held stocks of cattle and hay. The next day, the wind being unfavorable, the English vessels were warped up the harbor and formed a line fronting the Neck.

"The true object of Mowat's visit was made clear when he sent a let-ter ashore informing them he'd been sent to 'execute a just punishment on the town of Falmouth' and allowed them two hours to remove them-selves from the scene of danger. The vessels had orders from the English admiral in Boston to destroy any towns north of there in a state of rebel-lion. For some reason Mowat skipped over four or five other possible targets, singling out Falmouth for retribution. On the receipt of Mowat's letter, a committee went to parley with him in hopes of averting the de-struction. Mowat consented to postpone his orders the next morning, on condition that the town surrender its four pieces of cannon, small arms, and ammunition. Without hesitation the townspeople rejected the idea. But in order to gain time for the removal of the women and children, they promised a definite reply the next morning."

Lean found himself tilting forward a bit. He still wasn't sure that the various mentions of Old Tom Webster were worth his visit today, but he found himself being pulled into the story of Portland's history. He knew the outcome well enough from his schoolboy days, but the details were no longer strong in his memory.

"The town's committee visited the ship, and Mowat greeted them with kind words, even shedding tears at the repetition of his orders. But they couldn't delay the action for long. Mowat ordered the committee back to shore with only thirty minutes to escape the coming bombard-ment. At half past nine, all five vessels commenced firing. Cannonballs, bombs, incendiary shells, grapeshot, and musket balls all rained down on Falmouth without break until six that evening.

"In the meantime, English landing parties came ashore and set fire to various buildings. The confusion in the streets was terrible, people screaming and endeavoring to escape, children separated from their parents and not knowing where to go for safety. The inhabitants were so occupied in getting their families away, and the militia so scattered, that little resistance was made. The first landing party proceeded to Mr. Webster's house on India Street."

"The site of his earlier argument with a town resident over some un-known bit of business." Lean allowed himself a little smile. The mean-ing of it all was still unclear, but at least the threads of the story were starting to pull together.

"Precisely," Meserve said. "I think it rather peculiar that the landing party should make for this same locale as its first order of business. Webster had fled, and they searched through the house along with his attached shop, a sort of apothecary, then burned it all to the ground.

"Most of the old wooden town was soon just a sheet of flame. In the end three hundred families were left destitute. Over four hundred buildings were razed, including the new courthouse, the church, the customhouse, a fire engine, together with almost every store and warehouse in town. Only one hundred dwelling houses were left standing, many of which were damaged by balls and the bursting of bombs. When the first parish meetinghouse was taken down fifty years later, they found that the ceiling still held unexploded balls.

"The elegant and thriving town of Falmouth was ruined, with the naked chimneys of demolished buildings left standing as monuments of the attack. Still, this town did not lack a fighting spirit. What was left became a harbor for privateers, and it later received a special commendation from the General Court for raising two thousand men for the Continental Army."

"Certainly an interesting tale," Lean said as he stirred in his seat, readying the process by which he planned to extricate himself from today's history lesson.

Meserve forged ahead. "After the destruction of the Neck in '75, little effort was made to rebuild the wasted area until the war was over. Only a few houses were rebuilt prior to 1783, when news of peace was finally received. The people had a mad day of rejoicing, firing cannon incessantly from morning to night, and ended in accidentally killing one man by the bursting of a cannon."

Lean rose and stretched but still didn't succeed in slowing Meserve's speech.

"Another man, named Clough, who hadn't long since arrived in Falmouth, was killed during some manner of mischief a short way below the corner of Congress and Oak streets. And here again we see a suspicious side note made by the author in reference to that reported death: 'T.W. questioned by magistrate.' I suppose Willis could never confirm the facts about Thomas Webster, and that's why they weren't included in his final history. But it certainly raises an eyebrow, doesn't it?" Meserve smiled as he finished his presentation.

Lean sat down again. That last bit was not expected. In addition to some sort of running feud with a newly arrived British naval commander, Old Tom Webster may also have been involved in the death of another new arrival to the town after the war.

Helen nodded. "A fascinating story, don't you think, Archie? And now, over a century later, we have mysterious goings-on at two properties owned by this little-known man whom Willis suspected of playing such a conspicuous role in the bombardment of Falmouth." She looked sideways at Lean, whose mouth was tense and contorted.

"Is something the matter?" she asked.

"I was just thinking about that. A hundred years ago, they're after Old Tom Webster. Now people are digging around the places he used to own. They're all searching for something. And I was thinking that Frankie Cosgrove got shot because he got ahold of what they've all been looking for. But that makes no sense—they're still digging even after his death."

Lean tapped his knuckles on the chair arm. "Then what else are they looking for?" Helen asked.

"And have they found it yet?" added Meserve.

"I don't think so," Lean answered. "Jerome Morse bought the site of Tom Webster's old house on Oak and Free early this year. But whatever they're searching for wasn't there, because months later they start looking at the tailor shop on Exchange and the house on Vine Street, where Cosgrove's corpse turns up, all burned to scare folks away. But there's only pilot holes in those cellars, no real digging."

"Which means they're still looking," Helen finished the thought.

Lean nodded. "Mr. Meserve, you mentioned India Street as the original house owned by Old Tom Webster. Do your papers say exactly where that was?"

"No, it wouldn't exist anymore," the historian blurted out, as if it were somehow his fault that the evidence of the place was now lost. "The British searched there and burned it to the ground."

"Besides," Helen said, "if the redcoats found what *they* were looking for, then that later man, Clough, wouldn't have bothered to come looking for Tom Webster at the end of the war."

"And gotten himself killed," Lean said in agreement. "So it wasn't at India Street either. What properties are left?"

"The pastureland that Webster bought on Munjoy Hill," Helen replied.

Lean snapped his fingers in excitement over the possibility of one more location. "You said before you were still trying to pin that down. Any luck?"

Helen's face pinched up in disappointment. "Not yet. The old land records are sparse and inexact, but I'm still working at it." She tried to sound hopeful. "I could make another effort this afternoon if you'd like."

"Yes, please, anything you can find about the precise location would be immensely important."

"Of course." Helen smiled, happy to have what suddenly seemed like such a vital task facing her. "I'll telephone you as soon as I can."

Chapter 41

L EAN SET THE TELEPHONE RECEIVER BACK IN ITS CRADLE
and glanced at the wall clock in his kitchen. It was just after six-
thirty. He'd leave the house in about twenty minutes.

"Who was that?" Emma asked from the living room, where she was
sitting on the floor with little Amelia. The girl, not yet a year old, was
babbling away at the colored wooden blocks set out before her on the
rug.

"Helen Prescott. She's found something to show me. I'm to meet her
in a bit at the observatory."

"Will Perceval Grey be joining the two of you?"

Lean shook his head. "He's out of town. Still up at Mount Katahdin,
I think."

He'd gotten that information from Grey's landlady, who heard from
some young snitch of Grey's that the man had headed off to someplace
called Tarden. It had taken Lean a few minutes of pondering before he
figured out the real name had to be Katahdin.

"All the way up there, in the middle of the wilderness—whatever
for?" his wife asked.

Lean glanced out the kitchen window and caught sight of his son still
playing at some game with a couple of neighborhood boys. He returned
to the living room.

"Haven't the foggiest idea." That wasn't entirely true. Lean had several ideas kicking around in his head about what Grey might be up to. But
they had all collected into a vague, muddled heap of confusion involving
Professor Horsford's claims about the fabled city of Norumbega and Viking runes on stones and Chief Jefferson, the white man–turned–Indian
whom Grey had mentioned in connection with the Webster family.

"So that's why you're reading that book," Emma said. "Is that safe? Grey doesn't strike me as a true outdoor sportsman."

Lean sat down in his chair and picked up the copy of Thoreau's *Maine Woods* that he'd been perusing. He waved the book about.

"Certainly is a major chore to get there. As for safe, I suppose so. Though according to Thoreau, he'll have more than steep rocks to deal with. Listen to this." Lean flipped back through the pages of the book.

"Says here, 'The tops of mountains are among the unfinished parts of the globe, whither it is a slight insult to the gods to climb and pry into their secrets, and try their effect on our humanity. Only daring and insolent men, perchance, go there. Simple races, as savages, do not climb mountains,—their tops are sacred and mysterious tracts never visited by them. Pomola is always angry with those who climb to the summit of Ktaadn.'"

"'Only daring and insolent men'?" Emma pondered that for a moment, then added, "Sounds like you should have gone with him."

Lean chuckled. "Ah, my ever-loving and supportive wife. Whatever did I do to deserve you?"

"You can't recall either?" Emma smiled back at him. "Did you say you're meeting Helen at the observatory, really?"

"I knew it would be on Munjoy Hill, but yeah, the observatory is a peculiar choice." He shrugged. "She must have her reasons."

Lean was still wondering about Helen's choice of a meeting place as he stood outside the Portland Observatory forty minutes later. He glanced down the slope of Congress Street to the base of the hill where the open space of the Eastern Cemetery sat just to the left, out of his view. A city railcar had paused there as a second horse was hitched to assist in hauling the car up the steady quarter-mile slope of Munjoy Hill. After a minute, the horses started and the car lurched forward to begin its slow climb. Lean hoped Helen was aboard the trolley.

He glanced back over his shoulder at the observatory, a handsome building that was visible from practically anywhere in the city and throughout Portland Harbor. The brown wooden structure, built eight decades earlier as a signal tower for incoming merchant vessels, was domed and octagonal, giving it the appearance of a hilltop lighthouse. The observatory slanted inward slightly, narrowing from a base of thirty-two feet in diameter to less than half of that at its observation deck seven stories above the sidewalk.

The railcar reached the summit, and Lean caught sight of Helen's smiling face. She waited to disembark while the trolley stopped to detach one of the draft horses just past the observatory near the doors of Fire Department Engine No. 2. Lean took a few steps forward to greet Helen. He could see that she was trying to focus on him but wasn't completely able to avoid nervous glances at the observatory that loomed up right behind him. It had been atop that high point that she'd come face-to-face with a maniacal killer.

"I questioned your decision to meet here," Lean said, trying to keep his voice cheerful. "Thought this would be about the last place you'd want to visit."

Helen offered a tepid smile. "I haven't been this close to it since that night. But I didn't have a choice. The older land deeds are very obscure. Apart from the Eastern Cemetery, there weren't many points of reference hereabouts. Once the observatory was built in the early part of the century, it became the most important landmark on the hill. So I've used it to trace back to the plot of land that Thomas Webster bought."

"Right," Lean said, "it was all vacant back then. Makes sense for pastureland."

"Turns out he didn't buy it for livestock after all. He bought only an acre, and I found a reference to an intended observation tower, of the sort for telescopes and stargazing. It was never built, though."

"Odd. So where to from here?" Lean asked.

"It was north-northwest from the observatory, and as best as I can figure, it was just about five hundred seventy-five yards along to the south corner marker of the property he bought."

"North by northwest, so that would be . . ." Lean scanned the area to get his bearings.

"I think it's straight down North Street." Helen pointed across the way to where that more-or-less-perpendicular avenue ran off from them at a slight angle. "Some of the old records even refer to the pathway that later became North."

"Something's easy for once—excellent. I'll count the paces as we go."

They walked on in silence, except for the periodic announcements from Lean every time they completed fifty more steps. It was a working-class neighborhood and, on a warm summer evening such as this one, their progress was watched by many pairs of eyes lingering on front stoops. They passed the occasional bit of rowdiness or colorful chatter that Lean would have normally greeted with at least a hard glare. But tonight he kept his eyes forward, straight down North Street until they reached the end of the fifth block moving away from the observatory.

"Five hundred thirty-seven." He looked up from where they stood at the corner of North Street and Walnut.

"Now what?" Helen asked.

Lean knew that it was pointless to direct anger at an inanimate object, even one so large, but he couldn't turn his annoyed glare away from the massive embankment of the Munjoy Hill Reservoir that loomed before them just across the street.

"Unless you feel like changing into your bathing attire, I'd say we're at a dead end. He bought an acre, you said. We could fit that inside the reservoir four times over, even if it weren't covered with twenty million gallons of water."

"I guess there's a silver lining." She studied the embankment; the wall must have been two, maybe three stories high. "Whoever it was looking under all of Tom Webster's old premises has hit the same wall that we have."

"True, but then if they can't dig here, I can't catch them in the act. Can't believe it's a dead end. That's all I seem to be finding these days."

"Is there something else you're looking into?" Helen asked. "Anything I could help with?"

Lean let out a frustrated sigh. "A missing woman, missing for about sixty years. Probably passed on by now. And even if she were still alive, I doubt the pitiful old lady would have anything useful to say. Still, it's a loose end."

"No luck at all?"

"All I have is a name—Dastine LaVallee, and that might not even be right anymore. Not a trace of her in any of the city records."

"No offense, Archie, but there's got to be a better way to find a living person. That is, people have to live somewhere, and it's not inside the city records."

"If you've got any clever ideas, and the time to look into them, then have at it by all means. Personally, I've got other fish to fry. Starting with what to do next about finding Cosgrove's killer now that this trail has dried up."

"Poor choice of words," Helen said as they both stared at the reservoir. "Does Mr. Grey have any thoughts?"

Lean shrugged his shoulders. "I've got to get this new information to Grey. But he's being stubborn, as usual. He's worried that—" Lean stopped himself before he could stumble into the unwelcome topic of the danger that Helen and her daughter had found themselves in while helping in Lean and Grey's investigation the prior summer.

"That is, he insists on maintaining the appearance of not working with the police in this matter. Refuses to be seen with me in public and has banned me from approaching his apartment."

"If it would help, I could send him a message," Helen volunteered, "ask him to come around to the library to collect the notes and explain all that we've turned up."

Lean noticed the happy glint in Helen's eyes as she offered her assistance. He realized she hadn't seen Grey since her return to Portland, and this would provide an excuse to do so. The fact that she needed an excuse held meaning. The reticence that Grey had demonstrated whenever her name came up in conversation the past couple of weeks must not have been limited to his interactions with Lean. The deputy relished the idea of doing a favor for Helen while at the same time managing to annoy Grey. Besides, Lean was sure that a dose of Helen's company could only do wonders for Grey, despite the outward cloak of solitary reserve the man insisted on displaying.

"That would be a tremendous help." A smile spread over Lean's face as he handed the file of papers to her. "Thank you ever so much, Helen."

PART III

July 28, 1893

Pfister in his "Curious Criminal Cases" rightly
says: "The greatest art of the Investigating Officer
consists in conducting the inquiry in such a way
that the initiated at once perceive that there has been
'a directing intelligence,' while the uninitiated
imagine that everything has fallen into place of
its own accord."

—HANS GROSS, *Criminal Investigation*

[Chapter 42]

IT WAS LATE AFTERNOON BY THE TIME GREY SET THE THUN-
derstone on the desk in his study and took a seat. Though it seemed
like a week ago, it had been only yesterday morning that he'd gotten Chief Jefferson safely out of the woods surrounding Katahdin. His
guide had been able to fashion a poultice for the bullet wound, but the
hike back to civilization had stretched into four days. He'd left the feverish chief at the Hunt farm and paid the family there to take care of
the man during his recuperation. Before departing, he'd questioned Jefferson one final time about the circumstances of his obtaining the thunderstone. The man was in a weak, confused state but remained adamant
about his complete ignorance of who'd left the stone on his doorstep and
who'd stolen it from the attorney's office in the first instance.

Grey had left a letter behind, for Chief Jefferson's use in reporting
the murder of Louis Beauchamp to the authorities in Bangor. It reported
few details, only his having witnessed Beauchamp's fatal wound received from an unseen rifleman. The assailant had then continued to
fire on them, forcing them to flee the mountaintop. He left his name and
address as well as Deputy Lean's name as a reference. He didn't believe
that the local authorities would have any luck in tracking down the assassin. Furthermore, if Chief Jefferson reported the attack as intentional
murder, Grey expected the police to greet that accusation with skepticism. After all, why would they believe that someone had trekked days
into the wilderness and climbed all the way to the top of Katahdin just to
kill an Indian? The reason, and the responsible party, was in Portland,
and Grey wasted no time in returning there.

Leaning forward in his desk chair, Grey balanced the tip of the egg-
shaped thunderstone under the palm of his left hand. With his right he

slowly spun it, studying each symbol in turn, as he had so many times on the train ride home.

There was the now-familiar design matching the symbol he'd recovered at the Athenaeum. The next two in line resembled the traditional symbols for male and female. Next came a circle with a dot at the center, then two completely foreign symbols, and lastly one similar to a crescent moon. Grey pondered the collection of figures for a while before deciding they would need further study. He was tired and wanted to be done with this assignment; the recovery of the stone had drained him. Still, he couldn't ignore that the symbols remained an unresolved mystery. He would telephone Phebe Webster's house and arrange to deliver the stone that evening. Before that time, however, he would make a copy of the symbols for his own further consideration.

GREY REPOSITIONED the carrying case under his right arm and made a conscious effort not to put his weight on his walking stick. He gave the knocker three raps and waited outside the front door of the late Horace Webster's house. It was now solely the residence and property of Phebe, and he'd agreed to meet her there and turn over the thunderstone. He'd thought of having Rasmus drive him over, in the new carriage he was renting, but forced himself to walk in hopes that the exercise would help his legs. His thighs, shins, and ankles were still protesting the arduous climb and quicker, more jarring descent of Katahdin several days earlier.

Phebe herself opened the door, and Grey's face must have shown his surprise. She greeted him with a smile and took his hat and stick.

"Didn't mean to startle you, Mr. Grey. I've given the servants the evening off, so that we can speak privately, without interruption."

She invited him into the sitting room and poured him a cup of tea from a waiting pot. Grey set the case on a low table in front of them and flipped open the latches. Inside, the thunderstone sat nestled in a bundle of soft cloth.

"Remarkable, Mr. Grey. Not to say I doubted you, but I wasn't sure we'd ever see it again." She ran her fingers across the surface but left the stone in its place. "I hope retrieving it wasn't too much of a bother. Such a terrible fuss over a silly old stone. This will put Attorney Dyer's and Euripides' minds at ease anyway."

"Your uncle's been ill at ease? Has that caused him to be absent from work this week?"

Phebe gave Grey a quizzical look. "No, not at all. Whyever did you think that?"

"My mistake. But he's been acting on edge?"

"He's always acting on edge," Phebe said.

"Any more than usual?"

"He was a bit agitated after receiving a telegram three days ago. And rather anxious for another to arrive yesterday, but it never did."

"Who was that telegram from?" Grey asked.

"I don't know. Why all the concern with Euripides?"

"I'm curious about his ongoing interest in Chief Jefferson." He tried his tea. "There was, in fact, an unexpected incident in recovering the stone. Quite unfortunate."

"I'm sorry to hear that. Are you all right? I noticed you walking a touch stiffly."

"I'm fine, thank you," he answered.

"But the man who stole it has been found out. It was that Chief Jefferson after all, wasn't it? Has he been arrested?"

"I'm not convinced that Chief Jefferson was behind the theft."

"Who, then?" she asked.

"That I do not know."

"I'm surprised. I was sure it was him. So was Uncle Euripides. I'm glad to have it back," she said as she ran her fingers over the stone once more, "but still, it's a bit disconcerting not to have resolved the question of its theft."

"Some questions just take longer to unravel. Speaking of the unresolved, there is one more thing. You now have the thunderstone in hand. In return you promised to tell me all you know of your sister's current whereabouts."

"You have a commendable persistence, Mr. Grey. But all in service of what? The dear man who wanted you to find out now rests in peace. Why can't you let it be?"

"I was hired to discover an answer," he said.

"If it's the money, I'm sure we can reach some sort of arrangement."

"It's not that, Miss Webster."

"Well, I can see you won't be put off. Very well." Phebe smoothed the ruffles on her long skirt and clasped her hands in her lap. "My sister, Maddy. What is there to say? I think she was restless here at home. She always dreamed of traveling widely. Seeing what there was to be seen in the world. The spring of last year, she up and left with no real notice."

"Did she say where she was going?"

"She was supposed to be visiting some old family friends in Connecticut for a week or two. But the two weeks passed and there was no word from her."

"Did you contact these friends in Connecticut?" Grey asked.

"Yes, of course. We were all quite concerned about her. They said she boarded a train for New York. We were quite taken aback that we had no inkling of Maddy's plan."

"Was there any word from your sister after that?"

"Yes. Three letters arrived for me from New York City. The first came almost immediately. She didn't want me to worry. The final letter was in July of last year. She was staying with friends enjoying life in the big city and all that. Another letter came from Chicago, I think two or three months later. She mentioned a plan to travel west to San Francisco. Said she would write when she could. That was the last I ever heard from her."

"But your uncles both said she wasn't heard from after spring of last year."

"I didn't mention the letters to anyone. She asked me not to. She thought my grandfather or Euripides would send someone to New York to collect her. They would have, too. I'd prefer if you didn't mention that fact to Euripides or Jason."

Grey nodded. "You didn't share their concern?"

"Certainly I did. To some extent. But I also had much more faith in Maddy than they ever did. They still thought of her as a child. I knew she was capable of watching out for herself. In truth, I even envied her some. Off seeing the world—it's terribly adventurous. I've taken to working for Uncle Euripides this past year, just for something to do."

"I assume you still have those letters. I'll need to examine them," Grey said.

"I'm not certain I feel right about sharing Maddy's private letters."

"Miss Webster, you did promise that in return for the recovery of the thunderstone you would furnish me whatever information you had concerning your sister's whereabouts. Those letters are the only clues available. They might provide some indication of where she is now or who might have last spoken with her."

"Yes, of course. I'm sure I still have them somewhere. I'll need to look about. If you leave me your address, I could send them around as soon as I get them sorted."

Grey rose and started slowly for the front hallway. "Thank you. So what will you do with the thunderstone?"

The question stopped Phebe in her tracks. A surprised and puzzled look came over her. "I hadn't given it a thought until now. Honestly, it's been with the attorneys for so long I just forgot that I'd even have to decide. Oh," she said, and put a hand to her mouth, "you haven't let the police see it, take a photograph, anything?"

"No."

"Thank goodness. The last thing I need is to have Albert Dyer huffing and puffing about the terms of the old bequest and all that. Letting it be seen publicly is what got it boxed up in the lawyer's office in the first place. I don't suppose I can just set it out on the mantelpiece, can I?"

"Keeping it a bit more under wraps would probably be wise." Grey put his hat on and picked up his walking stick.

"Yes, after all, someone's already stolen it once, and a man was killed over it. Perhaps Grandfather's old safe."

"A reasonable solution," Grey said.

"Well, Mr. Grey, thank you once again for all your efforts on my behalf. I'll find those letters of Maddy's and send them over later this week, I should think."

Grey smiled and gave Phebe a slight bow of his head before departing. He made it as far as the sidewalk before he stopped. It had been less than three weeks ago that he'd paused in the same spot under different circumstances. The inquiry had become infinitely more convoluted and dangerous in that time. Grey still couldn't discern the true shape of what lurked at the center of the investigation. Men at the periphery of the matter, or who didn't even know what they were involved in, had died. His own life had been threatened on multiple occasions, by what he suspected were separate parties. Despite all that, a single thought entered his mind at that moment. He glanced back at the house to see if Phebe Webster would be in the window, as she had been on that first morning, watching him go.

He didn't see her face beside one of the curtains in the foyer or sitting room. Instead, on the other side of the first floor, he saw a figure. In the dim evening light, it was hard to make out any details, but the shape was too large, too masculine in its movements, to be Phebe Webster. Grey paused and stared. The figure moved out of his line of sight. Phebe had said she'd given all the servants the evening off. Grey hesitated a moment and then began to walk back toward the front door.

From inside there came a crashing sound—glass shattering. He heard Phebe Webster scream. Grey covered the remaining distance in a matter of steps, ignoring the flashes of pain in his aching legs. With his metal-handled walking stick raised up and ready to strike, he eased open the front door.

Chapter 43

G REY SLIPPED INTO THE FOYER AND TOOK IN THE SCENE instantly. Two strides and he brought his stick around with full force, slashing across his body. His target didn't have time to react. The man had Phebe Webster in his grasp, one hand across her mouth. He was turned three-quarters away, facing the entrance to the sitting room. By the time he noticed Grey, it was too late. The metal handle of the walking stick struck home behind the man's right knee.

He yelped, and one hand shot down to the injured leg. It was enough for Phebe to pull free from his grasp. At that instant a second man entered from the sitting room. He held the carrying case open and facing out from him, so as to display the thunderstone to his partner. He let the case fall from his hands and reached inside his dark brown frock coat.

Grey sprang forward, swinging his walking stick overhead once more. The man drew a revolver, but before he could aim, Grey smashed the stick down on his right hand. There was an audible crack as the metal handle met the gunman's knuckles. A thin spray of blood shot into the air as the gun clattered onto the polished hardwood floor.

With a glance back, Grey saw that the first man was no immediate threat. He was still clutching at his right knee and leaning against the wall with all his weight on his left leg. Phebe, recovering her wits after a moment, launched a kick into the man's left shin that sent him toppling over.

"Go on!" Grey shouted. "Get out of here!"

Phebe bolted through the open front door.

The second man cradled his broken and bleeding fingers, distracted from all else for the moment. Grey seized the opening to drive a fist into the side of the man's face. The thunderstone had rolled out when its case was dropped. Grey started toward it. The gunman reached out from where he lay on the floor and snagged Grey by the ankle. He went sprawling but managed to yank his leg free from the man. The first intruder had risen to one knee and had the same idea as Grey; he lurched forward at the thunderstone. Before he could grasp it, Grey swiped his stick along the floor. The angled handle snagged around the stone's curved surface, and Grey slid it away, out of the first man's reach.

Grey rolled to his side, then scooped up the stone as he got to his feet. Behind him the second man had recovered his pistol. He raised it with his left hand to aim at Grey. As Grey dashed out the front door, he heard the gunshot shatter glass in one of the small side windows. Phebe stood on the pathway to the street. She emitted a small shriek at the gunshot, and then, seeing that Grey was out safely, she turned and ran for the sidewalk. Within half a block, Grey caught up to her. They both paused and glanced back to see the two attackers appear in front of the Webster house. A couple of neighbors who had peered out at the commotion now disappeared back into their houses.

Grey sucked in a mouthful of air, wincing at the various pains shooting through his sore legs. He was about to urge Phebe on, but she had already started running again. They turned onto Pine Street. A horse-car had just passed and was thirty yards ahead of them. They chased it, following the rails that ran down the side of the street and garnering strange looks from the late-evening pedestrians whom they passed. As they drew even with the rear step to board the car, Grey pressed the thunderstone into Phebe's arms. With his free hand, he took hold of her elbow and swung her up onto the step. The effort left him a few yards behind the moving car, and his legs were straining as he caught up once more. He used his walking stick this time to hook the upright post at the end of the car and pull himself forward onto the step. Phebe made room and grabbed hold of his lapel, helping to get him steady on his feet. The pair of them collapsed into the two closest seats. Behind them, at the intersection, their two pursuers appeared and looked in the direction of the car but did not give chase.

"That'll be a dime, sir. Assuming you're paying for the lady, too."

At the sound of the creaky voice, Grey and Phebe looked up at the conductor. The old man's glassed-over eyes showed no hint of surprise or any real interest in their sudden arrival. To him everything was perfectly normal, all part of the routine. The absurdity of the man's humdrum expression after she and Grey had just fled for their lives was too much for Phebe. She was seized by a spasm of nervous laughter.

Phebe watched as Grey tried to answer the conductor in the affirmative but failed, too winded to speak. This caused her to laugh even harder. Grey dug a quarter out of his pocket, and the conductor made change with a look of utter boredom.

"Thank you for the fare, Mr. Grey," Phebe managed to say, "though, really, it's the least you can do after all the trouble you've caused."

He turned to her with a piqued expression and an eyebrow arched but said nothing. Phebe felt the urge to laugh rising once more.

Fifteen minutes later they were safe inside Grey's parlor. Mrs. Philbrick was out, so no one had seen them come in. Grey didn't light the gas jets until after he'd closed the heavy curtains. The nervous gaiety that had beset Phebe upon their earlier escape had now evaporated, giving way to the realization of how dangerous her situation had been. She sat in one of the spare chairs. Grey turned the lights up high. He could see that her face had gone pale, and so he reached for a decanter of brandy that he reserved for shaken visitors. Phebe accepted the tumbler in both hands with a tepid smile. After observing that a couple of small sips seemed to have a positive effect on her, Grey went to his phone. He rang the operator and requested to be put through to Archie Lean's residence.

Grey waited as he was connected and watched Phebe down the last of her brandy.

"What's this, Grey? I thought we we're each on his own in this thing. Need my help, don't you?"

"In a manner of speaking."

"I knew you'd come to your senses. What sort of trouble are you in now?"

"I'm not in trouble. It's Miss Phebe Webster." Grey glanced at Phebe, who was staring back at him with widened eyes. She marched over to the decanter and pulled out the stopper.

"Who, I should say, is no longer in any imminent danger either," Grey announced loudly for her benefit. He continued, in a quiet tone, giving Lean a brief summary of events and listening to the deputy's plan of action before hanging up.

"Do you feel safe going home?" Grey asked. "Deputy Lean is arranging to have men comb through your house. I suspect there's likely an officer there already, given the gunshot that attracted your neighbors' attention. He's agreed to post a man outside until morning."

"I don't think I could sleep a wink in the house tonight. The front window is shattered. Not all the staff will even be back until morning."

"A hotel, then. Do you have a preference?"

"I don't feel safe going anywhere at the moment. Those men are out there somewhere."

"I suspect they've been dissuaded from pursuing us further. They didn't chase the railcar, and one has some broken fingers," Grey said.

"But you drew the curtains as soon as we got here. That means you think they know who you are and where you live. They could be waiting outside this very minute."

"If it would put you more at ease, I could step outside and reconnoiter the surrounding area. Make sure that no one's lurking about in the shadows watching our every move."

"Step out and leave me here by my lonesome, with killers just waiting to get at me?"

"Don't take me the wrong way, and as they say, there's no accounting for taste, but I believe it was the thunderstone, not you, they were after."

The stone was set on his desk. Grey placed his hand on it.

"That useless piece of rock. I ought to bring it to the quarry and blast it down to bits of sand. I just want to be done with all this, feel safe again." Phebe placed her hand on the stone as well, her fingers brushing Grey's. "I don't want to leave here tonight."

Grey regarded her for a long moment. He could smell the scent of brandy on her lips, see the tension lingering in her eyes.

"Of course," he said. "I could speak with my landlady as soon as we hear her come in. I'm certain she could accommodate you downstairs for one night."

"I don't want to leave," Phebe said.

She leaned in, lifting herself up on her toes to kiss him. "I just want to feel safe, Perceval," she whispered.

Her arms went around him. A second later his hands slid around to her back, holding her close to him. Their lips parted for an instant before Grey kissed her again. He picked her up in his arms, overcoming the ruffles and underlayers that made up her full evening dress. She put her hands around his neck as he swept her across the study to his bedchamber.

Chapter 44

GREY HEARD THE DOWNSTAIRS DOOR IN THE HALLWAY close. He moved across to the tall windows that looked over High Street and watched his landlady, Mrs. Philbrick, exit and march down the street to begin her morning round of errands. The last thing he felt like dealing with at the moment were the scandalized looks, or even an audible gasp, from his landlady upon witnessing a woman leaving his rooms at this hour.

Rasmus Hansen was waiting atop the carriage to deliver Phebe Webster back to her house. Grey understood from Lean that a patrolman was still stationed there.

"All looks ready," he said.

Phebe gave him an apprehensive smile before checking herself once more in the mirror. She'd done the best she could with the tools and materials that constituted a gentleman's toilet, but her hair was far from perfect. Her makeup was a disaster, and, worst of all, the evening dress she was still wearing had no business putting in an appearance on a sidewalk at this time of the morning.

"Thank you, Perceval. I'm sorry for so much fuss. Not to say that I'm at all . . ." She waited by the door and hoped her eyes were doing a better job than her lips in explaining her awkward behavior.

He gave her a small nod. "You appreciate the discretion. And your perfectly understandable desire to avoid any potentially compromising public appearance is in no way a reflection upon your feelings or thoughts toward me and what's happened between us. Which feelings and thoughts are yours alone and need not be subjected to the undue rigors caused by outside speculation and rumor."

"Yes." She smiled at him again, this time without any hint of apprehension. "Something like that."

He escorted her down the steps to the front entryway. Phebe waited just inside the door as Grey stepped out to assess the situation along the sidewalk. Rasmus had the carriage parked directly before the stairs. From the base of the front steps, Grey gestured Phebe to come along.

"Say, Mr. Grey, isn't that the doctor's niece, Mrs. Prescott?" Rasmus asked from his driver's seat atop the carriage. "It is. Well, ain't this a fine old morning?"

Grey looked up the sidewalk. Just twenty paces along, he saw a brunette stepping away from a cab that had just parked. He instantly recognized Helen Prescott. She looked the same as the last time he'd seen her, almost a full year past. Even from this distance, her clear blue eyes stood out from the fair skin of her comely face. Her long, dark hair was piled and secured at the back of her head. She held a packet in her arms. From her stylish yet functional dress, he guessed she might have been on her way to work; perhaps she'd already resumed her post at the historical society. He glanced back up the steps. Phebe had not yet emerged. She seemed to be making some last-minute refinement in her appearance.

"Mrs. Prescott?" Grey said as she neared.

"Surprised to see me? Delia and I came home earlier than we'd planned."

"I wasn't expecting you"—Grey tried to manage a smile—"here."

Helen's smile flickered for a second, but she launched into an explanation. "When you didn't answer my note about collecting the information we found, I thought I would come by and deliver it for you."

It seemed she was about to say more when her eyes drifted to her left and a sudden focus appeared on her face. Grey already knew what she had seen and how she was interpreting it. Still, he couldn't stop himself from turning to look in that same direction. Phebe was coming down the steps. Her evening dress struck Grey as even more blatantly out of place than it had been just minutes ago. When he turned again to Helen, her eyes were full and wide, her lips pursed. The packet she'd been holding at her side was now clutched across her chest with both hands.

"Yes, well, I see you're . . . occupied. I . . . I should have telephoned ahead."

Phebe reached the bottom of the stairs. Though she greeted Grey and Helen with a curious smile, her voice was perfectly natural. "Perc—Mr. Grey, aren't you going to introduce us?"

"Yes, of course. Miss Phebe Webster, this is Mrs. Helen Prescott. From the Maine Historical Society. You're there again, I take it?"

"Yes," Helen answered. "As I mentioned, I have some information from Archie and Mr. Meserve. Some historical documents they wanted you to see. I thought it would be helpful if I brought them as soon as possible. I tried the other day, but Mrs. Philbrick said you were off."

"Thank you." Grey accepted the packet of papers from her. "Yes, this is most helpful. Thank you so much."

"If you want to discuss it, with them . . . I mean, you could . . ." Helen stammered.

"Certainly, I'll make arrangements."

There was an uncomfortable moment of silence during which Helen and Grey both looked down the sidewalk to see the cab that had delivered her already departing. It was Rasmus who brought the awkward pause to a merciful end.

"Mrs. Prescott's cab's gone off. I could take her, if it's not too much of an inconvenience."

"Of course." Grey turned to Phebe to assure her agreement. "It's the least I can do after she's come out of her way with this valuable information."

"Certainly," Phebe said with genuine enthusiasm.

After a stilted handshake between them, Grey held the carriage door for Helen, and Rasmus took her off down the street.

Grey hailed a hansom cab. When it pulled to the curb, he offered his hand to assist Phebe into the carriage. Rather than immediately accept, she cast a wary eye toward Grey.

"That was all very queer. Who was that woman, Perceval? She seemed rather upset with you."

"Mrs. Prescott was involved in a prior inquiry."

"Mrs.?"

"A widow," Grey said.

"Involved in a prior inquiry? I wonder if that's how you'll refer to me one day," Phebe said as she entered the cab, her tone slightly taunting.

"It was a professional association."

"It struck me as more personal in nature," she said as Grey settled into the seat beside her. Any hint of teasing had been replaced by a sincere tone that bordered on concern. "Is there something I should know?"

"No. Nothing that affects you."

"But it affects you, doesn't it?" she asked.

"Even in its abridged version, the story is not a short or simple one to tell."

"You're only succeeding in piquing my interest even further. And I'm not one to let the truth of a matter remain hidden from my view, any more than you are."

The driver, who was awaiting instructions, cleared his throat.

"Very well. I'll explain as we ride."

As they rumbled along over the paving stones, Grey gave Phebe a very general and vague account of the murder inquiry he'd conducted with Deputy Lean the summer before, starting with a murdered prostitute. Recognition flickered across Phebe's features. It wasn't surprising, given that the news at the time had been rather sensational. Grey omitted mentions of other related murders, only stating that evidence had come to light that this murder had been inspired by a fascination with spiritualism and black magic. That detail seemed to grab Phebe's attention. Even the most rational of people tended to have a strong reaction to the topic. Likewise he left out the connections to Portland's temperance union. He also failed to include mention of Dr. Steig's name or the true manner of that good man's death, only offering that both Helen and her uncle had assisted in the investigation and that the stress had ultimately proved too much for the older man and his frail health.

"That's terrible."

"The trouble didn't end there for Mrs. Prescott. The murderer and a female accomplice of his were aware of our inquiry and of Mrs. Prescott's assistance. They abducted her and her eight-year-old daughter."

Phebe's hand went to her mouth. "Is she all right? The girl?"

Grey nodded. "Deputy Lean rescued her from one of the bay islands.

The killer's female accomplice had her and intended to burn the girl alive."

Phebe's hand remained at her mouth. Her eyes had gone wider than Grey would have thought possible.

"She was pulled from the flames just in time," he assured her.

"What of the woman—the accomplice?" Phebe's voice trembled, barely more than a whisper. Her eyes harbored a look of deep horror.

"She died. The deputy pursued and confronted her. But she was quite deranged and took her own life—set herself on fire. Lean couldn't save her."

Tears escaped and ran down her cheeks. Grey handed her his handkerchief.

"I'm sorry, I don't know what's come over me," she said as she dried her eyes. "Still emotional after my own scare last night, I suppose. It's just horrific—the whole story. Whatever happened to the murderer? I hope you caught him."

"He died in a fall."

She was quiet for a moment.

"I don't remember hearing about any of this in the newspapers."

"It was not an investigation sanctioned by the police. There were conflicting considerations among city officials," Grey said.

Phebe had quickly regained her composure. "I suppose that to mean that there were influential people involved who would be embarrassed by the airing of the truth."

"One of several unfortunate aspects of the inquiry."

"It always seems to be the way. If a man has money or influence enough, the world never gets to know his true crimes. Walk down the street with a smile and a wave and we all remain none the wiser about the blood on his hands." The grief and horror in her voice yielded to a genuine tone of righteous anger. "It's shameful."

Grey's thoughts turned to Louis Beauchamp atop Katahdin, but he refrained from making any further comment. They arrived, and as Grey paid the driver, Phebe started up the walk. Her steps were tentative at first, but then she caught sight of her uncle in the window and she hurried on through the front door.

"Uncle Euripides, thank you for coming." She noticed that the mess had all been cleared away. The bullet-shattered window by the door was the only indication of the violence from the night before, the last bit to prove that anything untoward had transpired. "Wasn't there supposed to be a police officer?"

"He told me what happened, and I sent him off. Police loitering about my father's house like it's some dockfront saloon. Disgraceful." Euripides Webster noticed Grey in the doorway, and his body gave a slight shudder of distaste.

"And what in the world is *he* doing here?" Euripides looked Phebe over with a suspicious eye. "Most unbecoming. You should have gone directly to my house."

"Don't be insulting. Mr. Grey has been nothing but a gentleman. His landlady was kind enough to accommodate me in her rooms for the night. After the trouble here, I was quite shaken. Couldn't bear the thought of heading out of doors into the night again. It was all very disturbing."

"Yes, well, the staff is home now, and that window will be fully replaced before lunch. All good as new." He looked Phebe and Grey over, saw that neither of them was carrying anything, and a frown creased his brow. "So where's the stone, then? I'll take it for safekeeping."

Phebe's eyes shot from Euripides to Grey, her confusion and disappointment evident.

"I'm afraid that won't be possible," Grey said. "In addition to its involvement in matters of murder, it is now also a key piece of evidence in the criminal break-in here. The stone will need to be turned over temporarily to the police"

"Unacceptable. Phebe's not pressing charges in this matter." Euripides waved toward the broken window. "Therefore there is no criminal matter to pursue. The family property should be returned immediately."

"Dangerous men break in and threaten your niece's safety and you wish to exclude the police?"

"I shall see to her safety with privately hired men. Ones who can be counted on without reservation, men without other duties that interfere."

"Men who would scale mountains and commit cold-blooded murder if you ordered it?" Grey asked.

"What's he saying, Uncle?"

"I haven't the slightest idea. More of the man's nonsensical rubbish."

"During the process of my recovering the thunderstone, a man was shot dead atop Mount Katahdin several days ago. The gunman then tried to kill Chief Jefferson and myself," Grey explained.

Phebe let out a small gasp and stepped back from Euripides. "That day in your office, you said you'd see him dead before you let him have the thunderstone."

"What a man might say in the heat of a moment and the truth of him, his actions, are often two very different things, my dear. Something you'd be wise to learn before you get yourself into trouble." Euripides then threw a spiteful glance at Grey.

"It seems I'm in trouble already, and that I have quite a lot to learn. But right now I need to retire to my room and compose myself. This is all rather too much to consider at the moment. Mr. Grey, please retain the thunderstone for me, for the time being." She then turned to Euripides with a glare almost as stern as his. "Uncle, we can speak later."

"Of course," Grey answered, before adding, "I'll show myself out."

"I'll see to that," Euripides said.

Phebe made her way up the staircase but paused on the second-floor landing, out of sight of the two men. She listened as the voices moved toward the front door.

"The murder has been reported to local authorities," Grey said. "They'll recover the body soon, if they haven't already. The truth will come out—I mean to see to that."

"What truth. Some Indian fellow gets a bullet in his brain while out in the middle of nowhere. What can you ever hope to prove, Grey?"

"It was murder. You may just as well have pulled the trigger yourself."

"It's your word and that false Indian chief's against whose? Some unseen person with a rifle. That ought to narrow it down to every single man in the north country. You mean to discover the identity of this mountaintop hunter and then somehow connect his actions to me, all because of a heated comment made to a knife-carrying fraud who invaded my place of business."

There was a long pause, and Phebe imagined Grey stoically regarding

Euripides. When he spoke, his voice was cold and detached, the opposite of her uncle's.

"Odd, what you said a moment ago. I don't remember telling you the
man killed was an Indian or where the fatal shot struck him."

"You'd never be able to prove a thing in a court of law." Euripides'
voice was laced with venom, as if Grey had leveled an accusation rather
than an observation.

"Yes, there is that to consider. Good day, Mr. Webster."

Grey stepped out, and the door slammed shut behind him.

Chapter 45

HELEN MARCHED ACROSS THE LOBBY OF THE PORTLAND Public Library, heading toward the historical society's office. Her boss, F. W. Meserve, had requested some additional supporting material for his morning appointment with Grey. Helen meant to make quick work of her delivery and then disappear into the library's stacks for an hour or so. She had no burning desire for another awkward encounter with Perceval. The sting of humiliation was still fresh in her mind.

She tried not to think of the stupid, girlish anticipation she'd felt and whether it had shown on her face when they'd first locked eyes on the sidewalk. A moment later she'd seen the young woman coming down Grey's steps. The looks on their faces as she approached had raised an alarm. The woman's evening dress confirmed the worst. But that wasn't what had left the worst sting in Helen's pride; her own dress did. She'd spent such time picking out the right dress herself, wanting to make an impression the first time he saw her in a year. She wouldn't make the same mistake again. Today she'd dressed plainly. She didn't plan to see Grey, but if she did, she wouldn't have him thinking she meant to make any impression on him. Not now.

She turned the knob and entered the historical society. Meserve was not at his seat, so she stepped forward, ready to deposit the folder in something that passed for a clear space on her boss's desktop. A movement to her side, by the window, caused her to flinch. The sight of Perceval Grey made her stop in her tracks. She held the folder to her body.

"You startled me," Helen explained with a polite half smile.

"Forgive me."

"Mr. Meserve asked for these papers."

"He's just gone into the back. Should be here again momentarily."

"Well, I'll leave these for him, then. Please let him know." She started toward the desk again, but Grey spoke before she could set the folder down, freezing her in place.

"Mrs. Prescott, about yesterday morning, I feel I ought to explain."

"Ah, so that's what you *feel*." Helen paused to overcome the iciness in her tone that she hadn't meant to share. "It's quite unnecessary, Mr. Grey. There's nothing for you to explain. You were simply escorting a client out of your apartment, albeit in a furtive manner. And despite the early hour, she was clearly still wearing her evening gown from the night before. We're both adults, and we have no business prying into each other's private affairs."

"Still, I don't want you to think that I . . . That is, if I'd known you were back in Portland, I would have paid you the courtesy of a visit."

"Most kind of you, Mr. Grey. But you aren't obligated. Last night I read again the few letters you sent over the past year. In response to mine. You certainly never promised me anything."

"That's true. I only ever meant to show you kindness."

"I suppose I have no one but myself to blame. Let myself read into your politely worded concerns and regards a warmer depth of meaning. Assumed it was just your naturally formal, aloof manner coming across on the page. But that was foolish of me."

"You underwent a very trying ordeal. A shared experience like the one we had last summer, culminating with a life-threatening event, naturally produces a powerful, lasting bond. It would be quite understandable for other emotions and feelings to become confused with those produced by our adventure. But the light of day and the passage of time allow us to sort out those feelings, consider them objectively for what they truly are."

"I suppose that's all a very roundabout and rational way of saying that you never truly had feelings for me."

"Mrs. Prescott—Helen—you are an attractive woman with a keen intellect and forthright character; as daring and spirited a lady as I have ever met."

"But?" Helen watched him pause and struggle for a response.

"Why did you go down to Connecticut and stay away so long?" he asked.

"Is that what happened? You felt abandoned? I invited you to come and visit."

"No, it's not that. Please, tell me why you went."

"For Delia. She was so upset by all that had happened. The change did her good. I needed to take her away."

"Precisely. And it was the right thing to do. You're a wonderful mother, and I wouldn't have expected you to do anything else." ·

"She's the most important thing in the world to me."

"Of course—I admire your level of devotion. It's something I fear I could never provide to another. The same undivided devotion I have to my work."

"Undivided?"

"I'm afraid so," he said.

"You may have noticed that most bright, talented men manage successful professions and a happy personal life as well."

Helen paused a moment. She'd cast the thought out as an appeal to common sense. Grey's dark eyes regarded her from what seemed a great distance. What at first seemed such an obvious answer to the situation she now recognized as a futile effort. She let go of the line, commending that faded hope to the deep. "But then I suppose that doesn't interest you. The sorts of things that allow other men to find contentment in their everyday, humdrum existence. You'd rather look into those darker hearts, the ones that carry rage and failures and misguided ambitions. Whatever else spurs them on to criminal acts."

The door to the back room opened, and F. W. Meserve appeared. Though he expected both Helen and Grey, he still looked surprised to see them. He pushed his spectacles up over the bridge of his nose.

"Ah, there you are, Helen. Is that the material?" He reached for the folder in her hand and motioned toward one of the chairs. "I was just about to enlighten Mr. Grey about the details of our findings on Thomas Webster."

"I do have some other work to get to," Helen said to Meserve as she slid toward the door. "I'm sure you can manage without me. You're more familiar with the material anyhow. Mr. Grey," she added with a curt nod before departing.

Meserve spent the next fifteen minutes going over the historical notes of William Willis's *History of Portland*. Behind his thick lenses, his normally beady eyes gleamed with conspiratorial delight. Grey interrupted only occasionally for clarification or to see the documents himself. When Meserve was done speaking, Grey sat silent for a minute with his eyes shut, reflecting on it all.

Finally he stood and drifted toward the window. "There is only one important question concerning the information contained in these marginal notes. Is it true?"

"We have no reason to doubt Willis's veracity. He was known as a most upright individual, a competent and dedicated historian," Meserve said.

"Then why didn't he include the information on Webster in his final historical manuscript?"

"The family remained prominent. Perhaps he didn't want to slander the man," Meserve suggested.

"Unlikely. Old Tom Webster comes across as perhaps hotheaded or vindictive against Mowat but mostly as an overly fervent American patriot. The only justification for excluding the references is that they are unconfirmed hearsay. If the information was confirmed, however, then it would paint a most mysterious picture of Thomas Webster." Grey turned away from the view of the outside world and went to the desk. He picked up one paper after another, glancing at each and setting it aside as he continued to speak.

"Why did Mowat seek him out, only to be taken hostage immediately afterward and have Webster lobby for his hanging? Why would Webster try to kill Mowat with his long-range musket shot at the deck of the *Canceaux*? Did Mowat purposely forgo other ports and raze Portland strictly to get at Webster? Why did Mowat's first landing party go directly to Webster's, and, when there, why didn't they hunt for the man when he fled? Instead they only searched his house, then burned it to the ground."

The flourish of speculative historical questions was too much for Meserve. His jowly face quivered in excitement. "And if Old Tom Webster killed the stranger Clough at the conclusion of the war, that's twice that men came to Portland, inexplicably looking for him."

"He had something they wanted." Grey's thoughts turned to the legal offices of Dyer & Fogg. Perhaps it was the thunderstone, the same object that was the focus of such attention now, a hundred years later. Grey recalled Albert Dyer reading the old man's queerly worded bequest of the thunderstone.

Meserve's voice interrupted Grey's thoughts, a sense of caution now mingling with the historian's excitement. "Of course, as you said earlier, this all hangs on whether the historical notes are even true. There's no way to corroborate Webster's role in the burning of Falmouth. Whatever secrets he had, they went with him to the grave."

"Maybe not just *his* grave," Grey said.

"What do you mean?"

"This man, Clough, the one reportedly killed at the end of the war just near Webster's newly built house. We can't verify why he came to Portland or what he had to do with Webster, but if we can confirm his death at that time, it would lend some credence to the other rumors swirling around Old Tom Webster. Not proof by any stretch, but a thread."

"A stranger to the town—I suspect he'd end up in an unmarked grave." Meserve stroked one pointed end of his thin mustache as he pondered the issue. "The Eastern Cemetery even had an area designated as the Strangers' section, for those who died friendless or poor. Buried them two to a grave. Though I'm not sure when that was formally established."

"It's uncertain we could find this man's marker, but worth the effort," Grey said.

"Agreed. Almost like an archaeological expedition—how exciting! I'll need to check the cemetery records. Though even if he's unlisted, there might still be a marker."

Meserve scrunched up his face into a tight ball of academic curiosity as he hurried out of the room in hot pursuit of the answer. Grey, forgotten in the historian's wake, showed himself out.

Chapter 46

LEAN AND MESERVE WENT THROUGH THE GATE OF THE EASTern Cemetery on Congress Street, passing the granite receiving tomb on their right. Though located at the foot of Munjoy Hill, the cemetery was still raised enough to provide an excellent view looking out over the city's business district as well as the waterfront and the islands of Casco Bay. The two men proceeded down Funeral Lane, a worn, L-shaped footpath that led into the heart of the graveyard before curving off to exit at Mountfort Street. Lean's eyes traveled over the ancient burial ground. A fence of granite posts and black wrought-iron spikes wound its way around to form an irregular, almost trapezoidal, shape that enclosed the five acres.

It was not a modern cemetery, orderly and well planned. This burial ground matched the city it served, all the more interesting for its untidy, haphazard layout. A few trees dotted the cemetery, and the grass was overgrown in most areas. There was no great uniformity to the place. Some of the rows tended to be ragged and imperfect. Tombs, above- and belowground, mixed with headstones of all shapes and sizes. Tall bright marble, rounded granite slabs, and small, rough-hewn fieldstones all mingled with one another, most angled forward or back to one degree or another. Upright pillars stood beside cracked, tilting markers. Lean was left with the impression that a massive haystack of stone markers had been shaken out from the heavens to fall where they might, and his job was to find a granite needle in all this.

"A lot of markers to look over," he said.

"The city more or less ceased burials thirty years ago. Still, there's over three thousand known graves, hundreds of unknown ones. The earliest official plot on record is 1717, but the graveyard was established fifty years before that. The city's original settlers are all lost to time. But we do know that they were buried in the southern corner."

Lean looked that way, toward the sharp drop-off at the back of the cemetery. Twenty-five years earlier, the city decided to extend Federal Street on through to join Mountfort. A twelve-foot-wide stretch along the edge of the burying ground was cut away and a tall retaining wall set in the name of civic progress. Old bones, marked and unmarked, were simply hauled away and used as fill along the edges of Portland's artificially widening neck.

Meserve's voice rattled on in the empty space of the graveyard. "There used to be a grand old solitary pine there. A low rock wall ran beside the ancient burial ground, to pen in grazing cattle. A dozen Colonial militia were ambushed and killed by Abenakis hiding behind the wall when the town was attacked by a large French and Indian force back in 1690. Their bones were left unburied for two years before the area was resettled."

"Speaking of lurking Indians, I expected Grey to meet us here," Lean said.

"He did mention something of a prior appointment."

"Did he? How convenient." The man's ongoing insistence on separate approaches to the investigation continued to irk Lean. There had been messages exchanged and information traded, but Lean couldn't shake the feeling that Grey was holding back from him. He suspected the man had some conflicting interests due to his secretive side investigation involving the late Horace Webster and the man's granddaughter.

"In any event," Meserve assured him, "we won't need to search the whole cemetery. I thought we'd start near the plots of Old Tom Webster's family, in case he felt obliged to bury this man Clough. That'll be ahead, near where the mower's working."

Lean glanced ahead at a stoop-backed man under a broad hat lethargically pushing a reel mower. From that distance Lean couldn't tell if the thick-bearded man was elderly or just plodding along at the natural pace of an unsupervised fellow being paid by the hour.

"If Clough's not there," Meserve continued, "then we'll have to cast about in the Strangers' section and hope for the best."

When they came to the bend in Funeral Lane, Meserve led the way off the path, taking an angle across the grass. As they approached their target, the groundskeeper moved off, with his wheel-driven rotary blades clacking loudly through the grass. He probably figured them for a pair of regular, familial visitors and meant to give them a bit of privacy. It took Meserve only a minute to locate the headstone of Thomas Webster, bearing a winged death's-head. Close by, in a cluster, stood the markers of his wife, various children, along with their spouses, and a few grandchildren who had died at early ages. Lean and Meserve found, buried amid the family grouping, two apparently unrelated headstones. Silas Martin had died in 1805. The second marker was small enough that it couldn't bear its inhabitant's full name. Stacked atop each other on the narrow face were the words HERE LIES N. F. AGEE 1787. The men traded guesses as to the identities of those two: cousins, close family friends, or maybe just solitary men shoe-horned in to whatever thin spaces could be found in the cemetery.

Meserve noticed an even smaller marker, dark with age and with a top corner missing. From where he stood, Lean couldn't make out any inscription. The pudgy historian got down on his hands and knees to study the face of the stone. A moment later he reached inside his coat and drew out a piece of paper. Lean watched him press the paper to the stone and rub at it with a small lump of charcoal.

"You certainly came prepared," Lean said.

"I had the paper, but the charcoal was just sitting there right on the ground. Rather fortuitous, I'd say, given what it revealed." Meserve held out the paper.

Lean took the sheet. The missing section of the stone left the first few letters truncated, but he could identify the name as J. Clough with a 1783 death. "Most fortuitous indeed."

There were no other visitors in the whole cemetery. Lean's eyes landed on the stoop-shouldered man who was slowly pushing his mower toward the Mountfort Street side of the cemetery. He motioned to Meserve and strolled off in the same direction. They made it the majority of the way to the side-street exit when Lean paused. He was trying to study the groundskeeper without being thoroughly obvious. He noticed the three tablelike tombs close at hand along a narrow path. The celebrated occupants gave him an excuse to stop and linger.

He glanced at the lengthy inscription set into the marble of the center tomb. It began, BENEATH THIS STONE MOLDERS THE BODY OF CAPTAIN WILLIAM BURROUGHS LATE COMMANDER OF THE UNITED STATES BRIG ENTERPRISE WHO WAS MORTALLY WOUNDED ON THE 5TH OF SEPT.

1813. The word "molders" stuck in his brain and left him with an uneasy feeling, like having walked through a spiderweb that even after being brushed away leaves a clingy feeling of unease upon the skin.

Like most Portlanders he'd learned the story as a schoolboy. The young commander of the USS *Enterprise* had met Captain Blyth of the HMS *Boxer* in battle, and both captains were hit by cannon fire. Blyth was killed quickly. Though grievously wounded, the American commander lived long enough to secure the victory. After the British surrendered, he was presented with Captain Blyth's sword, only to refuse it. He ordered that it be returned to his counterpart's family in England with honor. Then he died.

The ships had then returned to Portland, where the city hosted a grand funeral honoring both the fallen commanders. The two men were buried side by each, at peace together for eternity. Two years later a junior American officer finally succumbed to the wounds he'd suffered in the battle and was entombed beside the captains. Lines of poetry commemorating the battle seeped into Lean's mind. A sly grin stole onto his face as he eyed the groundskeeper twenty yards away. Lean cleared his throat and from his diaphragm unleashed the lines.

> *"I remember the sea-fight far away,*
> *How it thundered o'er the tide!*
> *And the dead captains, as they lay*
> *In their graves, o'erlooking the tranquil bay,*
> *Where they in battle died."*

An exasperated groan issued from the groundskeeper, who announced, "Of course, your young Longfellow was still in short pants when that battle was fought."

Lean laughed. "I thought that might be you when we found the charcoal rub. And I knew that Henry Wadsworth Longfellow's siren song would lure you from that disguise."

"Less a song and more a trampling of history," the groundskeeper answered. "The tranquil bay where they died was up by Pemaquid Point—Muscongus Bay, not Casco. So he must have had some set of ears on him to hear the thunder of battle so many miles away."

"It's called poetic license," Lean said.

"A pretty phrase for something other than the simple truth."

"And I have a few more pretty phrases at the tip of my tongue if you care to hear them." Lean chuckled before noticing Meserve's perplexed stare.

"That's Grey under that ridiculous false beard." Lean turned to Grey and added, "Is that really necessary?"

"I'm still being watched," Grey said.

"Even now?" Lean couldn't resist scanning Mountfort and Congress streets for any signs of unwelcome observers.

Grey shook his head as he continued his charade of mowing the grass. "We're alone for the moment."

"Good." Lean looked back toward the patch of Webster graves. Grey had left a sloppy, random swath of cut grass in his wake. "Because I don't think you would have fooled anyone watching you closely. You missed a few spots."

"Not the spot that matters," Grey replied. "Clough's buried right near Tom Webster."

"Keep your friends close and your enemies closer, even in death, eh?" Meserve said.

"So, Grey, you think it's all true, then?" Lean asked. "Webster had something that Mowat was willing to burn Falmouth for. Later, after the war, Clough came looking for it as well and got himself killed by Webster."

"There seems to be at least a grain of truth to the suspicions about Webster's shady past. Captain Mowat burning Falmouth to get at Webster or something the man was hiding could be a plausible theory," Grey said.

"But where does that get us?" Lean asked. "If it was all owing to the thunderstone, then why? It's just a rounded hunk of granite."

"Quartzite," Grey corrected him.

"Ah, yes, an important distinction, that," Lean said. "What I mean is, I can't swear for Clough, but I'm certain that Mowat was no Indian. If the thunderstone was what he was after, it wasn't for some absurd Indian ceremony like that Chief Jefferson had in mind. There's got to be more to it."

Grey dabbed the sweat from his face with a handkerchief. "Maybe Professor Horsford was only half off the mark. The symbols on the stone obviously aren't Viking runes, but they are a sort of coded message pointing to something."

"Didn't the Websters tell you it's something to do with an old treasure? How about a buried treasure?"

Grey scowled at Lean, but the deputy plowed ahead with his reasoning. "Someone's been going far out of his way to dig below all the building sites that Old Tom Webster ever owned. And here's a little nugget I haven't told you yet. One of the properties was purchased a few months back. But the new owner must not have found what he was looking for, since he's already put it back up for sale. And the excavations at Vine Street and at the tailor shop happened afterward."

"How can you be sure the owner is even aware of the building's connection to Old Tom Webster?" Grey asked.

"The buyer is one Jerome Morse," Lean said.

"Jotham Marsh's flunky," Grey said as a look of understanding dawned on him. "The same one you punched in the nose last year."

Meserve flinched away from Lean, who assured him, "I promise—the man had it coming."

"So now what?" Meserve asked with a feverish look in his eyes. This was clearly the most excitement he'd had outside the confines of a book in quite some time.

A few moments of collective contemplation followed before Grey broke the silence.

"We know that Thomas Webster had the thunderstone at the time of his death in 1821. For the connection to Mowat and the killing of Clough to hold up, we need to know he had it as early as the Revolutionary War. Attorney Dyer may know the details. Also, he still has the original will and testament. I'll need to see the list of other property mentioned therein. Rule out the possibility that there's something else of value there besides the thunderstone."

"You go and confirm it with the lawyer, but I'm assuming all you'll find is the thunderstone." A resolve that had been absent throughout much of the discussion now returned to Lean's voice. "That's what Frank Cosgrove stole in the first place. So we need to decipher what those symbols mean. If whoever killed Cosgrove figures it before us and finds what he's after, he'll vanish without another clue."

Chapter 47

G REY SAT AT A TABLE NEAR THE WINDOWS OF THE ATH-
enaeum's second-floor reading room. Justice Holmes's telegram
of that morning had alerted him to the fact that the Boston police
had finally returned Eben Horsford's book. He'd responded with a pair
of telegrams to Boston along with the earliest train departure he could
find. Now the newly repaired manuscript of the professor's final book
was spread before him. He finished his last sketch of the twenty-four
symbols reproduced in the late professor's treatise. Grey glanced out the
window; there was nothing to see except some people passing under the
streetlamps and a few lit windows in the nearby buildings. He glanced at
his pocket watch. Father Leadbetter's telegram that morning, in answer
to Grey's, had stated he could meet at nine o'clock. The man was now
three minutes late.

The sound of tentative footsteps floated through the air and Grey
looked up to see Father Leadbetter in the entranceway at the far end of
the reading room. Grey raised his hand to acknowledge the man, who
smiled and did likewise. The former minister had replaced his ratty robe
with a proper suit, but it was old and worn, giving him the appearance of
some cloistered academic who hadn't stepped away from his studies long
enough in the past two decades to update his wardrobe.

"Sorry I'm late," Leadbetter said.

Grey motioned to the seat beside him. "Not at all. Thank you for
coming."

"My pleasure. Your telegram was most intriguing," Leadbetter said as he settled himself into the chair and angled the book for a
clearer view. "So these are the symbols you mentioned, eh? Well, let's
have a look."

"Thank you. Your expertise is most appreciated. I haven't had time to conduct the necessary research on my own. The Portland Library is sadly lacking in materials on Rosicrucian alchemical symbols."

Leadbetter smiled and nodded before he began to study the pages in earnest. His bony fingers turned each page with the utmost care as he worked through the book, pausing longer on some of the twenty-four images. Occasionally he muttered to himself, sounds that Grey tried to identify as indications of familiarity or puzzlement.

When there were no more symbols to consider, Grey asked, "Do you recognize any more of these as possible Rosicrucian figures?"

"Not Rosicrucian per se, but I do think that"—the older man paused as he did the mental arithmetic—"eleven of them could be said to represent basic alchemical symbols."

"And the others?"

"I could hazard a guess as to the origins or meanings of some if I were forced to, but I couldn't say for certain."

Grey flipped through the pages until he came to a pair of sheets each bearing a shape like a Roman numeral one. "What about these? It alone is a duplicate among the symbols, appearing twice in a row."

I   I

"Uppercase 'i.' Roman numeral ones. Something else entirely?" Leadbetter guessed.

Grey nodded and readied a blank sheet of paper. "The eleven symbols, then. Show me which ones they are."

Leadbetter started back to the beginning of the shapes. He flipped through, landing a finger and pronouncing an identity on eleven of the two dozen images: "Salt, lead, tin, dissolution, silver, mercury, iron, coagulation, copper, gold, sulfur."

As each of the symbols was identified, Grey quickly copied down each corresponding figure, collecting all eleven on a new single page. Then he studied this grouping.

"There are more than eleven symbols used in alchemy, correct?"

Leadbetter nodded his agreement. "Far more."

"So what do these mean? Why are these eleven chosen to be represented?"

"They are important ones, certainly."

Grey stared at the older man, awaiting clarification.

"Take them in groups." Leadbetter pointed to the images on Grey's page. "May I label them?"

Grey nodded his assent, and Leadbetter started his identifications.

"Salt, mercury, and sulfur are considered the Three Principles into which all things can be divided, allegorically speaking. They represent the form, spirit, and essence of things, more or less. We could discuss the philosophical subtleties of it for a long time, but you take the general flavor of the idea." Leadbetter gestured to the page again before continuing.

"We also have *solve* and *coagula*."

"I mentioned those when you came to see me earlier, when I showed you the picture of Baphomet. Two vital stages in the process of alchemy. *Solve* refers to the dissolution or breaking down of a thing into its distinct essential elements. Then, after purification, there is *coagula*. The coming together again, whereby the material is once again reconstituted, but now in its purest form. And finally there are the seven metals." Leadbetter labeled these each in order as he spoke.

"Lead, tin, silver, mercury, iron, copper, gold."

"You've mentioned mercury in two capacities," Grey said.

"Mercury has near-infinite capacities. It is the transformative and unifying essence, the alpha and the omega, the one and the all."

Grey was listening but focusing his attention on the drawings. "Very interesting."

"Do the symbols mean something to you?" the older man asked.

"Not all eleven, but——" Grey raised his index finger and then bent down to reach into his satchel. A moment later he produced another sheet of paper on which the seven images from the thunderstone were copied. "I am familiar with these seven, which appear among your eleven."

$$\text{☿} \quad \text{⚸} \quad \text{♀} \quad \text{☉} \quad \text{♄} \quad \text{♃} \quad \text{☾}$$

Leadbetter compared the two pictorial lists, then declared, "Well, obviously what you have there are the seven primary metals again. But I'd say you've got them out of order."

"Really? How's that?"

"You've ordered them starting with that one you showed me before, mercury. Truly it's lead not mercury that should be your starting point. In alchemy lead is the base metal, or, spiritually speaking, it represents the human body as the raw, base material. Lead is transformed through the alchemical process through the stages of tin, silver, mercury, iron, copper, and finally into gold, representing pure spiritual enlightenment." Leadbetter paused as he regarded Grey's papers. "Where'd you get your list of seven, if I may ask?"

"A different stone from that which held those twenty-four," Grey said.

Leadbetter frowned. "Do you suppose there's a connection between the two sources?"

Grey allowed himself a little smile. "Perhaps. But who can say what it might be?"

There was a moment of silence as each man realized they'd quickly come to the end of whatever path they'd been following or hoping to follow in the Athenaeum that night.

"Well, if it would help at all," Leadbetter said with a sudden burst of enthusiasm, "I could loan you some of my volumes on alchemy and the Rosicrucians. Maybe within the pages you could find some sort of explanation that would give you the answer you're looking for."

"That might be helpful indeed. I'm leaving tonight on the 10:15 to Portland. I could accompany you back to your rooms to collect the books."

Leadbetter waved off the idea. "No need for you to bother. I could hurry home and get them and meet you at the station. The B&M, ten-fifteen to Portland."

"That's most generous of you, Mr. Leadbetter. Thank you ever so much for all your assistance."

The two men headed downstairs, and Grey paused, making an excuse about needing to speak to one of the librarians. Leadbetter tipped his hat and hurried out the front door. Grey made his way toward one of the windows overlooking the entrance on Beacon Street. He couldn't fathom why the slow-moving Leadbetter had been so keen on making the trip to the North End alone to collect the offered books and lug them to the train station. It would have been simpler and quicker for Grey to accompany him.

He watched Leadbetter reach the sidewalk and turn right. Grey strode to a side door and exited. After making his way up a side alley he stopped at the corner to observe Leadbetter. A man in a dark overcoat stepped forward and placed a hand on the ex-minister, stopping the old man in his tracks. The man spoke to Leadbetter in hushed but urgent tones, seeming to berate the old man. Grey was about to step out and intercede when he saw Leadbetter say something in return. He shook his hands, palms upraised, as if explaining something. Then he pointed back at the Athenaeum. Both men glanced in that direction. Grey ducked his head back into the alleyway. When he glanced out again, he saw that Leadbetter and the shadowy figure had parted ways.

Grey paused in the darkness. Only now did he wish he'd called on McCutcheon to join him on tonight's task, but he hadn't thought his old colleague would be of any particular use at a library. He thought of the contents of his satchel and formed a plan. He had plenty of paper and even an envelope that would be large enough. What he needed now was a well-lit but inconspicuous spot, maybe an out-of-the-way café where he could complete his new task before setting off to the train station.

Chapter 48

GREY EDGED ALONG THE DARK SIDE OF THE MASSIVE, HANgarlike rail terminal. In his long, dark coat, he knew he'd pass unseen among the construction materials that littered the area. Five minutes earlier he'd observed Leadbetter waiting with a single book in hand near the entrance to the Boston & Maine line. Plenty of others lingered about as well, some of whom could have been the shadowy figure who'd accosted the old minister outside the Athenaeum an hour ago. Grey had paid a scrawny young paper hawker to go inside and verify the track number for the 10:15 to Portland.

He rounded the front of the terminal and peered into the dimly lit hangar. A smoky haze hung above the pigeons loitering in the rafters. Misty halos surrounded the lamps at the platforms and ticket windows far away at the base of the station. Grey stole into the wide-open mouth of the terminal like some Jonah entering the belly of a coal-fed behemoth. He crossed several of the rails that led from the colossal structure as he made his way to the train idling on Track 6 with thin wisps of smoke wafting up from its stack.

He was still early; the Portland train had not yet boarded. Grey clambered aboard at a coupling near the end of the still-vacant locomotive so that he could observe those milling about on the platform. He was met by a frowning conductor, who reminded him that they had not yet issued the boarding call. Grey feigned confusion, motioned to his walking stick, and claimed to need additional time to make his way aboard, owing to a gimpy leg. The unimpressed conductor directed him through the doors to the final car and into a private compartment.

With the room's gas lamp kept low, Grey peered from the edge of the small window. He saw Leadbetter enter the platform and scan the crowd that milled about, waiting to board. After another minute a rotund conductor hollered out the first boarding call. A nervous, almost panicked look overcame the former minister. Grey felt sorry for the man as he wandered aimlessly about the platform. Ever since the would-be assassin had tried to shoot him down outside the Seamen's Bethel, Grey had been noticing familiar figures lurking on the edges of his investigative activities—figures who reminded him of the one who'd waylaid Leadbetter near the Athenaeum earlier. Grey recognized that Leadbetter's confrontation might have nothing to do with this investigation. A man who'd done enough to get removed from the ministry could have plenty of people who bore him no goodwill. Still, when Leadbetter approached the train, trying to glance up into the compartment windows as he passed, Grey leaned against the interior wall, concealing himself from the old man's view.

He pulled the shade closed, turned the lamp higher, and settled into his seat. With his eyes closed, he directed his thoughts toward the puzzle of Horsford's twenty-four symbols and what they could reveal about the meaning of the thunderstone. There was obviously a connection intended. The seven repeated on Old Thomas Webster's thunderstone represented the seven metals in the alchemist's process of transforming lead to gold. Horsford's twenty-four symbols were copied from etchings on a rock near Portland. A rock along the coast would be visible to anyone, but Tom Webster had hidden the thunderstone, meaning it was those seven symbols that mattered most. They were the key to whatever he was concealing. But what did they represent? Just the alchemical elements, or were they a message, a code of letters or numbers? Were the twenty-four just a distraction to hide the seven? That made no sense. Why carve figures into rock if they meant nothing?

The two sets had to fit together. The twenty-four could be the base pattern or alphabet of the hidden message meant for the Webster family heir to the thunderstone. If so, it was an unusual sort of code, in that it contained a single pair of duplicate images. Two "I" symbols were included and placed next to each other. Grey latched onto those two "I" figures as the glaring anomaly, the likeliest key to unlocking this code.

The train sounded its departure and lurched to life, moving slowly away from the terminal. A minute later Grey opened his eyes at the sound of approaching footsteps. He only now realized that during the boarding process no one had passed by his compartment. In fact, he hadn't heard anyone else even enter the final car where he was located. His door opened, and Father Leadbetter stumbled into the compartment. Behind him was a stocky man with a flat, mean face and a pistol pointed at Grey.

"Don't try anything."

The gunman gave Leadbetter a shove, forcing him onto the seat next to Grey. Then the man eased aside to let two others enter the compartment. Grey instantly recognized Dr. Jotham Marsh and his fawning lackey, Jerome Morse. The two latest arrivals took the opposite seats, facing Grey. The gunman closed the door and remained standing outside, blocking the small window that looked into the railcar's aisle.

"Father Leadbetter, what a surprise. Friends of yours?" Grey asked.

"He was nice enough to alert us of your intentions as soon as he received your telegraph," Marsh said.

"Forgive me, Mr. Grey, I had no choice." Leadbetter's face was gripped by self-reproach.

Jerome casually drew a pocket pistol. Grey recognized the weapon as a Remington Model 95 double-barreled derringer. Jerome bent forward and confiscated Grey's walking stick, which had been leaning nearby against the wall.

"Yes, his alternatives were rather limited," Jerome said.

"A situation not unlike the one you currently occupy," Marsh added.

Grey glanced at the door and the gunman standing on the other side.

"Don't worry, Grey, we won't be disturbed. I've made arrangements with the conductor to ensure that we have complete privacy on this car." Marsh held out a hand. "Now, the pages you copied from Professor Horsford's unpublished manuscript."

Grey drew the folded pack of papers from his inside coat pocket and turned them over to Marsh. The older man flipped through the images while his young follower Jerome peered over his shoulder.

"Come, Grey, why don't you save us all a bit of time and trouble and tell me your conclusions as to the meaning of the symbols. Above and beyond what you've already discussed with your esteemed colleague here," Marsh said, with a nod at Leadbetter.

"Obviously intended as some type of code or cipher, but as to the meaning, I must say I haven't yet the faintest inkling."

"That's most disappointing," Marsh said. "I was hoping that you might stumble upon the answer I'm looking for and lead me to what I seek. It's why I let you live this long."

"Odd. I was sure I was still alive because I'm smarter than you, your incompetent thug can't aim a pistol from atop a carriage, and furthermore I'm smarter than you," Grey said.

Jerome scoffed at the last comment. "You said that already."

"You caught that? Very good."

Marsh put a hand on Jerome's arm before the younger man could do anything more than scowl at Grey. "Brash words from a man in your current predicament. But such arrogance is to be expected from one who has so fervently dedicated himself to his misplaced faith in objective reasoning. Yes, you possess an estimable intellect, Grey, but what has it gained you?"

Marsh pulled a silver case from his pocket. He opened it and readied a cigarette. "You scurry about, eyes to the ground, teasing out the little details that reveal their finite secrets, and then you puzzle out the answer to this incident or that crime. Who stole this thing, or who murdered that one wretch or another, as if any of that will ever matter. There are so many grand, universal mysteries that remain hidden from mankind. Yet you've devoted a great mind to answering only the little questions about the meager lives and deaths of utterly insignificant people. What a waste." After a deep drag, Marsh exhaled slowly through his nostrils. The two thin lines reached their nadir, then reversed themselves, rising in smoky tendrils that twirled about his face.

"The real shame of it is that now your intellect has failed you. And on the one occasion when it might actually have answered a question of monumental, even universal, importance. So if you are ignorant of the solution to our little riddle, then you are of no use to me." Marsh's tone held no threat; he was merely tossing out a fact.

"Those runes won't do you any good either," Grey noted. "They're only half of the puzzle. And I have the other half."

"Don't you think I was careful enough to make a copy of the thunderstone's seven symbols when I had the chance?"

"Of course," Grey conceded. "I just wanted you to verify my suspicion that you were behind the original theft of the thunderstone. And thus also responsible for the related murder of Frank Cosgrove. Disinterring his body and placing the burned corpse on Vine Street was meant to keep prying eyes away from the scene long enough to carry out the necessary excavations in the cellar."

"In part." The skin around Marsh's dour lips spread into a grim smile. "Fear has many uses. Its power upon weak and superstitious minds is not to be underestimated. That one act will continue to serve my purposes long after the specific details of Cosgrove's death have been forgotten."

"Yet when the thunderstone yielded no results to you, you handed it away, to throw suspicion down another trail." Grey saw a flash of annoyance in Marsh's eyes. Something about giving the thunderstone over to Chief Jefferson rankled him. That hadn't been Marsh's idea. Or something about the scheme had gone wrong. "You don't know what its symbols meant, so you had to keep digging up the cellars of every site ever owned by Thomas Webster."

"Yes, unfortunately, we had to try things the hard way. Until the contents of Professor Horsford's book came to my attention."

"And thus your need for Chester Sears to steal it."

"Who'd have thought a professional thief could make such a horrific mess of so easy a task?" Jerome said.

"Tell me about the cellars of Thomas Webster's former properties. What convinced you of the need to dig?" Grey asked Marsh.

"Vitriol, Mr. Grey. Pure vitriol."

Grey stared, awaiting a further explanation.

"*Visita Interiora Terrae Rectificando Invenies Occultum Lapidem,*" Jerome said, then translated himself. " 'Visit the interior of the earth and purifying you will find the hidden stone.' "

"The motto is from *L'Azoth des Philosophes,* a fifteenth-century work of the alchemist Basilius Valentinus," explained Leadbetter in a cautious voice. "It's a reference to the philosopher's stone."

"The Great Work," Grey said.

"Very good, Grey. You do pay attention," Marsh said.

"Yes, insane statements uttered by a man who looks like he ought to know better do tend to stick in one's mind."

Marsh chuckled, a cold and bitter sound. "I'm also glad to see you've kept your wit. It makes you slightly less annoying."

"I . . . I don't understand," Leadbetter stammered. "What's this to do with the philosopher's stone?"

"It appears that your old friend thinks he's close to actually getting his hands on it," Grey said.

"What? That's ridiculous," Leadbetter answered.

Grey watched as Leadbetter stared at him and then turned to study Jotham Marsh's face. The former minister's expression flickered from incredulous to stunned, then to appalled.

"Impossible. The stone—the Great Work—it's not . . . It's only a principle, an ideal to be pursued. It can't actually be obtained!"

There was a hint of genuine disappointment in Marsh's voice as he spoke to Leadbetter. "You taught me a great many things when I was younger. But the most valuable lesson you had to offer was that a man who abhors greatness will never achieve anything."

"You can't achieve something that's impossible," Leadbetter said, "that doesn't exist."

"You've forgotten your history, my poor fellow. The Count de St. Germain uncovered the mystery and completed the work."

"Anecdotes and rumors—never proved," Leadbetter said.

"The accounts of his wondrous life are rather convincing," Marsh said.

"It's always easy to convince one of something he deeply desires to believe," Grey said.

"And virtually impossible to convince a man with knowledge that he lacks wisdom. Since I have no need to convince you of anything, Grey, I won't waste my time trying." Marsh folded his hands, with a satisfied smile.

For a moment it seemed the man would let the matter lie, but then he could no longer deny himself the luxury of relishing his victory.

"Suffice it to say that there exists in nature a force immeasurably more powerful than anything man can create or you can comprehend. With it a single man, possessing the knowledge of how to direct it, could change the world. This force was known to the ancients, a universal agent having equilibrium for its supreme and only law. Its control is dependent upon a mastery of the great arcanum of transcendental magic. The Count de St. Germain possessed a device to channel this power, and soon it will be mine."

The train's whistle sounded two warning blasts; it must have been approaching a crossing. Grey waited until he was sure no more blasts would follow, then turned to the older man seated next to him.

"Father Leadbetter, didn't you tell me before that this Count de St. Germain was seen at the various European capitals and royal courts throughout the 1700s?"

"According to various tales and anecdotes. You have to piece them together, since he reputedly operated under assumed names."

"Until his death in 1784, I believe," Grey said.

Leadbetter nodded.

"So explain to me, Dr. Marsh, if you'd be so kind, how is it that someone in possession of this supposed philosopher's stone, this elixir of life, goes about dying?" Grey asked.

"Yet another example of how you fail to comprehend the true nature of things. Digging up this bit of history is like piecing together a discovery of broken pottery shards. You can fit most of them to the shape of a vase. But you, Grey, see a missing piece that leaves a hole at the bottom. Today water would drain from that hole, so you blindly conclude it must never have served as a vase. But I recognize the missing piece and see the true meaning of it all.

"You say he died, so he could never have held the secret of the philosopher's stone. I, however, say he only died because the secret of the stone was taken from him and his existing supply of the elixir could sustain him only until 1784.

"The count caught the attention of many famous and noble men and women of the age. Casanova's memoirs describe him as an accomplished charlatan. He was arrested in England in 1745 as a spy, and the Duke of York was reportedly obsessed with the mysterious man. He was a confidant of Louis XV and undertook secret missions on his behalf. He was present in St. Petersburg and had an active hand in the 1762 coup that raised Catherine the Great to the throne. He escaped arrest under suspicious circumstances in Amsterdam in the early 1760s. The matter was discussed in letters from Voltaire to Frederick the Great. The man who never dies and knows everything, he was called. After Amsterdam he fled to England.

"It was there that he attracted the particular attention of a man neither famous nor noble: Thomas Webster. Webster entered the count's service, and soon enough he stole the secret to the philosopher's stone. The count's agents chased Webster to the West Indies and then to Boston and finally to Portland, just prior to the Revolution."

"I see," Grey said with an exaggerated nod. "You're saying that Captain Mowat was acting under orders from this infamous Count de St. Germain when he razed the town and fanned the flames of the American Revolution."

Marsh shrugged. "The details are murky, but someone with authority was acting on the count's behalf. In any event, a revolution in a single nation is a small price to pay in order to recover the secret of the Great Work. St. Germain was still alive, but faltering, when a final, desperate attempt to recover the secret was made in 1783."

"When the stranger, Clough, came looking in Portland and Webster killed him," Grey said.

"Precisely," Marsh said.

"Yet, like the count, Webster died." Grey allowed himself to smirk at the absurdity of it all. "I must say, this wondrous elixir of life is leaving me thoroughly unimpressed."

"Webster was unprepared. He didn't have sufficient understanding to use it—to access the vast power and knowledge contained within."

"Wait a moment," Leadbetter urged, his rapt eyes fixed on Marsh, "I don't follow you. Even if the secret was written down and stolen, St. Germain would still possess the knowledge. Why would he pursue Webster? Why not simply use his mastery of alchemy to reproduce the stone?"

"It's not mere knowledge, though that is certainly required." Marsh grinned, reveling in the demonstration of his own superior knowledge. "What St. Germain had acquired, somewhere in his worldly travels to Persia or India, was an actual mechanism. A self-contained distilling and transmuting and collecting apparatus. The ultimate perfection of an alchemist's alembic, though that word does no true justice to the genius of this device. Germain's alembic is something like a lock and something like a key. Made of pure gold and inscribed in coded terms with the process to produce the philosopher's stone. It's hollow, and when the proper elements are added, in the proper order and with the proper processes followed, each one in turn, it functions in alchemical terms akin to the tumblers inside a lock turning, opening. Until the final step is achieved and the stone—or rather its grains are produced. It is that matter that can transform metals to gold. Or, when consumed, give eternal life. And with it true and ultimate understanding."

The train's whistle sounded, and the train began a gradual deceleration.

"Well, Grey, it seems I have rattled on, but at least my explanation has sufficed to keep you entertained and docile until I can be safely on my way. Thank you for your efforts." Marsh stuffed the folded papers filled with arcane symbols into his own jacket pocket. "Much appreciated. It may comfort you to know that when I decipher Tom Webster's riddle and locate Count de St. Germain's alembic, you will have played a small part in revealing the ultimate understanding of mankind and the universe."

"Well, that's something, isn't it?" Grey said.

"More than *something*, Grey. It's all that's left for you. I don't want your death to be even more inconvenient to me than your life has been. So I will take my leave of you at this stop and return to Boston. My never having been on this train, there will be no way for your tiresome bulldog Lean or any of your Pinkerton friends to tie me to your impending misfortune."

Marsh stood and exited the cabin. Jerome followed him into the passageway. The gunman standing in the aisle reentered the compartment with his pistol drawn.

"You promised he wouldn't be harmed," Leadbetter protested.

"It's these small lies that give us an even greater appreciation of the higher truths," Marsh said from the doorway to the compartment.

"What about him?" The gunman pointed at Leadbetter.

Marsh regarded the minister with contempt. "There was a brief time when I looked to you for learning. I suppose you may still be of some limited use to me." He then spoke to the gunman. "Once matters are resolved here, bring our old friend on to Portland. Keep him at the house, under watch."

The stocky, mean-faced man nodded. He took a seat opposite and aimed his pistol squarely at Grey's chest. The whistle sounded again, and the train slowed. Marsh and Jerome disappeared from view. Grey, Leadbetter, and Marsh's armed henchman remained seated in the isolated compartment.

Leadbetter looked at Grey with bitter defeat in his eyes. "I'm sorry, Mr. Grey. They forced me——"

"Shut your mouth, old man," the gunman ordered.

"Whatever Marsh is paying you, I'll sweeten the pot," Grey said.

"You shut yours, too." The man waggled the gun at Grey. "Shows how smart you are. He pays me fine. But it ain't the money anyway. He can do a hell of a lot worse to you than any lawman ever could. You were stupid to ever cross him."

Five minutes later the train was under way again. The three men in the compartment sat in stony silence for another ten minutes before the gunman stood and backed out into the hall of the empty railcar. He motioned at Leadbetter with the pistol.

"You stay here, old man. I don't want any trouble from you." He aimed at Grey again. "Hurry up, smart guy, on your feet."

Grey was about to stand when Leadbetter threw himself to the floor and clutched Grey's knees.

"May God have mercy on your soul," he pronounced. Then, in a whisper, barely audible above the muffled churning of the train's wheels along the rails, he added, "The stone—you can't let him get it. Ever."

"All right already. Come on!" The gunman motioned to Grey, who stood and joined him in the aisle.

Grey glanced back at Leadbetter; the old man's face was even paler than usual.

"Go ahead," the gunman said to Grey, "out to the back of the train."

No more than a dozen steps would deliver them to the rear exit. In the narrow aisle, Grey could sense that the man was several steps behind him, leaving plenty of space in order to avoid any sudden movements by Grey.

He was almost to the rear door when he heard a desperate, furious growl of a noise. Grey looked back to see Leadbetter in the aisle charging the gunman from behind. Leadbetter rammed into the man, and the two of them collapsed in a heap as the gun went off. Grey took two steps toward them, then watched as the old man's body slumped away from the gunman. A dark stain spread across Leadbetter's shirtfront. Grey waited a second to see the man move, but he was lifeless. Marsh's thug still gripped his pistol.

Grey bolted to the door and pushed it open. He stepped out onto the small exterior platform at the rear of the train and ducked to the side. The gunman fired twice. One of the bullets splintered the doorframe as the door swung closed. Grey stood against a short railing that kept him from falling off the platform's edge.

With one hand against the back wall of the car and the other on a pole that rose to the small roof, Grey lurched up onto the thin railing. The door to the rear compartment started to swing open. He knew he should just jump, but anger over Leadbetter's death surged up in him. Grey held tight to the pole and slammed his foot into the door. There was a satisfying grunt of pain as it smashed into the gunman's face. Grey looked back at the dark blur of the earth hurtling by below him. He picked his spot and leaped.

Chapter 49

HELEN HELD THE OLD BLACK WOMAN'S ARM EVEN THOUGH she was very steady on her feet for her age. They left behind them the Portland Alms House. It was where the woman, Dastine LaVallee, had spent the last several years of her life. The main structure, along with its few scattered outbuildings, had seen better days. Helen imagined that the same was true of the talkative lady next to her. She gazed sideways at Dastine as they walked. It took a long look at her face to see past the ravages of many decades and find hints of the pretty teenage girl who had once charmed the heart of a young Horace Webster. The left half of Dastine's face sagged under an old scar that started at her clouded-over eye and ran down to her jaw. Only the faint outline of an iris could be seen beneath the milky surface of the damaged eye.

On their walk up North Street the other day, Archie had mentioned his frustration in trying to find any trace of the woman. He'd been focusing his search on the records located in City Hall. Helen had instead wondered what type of life such a woman, one who'd suffered the early hardships Lean described, would have had. If indeed she was still alive and in the city, where would she actually be living? If she was not fortunate enough to be in her own family home, the choices would be limited. It had taken just a few telephone calls to locate the woman.

Helen made a polite reference to having enjoyed lunch, and now Dastine was fully engrossed in her litany of meal-related complaints.

"I was late to the table by an hour last Friday, fish day. I went to the kitchen and asked the cook for my dinner. She'd forgot me, offered me the leavings of the table. I went to Mr. Thompson and told him I wanted my dinner, and he came to the kitchen. Now, I don't know what he said to the cook, but it must not have been much. She only brought me a plate of small, soggy potatoes. I told her that no fish was with it.

She went back and put on a thin piece no bigger than my two fingers, without any fat. I told her to take it away, and I made a little stew of some hard crusts of bread and two apples for dinner."

"The almshouse does appear rather mean in its comforts. Wouldn't you be happier at the Home for Aged Women up on Emery Street? I searched for you there first."

"Oh, perhaps you're right. Let me just take a peek in my purse—I'm sure I have that hundred-dollar entry fee in here somewhere." Dastine released a delighted cackle, then gave Helen's arm a slight slap to let her know she was in on the joke.

After waiting for several carriages to go trotting past, they crossed the street and entered the western edge of Deering Oaks.

"I don't normally see the park during the middle of the day anymore. I like to come just after sunrise or else later in the evenings. When there aren't so many souls around. When I won't see so many children."

"I suppose they can be rather loud and bothersome."

"Oh, heavens no, Mrs. Prescott."

"Helen, please."

"Helen. It ain't that at all. Children are right to be loud. I'm afraid it's me that bothers them. Can't blame them for being scared. It took me years to get over this scar on my face. More years than some of the children have even been alive. And though I've lived long enough to see just about everything one person can do to another, seeing fear on a child's face when she looks at you, that never gets easier."

They crossed a forty-foot wooden bridge spanning a short gully. Below the structure a slow spring produced a thin trickle of muddy water that seeped down toward one of the long fingers of the park's duck pond a few hundred feet away. Archie Lean was waiting on a bench there and rose to meet them as they approached. Helen had already told Dastine about the deputy and now completed the introductions. Dastine eased herself down onto the bench overlooking the thin strip of springwater that couldn't quite earn the title of a brook.

"So, Mr. Lean, what makes a sharp young man like yourself come searching out an old woman like me anyway? Helen said it had something to do with Horace Webster." She motioned for them to sit beside her. "I was sad to hear about his passing. Is that what this is about, something of Horace's?"

She looked at him with a curious glint in her one good eye. Helen wondered if Dastine thought they'd come at an attorney's request. Maybe they'd tracked her down to bestow some money or else a sentimental item from their old romance that Horace had kept tucked away all these years.

"Not exactly," Lean said. "I'm sorry to say I haven't brought you anything from the late Mr. Webster. In fact, all I've brought is some questions about an old news article from the 1830s. It said you caused something of a stir by discovering some strange markings carved into a rock ledge along the Presumpscot River. Do you remember that at all?"

"Hah! Yes, I surely do remember, as clear as if it were yesterday. Maybe clearer, if you can believe it. The old days are still there, still sharp."

"So you stumbled upon the markings and then what? The newspaper got wind of the story?" Lean asked.

"Not exactly. I went right up to a newsman to tell what I knew. And I'd known about the carvings for a long while before I ever mentioned them."

"Why'd you wait so long?" Lean asked.

"'Cause Horace's father had threatened us. Said there'd be the devil to pay if we ever mentioned the marks on that ledge."

"So why'd you tell?" Helen asked.

"The same reason as I suppose anyone tells a man's secrets. To hurt him. Revenge for what he'd done."

Lean gave her a sympathetic nod. "Of course. You'd had a youthful romance with Horace. When Horace's father found out, he beat you severely. Is that how your eye was injured?"

"For someone who just met me, you know an awful lot about my life, Mr. Lean." Dastine glanced around, looking as if she wanted assurance that enough people were meandering by to come to her aid in case Lean and Helen started causing her trouble. She ran her fingers down the scar tissue on her cheek and shifted nervously on the bench.

Helen sensed that Dastine was weighing whether to end this strange encounter and get herself back to the almshouse. She already knew that the woman was a kindhearted soul, so she decided to play the best card they had to appeal to Dastine's sentimental feelings on the subject of Horace Webster.

"We're helping a colleague of ours who's searching for Madeline Webster, Horace's granddaughter. Before Horace passed, he asked for her to be found. She's gone missing, and now she may be in grave danger."

"His granddaughter?" A small, wistful smile appeared on the old woman's face. "What's that all have to do with those old stone markings? With me?"

"We don't know exactly, but something was stolen from the Websters. Whatever the robber was after, I think it has to do with those old markings," Lean explained. "In order to help Horace's granddaughter, we need to figure out just what is really going on here. I need to learn everything I possibly can. Before it's too late."

"What's the girl's name again? His granddaughter?"

"Madeline," Helen said.

Dastine repeated the name in a whisper. Several moments of silence passed, and her lips trembled with the weight of possibilities long since vanished, thoughts of a very different life she'd once dreamed of living. Helen guessed that the woman had never had any children of her own. Maybe because of the facial disfigurement inflicted by Horace Webster's father. She tried to imagine what that was like, a life alone. A life without her own daughter, Delia. She reached into her bag and had a handkerchief ready even before Dastine's eyes welled up. A tear dripped from the old woman's unseeing left orb. Helen offered the handkerchief, and Dastine dabbed briefly before passing it back. When she spoke again, there was no trace of anguish in her voice.

"You may know a lot about me and Horace, but you don't know everything. It wasn't some sort of fleeting romance between foolish young folks who don't know better. Horace and me, we loved each other. Very much. Yes, his father beat me and ruined my eye. But worse than that, he took Horace from me. You get used to seeing with just one eye. The pain in my soul, from having my love taken away—that was worse."

"You were cast out from the Webster house, and Horace was forbidden to see you ever again," Lean said.

"I still went out of my way to see him." She chuckled at her confession.

"From a distance, mind you, in public places where the crowds kept me from being noticed."

"He made no effort to see you anymore?" Helen asked with a hint of bitterness in her voice.

"He would have. I could tell by the look on his face whenever I caught sight of him. The joy that I'd known in him was gone. He'd seen how his father had ruined my face. I wasn't a beauty anymore. It hurt, thinking that might have made Horace stop loving me. But I believe that the real reason he never came looking for me was he knew what would happen if we was ever caught together again. His father might take it out on *him* some, but that man would sure as hell have killed *me*."

Helen gave Lean a quick shake of her head to delay any further questioning. Dastine LaVallee was a talker, and Helen suspected that if they let her go on as she would, she'd tell them more than they'd even know to ask.

"Well, of course that ain't entirely true. We *did* see each other one more time," she said.

"Despite the danger?" Helen laid her hand on Dastine's arm.

"I was terrified of his father, but then we were young and in love. We arranged a secret meeting. It was a spot where no one would ever see us. We'd gone there before to be alone with ourselves. It was our spot over by the Presumpscot River, not too far below the falls. I suppose maybe that's why I like it here by the little spring—just a hint of the same, without being enough of a memory to hold any grief in it."

"It's all water under the bridge anyway," Lean said with a smile.

Dastine cackled at the bad joke.

"That's why you were familiar with the Presumpscot," Lean said, "and why you knew about those ancient runes or markings."

"Hah! I knew about them 'cause they weren't ancient at all. My own *pépère* is the one who carved them into the stone. Horace's grandfather, Old Tom, had told him what to do, and *Pépère* got his hammer and chisel and did the work."

"Really? Say, if we brought you there, do you think you could still find the spot? The ledge that holds those markings?" Lean asked.

"Of course. It's like I said, the old times are still in here." Dastine tapped her temple. "I still see them as sharp as ever."

Lean's police carriage took them across Tukey's Bridge, through the town of Deering, and then along the winding roads through Falmouth. After a while of reminiscing over days both old and recent, Dastine nodded off. As they passed along the Presumpscot, drawing nearer to the falls, Helen woke the old woman. She recovered her bearings in time to recognize a curve in the road. They all got out and had to make it the last few hundred yards on foot. First they crossed a field and then ducked into a stand of mixed pine and hardwoods that ran along the river. Dastine relied on Lean for support as they made their way through the undergrowth and over the uneven footing down to the river. They reached a rocky section of the bank a short way north of where Dastine had meant to come out, but another minute and she recognized her spot.

"It was here that our trouble started. If you want to call it that. Horace and I would sit on this flat space, just below where the dip makes a natural seat. You could sit nice and peaceful as if you'd brought a chair from home and look out on the river."

"Did the Websters own this land, I wonder?" Lean asked.

Dastine settled herself down onto a rock much taller than the old one she'd mentioned, so as to avoid the need to bend her knees too much.

"Horace's grandfather, Old Tom, had bought it up years earlier. Had a whole stretch along the river here, but they didn't do anything with it. I had never seen it myself until I was sixteen years old. I came with Horace and his father and my *pépère,* who was an old man by then. He and *Gra-mère* had come from Basseterre, in St. Kitts, to Maine when they were both young. Horace's grandfather had brought them here, and they married and started their family not long after. This was all back before the Revolutionary War. So my *pépère* was an old man by the time I first came here. Still strong as an ox, though."

"Horace's grandfather, Old Tom Webster, was dead by the time you came here? He'd have been much older," Lean said.

"Yes, he died a while earlier. If I ever met him, I was too young to remember it. But he didn't die of old age," Dastine said in a conspiratorial tone.

"No?" Helen's curious stare begged her to tell more.

"Not according to my *gra-mère.* She always said the man was old, but no older than the day he first brought them to New England. They found him in his workroom, dead on the floor, some broken bottles near him. Family said it must have been his heart. But my *gra-mère*, she would always cross herself when she talked of him, said it wasn't natural. She would only mention it when no one was around but us. She swore there was evil done on the old man. Poisoned, is what she told us. Too late for you to investigate that one, eh?" Dastine said with a dry laugh.

"Maybe," Lean agreed. "Did your grandmother ever say who she thought poisoned him?"

"The same ones that were always chasing after him, I suppose."

"The same ones? Just a moment—there were men pursuing Tom Webster?"

"That's why he fled St. Kitts with my grandparents. Why he showed up on that island in the first place."

"Who were these men?" Lean asked.

Dastine shrugged. "Englishmen or other Europeans, *Gra-mère* never said exactly. But they knew he was in Maine. They'd found him here before."

"But he was no longer running away," Helen said, remembering her research into the properties owned by Old Thomas Webster. "So when they found him earlier, was that at the house on Oak and Free streets, the one he built at the end of the Revolutionary War? A stranger by the name of Clough was reported to have died close by there under 'mischievous' circumstances."

"That was all before my time," Dastine said. "But *Gra-mère* just said that she'd thought the men were done coming after him. That he'd taught them a lesson."

"And did she ever say why these foreign men were after Old Tom?" Lean asked.

Dastine's good eye lit up with a bit of childlike glee. "His golden puzzle."

"Which is what, exactly?" Lean tried to keep his voice level.

Dastine shrugged again. "*Gra-mère* would only ever whisper about it, and she wouldn't say much. She wasn't supposed to know about it. But sometimes she'd see Old Tom with it in his hands, a little puzzle box, all shining gold. And he'd be twisting it this way and that. She never knew what it was, but she figured he was killed over it in the end.

She used to tell me to behave or those men would come back." She let out a chuckle at the childhood memories of her grandmother's stories. "What do you make of that, Mr. Lean?"

"I'm not entirely certain. So I suppose I should just get myself back to the original questions that brought us here," Lean said. He'd been glancing about at the ledges but hadn't seen any traces of etchings in the rock. "Now, you were telling us about the first time you came here. You saw the markings."

"I just tagged along to help out any way I could. Like I said, *Pépère* had gotten old. Though you wouldn't know it by the way Horace's father bossed him about. Brought him here on account of he was the one who'd chipped out the markings in the first place. The river water coming down over the rocks can get going pretty good sometimes. It was wearing the markings down. Horace's father wanted *Pépère* to chisel them out again, deeper, to keep them fresh."

"And where exactly are the markings?"

"Oh, we haven't reached them yet. Come, I'll show you."

She extended a hand, and Lean helped her to her feet, then escorted her through the brush, another fifty yards downriver. They emerged onto a wide, flat ledge that sloped a touch toward the river.

"This is it," Dastine said with a nod. "They should be right over there."

Helen stayed by Dastine while Lean stepped to where he saw the faint marks on the rock. He crouched down just outside a circle, maybe three feet in diameter, of faded symbols carved into the ledge. The river bubbled past right along the lower edge of the rock. The water level wouldn't need to rise much for the river to flood over the whole face of the ledge. The river had defeated Lean's intentions. Once again the waters below the Presumpscot Falls had worn away the markings that Dastine LaVallee's grandfather had cut into the rock. The symbols were no longer distinct or legible. All Lean could do now was count them and confirm that Professor Horsford's book hadn't erroneously included a duplicate of the "I" symbol. That figure did appear twice on the rock, making the total number of separate markings there twenty-four.

"Seems your grandfather didn't cut the rock deep enough the second time either," Lean said.

"He did what he was told." Her voice rose as she defended her beloved grandfather. "If someone's to blame, it's that Old Tom Webster for not picking a spot back enough from the river in the first place."

Lean stood and surveyed the rocks about him. The marks would have been legible to anyone who knew where to look for them and could have been set down in several clear spots farther removed from the river. Maybe the marks weren't meant to last forever. Lean just shrugged and turned to another subject.

"Your anger at Horace's father is understandable. But why go to the newspaper with the story about the etchings on the rock? An odd choice of revenge against the man who'd beaten you so horribly and ripped your young love away."

"I was just a girl. A poor black girl with no means at hand. How else could I strike back at the man?" Although she was answering Lean, it was Helen she looked to for understanding. "It was actually Horace who gave me the idea. Like I said earlier, after the trouble we arranged our last meeting at our spot upriver. We came to say our good-byes, to hold each other for a moment longer."

Dastine turned and looked back the way they'd come, as if picturing the events of sixty years ago. "Horace was beside himself. I could see horror in his eyes when he saw my beaten, scarred face. This dead eye. He tried to pass it off as anger. And I suppose it was, in part. But looking back on it later, I realized it was horror at the sight of my face as well. He couldn't stand still. We walked along the bank until we reached the ledge here.

"The sight of that circle, all those carvings, it made something burst inside him. He went into a frenzy. Cursing his father. Saying the man cared more for this stupid circle than he did about Horace himself. He took up a rock and began smashing it on the ledge, trying to destroy those markings. But all he did was scrape up his hands."

Dastine LaVallee clasped her own hands in front of her, rubbing them back and forth like she was soothing an old ache.

"That put the idea in your head about how valuable the markings were to his father. The man was intent on preserving the marks and making sure they remained a secret," Lean said.

"He took so much from me," Dastine said. "This was the one thing

I was free to take from him. I brought the newsman right here. Even helped him make charcoal rubbings of each of the marks. He thought they were genuine. Carved by Indians or ancient travelers of some sort or the other."

"The truth wouldn't have made for much of a story. You wanted the newspaper to get everyone talking," Lean said.

"Seems so petty now. But then I hated that man more than anything in the world. I relished the anger he'd feel when the whole world knew about his strange little secret. It must have worked, too. I came back here two weeks later and saw that Horace's father had put up signs and hired a couple of rough hands to keep trespassers away. It was a very small victory in comparison to what he'd done."

"Not the *only* victory, though, was it?" Helen was remembering the anger she'd felt the prior Fourth of July, when she'd seen dismay in her uncle's face at the idea of Perceval Grey, an Indian, escorting her to the very public fireworks gala. "The paper reported that you found the marks while out for a romantic stroll with your beau."

Dastine smiled. "I wanted to stick that right under his nose. Say it out loud so he'd know right enough that me and Horace loved each other. And it was there on the page in black and white. Nothing he could do about it."

Lean couldn't think of anything to say that wouldn't diminish the old woman's declaration of her small and long-hidden claim of retribution against the man who'd so horribly wronged her. He could only nod and turn his attention back to the stone ledge. The author of the news story was the only one who'd definitely seen the markings and bothered to record them. His charcoal rubbings must have stayed in the files at the paper for years after. They remained stashed away for decades until Professor Horsford dug up the story and unearthed the drawings for his last, unpublished book.

Lean studied the circle of worn-down cuts. Horsford had presented the symbols in a linear series. He'd had to break the circle and select an arbitrary starting point to put the symbols in the order he'd selected for his book. Horsford had opted to commence with the symbol that looked like the first letter in the Norse runic alphabet. Lean wondered whether Horsford's book preserved the proper order. Did Horsford's order match the original, now-obliterated pattern?

"Have you ever shown anyone else this ledge since then?" Lean asked. "An old professor from Harvard, perhaps?"

Dastine shook her head.

"The newspaperman, you said you helped him make his charcoal rubbings to copy the marks. Did he do them in a row one after the other, as they were on the ledge, or did he just trace them out in random order?"

"He kept the order," Dastine said. "He was very particular. He thought if he could find out what they meant, they might spell out some message from whoever had written them so long ago."

"Maybe he was partially right after all," Lean said.

Dastine gave him a doubtful look.

Lean clasped his hands together and gave her a pleading smile. "I know I'm likely trying your patience, but please take my word for it. I'm neither as gullible as your reporter nor as mad as Old Tom Webster for putting these marks here in the first place. But I do believe that in some unknown manner these marks were left as a message of sorts."

Dastine shrugged, still unconvinced.

"Tell me, did you ever see any identical kind of markings at the Websters' residence that might have given Old Tom the idea for these ones? Perhaps on some strange stone they kept about."

"You mean that thunderstone?" Dastine asked.

Lean nodded. "I've heard that Old Tom Webster dug that stone up when he was clearing out earth for a cellar."

"And you think that maybe the marks on that old stone are what he was copying down here on the ledge?"

Dastine gave a shake of her head.

"Not the case?" Lean asked.

"*Pépère* told me Old Tom had found the stone, true enough. They couldn't believe how smooth it was. But the carvings on that, no. *Pépère* made them, too."

Lean gave a cautious smile.

"Is that good news?" she asked.

"To tell you the truth, I'm not sure. But it may be good news to somebody I know."

Chapter 50

Y OU KNOW I'M A SOMEWHAT RESPECTED DEPUTY OF THE
city police, not a delivery boy," Lean said as he entered Grey's
study and hung his hat.

Grey hadn't greeted him yet, and as Lean took in the room, he understood why. Grey sat cross-legged in front of his large chalkboard. At the center of the board were the chalk outlines of two dozen small rectangles arranged in a circle. These were labeled 1 through 24, and they bore evidence of various entries' having been crossed out and erased. Grey himself sat surrounded by a circle of twenty-four white paper rectangles. Lean instantly recognized those two dozen sheets of paper.

He'd received the special delivery the prior afternoon, marked from Boston but with no return address. Inside had been twenty-three small sheets of paper, each bearing a hand-drawn copy of a symbol from Professor Horsford's book. Grey already had the final page from their first visit to the Athenaeum.

"You got the envelope I left with Mrs. Philbrick last night, I take it. You were out." Lean waited for Grey to offer an explanation of his whereabouts, but none was forthcoming.

"So you've got the full set of twenty-four symbols from Horsford's Viking book. What do you make of them?"

The quick, unamused look from Grey confirmed that he hadn't made much progress in his attempt to uncover some sort of hidden pattern in the sets of markings from the book and the thunderstone. Lean decided to change the subject to one that he found more important and distressing. Grey had broken his own silence yesterday, arranging a clandestine meeting with Lean where each provided updates to the case, including

Dastine's memories and Father Leadbetter's sad fate on the train two nights earlier.

"On a much more distressing matter, I haven't seen any mention of Leadbetter in the Boston papers," Lean said.

"Nor has McCutcheon made contact. He'll alert me as soon as word reaches the Boston police. If Leadbetter's body was cast off the train, it will turn up sooner or later along the B&M line. If it doesn't happen today, McCutcheon's agreed to take the train himself. He'll man the rear platform so he can spot Leadbetter and have the poor man's body recovered."

A grumbling sound rattled around in Lean's throat for a few seconds before he finally put his annoyance into words. "That harmless old man gunned down. I can't stand the notion of doing nothing about it. I could arrest Marsh on your word."

"He's already bought off the conductor once. Essentially making that man an unwitting accomplice to murder. He'll have no trouble paying the conductor to say that Leadbetter was alone in the last car with me before he was killed, and he never saw Marsh on board. Then it's me who ends up facing murder charges."

"So I get to the conductor first, force the truth out of him. Have him identify Marsh."

Grey shook his head. "He wouldn't be careless enough to let the conductor see his face. I'm sure he had his crony handle the details and the payment. Besides, he's probably already got a dozen witnesses who'll swear they were with Marsh the entire night."

"Maybe, but what about Cosgrove's murder? You said he all but confessed to it," Lean protested.

"True, but there's even less evidence to convict him of that crime. Sorry, Lean, justice for Dr. Jotham Marsh will have to wait until I can find ironclad proof against him."

"Or die trying," Lean said.

"Your confidence in me is heartwarming. As for Leadbetter, I share your frustration, believe me. But there is nothing we can do on that front. For now."

"Then when? Sooner or later Marsh has to answer for this."

Grey nodded his agreement. "Among his many other crimes. The best I can do for Father Leadbetter at the moment is to see his dying wish come to fruition. And that means preventing Marsh from solving this riddle of Old Tom Webster's and finding this supposed alchemical artifact."

"That's what you're choosing to focus on?" Lean asked. "Not the real-life murders of two men but finding some mystical artifact that you've assured me doesn't actually exist."

"Correction, I've assured you that no actual alchemical device that creates gold and grants eternal life exists anywhere, least of all buried somewhere beneath the ground of Portland, Maine. However, it does seem quite probable that if Tom Webster went through all the trouble to create the thunderstone and this convoluted code of twenty-four symbols, then he would have completed his hoax. As you told me, Dastine LaVallee's grandmother told of Old Tom's having some golden item he guarded jealously. He obviously had faith in its hidden alchemical powers, and I suspect he did indeed bury it somewhere for safekeeping."

"If it's not real, why bother trying to find it at all?" Lean asked. "I think you've lost sight of the real crimes that have been committed."

"On the contrary, the fact that Marsh is willing to kill for the artifact makes it worth pursuing. I might be able to use his desperation to obtain the item against him. Cause him to make a fatal misstep. At the very least, we'd have the item in hand, the motive for these murders he's orchestrated."

"You confident that you can do that? Find it before Marsh, I mean. Judging by the sorry state of that chalkboard, I'd wager you haven't made great progress."

"It's true that I haven't yet had much success. But I take some degree of comfort in the knowledge that Marsh is having a harder go of it than I am. His set is missing the mercury symbol that I originally recovered at the scene of Chester Sears's fatal jump. In addition, once my suspicions were aroused that Father Leadbetter was under duress in Boston, I took the precaution of making duplicates of my drawings. I sent this set to you, in case I met some harm. I kept the second set of pages on my person, after I shuffled them. So now Marsh is attempting to decode a series of symbols that have been randomly reordered. His task will be almost infinitely more difficult than my own."

"So let's have it, then. What have you figured so far?" Lean made a show of studying the chalkboard.

"The twenty-four symbols are those carved into the ledge along the Presumpscot. Those are the symbols in Horsford's book. According to Dastine, the original news reporter accurately recorded the order in which the symbols appeared. But since they were carved in a circular pattern on the ledge, we don't know in what order Tom Webster meant them to be read."

"But you got from Leadbetter the proper order in which to read the seven on the thunderstone?"

"Yes, and if the thunderstone's intended as a code, as I believe it is, that order is vital. Those seven figures are the specific message that Old Tom Webster has drawn out of the code of the twenty-four."

"So it's down to a matter of deciphering what the twenty-four are meant to represent." Lean cracked his knuckles. "Two shy of the alphabet. I suppose that would have been too obvious."

"I've tried certain variations omitting pairs of letters, but to no use. The Greek alphabet has only twenty-four letters, but I could discern no obvious code."

"Might not be letters. Twenty-four hours in the day?"

"I considered that, a numeric code instead of an alphabetical one, but I feel confident that's a false trail."

Lean stared at the chalkboard, then began a slow walk around the circular formation of pages arrayed on the floor.

"It could be anything. Stare at it all long enough and you're likely to see anything you can imagine—or nothing at all. This is just grasping at straws."

"Yes, without knowing the key to the code, it would be next to impossible to ever decipher Tom Webster's riddle," Grey admitted.

"A key?" Lean asked. "Like what? Something common that anyone might know?"

"Unlikely. He's made efforts at concealment elsewhere. The key is apt to be something private. Something only his family would have access to. I was hoping it might be in the only other document actually handed down from Old Tom." Grey motioned toward the desk. "It took all manner of promises and veiled threats to get it out of the attorney's hands, but I did manage to take temporary possession of Thomas Webster's original bequest of the thunderstone."

"Well, that sounds promising." Lean moved to the desk and glanced down at the old paper.

"So I hoped," Grey said. "But I've read it two dozen times, and while I spy certain hints and references, I haven't yet grasped any overarching pattern for the code." Grey regarded Lean with a quizzical look and added, "Why don't you give it a read?"

Lean shrugged and sat down at the desk to get a closer look at the old page without having to touch it. The thunderstone sat beside it. He began to read the handwritten words.

Grey said, "Tom Webster stuck a line in there about heeding his voice. I think he meant it to be read aloud."

"Fair enough." Lean cleared his throat and glanced at Grey, who was still peering at him. Lean couldn't help feeling like a caged animal on display, being studied. "Why are you looking at me like that?"

"Sorry, like what?"

"Like you're waiting for me to say something off the mark. I'm only going to read what's written," Lean said.

"Of course, go on," Grey said.

Lean couldn't shake his feeling but went on with the reading anyway.

"Vary you not from these instructions or else the keepers appointed by me shall reclaim the thunderstone for as many of the earth's revelation about the Sun as shall be appointed you and until such time as you shall pass into the earth, and then the next generation shall have the right to claim the stone. In no company other than mine own blood shall you let the thunderstone be seen, nor shall its markings be presented in any form to others. To gather in the stone's meaning will won a soul a treasure beyond conception. Read what has been writ in the earth before

you and do not be verse to the teachings of the Lord. I alone should appear true and clear to you, and know my meaning is not to enumerate for you, each time I am seen among other fallacies. One can only find the measure of a man at the ends of his days, and understand that his true nature cannot be the base materials of his bodily wants, the needs of the flesh, what he shall drink and ate, but only what he has stood for. Look not to letters or words other than those of the thunderstone but heed my voice, only then shall you be rewarded, not in my name, nor truly in any human form."

Lean stood up and gave a shrug. "Doesn't exactly roll off the tongue."

"At first I attributed that to outdated speech and an exaggerated need to sound official. But I've begun to think that there's a method to his madly ineloquent phrasing." Grey approached and pointed toward the latter part of the document. "He says to ignore letters or words other than those of the thunderstone. That verifies the thunderstone's seven symbols as the specific words or letters he's trying to convey."

"He says that earlier as well, don't you think?" Lean asked, and pointed to the middle of the long paragraph. 'My meaning is not to enumerate for you.' He's stressing it's not numbers he's after."

"Agreed. I was also struck by that sentence. 'I alone should appear true and clear to you . . .' Then the bit about not enumerating anything. Followed by 'each time I am seen among other fallacies.' "

"What's he mean? When would Tom Webster appear among fallacies?" Lean asked.

"I don't believe he's referring to himself. Look at the phrasing he chooses. '*I* alone should appear clear and true . . . each time *I* am seen among other fallacies.' "

Lean looked at Grey, trying to guess his meaning. Grey nodded in the direction of the floor, where his twenty-four pages of copied symbols still lay arranged in a circle. At first Lean's eyes were drawn to the most familiar sketch of mercury's symbol. But after a moment his gaze moved over the other symbols and came to rest upon the only pair that was not unique. Two "I" symbols located adjacent to each other now leaped out, demanding his attention.

"The 'I' symbols," Lean said. "They're not to enumerate, not Roman numerals—he's using them in the sense of a pronoun. They're the true ones, and the others are the fallacies?"

"The twenty-four symbols are the code hiding the meaning of the thunderstone's seven, and yes, the 'I' symbols are meant to be the key. Exactly how remains a mystery."

Lean read the bequest again, this time to himself.

"It'd be a hell of a lot easier if the crazy old bastard just came out and talked straight. He can't even get half his words right." He noticed that Grey was staring at him again and had reverted back to his earlier quizzical look.

"What? It's true," Lean said. "He mentions the earth's 'revelation about the Sun' and not to be 'verse to the teachings' and all that."

"Obviously he means 'revolution' and 'averse,' not 'verse.' He, for one"—Grey stared at Lean—"has the good sense not to be distracted by poetry."

"Thank God," Lean declared. "With prose that bad, I'd hate the thought of him writing in verse. I can only imagine . . ." Lean's voice trailed off as the look on Grey's face went from amused to intensely focused. "It's happened, hasn't it? What you were expecting before, when you asked me to read. I said something—"

"Brilliantly asinine," Grey completed the sentence for him.

"Off the mark, is how I was going to say it." Lean's tone was offended, but he couldn't completely stifle a smirk.

"Poetry indeed!" Grey grabbed a scrap of paper and a pencil from the desktop. "We may just have it! Look on the page: Find all the instances where he misused a word."

Lean stood shoulder to shoulder with Grey and scanned the page. "Well, he says 'revelation' instead of 'revolution.'"

Grey finished jotting down that first word even as Lean spoke. He pointed ahead on the page. "He uses 'won' when he meant 'win.'"

"There's 'verse' instead of 'averse,'" Lean said as he watched Grey slide his finger back and forth across the lines of the yellowed page.

"He says 'drink and ate' when he should have said 'eat.'"

"That looks like all the mistakes." Lean rolled his hand, almost as if he were working a fishing reel, urging Grey to hurry on. "Read them back."

"Revelation, won, verse, ate," Grey recited with a grin.

Understanding slapped Lean in the face. "Your Bible! Where's your Bible?"

Grey spun half around on the spot, taking in his wide shelves of books all at once. "Not here. I left it at my grandfather's."

"What? The clue you've been waiting for—'Don't be verse to the Lord's teachings'—and you don't have a stinking copy of the Bible?"

Grey snapped his fingers, the look of defeat on his face giving way to hope. "Mrs. Philbrick."

The two men practically tripped over each other racing out of the room and down the stairs, arriving in a crescendo of thumps at the landlady's threshold. Grey pounded on the door, and they burst in as soon as she turned the knob. Lean managed an apology as both men stormed through the room, looking high and low for anything resembling a book.

"Your copy of the Bible, Mrs. Philbrick?" Grey demanded.

The landlady stood in the center of the front room wearing a troubled expression, very much confused by this turn of events.

"Please," Lean said in as calm a tone as he could, "we're really quite desperate to get our hands on a Bible."

She retreated back to what Lean guessed was her bedroom and emerged with the black-covered book outstretched. She eyed the two detectives with a hint of disapproval. "Can't say I'm surprised it's come to this."

Grey snatched the book from her and mumbled something that might have been appreciative in nature. He flipped it open toward the rear and began turning pages with more care as he neared this goal.

"Book of Revelation, chapter one, verse eight." He was silent a moment, handed the Good Book to Lean, and strode to the exit

" 'I am the Alpha and the Omega . . .' " Lean read.

He gently handed the book back to Mrs. Philbrick, smiled, and apologized for the inconvenience. He eased her door closed behind him and then pounded up the stairs.

Grey was already kneeling on the floor near the chalkboard, frantically rotating his circle of symbol-covered pages. Lean approached and saw that when facing the chalkboard and looking down at the circle, one of the "I" symbols now sat in the twelve-o'clock position.

Grey seized the thunderstone from his desk and handed it to Lean, whom he directed to the center of the circle of symbols arrayed on the floor.

"The code is in the Greek alphabet after all. The two 'I' symbols are the alpha and omega, the first and last letters of the Greek alphabet. The one on the right represents the alpha. The next symbol is the letter beta and so on until the circle is complete and the last symbol, the other 'I,' stands for omega. So start with the first symbol on the thunderstone, which according to Leadbetter should be the element lead." Grey pointed out the figure. "Match it to the position of the identical lead symbol in our circle of twenty-four."

"Done," Lean said as he rotated slightly to his right and counted off. "If 'I' is the first spot, then lead is the symbol located in the ninth spot in the circle."

"The ninth letter of the Greek alphabet is iota. Next."

Lean turned the thunderstone in his hand to the second marking, found the corresponding symbol for tin among the papers on the floor, and counted off its numerical position.

"The second symbol, tin, is located in the thirteenth spot."

Grey ran the Greek alphabet through his head, announced it as nu, and wrote that letter down on the chalkboard. They repeated the process until all seven of the thunderstone's symbols were compared to the positions of the twenty-four symbols in the circle and the corresponding Greek letters determined, falling in spots nine, thirteen, five, twenty-one, fifteen, three, and seven.

"Iota, nu, epsilon, phi, omicron, gamma, eta." Lean read the board, nodded thoughtfully, then declared, "I don't mean to sound, as you said, asinine—"

"Brilliantly asinine," Grey corrected him.

"Thank you. But I'm not getting whatever is meant to be understood here. Am I mispronouncing something?"

"You named the letters correctly." Grey set the chalk down and stepped back. "Greek was never my favorite. Put together, the letters would be read something like 'Een-eff-ogg-ay.'"

The room fell silent for a long moment, and then Lean said, "Well, there it is. Case closed."

"'Ine-eff-ogg-ey'?" After another moment of reflection, Grey said, "I suppose I shall need a trip to the library for a book on Greek. A native speaker would be better. It may be a name or some colloquialism."

He stood there, transfixed by the Greek letters on the board.

"Sorry, Grey. It's a disappointment to be sure. But it's not the end of the world. Remember where we started in all this? Me trying to figure who shot Cosgrove and then defiled his grave? We know that was Marsh's doing. And you were looking for that missing Webster girl. She's still out there. We both have real tasks left to do. Getting Marsh and finding the girl. Real live problems to work on. Forget this old crank Webster and his wild hoax. Let him keep his riddle. Time for each of us to let go and move forward."

Lean went to the hooks by the door and retrieved his hat. He felt bad leaving Grey there at a loss. But the man was nothing if not practical; he would soon move on to items that actually mattered.

"After all, some secrets are meant to be carried to the grave," Lean said, and glanced back. Grey was no longer staring at the board. He was watching Lean, and his quizzical look had returned.

"Again—brilliantly asinine," Grey declared. Then, enunciating the sounds carefully, he added, " 'In-eff-oj-ee.' "

"Come again?" Lean said.

" 'In effigy.' I think Old Tom Webster meant to spell out the words 'in effigy.' " A strained smile showed on Grey's face.

"Wonderful. You've solved the riddle and proved it's all a fake. 'In effigy.' Just a symbol, a parody. All a hoax. Now can we agree it's time to move on to catching a murderer?"

"Where are you going?" Grey asked.

"To see Marsh."

"I don't think that's wise."

"Maybe not, but the man's guilty of murder," Lean said. "I can't just leave it."

[Chapter 51]

LEAN WAS TOO RESTLESS TO SIT, SO HE WALKED THE FOUR blocks west from High Street over to Marsh's mystical thaumaturgic society on Winter Street. The quick pace as he crisscrossed the semifashionable neighborhoods made him feel that he was accomplishing something, or at least moving in the right direction. As he turned the final corner, the sprawling, peaked, three-story brick building came into view. A coupé-style landau sat out front with the rear cover down and a driver at the ready.

He waited at the corner a minute until an available hansom cab passed. The driver gave a queer look when Lean climbed aboard but only ordered him to pull around onto Winter Street and wait.

"Just sitting ain't free, you know," the squirrelly-faced driver said.

"Does it cost any extra to sit in silence?" Lean replied.

Five minutes passed. It felt longer as Lean's mind coiled itself ever more tightly around the idea of Dr. Jotham Marsh and whatever unknown, despicable ideas he was spreading within the innocent-looking structure. The man was directly responsible for two killings at least. Lean knew he shouldn't feel any more or less outrage about either one—murder was murder. But Frank "the Foot" Cosgrove was a career thief; he'd chosen a potentially deadly calling. Father Leadbetter, on the other hand, had chosen a life in which he'd tried to help people. And even after his ouster from the ministry, the man had lived a harmless life in a basement apartment surrounded by books and a decrepit dog. The old man hadn't deserved a violent death, followed undoubtedly by the loathsome tossing of his dead body off a moving train.

Marsh's actions in this case made Lean reconsider his thoughts from the series of murders a year before. Jack Whitten was clearly disturbed even from his youth, but how much had Marsh's occult teachings pushed the violent young man over the edge, past whatever grip on reason he'd ever had, into the realm of his depraved killings? He wondered how much Marsh was to blame for those innocent lives, and for the attempts on Helen Prescott and her young daughter, Delia. And apart from Whitten, what other fragile minds was he corrupting?

The image of the madly venomous woman on Cushing's Island, firebrand in her hand and spewing delirious threats, leaped into Lean's mind. He tried to banish her from his thoughts before she touched the torch to her dress. Her shriek echoed through Lean's head, and he imagined the smell of gasoline and burning flesh creeping through his nostrils. He forced an angry cough and spit over the side of the carriage.

A hundred yards away, Jotham Marsh came out the front door in a full-evening-dress suit of black broadcloth with a top hat. Behind him stepped a dark-haired woman in a brocaded silk evening dress of dark crimson with elbow-length black gloves. Last out the door was a younger man whom Lean recognized as Jerome Morse, Marsh's sniveling bootlick.

Lean had his driver follow Marsh's vehicle as it turned onto Pine and then entered Congress Street at Longfellow Square. Though intent on the man he was following, Lean couldn't ignore the sight of his favorite poet immortalized in cast bronze, comfortably seated, atop a short but broad granite block. Several blocks on, Marsh's landau pulled over in front of the Mechanics' Hall. This was home to Portland's Haydn Association, conducted by the city's resident musical genius, Hermann Kotzschmar.

Jerome stepped out first, followed by Marsh. The woman in crimson was still seated in the landau when Lean approached.

"Dr. Marsh."

It took a moment for recognition to appear in the man's eyes. "Deputy Lean, isn't it?"

He glanced at Jerome, who nodded, a look of angry disgust twisting his features.

"How's your face?" Lean asked Jerome, who glowered but didn't speak.

"Whatever can I do for you, Deputy?" Marsh asked.

"I'd like to ask you about the death of Frank Cosgrove."

"Who? Oh, that again. Your friend Mr. Grey asked me about that. Sorry, I still don't know anything of the matter. Now, if you'll excuse us, we don't want to enter the performance late. Quite unseemly, you know."

Marsh began to turn away, but Lean's question halted him. "Then what about the death of Father Leadbetter?"

Marsh locked back, shock written across his face. "I'm sorry, what did you say?"

"Shot dead while coming north on the B&M two nights ago."

"That's . . . horrible," Marsh sputtered. "I can't believe it."

The man's surprise struck Lean as so genuine that he paused for a moment before asking, "Are you denying you were present in that railcar with Father Leadbetter?"

Marsh gasped. "What are you saying?"

Jerome stepped forward a bit, though Lean noticed that the man didn't actually come within arm's length. "Doctor, should I—"

"No, Jerome, it's all right. Deputy, I'm stunned that you would think . . ." Marsh's voice trailed off in disbelief. "Very well, two nights ago I was actually in Boston, coincidentally enough. At a benefit for a friend. It lasted all night."

"So you have witnesses who can confirm this?" Lean asked.

"This is utterly preposterous. But if need be, then yes, I can obtain statements from a dozen reputable witnesses as to my whereabouts that evening. Physicians, attorneys, business leaders, some gentlemen from the statehouse."

An edge came into Marsh's eyes, and his voice was sharper when he spoke again. "*Reputable* witnesses, not some— What is he anyway, a private detective? Some eccentric half-breed who devotes his life to snooping around into other people's business. It's a free country, and Mr. Grey can do as he wishes—within the law. But you, Deputy Lean, are a sworn public servant. The people of this city, and your superiors in the city government, expect more out of you than baseless, and frankly absurd, allegations of misconduct."

"I have reason to believe that you're aware of the circumstances surrounding these deaths."

"You don't have any evidence at all to link me to either of these crimes. Do you know why? Because I haven't the slightest idea of what you're talking about. I don't know this Cosgrove fellow. Father Lead-better was a friend of mine, but many years ago. A kind soul, certainly no one I would ever wish harm upon."

"Not even if it meant getting a hold of this Count de St. Germain's alembic? The philosopher's stone?"

"Really, is that what Grey's filling your head with?" Marsh scoffed. "Please let me give you some advice. I think you need to reconsider where you place your faith. The philosopher's stone." He began to chuckle.

"What's next, Deputy? A leprechaun's pot of gold? Perceval Grey is an unbalanced individual. He seems to be obsessed with delusions about grand criminal conspiracies. Now, I don't blame you, the man can be very convincing. His people are like that—natural-born snake-oil salesmen. My dear fellow, don't let him reel you in. Your job is to protect the public in this beautiful city of ours. Not to let real criminals go free while you search for imaginary shadows that only Grey sees. We really do need to get inside. Is that all now, Deputy?"

"Yes, I suppose it is."

Marsh studied him for a moment, then chuckled again. "Yes, of course it is. I think you're realizing how foolish this all sounds. Good evening, Deputy Lean."

Marsh turned and hurried up the steps with Jerome at his heels. In the rush of the moment, he seemed to forget about his other, far more memorable-looking companion. Lean had also let the woman in the crimson dress slip his mind, until she bumped into him. He felt her face close to his, and her quick whispered words went through him like an electric shock.

"There's danger here."

The feeling was over in a second.

"Please watch where you're stepping," she announced loudly.

From atop the steps, Marsh turned back to see the woman separating herself from Lean and called out, "Come along, Mira."

"Terribly sorry, miss." Lean tipped his hat and apologized with a short bow. He watched her up the steps. It hadn't been a threat she'd whispered; there was more of a warning to it. She was almost to the top of the steps when she glanced back and met Lean's eyes. He saw concern there, maybe even true fear.

Chapter 52

Tom Doran sat looking through a line of trees at the grounds of the Forest City Cemetery in Cape Elizabeth. The sun was beating down on him in the open-topped hansom cab, and he wiped the sweat from his brow as he cursed the name of Archie Lean. This was the second burial ground that he and his man McCrink had trailed Perceval Grey to today. His first round of following Grey had been done in gratitude for the Indian detective's discovery of Doran's daughter the year before. This time the deputy marshal promised a favor. In Doran's line of work, as muscle for one of Portland's two Irish gang leaders, a favor with the cops was worth having in his back pocket.

Still, Doran had never been a patient man, and the tedium of the hot day was fraying his already thin nerves. At least this cemetery seemed to be taking less time. Earlier, at Riverside, Grey had wandered aimlessly while Doran remained hidden in the carriage. With his mammoth size, he was too easily recognized. The job of getting on the ground in the boneyard and keeping a closer eye on Grey's movements fell to his associate, McCrink. That fellow had been blessed with below-average size and a face, typically hidden in a haze of cigarette smoke, that was utterly forgettable.

This time Grey hadn't wandered much at all. He had met a man, maybe a worker at the cemetery, by the front gate. The two had spoken for a minute, and then the man had pointed. That seemed to be enough to tell Grey what he was looking for. The detective found the headstone within a minute or two. But now he'd been standing in the same spot for ten minutes. Doran didn't want to begrudge Grey, or any other man, whatever length of time he needed for mourning at a loved one's grave. Heaven knew Doran had spent many an hour at his wife's marker, too often with a bottle in hand. Yet the sun was hot today, and it was hard to believe, based on what he knew of Grey from their previous work together, that the man had heart enough to hold ten minutes' worth of grief.

Finally Doran saw Grey's dark outline turn and walk away. He was relieved that McCrink had enough sense to wait until Grey passed out of the cemetery before hurrying in to see what had captured his attention. The relief turned to annoyance quick enough. McCrink stood in front of the same marker, staring at it for what seemed an eternity. The man should just have read the name and rushed back to the cab so they could stick with Grey. Instead McCrink was now flapping a scrawny arm in Doran's direction, beckoning him to come and see.

Grumbling the whole time, Doran climbed down, pushed through the trees, and trudged across the graveyard to where McCrink awaited him.

"What in hell are you doing, lolling about gawking?" Doran waved an angry hand toward the road, where Grey's hansom had already passed out of view. "We'll have lost him by now."

McCrink's glassy eyes followed the sweep of Doran's arm, then trickled back to the headstone. When he cracked his lips apart to speak, his cigarette hung at the corner of his mouth, kept there by a dab of dried saliva and leaning over like a desperate man on the precipice of a high bridge.

"Oh, sorry," McCrink said. "But have you ever seen a gravestone queer as this?"

Doran finally glanced at the headstone that had so entranced both Grey and McCrink. The truth was that Doran had seen plenty of headstones in his day, passing through on the way to his wife's marker. And yet it was also true that few had ever struck him as peculiar as the one he saw now. There was no name. There were no dates of birth or death. The stone was clean and fairly new, well cut and pricey-looking. Four simple words crossed its face.

⮀ ⮀

LEAN STOOD IN his front parlor with Doran. Emma had excused herself and, with the baby on her hip, headed off to the kitchen. She was glad to do so, Lean could tell by the look in her eyes. Tom Doran didn't cut the sort of figure to put people at ease, particularly people intent on shielding their young children from all the dangers and brutalities that awaited in the world. His young son, Owen, was a different matter. The boy was clearly fascinated by the most mountainous example of humanity he'd seen in his six short years. Lean had tried to shoo him from the room three times. It was only when Doran growled at him in a way that was not entirely playful that the boy beat his own hasty retreat to the kitchen.

Doran gave a quick summation of that day's events, leading up to Grey's apparent discovery of something interesting at the Forest City Cemetery.

"Let's have it, then. Whose grave was it?"

"Couldn't tell you."

Lean's jaw dropped an inch in disappointment. "You didn't check to see?"

"Course we did. Weren't no name 'scribed at all. Nor dates neither."

"A blank stone. Really?"

"Didn't say that. Weren't blank. Just said 'My Sister, My Soul.' Nothing more."

"I never heard of Grey having a sister," Lean muttered. Of course, that didn't mean anything. He knew very little of Grey's family history. He knew that the man had been raised by his wealthy maternal grandfather. His Indian father had died in an accident when Grey was young. He gathered that Grey's mother had died tragically at some point. He'd never presumed to ask the man, but Lean remembered vague comments that led him to think the woman might have taken her own life.

"Is that it, then? Am I done with following Grey—done for good and true this time?" There was more than a hint of annoyance in the big man's gruff voice.

Before Lean could answer, the mail slot on his front door clacked open and a small white envelope dropped to the floor. It was past dinnertime; the postman had come hours ago. Lean strode to the front door and glanced out a side window. A scruffy boy, twelve years old or so, dashed away down the street into the darkness.

Lean bent and picked up the envelope. He tore it open with his thumb and drew out the single short page and read it to himself:

I know who shot that man Cosgrove. I saw it happen and am ready to tell everything I know. Meet me where he was shot. I don't want any trouble, so please come by yourself at midnight.

Cosgrove had been killed near the Munjoy Hill Reservoir sometime between midnight and dawn. It could be a woman passing by from a late factory shift. A prostitute on North Street looking for a bit of privacy also made sense for a witness in that area. But the note itself made him think otherwise. The message appeared to be written in a hurry but in a well-schooled, feminine hand. In addition, the paper was of high quality.

"What do you say? Done or not, with following Grey?" Doran had joined him at the doorway.

Lean held the message down by his side. He wasn't even sure how well Doran could read but didn't want to take a chance on the man's seeing the note.

"Yeah, all over," Lean said absentmindedly.

"Good. I suppose I should go round up McCrink and tell him to knock off."

Lean showed the big man to the door and stood there thinking. It seemed Grey had found whatever he'd been combing the cemeteries around Portland for. Now Lean was promised an eyewitness to Cosgrove's murder, the answer to the only question he'd had at the start of this inquiry. Things seemed to be wrapping up. Yet that had been the case before, the first time he'd worked with Grey. Just when they thought they'd had their killer, the truth had slipped through their fingers and Dr. Virgil Steig had paid the price. Lean decided he wouldn't let his guard down again.

It took a moment for the operator to connect him to Grey's number. Once he got through, he told Grey he'd just received an anonymous tip. He read the note but, in case the operator was listening in, altered the language to avoid any explicit mention of shooting or violence.

"She wants to meet me at midnight up at the site where the initial trouble was."

"You're certain it's a woman?" Grey asked.

"From the handwriting anyway. On expensive stationery as well."

A brief pause buzzed through from Grey's end of the line. "Could be trying to put you at ease, catch you off guard."

"I think it's genuine. Yesterday evening, just as I finished speaking with Marsh, there was a woman with him. She whispered to me to look out for danger. There was real fear in her eyes."

"Pale skin, dark hair, black fingernails?" Grey asked.

"Wearing gloves, but yes, that sounds like her. All dressed up in crimson."

"She actually spoke. Well, maybe she's taken a shine to you."

Lean ignored Grey's commentary. "This could be the break we need on Cosgrove and to get the inside details on all Marsh's activities."

"Possibly. What was his demeanor when you confronted him? If Marsh felt threatened, this could be a trap."

"He laughed me off," Lean grumbled, "knew I had nothing on him."

"Good," Grey said without a hint of sarcasm.

"Good?" Lean scoffed. "Being mocked by a murderer?"

"Being underestimated by one's enemies always imparts an advantage. How do you want to approach the meeting?"

"The note says to come alone, so I'll make myself conspicuous, stroll along around the North Street corner. You keep an eye out from nearby."

"Any additional patrolmen?" Grey asked.

"I don't want to risk her catching sight and getting scared off. Still, you may want to bring a pistol."

"Of course. Just before midnight," Grey said, with a finality that ended the conversation.

Lean hung up, started to turn away, then glanced back at the phone. Something nagged at his brain, but he pushed it aside. All his thoughts were on the crimson woman and the reservoir.

Chapter 53

GREY RAPPED THE BRASS KNOCKER ON THE FRONT DOOR OF Phebe's house and waited, but there was no response. It was past eleven o'clock, and the house was mostly dark. The front hallway was lit, as was one of the upstairs bedrooms. An uneasy feeling crept through him, and he knocked again, this time with his fist and more loudly. He heard no approach of footsteps or any other human sound from inside, so he tried the locked handle before moving off around the side of the house. A kitchen window yielded to him, and Grey managed to slide and wriggle his way into the darkened room. He walked to the front hall and paused when he heard a footstep on the stairs.

"Perceval—my goodness, you frightened me! What's going on? Has something happened?"

Phebe came down the steps. She wore work boots, heavy woolen trousers, and a dark brown field coat, with a wide-brimmed hat in her hand. All in all she looked as if she'd raided the wardrobe of some country farmer. "How'd you get in here?"

Grey was studying her appearance and managed nothing more in reply than, "Sorry. I took the liberty of letting myself in the back. I was worried when no one answered the door."

"I didn't hear you. And the servants have the night off. Mrs. Mullen must have forgotten to lock up. I really will need to speak to that woman."

"You gave them the night off? I'd have thought you reluctant do that, so soon after what happened the last time," Grey said. "And what of those private security men Euripides planned to hire?"

"Oh, I sent that useless fellow off. I suppose you're wondering why I'm dressed in this outlandish getup?"

"It did strike me as peculiar. Though, that isn't the first question that leaps to mind."

"Oh, really? As usual you've piqued my curiosity."

"Just how deeply are you involved in this deadly game you've all been playing at?" Grey asked. "What do you hope to accomplish?"

Phebe came down the rest of the stairs, frowning at his accusatorial tone. "What on earth are you talking about?"

"I suppose we should start with the original theft of the thunderstone from the offices of Dyer & Fogg. Though we both know it goes further back than that episode."

"The thunderstone? That's been resolved. You have it yourself. It couldn't be in safer hands." Phebe laid a reassuring hand on Grey's arm.

"Resolved, you say. There's still the little matter of Frank Cosgrove's murder. Who would care enough about that stone to kill a man? So few people had any idea the thunderstone was even in the lawyer's locked vaults."

"I don't know what you're aiming at, but in any event, the employees at the law office would have known of it. And as I already told you, I mentioned it in casual company any number of times."

"Yes, but apart from Chief Jefferson, only your family ever showed the slightest knowledge of, or interest in, the item."

"Chief Jefferson, then." She implored Grey with her eyes. "I always suspected him."

"He never stole it. It was delivered to him later, and no one was as surprised by that development as he was. Someone who had no use for the stone anymore arranged for it to be passed to Chief Jefferson. You were so very eager to have me find it. But it only became important to you once you realized that I still intended to locate your sister, even after your grandfather's passing. No doubt you hoped I'd give up the chase after that unhappy day. You saw the chief as an opportunity. You could cast suspicion in his direction, and I'd waste my time pursuing him across the entire state."

"This is ludicrous, Perceval. I don't care to listen to all this . . . this claptrap. Are you sure you're feeling quite well?" She led the way into the living room and lit the gas lamp.

"Not as well as I'd like, it's true. But please indulge me." Grey followed her into the room before continuing with his train of thought.

"Early on I suspected that the thunderstone was just a harmless hobby or obsession for your ancestor Thomas Webster. Not unlike Professor Horsford and his supposed Viking discoveries. After all, Tom Webster fabricated those rock markings along with the thunderstone. Ordered a servant of his to carve them. All an elaborate ruse. But why?"

"I wouldn't have the faintest idea what you're talking about," Phebe said. "Believe me."

Grey began to pace. "I might have, if there weren't other elements, and dangerous people, involved. It would have been easy to believe that you knew nothing of this at all. It makes no sense unless you know what you're looking at—and what other people are seeing. From the beginning nothing added up in this whole business. Least of all your role."

"Me? Perceval, you're making me nervous. Please let's sit and have a drink."

He paused in his movement and waved off the notion of a drink. "From the moment I first saw you, it was clear that you were a devoted granddaughter, caring for Horace in his final days. Your concern for him appeared nothing other than genuine."

"And I assure you it was," Phebe said as she poured a small glass of sherry for herself.

"I don't doubt. And what else became clear, in our talks, was the similar love and devotion that you felt for your sister, Madeline. You've struck me as a remarkably clear, coolheaded woman. Except for matters of your grandfather and sister. Those are the two instances when your emotions come to the surface. And where those two instances collided, that was where I began to suspect that not all was as it appeared with you."

They regarded each other in silence for a moment, neither one's face yielding any hint of emotion.

"I have some news regarding your sister. Though I suppose, in the strictest sense, it won't truly be news to you."

"Really? You mean you've received some word on her where-abouts?"

Grey didn't answer her question. He only stared at her a moment longer before speaking again. "Despite your obvious devotion to your sister, you never showed the slightest interest in having me actually lo-cate her. Why not? Was she really off gallivanting around the world, who knows where or with whom? There was no valid excuse for you to have resisted the idea of locating her, of freeing your grandfather from such a great worry on his deathbed. There can be only one reason: You already knew where she was. And you wanted to shield him from the pain of that knowledge. So no, I wouldn't say I've learned her whereabouts as much as her final resting place."

Phebe lowered her unfinished drink, the crystal clanking down hard on the marble-topped side table.

"I was at the Forest City Cemetery today. I've been visiting most of the burial grounds in the area over the past couple of weeks. Without much luck, until today. The overseer at Forest City instantly knew what I was looking for. He remembered it quite clearly. A young woman with burns to her face severe enough to prevent any possible recognition. She'd washed up on the shore. It was in the papers, but with identification impossible, and no one to claim the body or pay the cost, she was buried in the paupers' field. About a week later, another young woman arrived, with plenty of money. Enough to have the body exhumed. She was able to identify the corpse by a birthmark."

Grey watched Phebe's lips tense, but she said nothing.

"Your uncles didn't know she had one. I paid a visit to Dr. Thayer's office after hours. Madeline's records make mention of the mark's location: on her side, always under her clothing. Who outside the family could have identified her by that? This new young woman paid for a rather expensive headstone as well as a bit of extra money to make sure no word was mentioned to any newspaper about the deceased mystery woman's finally being identified. Even the headstone itself was meant to keep that mystery hidden. 'My Sister, My Soul.' A simple and stirring epitaph you chose. But it's like I told you that first day we met: Four words can be quite telling." Grey ceased his pacing and now waited on Phebe.

"So what if it's all as you say? Yes, I knew that my sister had died. I wasn't willing to inflict that blow upon my grandfather's weakened heart. I gave her a proper burial and tombstone. What of it? There's nothing to connect me to the theft of the thunderstone or handing it off to that Chief Jefferson fellow. Even if I did give it to that man, so what? It was mine to give."

"That was a point of indecision for me," Grey admitted. "Everyone expected Euripides to inherit the stone. Thus he had no cause to steal it. If some family involvement and motivation existed, as appeared so highly likely, it had to be you or your Uncle Jason. He's clearly more fanciful in spirit than you. I suspected him at first. That he was somehow involved with certain unsavory elements in the city. The kind with the imagination and resources to pull off that elaborate bit of skulduggery: stealing Cosgrove's corpse and burning it.

"But then you wept when I told you the story of Helen Prescott and her young daughter. The reaction was out of character for such a pragmatic woman as you. Especially considering that the young girl came to no ultimate harm. The only permanent victim in that part of the story was the murderer's accomplice. The unknown woman who tried to burn young Delia Prescott and, in the end, gave herself over to the flames."

Phebe looked unsteady on her feet. Grey stepped forward, took her arm, and guided her to a stuffed chair.

Grey spoke more quietly and let some degree of sympathy into his voice. "I suspect that you knew Madeline had been led astray, into acts of madness by some insane killer. But you would never have heard that part of the story before. The exact details of how your sister died, and that in her final moments of life she'd been trying to murder an innocent child. It must have been quite a blow to hear those words. That was not the sister you knew and loved."

"I've only lied to you about one thing that truly did matter, Perceval. You asked me why I cared more about recovering the thunderstone than I did about finding her. I told you it was because my sister hadn't been stolen from me. That was a lie. Madeline *was* stolen from me." The look of innocence drained from Phebe's face, replaced with one of angry defiance.

Grey nodded. "Stolen by that murderer Jack Whitten. He's already dead, but your work isn't yet done. There's someone else to be held responsible. Perhaps Dr. Jotham Marsh, Whitten's mentor of sorts. He was the missing connection. He's very knowledgeable about your ancestor's history, and about the thunderstone. He wanted it only to copy the markings, but he didn't know that you were going to hand it over to Chief Jefferson. That annoyed him—I could see it on his face when I mentioned that. He didn't want anyone else seeing the markings, maybe figuring out what they truly meant. But you never cared about what those markings meant, did you?"

"Of course not. It's all a fable. Some fairy story dreamed up by my senile great-great-grandfather."

"You cared only about your sister—and getting me out of the way on Chief Jefferson's trail long enough to do whatever it is that you mean to do. Those men who attacked you, that evening when I returned from my pursuit to Katahdin, were a ruse. Some of Marsh's men, I suspect." He saw the truth of that in her eyes, the first hint of shame or guilt he'd seen there. Was it because she'd faked the attempted robbery by those men or because of what followed later that night? It wasn't the first time Grey had wondered whether that part was also calculated in advance, only the first time he could read her face and see any hint from her. He pushed the thought aside; it didn't matter now.

"But if you don't believe in any of this alchemical nonsense, then what's the reason for your connection to Marsh? Did you offer him information about the thunderstone in order to gain his trust? Why?" Grey asked.

"Yes, we worked out that bit together. He wanted his men to take the stone back, so no one else could read it. And he agreed to stage the robbery, so we could divert any possible suspicion you might have had of me in the whole thunderstone mess. But you're wrong about my telling him anything of the thunderstone. He already knew all that. Uncle Jason told him everything about Thomas Webster. He's been in with Marsh for a long time."

Phebe stood and found her drink again. She threw the last part of it down her throat, steeling herself for what she would say next.

"Jason's the one who introduced Maddy to that cruel monster. My uncle saw how wide-eyed and bored with her life she was becoming. I thought it was just a silly phase, all this mystical, magical rubbish. By the time I realized how serious it was, I was too late. Marsh is an evil man. And Jason handed her over, his own flesh and blood. Jotham Marsh preys upon people like Maddy. People searching for something new and meaningful, no matter how ludicrous it sounds. People who are desperate to feel special and powerful."

Grey nodded. "Her death, her ever getting mixed up in any of this, is a tragedy. I won't deny that. But she hasn't been the only one to suffer. Why did Frank Cosgrove have to die?"

"That was never part of the plan. Uncle Jason was simply going to pay him for the thunderstone. Then, at the last minute, Marsh had a change of heart. Didn't want to risk Cosgrove talking. He said there was too much at stake, so he had one of his ruffians shoot the man." She pleaded her innocence with a long look into his eyes.

"I'm not the criminal here, Perceval. It's Marsh. You must see that. He's the one who kills anyone who stands in his way. He's the one who digs his claws into innocent souls, corrupts them with his madness, and sets them loose to do his killing. He has to be stopped. You know that. Help me do it. I owe Maddy justice."

"Justice? How, exactly? By killing Marsh? Or your Uncle Jason? The desire for revenge is born of pain, not justice."

"Killing's too good for Marsh. Not yet. I'm going to destroy him first. Expose him for the greedy, criminal lunatic that he is. Ruin him, see him paraded about in handcuffs. Ridiculed and despised in the street. And once he gets out of prison, or if he avoids jail, there'll be time enough to kill him then."

"Listen to yourself, Phebe. It's for the law to deal with Marsh and your uncle."

"They'd never be held accountable for Maddy's death. There's no proof of anything that happened with her. And I wouldn't let her name be stomped down into the mud."

"With your testimony they could be found complicit in Cosgrove's death," he assured her.

"And me as well. I never went to the police afterward."

"You didn't know that Marsh meant to kill Cosgrove. I'm sure the city attorney would grant you amnesty in return for your testimony."

"No. Jason and Marsh need to pay for *Maddy's* life—not that man Cosgrove's."

"How do you propose to accomplish all this?" Grey asked.

"I've worked it all out, made all the arrangements. As soon as Marsh and Uncle Jason started this insane alchemy talk and digging up my ancestor's buried treasure, I knew it would come to this. I knew all along they'd never find whatever they were looking for buried under one of the old family houses. Eventually they'd have to look in the last possible location. And there was only one way they could ever reach it.

"I've long since prepared certain incriminating documents. After tonight, when this is over, those documents will be found among Jason's papers. They'll expose his connection to Marsh's insane magic society. Engineering plans that show the weak spot. Journal entries revealing their plan to use the explosives he stole from Uncle Euripides' munitions works. The ones they used to finally complete their delusional plan and unearth the hiding place of Thomas Webster's magical golden formula or whatever foolishness it is that they believe in."

"Explosives—what explosives? You're actually arranging an explosion? Where? Don't you hear how crazed you sound?"

"It's already set. Jason and Marsh saw to that. All I had to do was go back and increase the amount of the charges." The firmness in her eyes wavered for a moment, replaced by another pleading look. "It's the only way. Help me do this, Perceval. You know it's the right thing. True justice never fully reaches men like Marsh and Jason in a courtroom. Fancy-talking lawyers will spin lies, and they'll walk free. This is our chance to see real justice done—tonight. Come with me."

"None of this will give you your sister back."

"No." She turned away from him. Her hands slipped into the large pocket of the field jacket, and her shoulders slumped as if she were finally accepting defeat. When she spoke again, there was still desperate hope in her voice.

"It will make them pay, though. All three men responsible for her death. Won't you help me?"

"Three men?" Grey repeated, confused at that last admission. "I don't know what madness you intend, but I can't let you go through with it."

Phebe turned around to face Grey again. Her shoulders pulled back straight, in defiance. Her right hand slipped out of her coat pocket, holding a pistol aimed squarely at Grey.

"I'm sorry, Perceval. I didn't wish for things to end this way between us. I was ready to forgive *you*."

Chapter 54

Tom Doran found McCrink lurking in the shadow of a building across the street from the Webster house.

"We're done," Doran announced quietly.

"Finally," the diminutive man answered. He crushed out his cigarette and readied himself to leave. "Thought you said this Grey fellow was smart."

"What do you mean?" Doran asked.

"Well, he's been in there a while, with the Webster woman, no doubt. I'm thinking he means to spend the night. One of the servants came out ten minutes back and took off for the day. Even had his luggage with him. And Grey's still left his driver right out front. Not being too sly about the fact that he's paying the young lady a long visit."

Doran decided to linger after he sent McCrink off. He lit a cigar while he stood there watching the house. Quiet minutes drifted past. His cigar was burning down toward the end. That was the deal he'd set with himself. When the cigar was out, he'd do something besides just stand there waiting for Perceval Grey to make an appearance. He took the cigar from his mouth, wanting it to last a few moments longer while he sorted out what to do next. The whole scene was queer. The house was dark. No one was moving around inside. The young Webster woman was still in there. Otherwise there'd be no call for Grey to still be nosing about. That had to be the explanation. They were inside moving about plenty, just not the kind of moving you do in a lit room in front of the window, where peeping Tom Doran can get an eyeful of you.

One big fat problem kept kicking around in his brain. Grey's carriage and his driver, Rasmus Hansen, were parked right there out front, beneath a streetlamp. Rasmus was reading the evening edition through for the second time. Doran knew the driver from before, when Rasmus worked for Dr. Steig. It was natural to get used to waiting around when you drove for a doctor who could be called out at all hours. But Rasmus was no fool neither. If Grey was inside with the Webster woman, Rasmus would be discreet. He wouldn't announce his employer's presence by parking directly out front.

After a last puff on the cigar nub, Doran tossed it aside and lumbered down the sidewalk toward the parked carriage. The horse whinnied at his approach, and Rasmus glanced past his paper.

"Big Tom Doran," the driver greeted him, with a crooked but genuine smile. "Wondering how long you were going to wait there, lurking in the shadows."

"You knew I was there?"

"Mr. Grey had your man pegged down as following us since we left High Street." The driver folded his newspaper and tucked it beside his seat.

"Well, what's he on about in there? I'm tired of waiting for him. When you expect him out?"

"Already. But I've learned it don't pay to expect Mr. Grey to do what you expected him to."

Doran snorted by way of acknowledgment, then asked, "That Webster girl got her hooks in him? You figure maybe he's in there working up a smile?"

"I don't reckon that," Rasmus said as a look of serious contemplation come over him. "He was in one of his gloomy ways when he climbed in. Like he gets when he's thinking too hard."

"That's not good for a fellow," Doran said.

"True enough, but you know what he's like. Peculiar. Seems to me the man's only happy when he's in a troubled mood."

"This is a waste of time. How long you mean to wait on him?"

"Don't know. He should be out by now, or soon anyway. And he don't like to be interrupted when he's up to things." Rasmus took his hat in one hand and scratched his scalp. "Maybe I could peek in or give a light knock. If Miss Webster's up, there's bound to be a maid or somebody awake. I could give a light rap, see if I can learn what's what."

"Go on, then," Doran urged him. "My feet are aching with all this standing about."

He watched Rasmus make his way to the front door and peek in at the narrow side windows. The man gave the knocker a timid rap. Then he pressed his ear to the door and listened for at least twenty seconds.

Doran was about to shout at him to knock louder when Rasmus waved him forward. Doran tromped up the walkway.

"Listen," Rasmus hissed at him.

Doran didn't hear anything other than a few faint sounds of carriages passing on the next block. He pressed his ear to the door as Rasmus had done. After a few seconds, he heard it. A faint metallic clanking sound. It almost sounded like heating pipes coming to life, but this was different, more urgent.

"What is it?" Doran wondered aloud.

Rasmus didn't answer. He stepped away from the door and moved along the front of the house, peering in windows as he went. When he disappeared around the corner, Doran gave in and followed. The windows were all dark and revealed nothing. He didn't catch up with Rasmus until he reached the back of the house. The driver had his head pressed close to a window that was not fully shut. From the moonlight passing through the window, Doran could make out that they were looking in on the kitchen. The clanking sound was still muffled but louder. It was irregular, several seconds of silence and then a burst of angry rattling.

"Don't you think this is queer?" Rasmus asked.

"Queer enough." Doran went to the back door and hammered on it with the side of his fist. There was silence and then, a few seconds later, an even more furious sound of metal clanging and rattling.

Doran returned to the window and lifted it wide. "Here, I'll boost you through."

As he readied himself to step into Doran's interlocked fingers, Rasmus paused. "But what if it's nothing? What if they're upstairs and all?"

"Then we hoof it fast around the corner. I was with you and you were with me, together minding our business over at Farrell's saloon for the past hour."

Rasmus slipped through the window and unlocked the door for Doran before lighting a wall lamp. The kitchen was neat and orderly, everything set to rights for the night. There was no sound throughout the house.

"Don't think there's anyone here," Rasmus whispered.

The clanging sounds started up again, and Doran led the way down to the end of a short hall. Rasmus loitered behind a moment as he found and lit a candle. Doran opened the door. The room inside was dark, but he could make out the white porcelain sink. It was a small water closet. There was a dark figure lying on the floor next to the sink.

"Shut the gas valve," the man on the floor growled.

A second later Doran heard it, the low, steady hiss of the gas jet on the wall left open. He glanced over his shoulder to where Rasmus was starting down the hallway with his candle in hand.

"Douse that flame." The big Irishman ordered before fumbling in the dark to turn the jet off.

"I'm handcuffed," the voice from the floor said. Doran recognized it now as Grey. "Is the key somewhere?"

Doran shouted the question back to Rasmus and then felt for Grey's hands. The cuffs ran behind the sink's drainpipe. Doran gave several strong yanks to see if he could dislodge the pipe and free Grey. The plumbing shuddered but held in place.

Rasmus appeared in the doorway with a key held up in triumph. "This was on the kitchen table. Give it a try."

It took Doran a moment, but he got the key in and heard it click. They helped Grey to his feet and guided the unsteady man back to the kitchen.

"Did you see her leave? Phebe Webster?" Grey asked them. "Did she meet anyone? Which direction did she go?"

Rasmus shook his head. "Never saw her. Some worker left out the side. Carrying a heavy trunk. Maybe a toolbox."

Grey pondered this for a moment. "Rasmus, is my bag still in the carriage?"

"Course, Mr. Grey."

"Right. I need you to get me to Deputy Lean's house, and quickly. Doran—get to the patrol station. If Lean's there, have him telephone me at his house. We need to find him. Now."

⁂

"ARCHIE LEFT THIRTY minutes ago." Emma's eyes wandered out past Perceval Grey, trying to penetrate the shroud of darkness beyond her front porch. "He was going to check in at the station, and then he had to meet someone."

"He didn't perchance say exactly where he was meeting?" Grey tried to keep his tone casually polite, but he noticed his own fingers tapping furiously on the doorframe and had to pull his hand down.

"I don't know. He didn't say. In fact"—her hand circled in the air near her head as if cranking up her mind—"I don't think he knew who he was supposed to meet. He mentioned that murdered man from a few weeks ago and Munjoy Hill."

"Where's Daddy?" The demanding voice came from the hallway stairs. Beneath a pile of tousled hair were a pair of blurry eyes and the aggrieved face of six-year-old Owen Lean.

"Back up to bed, young man."

"Has he done something with Daddy?" Owen pointed an accusatory finger toward Grey at the front door.

"Owen, you march right up those stairs this instant. I'll be up to tuck you back in." Emma stared after her son for a few seconds, making sure he started his grudging retreat to his bedroom.

"Sorry, Mr. Grey. Is Archie in some sort of," she asked as she turned back to the door and saw Grey already down to the sidewalk and climbing back into his carriage, "trouble?"

Chapter 55

R ASMUS HANSEN URGED THE HORSE ALONG WALNUT STREET toward the intersection with North. The Munjoy Hill Reservoir rose up in the moonlight at the far corner. It was set back slightly from the street front, leaving enough room for two small houses to squeeze in at the immediate corner. Farther down, past the impressive embankment, three stories high, stood two more houses. Otherwise the massive structure, holding twenty million gallons of water, dominated that block. Grey ordered Rasmus to slow as they reached the intersection. He peered down North Street, looking for any sign of Lean or other suspicious activity. In that direction the reservoir's steep embankment transitioned briefly to a more gradual slope that ended at the sidewalk. Across the street were a row of houses and a lamppost. That scene was too obvious and open to view. If trouble lurked, it wouldn't be near either North or Walnut Street but away, hidden from view on the vacant north or east side of the giant reservoir.

"Let's get a look ahead. Past the far wall of the reservoir," Grey said.

The carriage jolted and sped forward, then slowed after it passed by the few houses farther along, approaching the Eastern Promenade.

"Drop me at the corner. Then wheel about back to North Street. Wait there and keep your eyes sharp for Lean's arrival," Grey said as he slung his leather satchel over his head so the long strap ran across his torso. He hurried past some bushes that lined the sidewalk, leaving the greenery of the Promenade and the scenic but unappreciated moonlit vista of Casco Bay behind him. He skirted the two houses, one of which still had lights shining, along with a shed and a large barn. It wouldn't do to have the homeowners coming out their back doors and shouting at him as a trespasser or thief. He didn't wish to lose his only current advantage: that Phebe, along with any possible accomplices, thought he was still shackled on the floor of the water closet.

He passed through a scant grouping of trees and paused at the edge to consider the reservoir and its surroundings. The natural lay of the land sloped up slightly toward the reservoir before meeting the steeper sides of the massively thick retaining wall. That embankment rose at least thirty feet above the surrounding terrain. Grey listened but heard no voices or other sounds of activity at the reservoir. He was tempted to make directly for where a set of earthen steps was cut into the embankment not far from Walnut Street. They led to a five-foot-wide graveled walkway atop the wall, which circled the entire four acres of the water's surface. It would give him a commanding view but also instantly reveal his presence and make him an outstanding target. He abandoned the thought, opting to keep low to the ground while searching for the location of the night's threat.

If there was to be an explosion, it made sense for it to happen slightly to Grey's right, closer to the northeastern corner of the rectangular structure. There were no houses that way. Fields and trees alone would bear the brunt of any debris or destruction. This large and irregular city block was mostly undeveloped, virtually the last such open space on Portland Neck. It thinned to a narrow point above where the Eastern Promenade and North and Washington streets all merged in a triangle at northernmost tip of the peninsula. Below there, down the slope leading to the ocean, Tukey's Bridge stretched over to North Deering, across the outlet of Back Cove. Anyone mad enough to dynamite and potentially breach the reservoir would logically choose that direction, allowing the water to escape to the ocean unimpeded, with no danger to nearby houses or untimely pedestrians.

Grey walked slowly toward the rear of the reservoir. The moon was about half full, providing enough light to allow him to see any obvious movements. He stayed close to the edge of a line of bushes and trees, cautious and stooped in an effort to reduce his profile and make as little noise as possible. He alternated between watching the ground before him and keeping an eye on the reservoir as he walked. Halfway to the northeastern corner, he felt his foot snag on something, and he stumbled forward to his knees. He glanced about and listened for any reaction to his fall. There was nothing, but instead of spying any offending root or fallen branch that tripped him, he saw a thin wire stretching across the ground.

Kneeling there, he lifted it to his eyes. The wire ran off in both directions, the angle of its path indicating that it stretched from a thick stand of trees and brush directly toward the center of the eastern embankment of the reservoir. Grey took his satchel strap from around his neck and set the satchel on the ground. He searched through the various interior pockets that held his multitude of tools and all his equipment. His hand settled onto a thin metal file.

Grey bent the wire into a loop, slipped it over the edge of the file, and started sawing at the line. Within ten seconds the wire snapped. He stood up, still holding one end of the wire. He was about to trace it to its source, its detonation device, when he heard a distant voice. He dropped the wire, whirled about, and listened. He heard the voice again, off to his right, around the northeast corner of the reservoir wall. He sprinted forward toward it. Upon reaching the corner, he skidded to a stop. Forty paces in front of him, he saw a figure standing with his back to Grey, broad-shouldered and wearing a bowler. Another man, slender and all in dark shades, faced the first man, separated by only two steps.

Grey peered at the two men a second longer before recognition flashed into his mind. Just then he heard sounds of quick footsteps behind him. A shadowy figure was sprinting across the open grass, from where the detonator was hidden among the trees toward the reservoir's embankment.

Chapter 56

L EAN STOOD AND WAITED, A THIN RIBBON OF CIGARETTE smoke drifting past his eyes. He kicked at the ground on the back side of the Munjoy Hill Reservoir, close to the exact spot where they'd found the body of Frank Cosgrove weeks earlier. There was the occasional sound of foot or carriage traffic floating around the bulk of the reservoir, but all in all the midnight air was quiet and still. A single lamppost was visible over a hundred yards off on North Street, too far away to aid the limited visibility granted by the moon.

At long last he saw a man cross over the street, glance about, then continue on across the grassy slope just behind the reservoir. From the handwriting on the note he'd received, Lean had been expecting a woman. Since he'd made no effort to conceal himself, Lean now assumed, however, that the man was heading toward him with a purpose. He tossed his cigarette aside, readying himself for whatever the encounter would bring. The man stopped five paces short. He was slender and walked with a formal gait, as if he meant to be seen making an arrival, rather than just going somewhere. Lean guessed he was an older man, though the fellow was dressed darkly and the brim of his hat hid his features.

"Good evening," the man said. "Where's she at, then? Let's see what this big problem's all about."

The man sounded peeved and anxious, but Lean's ear still caught the underlying tones that indicated a very well-spoken gentleman.

"Just who is it you're looking for?" Lean asked.

The man recoiled and loudly demanded, "Who are you?"

"Deputy Marshal Lean. And who might you be?"

"That's none of your concern. I don't need to be accosted by the police, simply for being out having a walk."

The man backed away a step and started to turn. Lean drew his revolver. "Stop there, mister. I'm afraid you'll need to answer a few questions." He took two steps closer, wanting to get a better look at the man.

"I'll do nothing of the sort! Leave me be this instant, or I'll see you're relieved of duty permanently."

The man slipped his hands into his coat pockets.

"Afraid not. Hands over your head. Now!" Lean ordered. "And for the last time: your name?"

"Jason Webster," the older gentleman said through an indignant snarl.

"Lean! It's a trap!" The shouted warning rang out from a distance behind him.

Lean recognized the voice as Grey's, and his head and shoulders swiveled in that direction. In the faint moonlight, he spotted Grey at the corner of the reservoir embankment. As he started to turn back toward Jason Webster, something hard connected with the base of his skull just below his right ear. The few faint lights in his field of vision all exploded. He dropped to one knee and braced himself against the ground with his left hand. With the last strands of surviving consciousness left him, Lean focused on not letting go of his gun. He felt his body slouch forward and knew that his head was now pressed against the earth. There was no other attack. No other feeling or sound reached him. He wasn't sure how many seconds passed before his vision cleared and he raised himself up onto his knees again.

He moved his gun to his other hand and reached for the back of his head. He felt a large bump and the warm, slow oozing of blood. Groaning, he forced himself to his feet. Jason Webster was nowhere to be seen. Lean caught sight of the distant lamppost and used it to gain his bearings. He turned around and stumbled toward the spot where he'd seen Grey. He tried to move quickly, but he was still dizzy and found it necessary to keep his head bent forward, focusing on where he was planting each step.

He paused when he reached the corner of the reservoir. From atop the wall, quite a distance from Lean, came urgent voices. After a moment Lean's eyes picked out the dark shape of Jason Webster, equally far away. The man was scrambling, unsteadily, up the slope of the embankment. Webster was only halfway up the side when the whole ground shuddered. A loud boom shook the air. Lean kept his feet under him but watched Jason Webster get pitched back through the night to land and tumble head over heels down the slope.

As the rumble subsided, Lean heard Grey's voice shout something. He rushed forward in the darkness.

AFTER SHOUTING HIS warning to Lean, Grey had turned and raced back along the base of the reservoir wall. Ahead of him the runner covered the last few yards of open space to reach the corner of the reservoir close to Walnut Street. The figure was dressed like a laborer, but short and slight. If he hadn't known that Phebe was disguised, he might have been fooled. Grey was only halfway along the base of the wall, and she was already at the corner, climbing the steps chiseled into the hard-packed earth embankment. Grey veered to his right, trying to use his momentum to carry him up the slope of the reservoir's outer wall. After a few lunging paces, he leaned forward and continued scrambling upward on all fours, thrusting with his legs, scratching and clawing with his hands.

He gained the level edge atop the wall and pulled himself onto the five-foot-wide surface that ran along the entire course of the reservoir. He glanced to his right, assuming that Phebe had already raced past, headed to the northeast corner, but that way was empty. Grey turned back to his left, surprised at the sight of her bent down and handling some small contraption hidden from his view. It made no sense; he'd misjudged the location of the dynamite. Phebe was too close to the street. There were houses nearby, far too close for any sudden release of the reservoir's water. He sprinted forward.

"Don't!" he yelled.

Phebe looked up, paused, and then her right arm made a sudden movement. Grey saw a small spark near the ground. He watched her stand as he slid to a halt on the gravelly pathway. He was still five or six strides from her. His mind hadn't settled on what exactly to expect, but it wasn't this, an eerie stillness. A long second passed, then another.

Phebe turned back to the steps. Grey started toward her. The device may have malfunctioned, he could still disconnect it. In his second step forward, the ground jumped. A sound like a cannon blast filled Grey's ears as he fell to his side. He landed on his right knee, perilously close to falling into the reservoir. The broad expanse of water that had been deathly still now rippled angrily. Grey looked for Phebe. She'd fallen face-first on the pathway but was starting to get up.

The blast had been forceful but not devastating. It didn't feel strong enough to puncture all the way through the wide embankment. Maybe it was only meant to weaken the wall after all, to force the city to drain the unsafe reservoir, and thus provide access to the bottom and the imagined treasure lying beneath. Even as he exhaled, Grey realized that made no sense. Phebe's plans wouldn't be satisfied by a small explosion. She'd already admitted to increasing the intended blast. Euripides Webster's words, the day at the granite quarry, came shooting back into Grey's mind. Not a single explosion but a series of smaller bursts, expertly placed, could inflict the same amount of power as a single, large blast.

"Hold on!" he called out to Phebe.

A second explosion, larger than the first, sent earth flying in all directions. Grey felt something strike his head even as the force of the blast lifted him off his feet. He twisted in the air, then landed, splashing into cool darkness. He tumbled under the surface, taking in a mouthful of water before his head emerged into the night air. The world spun around him as he struggled to fill his lungs and orient himself.

His eyes focused on the cloud of dust that hovered over the site of the second explosion. The air was slowly clearing. Phebe would be off to the side. She was there, edging forward on her hands and knees. Only a few yards separated Grey from the inside wall of the reservoir. But he could see a thin seam, an opening created in the wall in front of him. He aimed for a spot off to his right, closer to where Phebe was heading. His arms flailed, and though he was sure he was kicking his legs strongly, they seemed oddly heavy and slow in the water. He stared ahead, trying to focus on his target along the embankment. He just had to reach it.

Dark, blurry spots appeared in Grey's field of vision, and he hoped it was only the water dripping into his eyes. His outstretched hand scraped against a hard surface, and he grasped for the wall. Fortunately, it wasn't a straight vertical surface. The wall sloped away, the same as on the outside of the reservoir. Grey lunged forward, his hands finding purchase on the dry earth atop the wall. To his left, Phebe had risen to her knees and was trying to stand. In his confusion Grey had somehow managed to swim past her, moving farther down the wall than he'd intended. As he strained to pull himself up, a third blast rocked the embankment. Grey lost his grip and slid back into the water but managed to keep his head above the surface. Clumps of rock and earth rained down around him. One struck him on the upper arm, but nothing worse followed. He dug his shoe tips into the wall and pushed himself forward again, dragging himself up out of the water.

The effort was almost too much. The world darkened and swirled before his eyes for several seconds as he lay on his stomach. He pressed his hands into the flat embankment, drawing some sense of stability from the packed dirt. Above the thin, buzzing sound that filled his ears, Grey thought he heard muffled shouts and distant screams.

He brought himself up to his elbows and looked ahead on the top of the embankment.

Phebe was only five feet in front of him. A scattered layer of dirt had fallen over her back. She wasn't moving.

"Phebe!" Grey's own voice sounded far from him.

He listened for a response. The buzzing sound was being overtaken by a new one, a heavy, rushing sound. Then he noticed, below and off to his right, a wall of water cascading down the outside of the embankment. He looked toward the ground, expecting to see the grassy field lit faintly in the moonlight. Instead the whole area was swirling and churning in a frothy, raging mass.

Grey looked past Phebe. Behind her the embankment had fallen away on both sides of the blast site. Even as he watched, the breach continued to grow, widening in a V shape. The force of the twenty million gallons of water trying to rush over itself and escape the reservoir was undeniable. The top of the wall crumbled, washing away like a sand castle caught in the undertow of a receding wave. As the gap in the wall grew, the roar of the rushing water increased in Grey's mind. He might as well have been beneath the ocean trying to hear over the waves.

The path atop the embankment fell away in chunks that left Phebe's feet hanging over the lip of the evaporating wall. Grey lunged toward her and grabbed her by the wrist. The contact roused Phebe; her head moved. She looked around, and her eyes found Grey, who was also lying flat but trying to pull himself backward and drag her with him.

He stared into her eyes and shouted, "We have to move! Come on!"

Phebe had lost the wide-brimmed hat of her disguise. A line of blood ran down from her forehead. Her eyes were glazed and uncomprehending. Her lips moved, but the raging water flooding out of the reservoir swallowed her voice.

Grey read her lips: *Perceval, help me.*

He lurched backward, trying to pull her toward him, but he had no leverage in his prone position and her body was like deadweight. Still holding her wrist, he forced himself up to one knee and got the other foot beneath him. He grabbed hold of her arm with his other hand and tugged. She started to slide toward him. Then the wall gave out beneath her legs and abdomen. Her body dropped away over the side. The force of the water pulling on her almost yanked Grey forward as well. He fell back into a sitting position and dug his heels in on either side of Phebe, still grasping her wrist. The breach atop the wall kept moving toward him, inch by inch, and with every passing moment Phebe dipped lower into the rushing water. It splashed around and over her, making Grey's grip wet. She started to slip from his grasp. Her nails dug into his flesh.

His eyes remained locked on her as he struggled to pull her close.

Help me!

He saw the scream pass through her lips. In the moonlight her eyes, dazed before, now seemed perfectly clear, endlessly deep, and locked onto his as she fell from his hand. Her face hovered there for an immeasurable instant, then disappeared, engulfed by the raging waters.

Pieces of the wall gave way beneath Grey's legs. He threw his body backward, fell onto his side, and rolled for several turns. As he got up onto all fours, he looked down into the avalanche of water. He could hear faint sounds of piercing screams and shouts filling the air. Phebe? He knew it wasn't her. Lean: Where was Lean?

To his side all was chaos. Millions of gallons of water, black in the night, rushed forward in an endless torrent. What should have been solid ground was a seething, hurtling cauldron. He looked just above it, and for a moment his mind didn't grasp what he saw. Large, blocky shapes floated above the water yet were a part of it all: houses. The few homes that lined Walnut Street were being consumed. They'd been two-story buildings before, but now the water and driving mud had risen in a wall to engulf the first floor of each

Grey looked away. He reached ahead, felt dry gravel and dirt beneath his fingertips, and clawed at it, pulling himself onward. He had no idea if he was beyond the danger of the wall's collapse. The world spun uncontrollably before his eyes; he knew only that he had to keep moving. Desperate cries cut through the water, swirling about in Grey's mind as he yielded his last tether to the conscious world. The ground seemed to fall away beneath him. There was darkness, heavy and tumbling, and then nothingness.

Chapter 57

THE HOSPITAL ROOM WAS DIM, THE CURTAINS DRAWN TO keep out the late-afternoon sun. The weak light and the nature of the news he was about to impart caused Lean's voice to drop to an almost confessional tone. "A young man from one house, though he was found inside the second. His father says he'd rushed in there to help get the neighbors out. But there wasn't time. A woman and her two daughters were home in the second place. They never had a chance."

Lean felt the unpleasant knot in his gut that he always felt when delivering this type of news to a victim's family. He wasn't quite sure why he felt it now, passing the information along to Grey. From his hospital bed, Grey watched Lean's face as he spoke, then stared straight ahead. It wasn't the first time Lean had ever wondered what was going on in the man's mind, only this time he was concerned for Grey.

A bandage was wrapped around Grey's head; he'd taken a cut near his left temple. The man's expression remained flat. Lean couldn't tell if he was just being his regular less-than-emotional self or if he was actually struggling to comprehend the full extent of what he'd just heard. The doctor had informed Lean, upon arrival, that Grey had taken quite a blow from the explosion and was likely to suffer lingering effects for several days.

"There's to be a full inquiry into the collapse of the reservoir, I assume," Grey said in a quiet voice.

"Not by the police. Euripides Webster has been busy. He's on very amiable terms with at least half the city council. They're very sympathetic to his tragic loss and listening to everything he has to say: that it's such a horrific and unexplainable coincidence that his brother and niece just happened to be passing the reservoir at that time. He's vowed to extend some rather generous charity to the families of the innocent victims in the houses that were destroyed." Lean's voice grew more sarcastic as he continued. "He's even willing to pay to have engineers examine the reservoir and determine the possible construction flaw that led to this disaster. If he can understand how this senseless tragedy happened, it might just take some of the anguish away."

"Most kind of him. The part about the charitable assistance anyway." Grey's tone was genuine and subdued compared to Lean's. "I'm sure his engineers will be able to find evidence of structural defects to blame for the failure of the wall. All of it a small price to pay to keep his family's name unblemished."

"Glad to see you haven't suffered any great damage to your reasoning faculties after all."

"Any problems with your bosses, the marshal or Mayor Baxter?" Grey asked. "How did you explain your presence? And mine?"

"Mayor's not any particular friend of Webster's, but he's not eager to turn a horrible tragedy into a major scandal. Especially if no good would come of doing it. And I can't see how it would. As for my being there, I told them the truth of it: I was supposed to meet an anonymous witness who might have seen Cosgrove get shot. You were there at my request." Lean dug out a cigarette and put it in his mouth.

"As for the events of the evening, I have no proof that Jason Webster was there for any nefarious purpose. He never actually said anything of the sort to me. The marshal and the mayor have both agreed to accept that the man may have been there innocently and mistaken me for an armed assailant."

"Very convenient," Grey said. "And I take it you're also willing to overlook the fact that this explosion was intended to murder you as well?"

Lean looked down at Grey with a mix of bewilderment and suspicion that the man was perhaps drifting into a confused state. "Me? What are you on about?"

Grey motioned to a small table beside his hospital bed. "There— inside the drawer. I had Mrs. Philbrick collect certain documents from my rooms and bring them here for safekeeping. Look inside. There's a photograph."

Lean opened the drawer and removed a folder. He pulled out a photograph of a young woman. He'd never seen the picture before. It was the one that Attorney Dyer had provided to Grey upon his acceptance of Horace Webster's request to locate his missing granddaughter. When Lean's eyes finally left the photograph, they were wide with disbelief.

"That's her—the woman from Cushing's Island last summer. Whitten's crazed accomplice. The one who set herself on fire!"

"Madeline Webster," Grey announced, his voice still restrained. "She was one of Marsh's acolytes. And Jack Whitten's mysterious female accomplice. The redheaded woman on the island and, I do believe, the same redheaded woman we briefly spied last year at the Salem train depot when we chased that impostor to his death."

"My God, I believe you're right. So that's what you'd been doing, visiting all those cemeteries. You knew that the sister was dead all along?"

"I had a suspicion."

"Why didn't you say something? Did Phebe Webster know any of this? Do you suppose it had any part in explaining her actions at the reservoir?"

Grey quickly summarized what Phebe had confessed to him about her sister's connection to Marsh, Jason Webster's role in getting the younger sister involved with Marsh's occult society, and Phebe's obsession with taking revenge on everyone involved with Madeline's death—Lean included.

"She figured that all their digging in basements would come to naught. Eventually they'd have to look under the only other site owned by Old Tom Webster."

"The pastureland on Munjoy Hill where the reservoir now stands," Lean said. "No way to dig unless they could force it to be drained first."

"I believe that was the original intent, only to weaken the wall, to present a danger that would require it be emptied, at least temporarily. Then Marsh could search for Count de St. Germain's alembic, the key to the philosopher's stone. But Phebe Webster supplemented the dynamite. She wanted a massive explosion. Lured her uncle there for the blast to kill him and do enough other damage to ensure an investigation that would incriminate Marsh."

"At the risk of taking innocent lives—madness," Lean said with a shake of his head. "How long did you know about her?"

"I was never entirely sure—until the end, that is. That's why I never mentioned her possible involvement."

"Hoping it wasn't true." Lean nodded in sympathy. "I wish none of it were. Wouldn't have to stifle the truth about some unbelievable plot to empty the reservoir, causing such horrible death and destruction, all for a chance to unearth some sort of mystical talisman that, to be sure, never existed. You are certain of that, aren't you? This golden alchemical gadget thing isn't real. It's not secretly buried somewhere beneath the reservoir?" There was a mischievous gleam in Lean's eyes.

"I am absolutely certain that no such item is buried anywhere near the reservoir. Marsh and Jason's idea to drain the reservoir and gain access to such a mechanism was completely unfounded."

"What if it wasn't, though?" Lean suggested. "Wouldn't that be something? A little device that . . . what? You put in lead or what have you and out comes gold dust. A lifetime of riches and an endless lifetime to spend it. Quite tempting."

"Yes, even to a man like yourself. One who, under normal circumstances, is levelheaded. More or less. And so we see the full extent of the danger. There's no firm proof that any such device ever existed. Just a bunch of wishes, lies, and rumors. Yet how many have died because of the ridiculous hope that it might be true? Even the *idea* of this thing is too deadly to be allowed to spread."

"Well, Jason Webster's out of the running now. But Jotham Marsh is still lurking about. And he obviously believes it. I don't like the idea of that man walking around, free to carry out more of his schemes. Phebe Webster wasn't wrong to say he's at least partly to blame for several deaths. Including hers, after a manner."

Lean's mouth drew tight, and his brow furrowed. "Did you really not know before the end? Were you hoping Phebe Webster wasn't involved in all this? Or did you suspect the truth, only you thought you could save her from her own madness? If you could have stopped her sooner."

"She would still be alive. As would those four needless victims of the reservoir's breach. Yes, I am painfully aware of those facts." Grey paused, gathering his thoughts. "Add to this the fact that Jotham Marsh will remain at large, once again unaccountable for his wrongdoings.

With Phebe and Jason Webster gone, only his own fanatical followers have any knowledge of Marsh's crimes. And they'll never testify against him. He's got the entire criminal element in the city frightened of his occult powers."

"He's even tried to kill you twice. What do you plan to do about him?"

"I'm not immediately concerned that he's planning any further harm against me, you, or anyone else. He still thinks that St. Germain's alembic, the device that Old Tom Webster supposedly stole and later buried, is somewhere under the reservoir. He'll likely be devoting his full efforts over the coming weeks and months to trying to find it. But your point is well taken. There will come a time, sooner rather than later, when I will need to obtain inescapable proof against him of one crime or another. He's too great a threat to be allowed to escape justice for very much longer."

"You know that if there's any way I can help . . ." Lean left the offer hanging in the air.

The door opened, and a stern-faced nurse in an overly starched uniform barged into the room.

"How are we doing, Mr. Grey?" The nurse didn't wait for an answer before announcing, "Time for me to change those bandages."

Lean stood by silently while the nurse unwrapped the old bandage, revealing a small bump and some dried blood on the side of Grey's head. Grey ignored her actions; he was instead regarding Lean with his full attention. Finally he gave Lean a solemn nod.

The nurse rambled on. "Mr. Grey, I'll have to insist you get some rest soon, but you do have one more visitor, if you feel up to it. Any new complaints?"

"The décor is numbingly bland, the air in here is stagnant, and that cup of tea you brought tasted as though it were wrung from an old dishrag."

"Isn't he just the dearest thing?" the nurse said to Lean.

"And to think I was worried about how your recovery would go. Well, I'll be off, since you have someone else who actually wants to spend a few minutes with you."

"Who knew I was so well liked?" Grey said.

"Trust me, you're not." Lean headed out the door, saying, "I'll check in again when I get a chance."

The nurse finished wrapping a new bandage. "Should I show her in?"

"Give me a few minutes, please. I'd like to dress first."

"Whatever for? You can't go anywhere yet."

"Oh, I'm quite sure I can manage," Grey said.

"The doctor won't allow it."

"I'll gladly disabuse him of his concerns after I see my visitor. Thank you."

A few minutes later, there was a quiet rapping at the door and Helen Prescott eased into the room.

"Mrs. Prescott. This is a surprise." Grey slipped on his coat.

"Hello"—she paused for half a second, unsure of how to address him—"Mr. Grey. I just wanted to stop in. I can't stay long. Delia's waiting."

"Quite all right. I'm preparing to leave myself."

"Already? Well it's good to see you're feeling better. Are you sure you're well? Does it hurt?"

"Only when I speak, or look at something, or think." He took a step from the center of the room, moved closer to his bed, and laid a hand on the footboard.

"I'm sorry," Helen said. "It's really quite awful, everything that happened there by the reservoir. All those poor people. I saw Archie on the way out. He told me something of what happened." She worked herself closer to Grey's side table, where she busied her hands rearranging a vase full of flowers that didn't need tending.

"He said Phebe Webster was among the . . . that she was at the reservoir. You'd pursued her there. That she was involved with this whole matter. He thinks you may have suspected her all along. Even . . ." Helen sounded as if the words were physically lodging in her throat. "Even that morning, when we met outside your house."

Grey didn't speak right away, and Helen finally met his gaze.

"Is that true?" she asked.

"What can I say to you, Helen? I would offer some kindness or comfort if I knew how. Did I truly have strong feelings for her? Or did I suspect her of being part of a criminal conspiracy all along and only sought to gain her trust in order to uncover her actions and motives?"

Grey studied Helen's face for a moment as if he were trying to see inside her.

"Which answer would you honestly care to hear from me? Which one would make you despise me less?"

She stared at him there, supporting himself with a hand on the hospital bed, his gaze foggy and pained.

"I don't despise you, Perceval. Not at all." She wondered whether he shared any of her sentiments at that moment. "I'm . . . I'm sorry. I shouldn't have come now. Maybe some other time we could talk. Later, once you've had a chance to . . . When you're feeling better."

Grey managed only the faintest of nods, and Helen quickly turned and left the room. He glanced out through the gap in the curtains before shielding his eyes from the light and turning away again to face the empty room.

Chapter 58

GREY ARRIVED A FEW MINUTES EARLY AT THE EASTERN Cemetery. He'd chosen it as a convenient, open location for the meeting. It was only a short walk from the site of the reservoir disaster, and Grey had wanted to get his first look at the destruction he'd been unable to prevent two nights earlier. Dozens of gawkers still lingered there at the fatal site. The swath of destruction was startling. A massive wall of earth and mud had sloshed down the slope. The two houses and a barn that had stood in the way were pushed along, crumpled, and smashed as if they'd been no bigger than children's toys. Mud remained piled up close to the empty second-story windows. Apart from Phebe and Jason Webster, four other souls, including a mother and her two young daughters, had perished beneath the wall of water, with its onslaught of earth, massive paving blocks, and heavy piping.

He remembered the last moments before he'd lost consciousness, the shouts and screams coming from those houses. That water, the idea of its weight, pushed down on Grey's mind, and he barely recalled just having walked downhill to the cemetery. He ended up a short way past the headstones of Thomas Webster and his kin. He stood there, deep in thought, as still as one of the monuments. In his coat pocket, he felt a single sheet of paper, the original bequest of the thunderstone written by Thomas Webster eighty years earlier. Attorney Dyer had been livid when Grey had lied and explained that the document had been lost in the reservoir flood. However, Grey had calmed the man by telling him that if the document were forgotten, Grey would keep quiet as to the Webster family's role in that disaster. He even managed to turn Dyer's annoyance into a smile when he informed him that the attorney could keep half the five-hundred-dollar commission owed Grey for locating Madeline Webster. Dyer was to spend the remaining half relocating

Dastine LaVallee from her sparse room at the Portland Alms House and paying her entry fee to the more comfortable surroundings of the Home for Aged Women. There would even be spending money left over for her.

Grey's thoughts turned to Thomas Webster's riddle—his play on words, as it turned out. The bequest in his pocket had been the key. It had allowed Grey to break the code of the twenty-four symbols etched by Webster. Allowed him to sound out the seven Greek letters represented on the thunderstone that gave the location of Webster's buried treasure. Een-eff-ogg-ay: in effigy. Those words were the name that hid the Count de St. Germain's alembic, the golden key to the supposed philosopher's stone. He glanced at the earth covering Thomas Webster's grave. Nearby was Thomas's son George. Lean had reported that both men's graves had been disturbed sometime last year. The seemingly inexplicable act had been marked down to desperate grave robbers hoping to find a bit of jewelry or some such.

Of course, that wasn't the case at all. Jotham Marsh, with the likely assistance of Jason Webster, would have been behind the attempted grave robbery. They had surmised that the reputed treasure was buried, but they didn't know where. One of the old graves was a natural guess. It fit with the mythos of the Rosicrucians, the legend of their founder Christian Rosenkreuz's own secret burial chamber, and the society's motto of VITRIOL: *"Visita Interiora Terrae Rectificando Invenies Occultum Lapidem."* Jerome Morse had translated it for him on the train: "Visit the interior of the earth and purifying you will find the hidden stone." Grey smiled at Marsh's failure. If only the man had realized how close he'd been to unearthing the true location.

The faint scratch of an approaching step on the gravelly surface of Funeral Lane sent those thoughts fleeing to the corners of Grey's mind. He looked up and shielded his eyes. His headache persisted, and the sunlight only made the piercing sensation in his brain worse.

"Looks like your luck hasn't gotten any better since the last time we met," Chief Jefferson said, pointing toward the side of Grey's head. The bandage there poked out from beneath the edge of his hat.

"It could be worse. I could be your man, Louis."

"That's true enough." The faint smile on the chief's lips faded.

"About that," Grey said, eager to break the awkward silence he'd just created. "It would never stand in court, but I know it was Euripides Webster who sent that sharpshooter up Katahdin."

"I wondered if it might be." Chief Jefferson tugged at his unshaven chin. "What are you expecting I'll do with that information?"

"Nothing, if you're wise."

"Not many have accused me of that. Louis Beauchamp was as good a man as any you've ever met. Deserved better than to be murdered. A hard injustice to swallow, that."

Grey nodded. "And revenge is sweeter than life itself. Or so say fools and madmen."

"I wonder which one am I."

"A madman wouldn't think to wonder."

Chief Jefferson chuckled. "That's a bit of comfort, I suppose. Well, I thank you for the information in any event. I'll have to think hard on it."

"You might do better to think *long* on it. I'm sure it's no secret that you've quarreled harshly with Euripides. If any suspicious harm were to befall him in the near future . . ." Grey finished the sentence with a shrug.

The chief nodded as he considered that angle. "Yes, I'd count myself lucky to have a solid alibi for my whereabouts on that unfortunate day—*should* it come to pass."

The chief shifted his feet about, looking like he was ready to move on before Grey stopped him.

"That's not the only reason I asked to meet. My driver's there." Grey nodded toward Mountfort Street. "He's waiting to hand over the thunderstone to you."

The chief's mouth dropped at the unexpected news.

"You were right, in a sense. It does hold a great power. One that men were willing to kill for, even when they were only hoping and guessing at what its power might truly be. It's a very dangerous stone."

"Not when it's in the right hands," the chief said.

"I agree. So promise me one thing," Grey added.

"Anything you like," the chief said.

"Carry on with your original plan. Put that stone on Katahdin or somewhere else where no white man will ever find it. Not for a hundred years at least."

Chief Jefferson's eyes narrowed, and he tried to read Grey's face, but he was having a hard time keeping himself from peering at the carriage, where his long-sought treasure waited.

"Of course." The surprise started to wear off, and Chief Jefferson shook Grey's hand. "Thank you, Grey. This means so much to me. And to our people."

As if the older man felt a sudden urge to reciprocate Grey's act of goodwill, he finally seemed to take in their immediate surroundings. His eyes focused in on the shabby-looking knee-high stone directly next to Grey.

"Stone that small, whoever lies there must have been the shame of the Webster family. And that takes some doing."

Grey could feel his own facial expression flinch. The chief must have seen it, too.

"Not to speak ill of the dead at all. That poor young woman seemed a kind soul."

Both men looked away from each other, trying to end the suddenly uncomfortable exchange. The little headstone served as a magnet to distract each one's attention.

"Not actually a Webster buried there," Grey pointed out.

"Oh, one of your folks, is it? That's a mighty coincidence, so close by all these Websters." Chief Jefferson bent low to read the name on the small grave marker.

"No relation of mine, I promise you," Grey said.

" 'Here lies N. F. Agee,' " the chief read the name out slowly.

"N. F. Agee." Grey repeated the name a second time, sounding out the syllables more quickly: " 'In effigy.' "

Chief Jefferson almost grimaced, as if he'd suffered a sour taste or a rotten joke. "An unfortunate use of initials for a dead man. 'In effigy'—do you suppose he was burned or just hanged?" The chief grinned.

"Neither, I think. Simply buried."

"Simply buried. What more is there to say?"

"Nothing," Grey said. "Best to leave it as it lies."

He requested a cigarette from the chief. The man handed one over, then struck a match for Grey, who gave a few hesitant puffs and offered his thanks. Chief Jefferson tipped his hat and gave Grey a smile before heading off alone, a sudden vigor in his step as he made for the waiting thunderstone.

Was it truly best to let it lie? Too many lives, innocent or otherwise, had already been lost during Jotham Marsh's mad, desperate search for whatever was buried in the false grave of N. F. Agee. Marsh would be preoccupied for months to come, searching beneath the ruins of the reservoir to locate the mystical alembic, the Count de St. Germain's secret mechanism for producing the philosopher's stone. But eventually Marsh would realize the truth: that it wasn't there. Then what? There was no way to predict what course he'd take next and how many more might suffer as a result. Grey decided on what he would have to do. Not now, when he was still likely being watched. Sometime in the months ahead, he'd have to come back and dig up the alembic himself. And when he had it in his hands, this alleged key to unlocking limitless wealth and the secrets of the ages, what then? The thought made his head hurt even worse.

Grey glanced about and saw no one taking note of him from either of the streets running along the Eastern Cemetery. He drew Thomas Webster's bequest from his pocket and held the cigarette to a corner of the ancient, yellowed page. He puffed a few times. The brittle paper smoldered briefly, then caught fire. Grey watched the flames devour the final written words of Thomas Webster. When the heat threatened to scorch his fingertips, he set the burning page on the grass in front of the pathetic little tombstone of N. F. Agee and waited until the fire died away, leaving only the blackened, crumbling remnants of the page.

Grey stepped down on it and twisted his shoe, obliterating the sole copy of Thomas Webster's bequest of his precious thunderstone. The heart of the old alchemist's last testament, and the key to his riddle, joined the earth beneath Grey's foot. The edges of the paper exploded into small black flecks that scattered on the wind, chapter and verse.

October 13, 1893

MIRA WALKED UP TO THE SECOND FLOOR AND ALONG THE hallway, past the tall windows that framed the sight of a slow-churning mass of dark gray clouds. Though she'd been longing for the return of sunlight, she didn't pause to consider the view. The parcel in her hands had monopolized her attention. She could feel a box inside the plain brown paper wrapping, and she was intrigued; it felt heavier than its size would suggest. Urgent voices leaked from Jotham Marsh's study, but she eased the door open without knocking.

Marsh was seated behind his desk, poring over a selection of old and new maps. Jerome stood just to the side, also peering over the material as he was expected to do. It was a familiar sight in the past two months, as Marsh had grown ever more focused on the exact location of Thomas Webster's single acre of land beneath the ruins of the Munjoy Hill Reservoir. This time a third man joined them, a heavyset fellow in dusty work clothes. His mud-encrusted boots had been removed downstairs, just inside the front door. Left standing here in his stocking feet, he looked like a little boy—though swollen to grotesque proportions and sporting a thick mustache—being scolded by his father.

"You've missed it, then," Marsh declared. "Moving too quickly these past couple weeks."

"The men are thorough, sir, just as instructed. It's the heavy rains—they've softened the earth. Made it easier to cover more ground," the portly workman explained.

Not wanting to acknowledge the reasonableness of that answer, Marsh shifted his attention to the parcel in Mira's hands. He questioned her with a glance.

"Just delivered. No return address on it." Mira caught a glimpse of herself in the large mirror on the far wall behind Marsh's desk. She tried to control the look of undue interest she saw on her face.

"Well, go on, open it." Marsh returned his attention to the maps spread out before him.

Mira set the package on the corner of the desk and used a letter opener to slice away the string that bound the wrapping.

"It has to be there. I know it is," Marsh muttered. "The old survey was wrong. We'll just have to move the southern corner's starting point farther in. Twenty yards more both to the northeast and the northwest."

Mira opened the box and lifted the single page set atop the contents. She unfolded it and read aloud: 'My good doctor, it's been such a pleasure to observe your current efforts from afar. After witnessing the dedication and thoroughness you've brought to bear on this endeavor, I felt compelled to pass along this small token of my appreciation. It's the least I can do after all the kindness you've displayed in letting me live this long. As you put it.' "

Marsh's bemused look turned to a scowl as Mira read the final two sentences. "What's in there?"

She drew out a photograph and offered it to Marsh. He snatched the picture from her hand. The image showed a hand loosely clutching a bright metallic object, roughly cylindrical and maybe eight or ten inches long. It appeared to have several gearlike dials on its exterior, as well as a short type of funnel extending from the top.

"The alembic—Grey has it!"

Marsh looked up and stared at Mira. From inside the box, she had picked up a small black velvet bag with gold drawstrings pulled tight. She cradled it in her hands as she stared back at him, her eyes wide in anticipation.

"It's heavy," she whispered.

"Here!" he hissed at her. His outstretched fingers wriggled uncontrollably, motioning her to hand it over. "Careful."

Marsh set it down as gently as if he thought the bag itself were about to disintegrate. His fingers pulled at the strings until they came loose, and he slid his hand inside the bag and drew the golden object out into the light. Rapturous delight crumbled into utter despair in the second or two that it took his mind to grasp what he was seeing.

His gaze shot to the photograph and then back to the distorted lump of gold upon the desk before him. The funnel was still there, and he could make out the shape of one of the prominent dials on the alembic's side. But the thing itself had been melted down, collapsing and rehardening into a shapeless mass. All traces of its alchemical markings, the secrets to its proper use, obliterated.

"No! He couldn't have!" Marsh grabbed the golden mass off the desktop. He turned around, unable to bear the looks on the faces of Mira and Jerome, watching him suffer this ultimate failure. He was rewarded by his own incomprehensible likeness, glaring back from a mirror on the wall.

"This is *not* possible!" His arm whipped around in a furious blur, and then the melted alembic hurtled from his hand. It struck the center of the mirror and dropped to the floor. A few shards fell, but most of the mirror hung in place, a spiderweb of cracked glass that now held the seething, fractured reflection of Jotham Marsh. "Dead. With my own hands—I will see him dead!"

Acknowledgments

First and foremost, I'd like to thank my wife, Cathy, not only for being my first reader but for all the help and support she provides every step of the way.

I'm very grateful for my editor, Sean Desmond, whose insight and good judgment helped shape this book and bring it to a satisfying conclusion. I'd also like to thank my publisher, Molly Stern, as well as all the people at Crown whose efforts have contributed to this series including: Julie Cepler, Ellen Folan, Meagan Stacey, Annie Chagnot, Christopher Brand, Lauren Dong, Stephanie Knapp, and the sharp-eyed Maureen Sugden.

At William Morris Endeavor, many thanks to Erin Malone and Suzanne Gluck for their never-ending faith and support, as well as Cathryn Summerhayes and Tracy Fisher.

A book of this type requires a significant amount of historical research, and I'd be hard pressed to recount every source. However, I often turned to Edward H. Elwell's *1876 Portland and Vicinity* along with various documents and photographs on the Maine Memory Network at www.mainememory.net. The character of Chief Jefferson was inspired in part from material found in *The Life of John W. Johnson* on the very informative www.nedoba.org website.

This story features a fictitious final manuscript by Professor Eben Norton Horsford referencing Norse runes at Portland, Maine. With regard to the professor's actual theories on Viking explorations in New England, I'm indebted to his other existing works, as well as Rasmus B. Anderson's *The Norsemen in America*, and Gloria Polizotti Greis's wonderful article, "Vikings on the Charles or, the Strange Sage of Dighton Rock, Norumbega, and Rumford Double-Acting Baking Powder."

To the extent that my descriptions of the Boston Athenaeum are at all accurate, I credit that institution's publication: *The Athenaeum Centenary*. Any and all errors in portraying the building's layout are entirely my own.

The 1775 bombardment of Portland by Capt. Mowat is described by William Willis in his *The History of Portland from 1632 to 1864*. However, I have made alterations to that work to suit my needs, including fictional references to Thomas Webster. Similarly, I made certain abridgments and omissions to Frederick Jackson Turner's seminal 1893 paper, "The Significance of the Frontier in American History," as necessary for the flow of the story.

Like Mowat's attack, the collapse of the Munjoy Hill Reservoir was another real tragedy suffered by the city of Portland. Four people died as the result of a flaw in the reservoir, and I meant no disrespect to their memories by reconstructing the events of the collapse in a much more dramatic fashion. Details of the collapse were gleaned from various newspaper accounts as well as John R. Freeman's "The Bursting of the Distributing-Reservoir at Portland, Maine, August 6, 1893" in: *Journal of the Association of Engineering Societies,* Volume 13, 1894.

In addition to my personal experiences on Katahdin, I used a variety of sources to re-create what a trip up the mountain may have been like in the late nineteenth century, including Elizabeth Oakes Smith's 1849 newspaper account of her journey, as well as the later words of Percival Proctor Baxter. To the latter, I am, like all Mainers, deeply grateful for the continuing gift of Baxter State Park and Katahdin.

About the Author

KIERAN SHIELDS is the author of Grey and Lean's first adventure together, *The Truth of All Things*. He lives along the Maine coast with his wife and two children.

A Note on the Text

This book was set in Fournier MT, a typeface created by Monotype in 1924, based on type cut by Pierre Simon Fournier circa 1742 in *Fournier's Manual Typographie*.